Bertie's Retreat
... a new start

a novel by

George Macpherson

Grande Vigne Press

Other books by the same author:
Fiction:
Bagamoyo Spring – a novel
The Floating Island – a tale of Africa
Okavango - Another Life
Expressions of love
The Glebe Field – a novel set in Cornwall

Non-Fiction:
Home-Grown Energy from Short Rotation Coppice (Farming Press)
First Steps in Village Mechanisation (Tanzania Publishing House)
Computers in Farm Management (Northwood Books)
Namna ya kujitengenezea gari la gurudumu moja (How to make a wheelbarrow) (Tanzania Publishing House)
Farming with the BBC (In Bulgarian – BBC World Service)
Farming with the BBC (In Romanian – BBC World Service)
Farming with the BBC (In Albanian: 40-part radio soap opera – BBC World Service)

See the end of this book for more details

BERTIE'S RETREAT

First Published in 2014
Copyright © George Macpherson 2014

All rights reserved. No parts of this publication may be reproduced, stored in a retrieval system or transmitted in any form or by any means, electronic, mechanical, photocopying, recording or otherwise without prior permission in writing from the publisher.

ISBN 978-0-9566386-5-6 (UK)
ISBN 978-1502732637 (CreateSpace)

Distributed by Amazon Kindle Store
www.amazon.com (USA and World)
www.amazon.co.uk (UK only)

Published by Grande Vigne Press
London, United Kingdom

Website: www.grandevignepress.co.uk
Email: tombayliss(at)googlemail.com

The moral right of George Macpherson to be identified as the author of this work has been asserted in accordance with the Copyright, Designs and Patents Act, 1988 Trademarked names appear throughout this book. Rather than use a trademark symbol with every occurrence of a trademarked name, names are used in an editorial fashion, with no intention of infringement of the respective owner's trademark. The information in this book is distributed on an "as is" basis, without warranty. Although every precaution has been taken in the preparation of this work neither the author nor the publisher shall have any liability to any person or entity with respect to any loss or damage caused or alleged to be caused directly or indirectly by the information contained in this book.

This book is a work of fiction. Names, characters, businesses, organisations, places and events are either the product of the author's imagination or are used fictitiously. Any resemblance to actual persons living or dead, events or locales except where specified in fictitious situations is entirely coincidental.

Grande Vigne Press

Acknowledgements and apologies

Had things been different, parts of Wiltshire might have been as in this book. They may yet change, but the reader must forgive the way in which the county's geography (and society) has been pirated, because this is a fairytale, albeit not for children. Maud Heath was real and evidence of this is as fresh today as it was in the 15th Century; the River Avon too is still running – sometimes in flood mode, but Tytherton Kellaway isn't there, nor its manor with Roman Temple.

Many of us need somewhere to recuperate from today's reality – to paint, make music, fish or simply pick up an undemanding book. Jeffery Farnol wrote such novels (1910-1952), full of gallantry, noble heroes, feisty women, passionate love, reformed villains, and prize fighters.

Tales like *Beltane The Smith* and *Money Moon* transport their readers into lands distant from the horrors of the Boer War and mass murder of World War One. His books may be scorned now, but for those of us whose fathers loved them, and who themselves have found in them, refuge, (despite the quaint language, bad English and often, difficult dialect), they still come down from the shelf.

Bertie's Retreat, set in today's world of unrelenting pressures, clamour, and disasters that we are impotent to resolve, is a tribute to Farnol. I don't apologise for *my* punctuation, capital letters, orthography or language but warn that it, like his, may not be 'conventional'.

A warning too, to those who prefer euphemisms and virginal purity when it comes to personal relationships. Who was it who first said 'never explain, never apologise'? It seems to be an arrogant attitude and there are various claimants as to who coined the phrase originally: so let me explain that my plea for tolerance in this matter should be taken more as a warning on the packet, such as 'may contain nuts'.

Many thanks, as ever, to Jane my wife, for her tolerance, criticism and love during the writing of this book; to Richard Cowen for my photo on the back cover, and to both him and Hilary Northcott for their invaluable help in weeding out errors, incongruities and typos – some of which may have crept back.

My thanks to Tony Frazer of *Just Do It Publications* and Tristan Bolton, artist and author, for their advice and assistance with artwork, text preparation and uploading. Tribute too, to Wikipedia and Google for answering so many of my questions with such amazing speed.

George Macpherson *Somerton, November 2014*

BERTIE'S RETREAT

CHAPTER 1

Bertie was angry. That *woman* had been given the one role he really wanted. Both The Chairman and The CEO knew how much it meant to him and how suitable he was for the post. It needed a strategist who would shake off the firm's fading image: someone with flare and daring to bring in some really big accounts. Tracey McGrath looked great and talked big. The fact that she was also sleeping with The Chairman might also have had something to do with it. That, however, like all major issues in the higher echelons of this business, was not discussed. Why The Chairman's wife didn't appear to know about it was a mystery, unless it suited her 'fond friendship' with her old friend Deidre, with whom she spent so much time.

Bertie had been open about his ambition, telling The CEO during his annual assessment last week what he would do in the role of Executive Director. His confidence was based on his track record over the past five years: rising from the Account Executive who looked after a pizza company to becoming Ogle Associates' chief lobbyist in Westminster and Brussels for their last major client, a multi-national conglomerate.

The Board had, for once, been daring, by appointing someone so young to such a responsible position but it was not only Bertie's sharp mind and charm that gave them the courage to act so apparently rashly. He was remarkably good looking. For a start he was tall and broad: not an ounce of surplus weight but light of foot and supremely fit. He was naturally active, often shunning the big leather swivel chair and conventional desk from which he welcomed clients and staff, to stand at his high working desk. He fetched what he needed from other floors via the stairs. He found this refreshing and invigorating: far quicker than waiting for someone else to deliver. It helped make up for not having time to go to a gym or submit to a personal trainer. He would make a game out of timing his ascent per landing, or seeing how many steps he could scale at a time up the concrete crevasses of Ogle Tower.

Since that bold appointment the board had begun to lose its daring. The last Executive Director's burn-out had frightened the board. His descent into alcoholism had finally come to light when he failed to turn up for the foundation stone ceremony for a new bank – the one pledging itself to 'trustworthy banking'. He had arrived late, inebriated. It had been Bertie's job to divert him from the Royalty poised to pull the silken cord.

The CEO had made a recording of Bertie's assessment interview on his desk monitor. It saved him having to take notes. On this occasion the resulting document had so inspired him that he studied it carefully before selling Bertie's ideas to The Board as being his own. He had also built them into the job description for the replacement Executive Director. Young Bertie Lamotte would have been his choice but The CEO, being one of the few who *knew* about Tracey McGrath and The Chairman, realised he was on a sticky wicket.

In the event, his choice was bowled out and the chief executive had to concoct a story that might placate Bertie to keep him within the company. The difficulty was finding an incentive that might persuade him to stay. He knew Bertie didn't *need* the job, being one of the very few with private means. The Lamotte family had 'old money', mainly derived from the slave trade, and gold mining in South Africa. Their wealth had been enhanced over the past fifty years by judicious investment and careful, but legal, tax avoidance.

Bertie only worked because he enjoyed it, having exhausted most available expensive pleasures that London, Paris, New York or Monaco had to offer. He had lost interest in his yacht, moored in Falmouth and the Aston Martin saloon, which had played such an important part in his life while at university. He had no desire to run a business of his own, with its inhibitions and baggage. It suited him to be loosely attached to an organisation that allowed him maximum scope for his off-the-wall ideas.

Bertie's passion was presenting the world with new concepts and innovation. They fired him up to work the incredibly long hours for which he became known. His research was so thorough that figures he presented were respected and generally acted upon. His reliability and judgement were considered excellent. Members of Parliament had grown to trust his evidence.

Unlike some of his greedy ancestors he was honest. For a while, during his teens, he had been a devout member of the chapel choir at Eton. His love of singing and music was to remain an important part of his life, though later he avoided organised religion and its confused hierarchies. The other remnants of his impressionable years in chapel were the ethics, which had captured his intellect; his accountant soon learned that tax evasion was out of the question. To sum up, Bertie Lamotte was an asset Ogle could not do without.

Tracey's appointment, however, had hit him like a ten-tonne truck on a zebra crossing. He was still in outraged shock when The CEO delivered his attempt to keep him in the group.

"Bertie, The Board needs you," he pleaded. "No one else brings in new business like you do. Clients take to you immediately and love your creativity. You would be wasted as Executive Director – all that boardroom politics. Your strength is in your talent for innovation and ability to convince people of its worth. We want to offer you a significant salary increase and a new title."

Despite his anger, Bertie did what he had learned to do at school: hold his fire until he had worked out tactics. It had saved many a black eye and avoided wasteful conflict. What he would have liked to say was that most of the new clients he had wooed into signing up had left again as soon as they could, disappointed by the lack-lustre approach shown to them by the rest of Ogle's personnel. As Executive Director he could have chopped out some of the dead wood and taken a stand during board meetings: what was the good of bringing in new clients only to fail them?

"I'll certainly think about it," he said, "and I'll let you know tomorrow."

That last word was the one which dashed The CEO's hope. The Board, in its usual indecisive way, had allowed Bertie's contract to drift right to its end without any commitment for re-engagement.

Bertie found himself in a very strong position. Tomorrow he was 'off contract' except for the five weeks holiday he was owed. If he wanted to, he could simply leave!

Striding homewards that evening across Hyde Park to his house in Bayswater he walked off some of the adrenalin that was distorting his mind. Decision-making must wait until he felt more in control of his emotions. It was a technique he had absorbed from his mother, who had had to deal with an irascible husband. Bertie had often taken cover behind her calm and loving resilience as she manoeuvred his father away from confrontation and towards her own wishes.

Should he accept the Board's offer and wait for the next opportunity of achieving this goal? There were many factors to make that attractive: like the happy hours he spent with his teams. He was very fond of them, treating them more as he had been treated by his tutor at Oxford, than as line manager. He had watched them develop their abilities and grow into dependable and talented operators. It went further than tutorial supervision. For several of his protégées he had found it necessary to provide peri-parental care. More than one had wept on his shoulder when crossed in love. They were the nearest he had to family, apart from his beloved mother back in Suffolk.

If he did *not* accept the concocted position, which was never likely to achieve much, the alternative was to unplug himself from Ogle altogether. He had never considered such an option, living in hope that he could rise to a position from which he could influence its path. The appointment of The Chairman's concubine had now scuppered that possibility.

Kicking at the few remaining autumn leaves, survivors of this winter's gales and torrents, he came to a halt. Leaving Ogle would mean not seeing these people. He would miss them terribly. His emotional life outside work was minimal. He had few other friends. His colleagues at the office speculated as to whether he had a secret personal life – perhaps being a closet gay; or one of nature's solitaries.

At twenty nine he was unattached, but contrary to the views of those who thought they knew him, he was very much aware of his physical and emotional needs repressed by work. Since leaving Worcester College his whole existence had been devoted to the career that had brought him to this moment, but how many times had his eyes been drawn to the shapely bottoms trotting past on fine horses in this park? How often had he stopped himself from taking one of his adoring female team into his arms to console her? Instead, he would force himself to listen to her woes while revelling in the beauty of her tearful eyes and longing to kiss that tempting neck behind the trembling ear-ring.

He was inexperienced enough not to be aware that an extra blouse button had been undone before the interview to reveal that extra swell of cleavage and promise of other rose-tinted delights.

Standing in Hyde Park, Bertie began to get chilly, his hand on his chin, index finger pressing his upper lip.

Then it hit him, as his mind drifted away from Ogle's shaky future, suddenly unimportant – irrelevant! It was as though someone had reconnected his mental power supply. A surge of excitement went through him. It could work! In a stroke it resolved losing everyone and everything, because it need not *be* 'for ever'!

"I could leave just for a couple of months to clear my head," he said out loud. They might be glad to have him back when they realised how bad their prospects were; he knew there were at least two other clients putting out feelers for 'fresh approaches' to their marketing.

Other people could call it a sabbatical, or study leave – perhaps a career break – but something new and even more intoxicating was sparkling into his head. It had echoes of the road to Damascus and was so powerful that, over-ruling his customary self-control, he allowed a childhood dream to topple his common sense and go into a star-burst of possibilities.

"I'm going to go and seek my *fortune!*"

In this Eureka moment he reached for the sky as he shouted his proclamation. A woman passing in the other direction pulled up her collar and hurried on – another nutter best avoided.

She need not have worried: he hadn't even noticed her as he celebrated his inspiration. He had just recruited a new client:

someone he had known for years: himself! He had already answered the first magic question: 'what can we do?'

Usually this referred to 'raising our profile?' or 'getting them to change their minds?' Best of all was 'finding a completely new approach?' It would set his motor running when he woke at five in the morning, raring to go, his mind chasing vague ideas to see where they led. This time, the horizons were endless.

His effectiveness in exploring the viability of possibilities was partly due to hours of donkey-work, learning everything about his targeted client, their products, motivation, talents and potential. He would study their field, and the competition, in great detail; and then, propelled by deduction, whim and inspiration, he would carry them far beyond their normal parameters of expectation with his proposals.

Solutions for his new client – himself, Bertie Lamotte, would be equally original, recalling all the thrill and promise of so many tales he had read when he finally conquered the printed page at the age of seven, (much to the relief of the prep-school and his mother, in the days when dyslexia hadn't become popular but 'slow' could give a chap a bad reputation).

Bertie had watched many of his favourite team members go through the same life crisis, wanting to spread their wings after a spell at Ogle. They would begin taking unexplained time off and receiving calls that made them hunch over their desk pretending to look natural as they spoke softly with a head-hunter or career coach. He used to pity them, putting so much at risk as they stepped into the uncertainty of a new workplace, strange colleagues, bosses and company ethos. They might gain no more than half a step up, with a mildly elevated title: from 'Account Manager' to 'Account Director', with a pay rise worth more to the Inland Revenue than to their own bank account. For him it was different.

"I'm *incredibly* lucky!" He clapped his hands.

The pigeon, which had landed nearby in the hope that Bertie might be about to eat a sandwich, took off hastily.

A few spots of rain brought Bertie, temporarily transformed, back to earth. He remembered which way he was going and set off once more, a spring in his step. Tonight he would allow himself to break his routine of going straight home to catch up with the journals over a stir-fry. He would drop by a wine-bar! He might even stay for supper to celebrate his latest deal – the most important so far.

What pleasure! Sitting there with some delicious salted cashew nuts and a glass of Madeira getting to know his new client. The wine bar was warm and dry and he found exactly the right table, set for one, in a corner next to a potted palm: discreet but not secluded: perfect! He could hold a meeting with himself – if he kept his voice down no one could hear him and think he'd gone completely bananas; but *listening* to what was on offer always seemed simpler than reading about it.

"How much do you have in mind to spend?" He asked himself, after the formalities and first few sips and nibbles. He took out his pocket notebook and jotted down the date and a pound sign, followed by a question mark. Writing notes was less likely to draw attention than if it were *all* out loud.

"Well, actually, money doesn't come into it," he replied. "It's no problem: there should be enough for anything you come up with."

"Are we talking tens or hundreds of thousands?"

"As I said, we needn't discuss it," Bertie tried not to sound irritable as he reached for another small handful of nuts.

"So – what kind of activity are we discussing?"

"It rather depends on what you suggest!" Really this man was being slow to twig what was needed. "*Try* me with something! I want adventure, achievement – success; love! I'm thinking about going off to seek my fortune."

"Well, looking at your present occupation I can't help agreeing you seem to be in somewhat of a rut."

"Exactly! This could be my opportunity to break out. I know I must get away from the position I'm in, which is far too cosy and totally infuriating."

"How about going off somewhere? Does that appeal?"

"What do you mean?" Bertie was curious.

"Pack a rucksack with just a few things and 'set out' – see where you finish up."

"What? Leave the house and everything – simply disappear?"

"No – you don't want to frighten people. Think of your poor mother, she'd be worried to death. So would your housekeeper. You could tell them you were 'off on a retreat'. They've got your mobile number, but ask them not to call you unless it's dire."

"But how long for?" He took another note.

"Traditionally it's for a year and a day," Bertie answered.

"I suppose it is," he replied. "And there's usually a princess in it somewhere, isn't there?"

"You can't leave it alone, can you? You've been telling yourself that for years and, to be frank, that's one of your weaknesses," he confessed to himself as tactfully as he could.

"Mine, or theirs?" asked Bertie, offended; "I can't help it if they turn out disappointing."

"Perhaps you have been going after the wrong sort?"

"My own fault again, I suppose!"

"No – I'm just trying to think laterally. You've always been so easily knocked over by a pretty face; and you've always been so undiscriminating! I remember at prep school you really fancied that boy Lawrence, who looked like Kylie Minogue. That was a silly mistake: he was a new-bug when you were in the top form."

"I didn't think anyone suspected that." Bertie was now uneasy. "There wasn't much else to fall for at *that* school, was there? Perhaps Matron?"

"And I remember you playing with yourself and dreaming of your own harem, full of girls with perfect breasts." His old guilty conscience was getting back to its favourite gripe.

"Now I say! That's far enough! This is not the Inquisition! It's not at all what I want to talk about. I want to know what I'm going to do tomorrow when I set out to seek my fortune. I just happened to mention the possibility of there being a princess about and you let it take over the whole conversation."

"Doesn't it always?"

"Well – not with other clients. They all seem to have that side of their lives under control."

"That's what they want you to think. Underneath they might be even worse off than you; but since you want to *avoid* the most important thing in the whole world – our very reason for existing – I suppose we shall have to change the subject."

It seemed like a good time to refill his glass, so Bertie addressed the barman, who had been smiling to himself, watching the conversation.

"You've been nodding away to yourself," said the barman. "I've been wondering what you were going on about! You seemed to be enjoying it."

"I suppose I was," said Bertie. "I'm trying to make up my mind about what I do next."

"Well, you could pay for what you've had so far," offered the barman. "After that – you could nip out for a film, or stay here for something to eat; even go home and watch telly. There's rugby on tonight!"

"I might do any of those things later – but what I have to decide now this minute is what I do tomorrow. I've just resigned from my job: not that I've told them yet."

"You don't look sorry."

"I'm not! I feel liberated: carefree; but a bit nervous about what comes next."

"Take a break – stay cool. Go away for a bit, if you can afford it. I would if I could but I can't; so I've got nothing to worry about, unless people stop coming in for a drink. I know what *I'd* do – get sacked and sign on. Couldn't you get them to make you redundant?"

"No, afraid not! But someone else suggested going away. It's a point." Bertie paid for his next drink and accepted a new pannikin of nuts, returning to his interview.

"Well – that's a practical suggestion isn't it?" He asked himself.

"It is, actually. The question is where: and how?"

"You won't want the car, will you? All that traffic! Tell you what: first thing in the morning – go to Paddington and get on the next train that leaves. Keep going until you feel you've got far enough away from London – then get out and see what happens!"

"You're on, dammit: I shall!"

The barman noted, with some amusement, that his customer seemed to leave with a sense of purpose. Bertie and his new client made their way home, popped something in the microwave and enjoyed supper on a tray, watching snooker to calm the excitement. They merged, showered and had an early night.

Bertie had been right: the nearest station to get himself away from all these bricks, shiny wet pavements noisy diesels and hissing tyres was Paddington and the following morning, having phoned his mother in Suffolk and his housekeeper before she set out from her home in Wembley, he arrived at the ticket office at about ten.

His grey knapsack was one of those with a frame that kept its copious canvass bag away from his back, allowing the air to circulate. It had umpteen pockets of varying sizes into which he could stuff gloves, socks, a sun-hat, battery chargers, his tablet, mobile and first aid kit. Larger garments and essentials went into the main compartment, folded and pressed down tightly. It finished up quite weighty and he needed to wear his walking boots before shouldering such a load. The boots went well with plus-fours and long woollen socks so he put them on, too. His warm outdoor jacket with emergency hood, sheepskin gloves and fur hat with ear flaps completed today's outfit, along with the thumbstick.

"You've just missed the Hereford train," he was told. "The next departure is for Swansea, via Bristol."

"Bath should cover it," he told the surprised booking clerk. "That should be far enough."

"Single or day return?"

"Single, please."

"Day return is cheaper."

"OK, day return, then." He could always ditch the return half, which probably lasted only three months.

"If you hurry, you can get the ten twenty on Platform 7. First stop Reading, and then all stations to Bristol Temple Meads."

"Thank you!" Bertie paid and set off for Platform 7.

Hardly anyone was heading west. Bertie had the carriage almost to himself so he dumped his knapsack on the seat next to him. In just a few minutes the train gave the slightest jolt and the platform began to slide away from around him, giving way to high blocks of dripping flats and deserted balconies. Gaudy initials in weird styles defaced every vertical surface, making this part of Paddington all the less desirable. Someone had described such graffiti as 'primates marking their territory – rather as dogs urinate on lamp posts'. Bertie wondered whether the 'artists' would welcome such a description and whether it might make them desist, and disguise their nearness to Cousin Monkey.

Even the packed Underground trains had been vandalised with spray paint, making them look part of this junky land. Escape from London and its defiled walls became all the sweeter.

Before long the speeding train passed all the sleek Eurostar rolling stock, resting in newly-built sheds and steel-fenced sidings; it whipped through Ealing and Southall, lost a race with a jumbo-jet, nose-up and heading for the clouds from Heathrow; and overtaken traffic crawling along the M4. From then on, most of the view was hidden by high-sided cuttings, still green and leafy despite the time of year. Strange, but this winter had not been cold long enough to leave the countryside withered and brown. Perhaps it would be a late spring? Emerging into less undulating landscape the scene changed to that of a river delta, although not by design.

The Thames had spread for miles each side of its usual course, asserting its dominance over its own 'Thames Valley'. No wonder the TV news had spent so much time showing people being rescued by canoe, tractor and trailer. Perhaps this was *not* the best time of year to 'take to the countryside'. Bertie was tempted not to throw away the return half of his ticket.

After Reading, however, the land began to dry out a little and by the time the train arrived at Didcot Parkway the landscape was still dreary but not as sodden. He looked for the huge cooling towers and mountains of anthracite but they seemed to have disappeared: strange; until he remembered seeing them being blown up at dawn on TV news. Certainly, Didcot didn't tempt Bertie to disembark. It did not look at all exciting. Nor did the next stop, Swindon, although Bertie quite fancied a look at the railway museum about which he'd heard.

Soon after Swindon, the train slowed down to a snail's pace, allowing him, seated on the left, facing the engine, a better view of the scenery to the south. Rolling hills and groups of ancient houses, some of them surrounded by farmyards and muddy lanes. He had been this way many times before and one feature that had always stuck in his mind had been the circling Hercules aircraft. Today there were none and he recalled that the Royal Air Force had moved this part of Transport Command from Lyneham to Brize Norton in Oxfordshire. In the old days it had always reminded him of bees, buzzing around a hive. Some of them might have been coming back from Afghanistan, carrying wounded soldiers – or even coffins of those killed on dusty roads outside Kabul. They might have been taking first aid relief to the sites of recent earthquakes or tsunamis – or spares for drones waiting to resume their lethal pursuit of bearded groups in pick-up trucks escaping to the mountains north of Kandahar.

Now, though, the skies around Royal Wootton Bassett were empty. He could see the outline of the town on top of the escarpment. It must be so much quieter there now; in fact, the low speed of the train, the rays of sunshine illuminating patches of meadow and stream both sides of the railway; the lack of graffiti, the scattered houses and not a soul in sight, all added up to what Bertie thought he needed.

This could be where to refresh his mind, blow away the frustration and fatuous chasing of targets, pitches, deadlines, margins, profit, corporate greed and 'competition'. He put his hat on when the guard announced: 'Chippenham next stop'. He was getting off.

CHAPTER 2

It was the softness of the air against his face that caught Bertie's attention, once the train had eased itself away towards Bath. As the other three passengers took the exit, he stood on the platform getting used to the weight on his back and shoulders. The bottom of the knapsack frame put comfortable pressure behind his waist and the shoulder-straps pulled him upright.

"Very good for my deportment," he thought. "After a few days walking, I shall stand like a guardsman." He took a deep breath.

There was something kind about the breeze into which the train had now disappeared. No chilly edge to sting his cheek; no fumes of diesel or hot brake linings, roaring buses or swearing cyclists. It was suddenly .... quiet.

The gentle wind stirred a flag over a nearby carpet shop: that was all that moved. This same air might have passed over Bath, Bristol before that, but it hadn't picked up the particulate soup of pollution that filled his lungs in London. It must have arrived recently from blowing the sea, purifying itself of New World dust on thousands of miles of Atlantic rollers before rising over the Irish coast to be washed by pouring rain across the Caha mountains and Bantry Bay; finally skipping its way eastwards, across the Celtic Sea to Wales, until, here it was, almost spent of its energy, about to rise above the first slopes of the Cotswolds.

To Bertie, filling his lungs, the air felt as fresh as it must have done when it first made landfall west of Dingle. It was so different from those angry gales which, already this winter had been tearing at roofs, trees and high-sided lorries, swilling walls of rain against windows, inundating fields and homes.

Today's gentle air carried promise of spring, memories of summer. Perhaps it was the assuaged remains of the last hurricane that had raged over the Caribbean and Florida before heading north to frighten New York. Maybe it had bounced off that terrifying Arctic surge that had recently dropped the USA into deep freeze, before heading out to sea.

Like a giant relaxing after destructive anger, ready to caress the world again, the warm breeze invited him to head south. It suggested that 'North' might be cold and dark, while its spirits from the skies of Antigua, St Kitts and Martinique offered enticing echoes of calypso and the rustle of palm leaves.

South it had to be: also it was downhill, giving Bertie's legs a chance to limber up after sitting on the train. Going up hills with this load was not going to be as easy.

It didn't take long, down to the bridge over the Avon in the middle of town, where traffic once again filled the road (and his head with noise), chasing away the Caribbean welcome. To continue on this main road was not tempting; besides, the other side of the bridge, was all up hill.

Looking for an alternative, Bertie found a path down to the riverbank. He took it and headed up river. He wanted to be away from suburbia and, further downstream, the waterways around Bristol, with massive ships disgorging regiments of glossy cars with no number plates.

He had little idea where the Avon came from, but from the glimpses upstream he'd caught from the train, the countryside had looked green and rural.

As he left the last suburbs of Chippenham behind, calm returned. He inhaled the scent of last autumn's leaves and the hints of contented cattle and hay. From the hedge came the rustle of a blackbird, moving twigs to reveal the next tasty worm; further away, the sound of a rabbit, stamping to warn its family of Bertie's approach with his stick and knapsack. He noted the tiny green buds on the brambles and the lamb-tailed catkin flowers of hazel with their promise of Spring.

His legs got into their stride, in step with his heartbeat and for a while he forgot the weight on his back as he covered the ground. It was exciting: the beginning of his year and a day!

This exuberance released tunes in time with his footsteps and he began to whistle 'I'm off to see the wizard'.

For him this was rare. The last time he whistled was when he was staying at his mother's for the weekend. It had convinced her he must be in love, or had pulled off some special deal. She remarked on it and was disappointed to find it was because Chelsea had won at home. She lived in hopes he might find someone to divert him from his obsessive working.

He was surprised how loud his whistling sounded in this environment, and tried a few grace notes and trills in higher octaves to see whether he was still as good as he had been at school. He had lost neither his volume nor technique, and it was satisfying, stepping out to his own music, blowing away his boredom and frustration.

Wrapped in his happiness, he didn't hear the horse and rider trotting on the grass edge of the path behind him. The soft turf conspired in this, but it was a girl's voice that made him jump out of his skin.

"I say – excuse me – would you mind *not* whistling? It makes my horse want to stop and pee and I'm timing this route."

Bertie had stopped and was standing back to see what had given him such a fright. It turned out to be a young woman on a tall bay horse, ears pricked, trotting past with little more than a glance; more interested in the path ahead than this loaded pedestrian.

"Thank you!"

This crisp acknowledgement was made without changing the pace of the horse, and with barely a turn of the head on behalf of his rider, rising and falling with ease in the saddle.

Bertie, the perfect gentleman, barely had time to touch his hat to the lady – something he had learned from his father at an early age – before the horse and rider, after filling his view and full attention, were past. He watched them out of sight, making various observations while resuming his journey.

He noted, from the rear, that the horse was a stallion and that the rider was very nicely shaped, immaculately dressed in hacking jacket and seamless jodhpurs tucked into shining boots. She was holding the reins in one hand while clasping what might have been a stopwatch and riding crop in the other.

Despite Bertie's long-legged progress along the path, the rider soon left him behind. It reminded him why horses had been the major means of transport for so many centuries. They were so effective: the rider went fast; and had the advantage of much better vision, given that extra height. As she sat on this great animal, she could foresee hazards sooner than the man on the ground – even sooner than the horse itself. She could relax and be carried at a pace to suit herself while controlling the direction of travel. This configuration was the equivalent of a modern four-by-four. Bertie concluded that today's articulated lorry matched a team of Suffolk Punches harnessed to a hay wain.

Without thinking, and since it didn't matter where he went, he followed the trail left by the horse-shoes, hardly noticing that the path now turned away from the river. Instead, it followed a stream that merged from the right. He chuckled as he stepped over fresh horse droppings. It contradicted something he had just been thinking, that, unlike today's transport, horses didn't pollute with their exhaust. On the other hand, the droppings would be well received by all kinds of flora and fauna as nutrition and habitat: very satisfactory.

His mind went further: the 'equine sports vehicle' wouldn't finish up in a scrap yard. At worst it might be eaten by some foreigner or canned for pet food, but it wouldn't be wasted. Even if it were lovingly buried in a horse cemetery, nutrients would seep through the soil back into plants and trees; and before it wore out, the stallion might father foals, providing replacement power sources, ready made with utmost economy for their owners, though not always with a chosen colouring or sex.

That fine young woman could probably charge money for her stallion to copulate with chosen mares. In place of a bill for a service she would be paid for it! No need for brake linings or software updates. He had to concede there *were* costs – iron shoes instead of rubber tyres, hay, oats and protein supplements instead of petrol; and veterinary cover substituting for oil changes and repairs.

There were further advantages. For example the rider could scrape past gateposts and bump into obstacles without having to leave her steed at the panel beater's for days. Her transport grew its own repairs.

He concluded there was still much to be said for the horse as an effective, healthy and ecological way of covering the ground, carrying loads and providing traction – as long as you had time and a good mackintosh.

His daydreams were interrupted as the horse's tracks diverted off the path and on to the road, which the path now followed. The footpath continued as a pavement to the highway, but later mounted a long, unusual causeway supported by a series of small brick arches. He could see that, before culverts had channelled a stream under the road, it must have been difficult for a pedestrian to cross. There was marshy ground each side and he counted sixty-four narrow arches as tall as a man, spanning it. At the end of the dry crossing Bertie stopped to read a Perspex-covered information plaque beside the path. It told him that a widow, Maud Heath, had paid for this causeway and path, not only to be built, but maintained in perpetuity for people wanting to walk from 'Wick Hill to Chippenham'. She had become rich from selling the hundreds of baskets of eggs she had carried along this route.

Maud Heath was childless, it said; and when she died in 1474, she had bequeathed a legacy 'for the good of travellers' who would use the path along which she had tramped to market several times a week for most of her life. 'Even today', said the notice, 'the charity maintains the path, using her bequest'.

Bertie was both impressed and enchanted. What a fantastic achievement! After more than five centuries, her practicality and generosity was as good as new! So was the path: the arches of this causeway looked as though they had been built comparatively recently, possibly in 1750: that recent! The year 1474 seemed *so* long ago.

Unlike benefactors who made contributions to the building of cathedrals and shrines she had not done this from guilt, to save her soul, but in sympathy with all those who, like her, had to spend the whole day selling eggs in Chippenham market with wet feet: admirable! With this unselfish act, unlike the penitence of the wealthy, which burdened generations with endless fund-raising to repair roofs and save spires, she had endowed the path in perpetuity. It was self supporting: even more admirable!

The notice had an arrow pointing towards a distant hill, with a note saying that, two hundred years after she had died, the trustees had erected a pillar and statue to her honour. He could just see it in the distance.

While still enjoying the thought of such a public-spirited woman, Bertie wondered whether this morning's intrepid horsewoman might even be her descendant. He didn't know what Maud Heath looked like but this girl certainly had fine looks. In that brief glance he had only seconds to gather this impression but she was, as his mother might say, 'striking'.

She had not been smiling or frowning – but was focused on her task as she checked her stopwatch, barely nodding in his direction as he stepped hastily out of her way. The dark strap of her riding helmet contrasted with the pale skin of her face. She had Bertie's favourite nose – straight – a perfect length with discreet, non-demonstrative nostrils. He approved too, of her eyebrows – natural. He didn't have time to see her eyes, noting only that they were large.

A few minutes later Bertie stopped, as he realised the hoofprints had disappeared from the side of the path. He felt suddenly lonely, as though he had been walking with a companion, now gone without warning.

The horse certainly was not Pegasus: it could not have taken to the air. They must have turned off while he was thinking about Maud Heath, but where? He retraced his steps until he detected a narrow gap in the hedge. He hadn't noticed it before, being miles away in his thoughts, but now he could see that the horse and rider must have pushed through the long grass into what appeared to be a wide untrimmed hedge going uphill towards the south east. He stepped through the grass, emerging into a muddy path that disappeared into a tunnel of tree branches and ivy. The overgrown lane must have once been wide enough for heavy horses, stamping for grip as they hauled wagons up the slope, over the centuries, carving their way into the soil and chalk, their steel-clad wheels creating something like a railway cutting. The hedges each side had grown limbs across, meeting high in the middle like a church aisle. Evergreen creepers on the branches shaded out most of the sunlight.

There was nothing saying 'PRIVATE' and Bertie reminded himself that he had no particular agenda, no meeting to attend and nobody looking for him. He looked at his phone: no texts and no emails – and incidentally, no connection. This must be a blind spot. Never mind – he could climb a hill later and pick up a signal if he needed it.

This lane looked tempting and he wanted to follow the fine horse and its rider. The tunnel was not long. It rose to the surface as the slope levelled out and, emerging into sunshine, led across a meadow. The hedges gave way to what was left of post and rail fencing around the grassy field. Many posts had fallen over and most of the rails had dropped out from one end or the other creating a dilapidated and ineffectual border that could keep nothing in or out. He trudged on, following the marks of the horse-shoes: the path must lead *somewhere*.

If this place was worthy of a visit from such a tidy ensemble it might be of interest to him, too, especially if he got the chance to meet the young lady in person. After all, he was seeking his fortune, which, he reminded himself, usually included a princess.

Where the meadow ended, Bertie realised this wasn't a lane, but an almost abandoned drive, because it now opened into an avenue of tall trees, at the end of which were high stone gateposts, their rusty iron gates permanently open, held in place by brambles and saplings.

On one side, almost hidden by undergrowth, was a tiny cottage. Single storey with pinkish roof tiles, it had a green front door, and a green-framed window each side.

Bertie guessed one window might be the living room, and the other, a bedroom. He pictured a short passage leading back to a kitchen and other small rooms. The cottage was plainly lived in: a thin plume of smoke rose from the ornate chimney; better still, the front door was beginning to open. Bertie would have the chance to find out more about this intriguing establishment.

"Thank goodness you come along," said a weak voice. An elderly man had appeared at the door, supporting himself as best he could by hanging on to it. His knees began to give way and he sank to the ground. Bertie slipped off his knapsack and knelt down beside the gasping figure.

"What is it? Are you in pain?"

"'Tis my chest: terrible! Pressure!"

"I'll call an ambulance," said Bertie, then realised he had no idea where to say he was; once he could get phone signal. "Where are we? What's the address, so I can tell them?"

"'Tis The Manor Lodge at Tytherton Kellaway. That's where 'tis: oh, dear dear!" At this, the old man put his hand on his chest and passed out, his face drained of colour and breath coming in short gasps. Bertie, grateful that he had recently attended a health and safety day course at Ogle Associates, made sure his patient was still breathing, then quickly loosened the man's collar and pulled the knapsack closer so that he could raise his legs to rest on top of it. A little colour returned to the wrinkled face.

"What's your name?" Asked Bertie.

"Reg – Reg Haines; oh dear!"

Bertie took off his own scarf and folded it to make a cushion for Reg's head.

"Can I get you a blanket or something?"

"In there," Reg pointed.

Bertie went into the house, searched first one room, the sitting room as he'd predicted, and then across the passage – the bedroom, where he found a thick blanket, which he took outside to wrap around the reclining figure.

The 'shock position' seemed to be working. Reg opened his eyes.

"Dear dear," he repeated. "That was painful!"

"Is it better yet?" Asked Bertie.

"No!"

"Shall we get you indoors?"

"Can you? My legs are terrible weak." He tried to raise one from the knapsack, feebly.

Bertie leaned over and picked the thin body up as he might have lifted a sleeping child, and carried him carefully into the bedroom.

"Have you got an aspirin anywhere?" Bertie asked.

"In the bathroom at the back there – in the wall cupboard somewhere," said the man, closing his eyes again. Bertie went to find the pill, discovered the kitchen too, and brought back a glass of water.

"Here," he said, "take this, it will do all sorts of good things for you."

That was something else he'd learned – it was the first thing you should do for a suspected heart attack, and chest pains or tightness were a fairly sure signal. It helped 'reduce blood clotting, allowing the blood to flow more easily through the heart's own arteries'. Bertie had found all the talk of blood rather distasteful, making him feel queasy, but he remembered the essentials, resolving that in future he would always carry an aspirin in his wallet, just in case something like this happened again; perhaps even, God forbid, to himself.

"Where's the nearest high ground – so I can telephone for an ambulance?"

"No need for that," said the old man; "there's a phone in the hall by the coat hooks."

Bertie felt a bit of an idiot: he should have asked. He went in, made his '999' call and returned to reassure Reg that help was on its way.

"I'm sure you'll be fine," he said. "Do you have a hot water bottle?"

"Right there," said Reg, pointing to the end of the bed. Bertie found the rubber bottle, cold in its knitted cover. He took it to the kitchen and boiled a kettle, returning with it to warm and comfort his new acquaintance.

"How's that?" Said Bertie.

"Helpin', thanks; but I don't know what come over me. I'm eighty six and never been ill in m'life: not 'til now. It still don't feel too good, I tell 'ee."

"I'm sure it doesn't Mr Haines, but don't worry, they've got these things well worked out these days. I expect you have some small problem with your arteries: they'll soon get you sorted!"

"I suppose I'll have to go to Swindon. Who's gonna look after my poor cat?"

Bertie hadn't seen a cat but assumed there must *be* one. Reg seemed in good command of his wits.

"That's a good question. Do you have anyone you can ask to come and feed it?"

"Only Her Ladyship; and I'm not sure she can make it this far. 'Er leg's that bad. But if you don't mind telling her what's happened – and mention the cat – I'm sure she'll think of something. She's still sharp as they come!"

"Where do I find her?"

"Just go up to The Manor, through the gates here. You can't miss it; but you'll have to bang 'ard on the door. 'Er's a bit deaf. Ouch, my chest!"

Bertie decided his cat report could wait: he stayed, ready to carry out resuscitation if necessary.

The ambulance men took twenty minutes to arrive, complaining it had been hard to find a passable road into the Manor and then trace Lodge Cottage. They congratulated Bertie on his prompt action, which might have saved the old boy's life, giving him the aspirin. They gave Reg oxygen and checked him over quickly before carrying him off to hospital. Before he left, Reg lifted the side of his oxygen mask to thank Bertie for his intervention and tell him not to forget about the cat. The paramedic said Reg shouldn't worry about the cat, his own health was more important. Replacing the mask and checking the flow, he told Reg he was sure 'the gentleman would take care of everything!'.

Bertie did as asked, locked The Lodge door, shouldered his knapsack and made his way towards the manor house, a glimpse of which he could see, some distance ahead.

If he had not been told someone lived there, he would have thought The Manor must be derelict. He strode up to the end of the weed-covered drive, made dark by the rhododendrons, high and dense at each side. They thinned as the drive opened into a circle, where Bertie found himself facing the shabby remains of what must once have been a splendid but small manor house. It had three tall windows each side of the imposing entrance with its six steps leading up to a porch supported by Grecian pillars. This was crowned with a triangular stone pediment bearing a coat of arms. Bertie couldn't make out its detail because so much had crumbled away. The steps, wide at the bottom and narrowing as they rose, had a low wall at each side, supporting rusty hand rails. A stone ball decorated the top of each pier at the base of the steps.

From the roof, all kinds of plant life had established itself, leafless brambles hanging through nettles. A long dark smear down the wall between two of the elegant windows indicated a blocked gutter, which must have been overflowing for years. The windows were dark, a few broken panes covered from the inside with plywood.

Bertie mounted the steps and raised the ring knocker, held in the jaws of a cast iron, once painted lion's head, and gave three bangs that he could hear echoing the other side of the door. He waited some time and was about to make another attempt at raising attention when there was a loud 'clack', as the latch was raised. The door opened and a tall, stooped lady, leaning on a walking stick, appeared. Her smile offered a favourable reception and Bertie doffed his hat, which he then held between both hands across his middle.

"Good morning; may I help you?" Her voice was deep and cultured.

"Excuse me, but are you Lady Veronica?"

"I am; and who are you?"

"I'm Bertie Lamotte. Rather serious news, I fear. I was just passing the Lodge Cottage and found Mr Haines in some distress. Don't worry, though, he's being taken good care of. He's now in an ambulance on his way to hospital, but he asked me to tell you he may be away for some days, and wondered whether you might be able to arrange for his cat to be fed."

"Oh dear! Poor Reg: I do hope he's not seriously ill, we do depend on him. You'd better come in, young man. You can leave your knapsack by the door here." She stood back, ushering him in and pointing to where he should unload his burden. Bertie looked round as he followed her across the hall. Opposite the front door a wide oak staircase rose to a landing. Passages lead off from either side at the bottom, presumably to the kitchen and servants area. On the right and left sides of the hall, double doors of polished walnut with brass handles looked as though they must open on to the rooms with the large windows he had seen from the outside.

Lady Veronica opened the door on the right and as they walked in, Bertie felt the warmth from a great fireplace the other side of a large drawing room. There was a long sofa in front of the fire and two high-backed leather arm chairs completed a semi-circle of comfort facing the glowing logs. She closed the door and used her stick to push a draft-excluding sausage pillow back into place.

"I do feel the cold, you know. Please sit down." She pointed to the chair on the right of the fire. Bertie sat down and looked around. The big windows made it a light room, although he would have pulled the long and dusty curtains even wider, had it been his house, to gain maximum brightness. On second thoughts it might be safer not to move them. By the look of them they may not have been drawn since World War II and might disintegrate.

By one of the windows was a writing desk, on which stood ranks of silver-framed photographs. Around the wall, portrait paintings, in which Bertie thought he detected a family likeness to his frail lady host, depicted several generations. They added to the faded splendour of this imposing room.

"Please tell me about poor Haines, Mr ...." She needed reminding.

"Lamotte – Bertie Lamotte, your ladyship."

CHAPTER 3

"I would have asked Arabella to feed the cat, but she's obsessed with a cross country event in two weeks' time for The Hunt. She's my late husband's niece, you know – doesn't live here but just pops down when she wants to. I haven't seen her since breakfast. For the last two days she's been disappearing all day: says she's working out how long each 'leg' will take."

"I think I might have seen her," said Bertie, taking interest. "About twenty, very smart – riding a large bay?"

"That sounds like her. Did she speak to you?"

"She asked me to stop whistling!"

"That was definitely her. She can't bear people whistling."

"She suggested it might hinder her progress because it ... affected the horse," Bertie put it delicately. Lady Veronica laughed:

"The truth is it affects her, not the horse. Like yawning, you know – rather infectious! She would never admit it: lovely girl but very proud and terribly bossy. Takes after my late sister-in-law, bless her. She's only staying until the weekend, then she's off back to London. I'm afraid Haines's cat won't be important enough to get her attention and I don't know who else I might ask. I suppose you aren't staying near here, are you, Mr....... my memory you know...?"

"Lamotte – Bertie. Please call me Bertie, everyone does."

"Yes of course! Thank you, Bertie. You have already been such a Good Samaritan, rescuing poor Haines. I'm so useless with my leg. I'm not sure whether I shall fare any better than the cat! Arabella is so wrapped up in her own affairs the rest of us are rather ignored."

"I did get that impression," said Bertie, with a polite laugh. "It was a bit of a Royal Occasion as she swep' past."

"That's the trouble with being so good-looking! Pretty girls are spoilt from childhood; they grow up thinking they deserve it. Years later they realise it's pure luck, having such an advantage. Beauty might run in the family – it might *not*!"

"If I may say so, Lady Veronica, from the photos on the desk over there, you too, may have been fortunate in that direction. That *is* you, isn't it?"

"Oh yes, dear boy! I *was* very fortunate: often used to get my picture in Tatler, back in the fifties. You might have seen me in old newsreels, trailing along behind the Queen at the Coronation; but I fear I was rather like Arabella in those days – headstrong and wilful. It was pure good fortune, though. My father, being a Duke, married the loveliest woman he could find, and I inherited a title and her looks – but it had nothing to do with the real me. Looking back, I don't think I was a very nice girl at all!"

"I'm sure you weren't as bad as all that!"

"You should have met me! I was a little beast! My poor husband had a terrible time of it. He suffered for fifty years before escaping ten years ago with a heart attack. By then I'd spent most of his money and given him, in return, high blood pressure and grey hair. I didn't realise what sacrifices he made for me until he was gone, by which time this place had begun to run down. Mind you, we had a riot of a life for a good while!" She gave a wry smile. "I suppose I'm paying for it now, with only poor Haines to do just about everything. I'm so useless with this leg of mine."

"And what about the lovely Arabella, won't she help out until Mr Haines gets back?"

"I fear not! She's not that sort of girl. The Manor is simply a convenience where she keeps the horse; and I'm a nagging old woman who irritates her."

"Don't tell me Mr Haines looks after the horse as well!"

"No – I don't allow it! Without Haines I would have to move into an old people's home and she knows she would lose her stabling as well as the kudos of 'The Manor in Wiltshire'. Her friend, Melissande, The Rector's daughter here, acts as groom. I expect Arabella pays her something for the privilege, but I bet it's not much!" She made a face.

"They were at school together; Melissande a charming girl but Arabella does exploit people, given half a chance. Her mother always used to call her a 'narcissist'. I've no idea what that means precisely, but I suppose it takes one to know one and a psychiatrist confirmed it when she was about fifteen! Her mother was at her wits end."

"This puts you in rather a difficult situation," said Bertie, with sympathy; "no one to look after the cat!"

He was wondering how Lady Veronica would survive without her faithful retainer. He found it hard to believe that she herself had been as unpleasant as she made out, otherwise she would not have made him feel so comfortable in her presence. Her own plight did not appear to be foremost in her mind: rather, her concern was for Mr Haines's cat.

"Poor animal! If I lived locally, I'd offer to have it to stay," he added.

"It's a she – spayed female; a sweet little thing. She helps keep down the mice; The Manor is part of her territory. She only goes home to be fed; and when Reg has lit the fire. She likes her comforts. You say you don't live around here. Are you from far?"

"I live in London – but not for the next year. I've no idea where I'm going to be when I go on from here!"

"How extraordinary. Are you in some sort of trouble? You must forgive an inquisitive old woman! I shouldn't ask such questions."

"Well yes, and no," said Bertie. "It's not the sort of trouble that should make you nervous – no need to worry. The truth is I *am* a runaway: not from any crime scene – Heaven forbid! It's just that I feel I've reached a stage of life where things need drastic change. I'm nearly thirty and all I've done is accrue money for myself and other people who don't really need it."

"That's fascinating," said Lady Veronica. "What do you do? Something in the City? They've been in awful trouble lately!"

"Almost as bad: I was a marketing director at an agency called Ogle until yesterday. Our main task was to cultivate the favours of Members of Parliament and other influential people, so they would bend to the will of our clients. One has to be very discreet about such activities these days: lobbying has become a dirty word. We also organised campaigns to persuade people to eat more margarine, chocolate and hamburgers, then take holidays in the Costa Brava. We spent millions on it!"

"That doesn't seem *so* undesirable."

"It's not something I'm proud of. We often bend the truth to make it suit The Frantic Quest for Profit."

"Oh really? I'm not sure *quite* what you mean, because I thought there were strict regulations about what you could say."

"Well, aside from politics, take margarine: although we'd never call it that. These days we'd say something tasty like 'golden spread' or 'butterworthy'. The margarine I've been helping to promote claims to reduce cholesterol while giving you a good time eating it. What we didn't tell you was that you have to consume large quantities before it has any effect – by which time many of us are bursting out of our waistcoats and walking around like jelly blobs, totally obese!"

"I see! It does seem rather too good to be true, but I do ask Haines to buy it for me. He does my shopping you know: such a treasure. I don't know what I'd do without him. However, we're talking about *you*, not me. So now you've put all that behind you, what comes next? What *is* this drastic transformation? You don't *have* to tell me – I know I'm being *terribly* nosey!"

"Actually I've no idea! That's what so exciting! This morning I decided to do what they used to do in all the best fairy stories. I packed a haversack, my version of Dick Whittington's knotted handkerchief and stick, and took to the road! Well, railway first and then road. I've given myself a year and a day before I go home."

"Don't tell me! You're going to seek your fortune: how romantic!"

"Well, yes!"

"What fun! But with no cat! I think we can solve *that* problem! Although I'm not sure the cat would agree to leave her job and take to the broad highway: it's a rare cat that would do that. Perhaps if you were to stay here for a while to get her on your side?" They both laughed and Lady Veronica rose painfully to her feet.

"I suppose you wouldn't like to help me make some coffee, would you?"

Bertie could hardly refuse. Obediently, he trailed after her into the hall and down the passage by the staircase. It led past a small office, presumably the butler's, and into a high-ceilinged kitchen, which looked as though it hadn't been updated since before the World War II.

An unpolished table filled the middle of the kitchen. Rows of iron pans hung above a long, black cooking range with four oven doors. A wide shelf ran down one side of the room at waist height. Electric sockets had been fitted and Bertie detected an electric kettle, a toaster, and a small portable grill with double hot plate, from the sixties. A large and ancient refrigerator stood where the shelf ended, next to a tall window. The floor was made of large grey flagstones and the whole room was clean, apart from the dust and cobwebs above 'easy reach' level, and, as Bertie's late father would have described it, 'shipshape'.

"You'll have to excuse me," said Lady Veronica, "but I shall have to sit down. It's rather painful, standing up." She lowered herself into the carver chair by the range. "Now: do you see those cups?" She pointed. "I think they will do. The sink is over there, and the kettle's on the worktop. I hope you don't mind terribly, running around for me."

"No, it's a pleasure," said Bertie. The prospect of coffee was attractive after the morning's adventures. He wondered how old Reg was faring. Was he still on a trolley in the hospital, or by now, wired up to monitors and on a drip? Poor chap: not much fun.

Bertie filled the kettle and carried it back to connect its lead, which, sheathed in woven silk, was truly antique. The plug had round pins set in Bakelite. Bertie hadn't seen one like that for years.

"My goodness, this *is* interesting!" He commented, switching on the power. "We used to have these when I was small."

"It was my husband's parents who modernised this kitchen after The First War," said Lady Veronica. "He and I never bothered, as long as something edible came out of it. Cook must have had quite a hard time before she retired although she never complained."

"Is she still around?" Bertie enquired.

"No, the dear soul died twenty years ago in a nursing home. We couldn't look after her here, although she stayed in one of the estate cottages until she got too infirm: her cottage is still empty. You will find a jug over there." She pointed again. "I find it's the easiest way to make coffee, as long as you warm the jug first."

As Bertie collected the jug he noticed the small blackboard on the wall by the fridge. On it was chalked 'milk, eggs, bread and potatoes'.

"Haines' shopping list," said Lady Veronica, watching him. "It's a bit of a worry really; I don't know when he'll be well enough to go to town again and I don't drive. I suppose I could ask Melissande; although she has enough on her plate, looking after the horse *and* running The Rectory. Her mother's not at all well."

"It does all seem rather fraught," sympathised Bertie, holding his chin and looking solemn. Thank goodness his own mother was so fit and independent and there were plenty of funds to ensure she could keep employing the couple who looked after her, the house, gardens and car in Suffolk.

"I'm sure something will turn up: it always does – or has done, up until now," said Lady Veronica, putting on a brave smile. "There: the kettle's boiled and the coffee's on the shelf there."

She directed Bertie to find the biscuits, sugar, cups and tray; and suggested a jug that might be ideal for the milk, which they agreed might benefit from a few moments in the micro-wave.

Settled beside the log fire in the drawing room Bertie felt very much at home, despite the tired surroundings. Even the spiders seemed to have lost heart, their cobwebs no longer displaying the symmetry of their labours, but hanging dusty and lank from curtain rails and the two chandeliers that must have once looked so splendid. He enjoyed the coffee and leaned back, relaxing. For some reason, he couldn't help smiling. This was all so completely unexpected.

By now he should have been miles away; instead, he was being swept up in several dramas: being rebuked by a 'princess'; rescuing an ancient retainer; making coffee for a dowager in distress. He had a strong intuition that he was about to be allocated a cat with which to continue his adventure. He was not wrong.

"I know it's an awful imposition, but if you were staying close by, I might ask you to pop in for a few days...... just to feed the cat." Lady Veronica's tone was carefully casual.

"Well actually, I hadn't thought of staying in this area;" said Bertie, "but now you come to think of it, it might not be a bad idea. I wasn't *going* anywhere in particular, which must sound a bit daft – but there you are!"

"I don't think it's at all daft! I'm fascinated, dear boy: giving oneself a year and a day to make a new start is so original in this day and age!"

"I suppose it's not something most people do," said Bertie, "unless you call it a 'sabbatical'; or 'a year out' if you're younger, and I've often envied the jobless who seemed to manage to go surfing in North Cornwall every weekend, coming back to London on Thursdays to collect their allowance and visit the Job Centre. They seem so content!"

Bertie tasted his coffee as he warmed to his theme. "Perhaps they've *made* their fortune. It depends on how you define 'fortune'. They certainly can't be seeking great riches – which doesn't come from drifting about in the rollers waiting for 'the big one'; but they must feel it's all worthwhile. They get their reward in those few seconds when they sweep towards the beach in front of a wave that can't quite catch them," he went on, waxing lyrical. "Most exhilarating, I imagine. They can discuss it for days with their friends as they drink their cider and smoke strange weeds."

"How Bohemian! So might you continue towards Cornwall?"

"Not yet, anyway! I suspect I'd soon get bored: not too keen on being wet and cold."

"Do you have any idea of what you might want to do?"

"I haven't a clue!"

"How exciting: and brave!"

Lady Veronica then continued her interrogation, which Bertie found most agreeable; few people had shown so much interest in him recently. No one at the office bothered to ask about his wishes or dreams, but now he was able to talk about the events of the past month, and, being the kind of woman she was, Lady Veronica learned a lot more about this personable young gentleman. Bertie imagined it must be like the first interview at the Job Centre, relating a summary of his background and career so far, but was enjoying it.

Lady Veronica, having ascertained that 'fortune' in his case did not mean money, and that no other goals had yet become clear, suggested that it might be a good idea to give himself a period of reflection.

"I can see that your recent life has been at such a pace that you cannot simply *stop*, and then expect to think clearly about what to do next. Don't you think it might make sense to slow down in a leisurely way, and allow your soul to catch up with the rest of you?"

"I must say that sounds tempting," said Bertie, mellow in the quietness of this faded but noble room. Lady Veronica allowed him time to ponder.

He ruminated on gatherings that must have been held here: what parties, what laughter; and doubtless what crises and tears. Looking across at Lady Veronica, elegant in her navy blue twin set, pearls, tweed skirt and Puffa body warmer, he saw her as a living connection with life before he was born, which he pictured as so gracious: when crowds came out in their thousands to greet the King and Queen; when heroes like Sir Stanley Matthews, in shorts down to his knees, was scoring impossible goals at Wembley; and when the nation united to defeat first the Kaiser and then the Nazis – with a little help from their American allies. Being here was like seeing the old newsreels in full Technicolor for the first time. He may not have been born then, but it all felt so familiar: like the Beatles and Pat Boone. He returned Lady Veronica's warm smile, as though being ready for her next intervention.

"I'd be delighted to offer you accommodation here, if you'd like to stay for a few days. These might be just the surroundings to give you time to contemplate your next move," she suggested. "Nothing much *happens* here and it would be lovely to have some company."

At that moment, a cat appeared at the window and Bertie's attention was drawn by the tapping of the buckle on its collar against the glass. From the smears on that pane, this was not the first time it had used this technique.

"There! She always does that when she wants to come in. Would you be so kind as to nip out to the front door and let her in. I usually have to, because she doesn't give up until I do:

probably good exercise for me but I'd be so grateful: this morning's been quite hectic enough already!"

Bertie did as requested and the cat, hearing the door latch, was ready to slip past him. Tail up, it marched into the drawing room, rubbed against Lady Veronica's legs and sat beside her until Bertie resumed his place. Then it came to jump on to his lap, where, after several turns, it settled down and began purring.

"You are definitely in favour," said Lady Veronica. "She doesn't take to everyone."

"Cats don't usually like me," said Bertie. "My mother has two and it always makes me laugh because, as soon as I arrive, one of them arches its back, fur on end, and spits, just like cats in the old Punch cartoons or Beano. I've no idea why."

"Strange animals; although I must confess I do enjoy this one. She makes me move about and she *does* provide some affection – even if it is cupboard love. You can see she's endorsing my invitation."

"Very tempting," Bertie repeated.

He considered his options. It would certainly be an opportunity to look at life from a new perspective. Doubtless he would be called upon to do menial tasks but that, in his experience, could be strangely relaxing: like when he decided to take a week off to paint his sitting room, soon after he moved to Bayswater. The house-warming party had ended a bit 'over the top' and various puddings had finished up on the ceilings and walls: great fun at the time but in the painful light of next morning, when the last of his now ailing friends had left, he found he couldn't remove the stains of summer pudding or chocolate fondant. The decorators had finished a few days earlier but not collected some of their equipment. Bertie tried his hand at re-painting the affected parts, but the result was still patchy, so he went back to square one and applied two coats over the whole room, even sanding and re-glossing the door and window frames, finishing on his knees to bring the skirting board back to perfection.

Like the painters, he had kept his radio on all the time and, as his hands carried on the work, his mind had free range. This proved both soothing and productive. The consequent campaigns from Ogle had been given quite a boost. A few days in Tytherton Kellaway might be intriguing and refreshing.

On the other hand, he had half expected to finish up today at some pleasant country inn, enjoying a leisurely dinner before an early night in a four-poster – perhaps watching a film before going to sleep. But what about tomorrow? There would be yet more decisions: should he keep walking? If so, where to? All a bit aimless, but staying here, he needn't think at all! Simply do as requested for a while – maybe even a little cooking. Add to that the prospect of a further brush with the dangerous Arabella and one had an extra dimension of desirability.

Bertie made a quick decision, based on no research, facts or profound reasoning, which for him was another first: and one that was to change his life for ever.

"I say, that's a frightfully generous offer, Lady Veronica: I'd be delighted to accept your invitation – if you will let me stand in for the inimitable Mr Haines, as best I may."

"Excellent! I'm delighted! That would be *such* a help. Anyway, look: the cat's gone to sleep. You can't move for a while: it would be so cruel to spoil her nap. Let's get down to some practicalities, shall we? Do you drive?"

"Yes I do. I had thought I was going to substitute my boots and stick for the car for a while, but in this weather it's not very tempting. Perhaps in a few days it will improve, by which time Mr Haines will be back on station. Do you have a car?"

"I do indeed: it's not in the best running order but managed to pass its MOT a month ago, so it's not illegal; and it's insured for any driver. If I give you the key, you could perhaps take me to visit Haines in hospital. I do hope he's all right. I'm sure he'd welcome a visit, if he is not too ill. We could take a few necessities for him. Perhaps I could leave that to you? He must have an overnight bag somewhere – although I can't remember the last time he went anywhere. I'm sure you know what a man needs for a few nights away – pyjamas and suchlike. From what you say, you yourself seem to have spent little time in your own home recently – always at airports and stations. On the way back we can stop at the supermarket and collect a few things to eat. I'm not sure what's in the larder!"

"What about us going out for some lunch," suggested Bertie, foreseeing that there was little promise of such a luxury at The Manor. He had observed the emptiness of the fridge when looking for the milk.

"What a good idea, but I have to confess it's not something I often do," Lady Veronica seemed reluctant. "Not for any medical reason, if that's what you were wondering," she added hastily. "I hardly like to confess, but I suppose it wouldn't take you long to deduct that it's a matter of .... resources."

Bertie understood at once. It hadn't taken long to observe that the one major deficiency at The Manor was that of money.

"Please don't worry about that," he said, reassuringly. "This is my invitation: you have been so kind and your cat has declared me 'persona grata' and it will be a great pleasure to take a lady out to a hostelry of her choice, although I'm afraid the cat will find it somewhat trying as I transfer her from my lap to the chair."

"She won't mind at all, now you have warmed the chair! But how kind of you, Mr......"

"Bertie .... Bertie Lamotte,"

"Yes, of course, Bertie – I'm so forgetful. It's terribly good of you, to take a poor old woman out when you hardly know her: most generous. Are you sure that's no trouble? I'd hate to impose at such an important time of your life. I should let you conserve your savings."

"I am most fortunate, Lady Veronica, in being shall we say, 'comfortably off', by a frugal and well-organised set of ancestors; and during the past few years my own good luck has enhanced their efforts, regarding finances."

"That's a great relief, because I fear I can't offer you much more than board and lodge, and the 'lodge' might be very sparse. Dear Haines lives on his pension and does 'duty for house', rather like the clergy, doing 'house for duty'. It has been a most satisfactory arrangement and to a large degree, he provides for me as well as himself, from his efforts in the walled garden here, which I shall have to show you. It really is a delight."

"Gardening is something I've never really tried since childhood," said Bertie. "It turned out to be rather a failure – we had such a dry summer and I found watering cans rather heavy. Nothing much came of it."

"Haines has green fingers – and the rain has done more than enough watering this year, hasn't it? I can hardly remember when we had a dry week. Now, can you give me just five minutes while I put on a hat and powder my nose. If I'm lunching with a handsome young gentleman I want to look my best."

"What about your niece? Do you think she would like to join us?"

"I was hoping we might have left before she comes back. I think she was planning to go back to London this afternoon."

CHAPTER 4

Visiting time at the hospital in Swindon coincided nicely with Bertie and Lady Veronica's emergence from lunch at her chosen pub in Wroughton, near the hospital.

"We'll get well away from home, just in case Arabella drops in and finds us," Lady Veronica had said. She had visions of her niece protesting that 'you could have waited for me!' Her Ladyship wanted Bertie to herself for a little longer. From lunch, they could go straight on to see how Haines was faring.

He was looking remarkably spry, sitting up in bed.

"They want to keep me in for a few days," he told them. "I feel perfectly OK, but 'tis something about my blood: they want more tests to find the best pills. I'll 'ave to take 'em every day from now on: damn nuisance – but better than being dead!" He chuckled and patted the bedclothes to make the bed look even tidier.

"They took me up to the operating theatre and put in some kind of plumbing to keep my veins open: a stint or something. They said I'd be fine, once my body had got used to it." He nodded at the memory.

"I was awake for the whole thing, but a nice young nurse held my hand – the one they weren't messing with – and kept me chattin'. It's still sore in 'ere," he complained, patting his chest, "but nothing as bad as when I first come in! That was bad! Never had nothing like that, never in my life. I'm surprised I've got any blood left – they keep takin' samples. Just look!" He pointed at small plasters in the inside of each elbow. "I'm like a bloody pin cushion!"

When Reg heard that Bertie was to hold the fort for a while, he was relieved.

"I've been quite worried about the cat," he told Lady Veronica. "Wondering how you'd manage." He waited until she went away to speak with the ward sister, before telling Bertie he was even more worried about Her Ladyship – she couldn't manage to do much for herself.

"She do depend very much on me, these days," he said. "But I can't mention it: she pretends 'tis the other way round! You know what these ladies is like! Terrible proud! She ought to be in a home, really; and Miss Arabella is no 'elp at all. She makes more work, if anything. She comes down 'ere, 'elping 'erself to all she wants, and we have to jump to it if she wants something. I pity any young man who finishes up with her!"

He couldn't say more because Lady Veronica was back from the briefing on his condition she had demanded, very sweetly, from the ward sister.

"That's very satisfactory," she said. "Apparently you did the right thing ... ... Bertie: there – I remembered! Yes, the right thing, giving him an aspirin. I really didn't know that was the procedure, did you, Haines?"

"No Ma'am, I didn't, but I'm glad this gent did! Done me a lot of good that did! That's what they said: might have saved me bacon! So thank you very much, sir."

"Glad to be of service, Reg, if I may call you that," said Bertie. "Lady Veronica has been kind enough to ask me to stay around for a few days, and I've been wondering whether it would be all right for me to stay in your house. I could be keeping an eye on things. It would keep the place aired, and the cat would know where to find its food."

"That's a grand idea," said Reg: "you can use the spare bedroom. The bed's made up in case I get any visitors – which ain't very often, but you never know! You've got the key, 'aven't you? Well, there you are! There's a bit of grub in the fridge and the cat food's in the pantry – the little door off the kitchen. I shall be able to rest much more easy, if I know someone's there. That's grand!"

"Are you sure you don't want to stay at The Manor?" Lady Veronica tried not to show her disappointment. "We have several rooms for visitors and I assure you they are perfectly habitable! Haines' spare room is hardly spacious, if you'll forgive me, Haines." She smiled graciously at her lodge keeper.

Bertie realised he must tread delicately if he were to avoid 'an atmosphere' between the two over his accommodation.

"Normally, of course, I'd be delighted to stay at The Manor, your ladyship, but I think it really would be best for the cat – as well as for our patient here – to return to a warm, inhabited house, after a spell in hospital. It would deter burglars, too. Perhaps when Reg has been home for a day or two I might take you up on your offer. It's most kind of you!"

Before leaving, Bertie noted the telephone number of the phone by Reg's bed and promised to give him a call the next day, to find out when he needed collecting,

"How's that ole car going?" Asked Reg.

"We didn't rush things," said Bertie, "and she managed the hills with ease!"

"You want to watch that handbrake," advised Reg. "It tends not to go down all the way, and after a bit, you get a bit of smoke and a smell. Then you know 'tis time to do something."

Bertie was retrieving the Gate Lodge key from under the flowerpot, when a small four-by-four drew up next to him from the direction of The Manor. It was Arabella.

"You must be the new man," said the young lady. "Welcome to The Manor." She gave him a lofty smile then delivered her first request.

"When you get a minute, could you replace the bulb in the outside light by the stable? It blew just as I was leaving last night. My groom won't be able to see her way round this evening when she comes to feed up: very trying!"

"It will be a pleasure – if I can find the stable," said Bertie. "Did you get your timings?"

"Yes. How did you know I was doing them?"

"You passed me this morning. Remember? I was whistling!"

He couldn't resist teasing; in any case it gained her attention and kept her close enough to look at. His eyes sparkled as he took in every detail of her, now dressed for town, a close fitting sweater giving clear publicity to her perfectly shaped torso and slender but strong arms. He noted in particular, her hands: attractive enough for the kind of work he often commissioned for skin cream or nail varnish ads.

Her voice, which, on the phone might have been mistaken for that of a young man, made the hair on the back of his neck tingle. He wondered if it was smoking after lights out in the dorm that had kippered her vocal chords, giving that deep and husky tone; but come to think of it, she did sound a little like her aunt, although it couldn't be genetic; or indeed, her aunt might, in the past, have smoked. Her accent was straight from Benenden or St Mary's: top drawer. She really was quite a girl!

Arabella was not, however, going to be wound up by his mischievous mention of her little problem. Rather, she preferred to engage in a little verbal sword fighting. With a hint of a smile, she pushed herself back from the steering wheel to get a better look at him. She liked what she saw.

"Oh it was you, was it?" She was beginning to suspect that he was no ordinary hired hand. His bearing and accent were more those of her pals in Belgravia.

"But I did stop, as requested," he continued.

"Quite so, thank you," she replied haughtily, not wishing to pursue this line of conversation. She put the vehicle in gear.

"Well, can't hang about. I want to miss the rush hour – better go!"

At which she wound up the window and drove away, turning off the drive from which Bertie, earlier that day, had emerged on foot. He guessed it was the track leading to the public road.

He picked up the provisions from the supermarket they had passed on the way back from Swindon. The bagful he had bought for himself contained a lot more than Lady Veronica's and the careful way she counted out her coins had touched Bertie's heart. His mother was far less frugal and always enjoyed her shopping. Lady Veronica plainly found it painful and difficult. How sad, he thought, that a fine lady should be reduced to this penny pinching. He looked away as she paid at the checkout, to save her embarrassment.

As he opened The Lodge cottage door the cat appeared, gave him a quick rub on the shin, and was first indoors. She led him through to the kitchen and sat watching as he took stock of his new surroundings.

Bertie could see she was ready to give him a little time to unpack before demanding her supper: or maybe it wasn't quite time yet?

Later, having fed the cat and put a hot water bottle in the spare-room bed, he ate, cleared up, and sat down in Reg's armchair by the fire. He had been tempted to catch the TV news but decided against it. It was time for him to work things out for himself. He had poured a small whisky and sparkling water from the provisions he had bought earlier. He took a sip.

No one could overhear him, except the cat, which had decided once more that his lap was the best place. It ignored him when, speaking aloud, he began proceedings.

"Bertie, what have you got yourself into?" He waited.

"And why on earth did you want to stay in this miserable little lodge when you could have been staying in such an historic and splendid manor house?"

It was time to explain: perhaps it would help him work things out.

"Well, for a start, I'm warm," he replied, "and I doubt very much whether it's warm up there." He indicated the direction of The Manor with his thumb.

"It would have been rude *not* to sit and talk with Her Ladyship until she decided to retire; and I'm simply not used to having long conversations in the evening unless I'm 'out' somewhere. I do prefer my own company, don't you, Cat?"

The cat made no reply as he stroked its head.

"Knowing you", Bertie said, meaning himself, "I suspect there's more to it than that. I can guess what you've got in mind."

"You are always so suspicious. Don't you trust me?"

"Not really: you often have ulterior motives and I suspect, in this case, that you were hoping, sooner or later, to get that gorgeous young thing on her own somewhere. You tried this afternoon; but you slipped up a bit there, Bertie! She still drove off!"

"Well of course she did! She probably has to go back to work; but at least I was able to make her aware of my existence. She really is a most desirable creature and I fancy her madly! From the look in her eye I suspect she found me interesting, too!"

"Are you going to tell her you're a baronet? She might be impressed."

"No I'm not: don't forget she's the grand-daughter of a duke! I expect baronets are two a penny where she hangs out. I bet she works in some posh office in Mayfair. Let her do her own research. She doesn't even know my name yet but at least I know hers!"

"Her aunt says she's a real Tartar: doesn't that put you off?" Bertie sounded disapproving and was trying to warn himself.

"Not at all! It will make a change not to have some girl going all gooey simply because I've got a title. She might be more interested if she thinks I've got a bob or two. They plainly need it at The Manor: the place is falling apart."

"That's not very romantic!"

"Who says I want romance? I wouldn't mind a bit of a frolic, though!"

Bertie thought about that for a while. So far this interview was getting nowhere. He cleared his throat.

"What are you thinking about now? No, don't tell me! Sex! But I can sympathise there, she is very dishy!"

"I suppose I was – my mind just drifted."

"It usually does – and brought you a lot of anxious moments. That's not what this meeting is supposed to be about. You've got to decide what to do next. Here you are, supposed to be seeking your fortune, and all you have done is to land yourself in a poverty-stricken remnant of English aristocracy with a whole new set of responsibilities. It's not just the cat! You are going to have to bring in logs to keep the old lady warm – and keep her fed. What about the fortune you are supposed to be seeking? Are you going to stay here and dwindle, along with the rest of the inhabitants?"

"The Lovely Arabella certainly isn't dwindling! I'd say she was blooming!"

"That was the sweater – she has got a lovely bosom, I admit."

"And I noticed that her eyes are similar in colour to those of the cat – sort of amber; and she certainly knows how to use them; and did you take note of her perfect bottom? Some girls look so good in jodhpurs don't they?"

"Well, if they have nice bottoms. This one certainly did: I'd love to give it a pat."

"Well for goodness sake don't do it until you get to know her better: but Bertie *leave* all that! We're trying to discuss your career."

"I've just realised I might not have one if I don't replace the missing light bulb! Sorry, Cat, but I'm going to have to leave you for a bit." The cat made no objection as Bertie stood up.

The meeting having come to an abrupt halt, Bertie searched the kitchen cupboards, found a light bulb, put on his coat and hat, dug out his torch and made his way through the darkness to the stable, next to the garage where the ailing car was recovering from being driven by someone it didn't know.

Bertie had the torch directed up at the guttering and upper wall of the stable, searching for the defunct light, when he walked into something large that fell over with a clatter. He identified it as a bicycle as it barked his shin and made him drop the torch, which went out. Groping about in pitch dark he found the torch, but his shin was hurting so much it needed rubbing before he did anything else.

He swore fiercely, under his breath. It was something he had learned to do at the office when things went wrong. With open plan, if you bellowed expletives, giving yourself a measure of relief from your pain and frustration, there would be instant protests from at least one born-again evangelist further down the carpet.

In his head, he shouted: "Shit! Fuck, and ouch!" Being silent it meant that another person, who had emerged from the stable to see what had happened to her bike, was not aware that Bertie was on one knee rubbing his shin in the pitch dark.

To her, the silence indicated she had not propped the bicycle properly. She was intent on picking it up at once, to avoid falling over it after feeding the stallion.

The obstacle that her legs encountered did not feel like a bicycle. Her hands, reaching out to seek the fallen machine, also met something they did not expect: Bertie's hat, knocking it off. She tripped over his boot, which extended behind him as he knelt.

Both parties suffered a shock: Melissande, (for that's who it was), being a practical country girl, assumed it was an intruder. She was instantly ready to strike as soon as she could identify a target.

Bertie, feeling like an intruder, unfamiliar with the surroundings and a guest to the area, adopted a defensive attitude, arms clasping his head. This was just as well, because

Melissande losing her balance, fell over him, fists clenched, adrenalin pumping.

Bertie knew someone was landing on him but, to his relief, it didn't feel dangerous because his nose signalled that whoever it was, smelled delightfully fragrant. In that fraction of a second he detected Devon violets and spring flowers.

Perfume always caught his attention. Some scents he liked a lot; others he hated and would change seats in the train to get away from brassy perfumes on the type of women who needed heavy applications before they could smell them at all. This scent, which he loved, prompted an unaggressive response and he allowed himself to roll over, becoming a soft landing place for his assailant. The next thing he knew, his face was very close to Melissande's, and her hair was tickling his ears.

Melissande had not been able to stop herself tumbling over Bertie's boot and, as he was pushed over, there was little she could do to break her fall. Bertie's being there saved her.

In that same split second, when her face brushed his, she, too became aware that this was no down-and-out vagabond or burgling prowler. The gasp that Bertie gave as her body bumped down on his, carried the slightest whiff of the best whisky, reminding her of her father's good-night kiss. She picked up traces of expensive aftershave, which gave off memories of visits from bishops and dignitaries who couldn't resist picking her up when she was small so they could look at her and hold her close. Until the age of about seven she had been the sort of child that people wanted to hold in their arms. She had been so pretty and full of smiles. That all ended when she went away to boarding school, paid for by her grandparents. She began to wear glasses, making her look studious; and, as she grew taller she became more reserved and too big to pick up.

In the present incident, being in complete darkness, it was their senses of smell that had avoided any unpleasantness.

There were, however, two consequences – Bertie's sore shin and the disappearance of Melissande's spectacles. Melissande feared they might be broken.

The pleasing aromas, however, led both of them to apologise rather than say "Who the Hell are you?"

Bertie got his apology in, first.

"I'm terribly sorry – I was just coming to replace a light bulb, then I fell over this bike. Are you all right?"

"It's my fault. I do apologise: I shouldn't have left the bike there – but I couldn't see! It's so dark. You poor thing, I landed on you with all my weight – I just couldn't stop myself! Did I hurt you?"

"It's OK – only my shin – lost a bit of skin on the bike but I shall live, don't worry."

He rose to his feet, and reaching down, found Melissande's arm, then her hand, which he took and helped her to stand up. He didn't let go immediately, making sure she didn't lose her balance, and, for a second or two, she allowed the contact, before retrieving her hand.

"Just a tick, I'll find my torch, if I can," said Bertie. He groped around for it on the ground.

"Ah, here it is!"

"Can you point it into the stable, I'll put the inside light on," said Melissande; "I was just feeling about for it when I heard my bike fall over. So sorry to make things worse for you. I had no idea anyone was here. It gave me quite a fright!"

"I've only been here since this morning," said Bertie; "I was commanded to replace the bulb before 'the groom' came to put the stallion to bed."

"Well, I'm 'the groom'; and I guess you must have met Arabella."

"I did, but, how do you do?" He extended his hand in formal greeting; she gave him hers for another, appropriate moment.

"I'm Bertie – and I just happened to be passing this morning, when all kinds of things took place: quite a long story, really, and I'd be delighted to relate it, but I think we ought first to replace that bulb, don't you? Let's see if it survived in my pocket."

By some kind of miracle the bulb was still intact. In no time, Bertie had found something to stand on, reached up and replaced the light; and Melissande made sure that the stallion in his box had plenty of hay, water and clean straw.

"Is your bike all right?" Asked Bertie.

"The handlebars seem to be pointing sideways," said Melissande.

"We can soon fix that." Bertie stood the bike up, took the front wheel between his knees and rectified the problem with ease.

"I can check them for you in the morning to make sure they are firmly in place – but you should be safe if you go slowly tonight. Do you have to go far?"

"No, it's only five minutes. I live in The Rectory, by the church."

"Ah indeed! I heard about you from Lady Veronica. Your father's the vicar, is he?"

"Rector, actually." Said Melissande, not unkindly. Bertie felt he was being educated.

"Oh, is there a difference?"

"It's all about money. A vicar runs a parish which gets its money from somewhere else, usually the diocese; but a rector is the priest of a parish that pays for him with its *own* money – bequests and so forth."

"Sounds expensive!"

"It's not when you see how little my father gets; but he doesn't complain – it's his choice! He could have done other things; he's quite brainy."

"This all sounds most interesting," said Bertie; "I'd love to hear more about church matters: I hardly dare tell you, but I've always left that to the rest of the family, apart from singing in the school choir, which I enjoyed. We didn't bother about much, other than singing and making sure people didn't see us larking about. But do you work in the parish, too?"

"No: I'm home partly because my mother's not very strong and needs help about the house; and partly because I'm not sure what to do next. It's a long story; I wouldn't want to bore you with it and I must get back now – help my mother get to bed."

"I'm sure we'll meet as we go about our duties in the next day or two," said Bertie, politely. He gave her a quick summary of why he was helping out. Melissande said she would relay the news to her father who would doubtless want to visit Mr Haines in hospital. Then, picking up an empty bucket she said:

"Thank you for fixing my bike – and yes, good night! This outside light is on a timer but the inside one needs switching off. I'll do it, don't worry."

It occurred to Bertie that old Reg probably made sure Her Ladyship had enough logs by the fire before he went off duty, and since it was only about nine o'clock, he decided to check that she was keeping warm. Their doctor in Suffolk had drilled into him that 'older ladies need to keep warm'; so he had a wood-pellet heating system installed, giving his mother automatic central heating which did as it was asked by the thermostat. This was convenient if not, perhaps, quite as comforting as a wood fire in the hearth.

In the dim light of the new bulb, he made his way from the stable yard towards The Manor House. Things in general were looking up. Perhaps he need *not* be in quite such a hurry to leave Tytherton Kellaway. These were beautiful surroundings; he was plainly needed – at least for a few days – and it was genuine need, not some fatuous cause like eating more high-cholesterol burgers.

It was rather good, too, meeting young ladies, apparently unattached, one of whom was very attractive, if rather pleased with herself; the other, interesting and intriguing, perhaps less self-centred.

His mind wandered away from whether to stay or not and back to the latter. He had no detailed idea of what she looked like, in the poor light during their unconventional introduction. She was certainly fragrant, softly but well spoken and plainly dutiful but he wondered about her figure and appearance when not hidden in a scruffy Barbour and sou'wester.

"Concentrate!" Bertie's sensible self prompted him. "You've drifted back to the usual subject. Look what happens as soon as you get away from the office! You'll degenerate if you don't dwell on the matter in hand. You are supposed to be bringing in logs, remember?"

He found the back door at The Manor still unlocked and Her Ladyship huddled by the last embers of the drawing room fire.

"Oh Haines: I wondered where you'd got to," she said. "I've been getting quite chilly."

"It's me, Bertie, Lady Veronica. Poor Mr Haines is still in hospital in Swindon."

"Dear me, of course he is – how stupid of me; but he usually comes in to wake the fire up a bit, after supper. It slipped my memory that he was ill."

Bertie discovered that, as a rule, Reg not only stoked the fire, but made cocoa for Her Ladyship, before locking up and returning to the Gate Lodge. It seemed that events, once again, were going to make Bertie's decisions for him. If he didn't stay for a day or two, things could go badly wrong at Tytherton Kellaway. They might also prove rewarding. After all, what kind of fortune was he seeking? He had his wherewithal, his health and his freedom. He had already picked up a charming old lady, a friendly cat, and somewhere to sleep where he could think his own thoughts.

"Better just get on with it, Bertie," he told himself.

CHAPTER 5

It was the door of a big white van being slammed that woke Bertie next morning. This was followed by persistent knocking on the Gate Lodge door. Whoever it was, sounded serious and was not being at all patient. It was annoying and, to say the least, rude.

"All *right*, damn it!" Bertie shouted with maximum volume. "I'm *coming*!"

The banging stopped and he could hear someone stamping as they waited in the cold.

"Is this Tytherton Kellaway Manor?" Said a fat man with a shaven head. His companion, who looked like an all-in wrestler, stood a couple of paces behind.

"This is part of it," said Bertie, now composed. "Can I help you?"

"Yes, sir. We are High Court Enforcement Officers. Here is our identification; and this is our warrant." He produced his ID card in one hand and a paper in the other. Bertie made no move to receive it.

"We've come to collect a payment of eighteen thousand pounds, or goods to that value; and I must advise you, sir, that we charge for our time: so the quicker this can be done, the less expensive it will be for you."

"Not for me, actually," said Bertie. "I'm only a visitor. This is the Gate Lodge; the Manor is further up the lane. The owner, I fear, is rather frail and from what you say this is going to be quite a shock for her. I wonder whether you would like to come in for a few minutes while I nip up to break the news to her. I'll show you where the kettle is and you can make yourselves a cup of tea."

The bailiffs were surprised at the civility of this gentleman, but looked at each other and nodded.

"I will stay here, and Tom can come with you," said the fat man. "He can wait inside the door while you talk to the owner. That all right, Tom?" Tom nodded again.

At the Manor, Bertie found Lady Veronica in the kitchen having trouble with the electric kettle. She was relieved at his arrival.

"How fortunate .... Bertie! I wonder whether you can help me with this. Haines usually does it and I'm all behind with breakfast."

"Certainly dear lady; may I suggest you go back to the drawing room and sit by the fire; I will bring you some tea in just a minute."

"How kind! The fire is still glowing nicely – you must have chosen precisely the right logs last night."

Bertie was quite proud to hear this. Log selection was a skill he had learned in Suffolk before he installed the central heating. Lady Veronica returned to the comfort of her armchair and Bertie did as promised, allowing her to have a few sips before informing her of the catastrophic news; adding that perhaps there might be a mistake.

"My dear, how frightful!" Lady Veronica was indeed shocked at the news, "I had no idea!"

Bertie knew about bailiffs, because a friend of his in London, having been unable to pay some card table debts, had suffered such a visit and called on Bertie to help 'bail' him out, as his friend joked later. On that occasion it had been a matter of six hundred pounds and, as expected, the friend soon repaid him. Eighteen thousand, however, was a bit steep if you had only known someone for a less than a day.

"They must have warned you first," said Bertie. "They can't just land on you like this. Are you sure you didn't sign for a letter of some kind in the last week or two?"

"I might have," said Lady Veronica, "or it might have been Haines. The postman always leaves the mail at the Gate Lodge. Haines brings it up to me and leaves it on the hall table. Let's go and have a look." She reached for her walking stick.

Bertie accompanied her into the hall. On the table was a pile of brown envelopes.

"It might be among these," said Her Ladyship. "I've been meaning to look at them for some time now, but they are usually bills of one kind and another and I simply haven't had the courage to look. Someone from the bank actually came to see me a few weeks ago: all the way from Bristol, and told me I must be very sparing with cheques, because my account was running very low."

"That can so easily happen," said Bertie, comfortingly.

"My husband used to deal with all that; and before he died he warned me that I'd have to stop spending, except on essentials; and that's what I've done: but now it's come to this. What on earth shall I do? Can they really just come in and help themselves? How frightful!"

"I think they can be persuaded to make a list of things sufficient to pay the bill if they were sold. They'll put stickers on now, and come to collect what they've chosen another time if you still haven't paid up. In the meantime you mustn't sell them or give them away."

"What ever shall I do?" Lady Veronica was becoming even more distressed, wringing her hands.

Visions of something like this happening to his mother flashed through Bertie's mind and it was painful to see things unravel like this for someone else.

He couldn't shrug it off as being someone else's responsibility: he was a participant in this drama as a consequence of following a track left by a horse carrying a rider whose pretty face and nice bottom had caught his fancy. This escapade was changing from 'seeking his fortune' to 'finding a ruin', aided and abetted by his carnal instincts. His inner self, usually quiet in situations like this, began to address him.

"Face up to it Bertie! You didn't expect to find your fortune without a few hiccoughs on the way, did you? Just think! In the old days, a chap would have to kill at least one dragon and slay several knights before even catching a glimpse of a fair princess. You've been dead lucky – meeting a fair maid, rolling about on a stable floor with another who smelled nice and sounded delicious – and now you've found an old lady in distress. Buck up – do your stuff! Show a bit of leadership! There's no one else – poor old Reg is lying in hospital; the lovely Arabella isn't much help – you're the old dear's last bastion!"

By this time, Her Ladyship was shedding a tear. She had produced a tiny lace handkerchief from her sleeve and was touching it below her eye, waiting for him to speak. Bertie took up his own challenge.

"I think you should invite them in; allow them to make their list and stick on their stickers. If we keep them waiting, they charge a fortune for every minute and they'll want you to pay for that, too, so the quicker we get them in, the less expensive it will be. We'll at least gain time to work something out."

"Very well – let's do *that*, Bertie. What a *mercy* you are here! At least you can keep an eye on them."

"You go back and keep warm; I'll see to everything; and don't worry! I'm sure there's a solution."

Bertie wasn't at all sure there *was* a solution but he was concerned about Lady Veronica's blood pressure. An untruth seemed appropriate if it prevented a possible heart attack. He'd already had to deal with one cardiac incident the day before and here was an opportunity of avoiding another. This place and its owner really had hit the bumpers of age and economic collapse.

The bailiffs were very efficient. They made a quick recce outside, first rejecting the idea of taking the car.

"It ain't worth nothing!" Said Tom. "I'm not sure about the 'orse."

"That belongs to someone else," Bertie informed him.

"It might be hard to cash in, too," commented the fat man. "I think we'd better start looking inside the big 'ouse: there isn't much out 'ere, is there Tom?"

Watching the bailiffs making their assessments in the drawing room, Bertie stood with his back to the fire to give Lady Veronica some moral support as she sat stiffly, trying to ignore the invaders but wanting to see what items they would eventually carry off.

Eighteen thousand pounds was a lot of money to raise at auction. The bailiffs were picking up the silver photo frames, sticking little dots of red paper on one after another before replacing them with care.

"Don't worry," said the senior bailiff, "they peel orf all right if you pay up before we 'ave to take 'em. These bigger labels won't spoil the furniture either," he concluded as he blew away a cobweb and stuck a printed notice on the glass-fronted antique cabinet in which colourful and fragile Chinese porcelain was displayed.

By the time he had finished, there was not much left without a sticker or label. Bertie dreaded to think what it would be like if the threat of collection were indeed carried out. It would be devastating for the old lady.

The last straw was when, before moving to the dining room, they placed labels on the two armchairs and sofa.

"Very nice pieces, if I may say," commented Tom. "They'd fetch quite a bit, I'm sure."

Bertie could take no more. If he wanted to accompany the men into the dining room, he would have to leave Lady Veronica on her own, and it worried him. She was already pale and tense, hugging herself as though freezing cold. He was afraid she might go into shock. For the first time in her life she was having to face the reality of running out of resources; tasting what so many others must have experienced, and here he was – just watching and saying 'there there!'

"What a funny way to seek a fortune!" His alter ego spoke out loud before Bertie could stop it.

"What did you say?" Asked Lady Veronica. "I see nothing funny!"

"No, no: nor do I – it was just me, trying to make up my mind," said Bertie hastily.

For the second time in a matter of days, he made a decision without proper consideration or research; certainly without having facts on which to base a balanced view. He addressed the bailiffs:

"I say: what would it take to stop you chaps doing all this labelling. It really is most distressing. You realise this poor lady will be left with an empty room and nothing to sit on!"

"Well, sir: that's the way it is, I'm afraid. It's what we do. The High Court gives us a warrant and we carry it out; and there's nothing much this lady can do except part with the goods, or of course, pay up."

"Can you give her some time to find the money?"

"With all respect, sir, I suspect the High Court has already done that. No – we have to take possession of the goods – or the money – before we leave; and as I say, the longer we spend nattering about it, the more expensive it gets."

"Will a cheque do?" Asked Bertie.

"No sir, it won't. But something like a debit card or credit card is just fine; or a bank transfer, wot we can verify, would do."

"Very well – let's get down to business. Have you got one of those gadgets for credit cards?"

"We have indeed, sir."

"Well I think if I used a couple, and topped up with my debit card, we can raise the cash here on the spot."

"Bertie you mustn't. I'll never be able to pay you back!" Lady Veronica intervened from her chair by the fire. By now she was truly upset and beginning to sob.

"Dear Lady Veronica, don't worry. This is purely an emergency measure and I'm sure we can work something out afterwards. We shall sort it out in no time – you'll see!"

He walked over and put a reassuring hand on her shoulder. She clasped it with both hers and he felt how cold they were. As he looked at the blue veins and brown patches of old age on the slender hands he knew it was the right decision. After all, it wasn't as though it might make him go bust – there was plenty more where that came from. Gallantly, he donated his handkerchief for the old lady to dab her eyes.

The cologne with which he had scented the yet unfolded kerchief, gave instant comfort: it reminded Lady Veronica of the occasions when her late husband had stepped into the breach with such assistance. She remembered, too, with some guilt, that previous crises, like this one, had been caused by her overspending.

The mobile credit card reader refused to work.

"No signal," complained the fat bailiff. "We'll 'ave to go up a hill somewhere. You wait 'ere, Tom. I'll go with this gentleman."

Bertie, being unfamiliar with Tytherton Kellaway Manor and its surroundings, had to ask Lady Veronica where they might find the nearest higher ground. She pulled herself together and suggested the knoll beyond the walled garden.

"There's a stone folly up there, built on a mound. It's supposed to look like a Roman temple – built by my husband's great great grandfather. It's quite high – you get a view of the whole valley. Try there."

Watching and waiting while the card sent its electronic prayer to the Great God 'Bank', Bertie felt it was an appropriate ceremony to be taking place in such a hallowed setting, equivalent to a Roman sacrifice of old, though less drastic than sacrificing a young girl to appease the deity. He wondered whether the Romans, two thousand years earlier, would have received as rapid a response to their plea.

"There we go!" Said the fat man. "That's one done. Make a note, will you, Tom. Five grand down, thirteen to go."

Relieved that, from this point on the Manor, connection could be made with the modern world, Bertie began to be less tense and, between handing over cards and seeing the debits confirmed, had time to admire the scenery.

As the rainclouds retreated over the hills behind him, great beams of sunlight pierced the greyness, lighting up meadows, which glowed green on the flat, low-lying land the other side of The Manor house. He could see the avenue and beyond, the dark foliage hiding the tunnel of a lane that had led him to this extraordinary place. His eye followed it between pastures towards what must be the Chippenham road and Maud Heath's causeway, in the middle distance.

To the right of the lane several fields were almost completely flooded. The sun was glistening from them as a breeze ruffled the surface of the water. It would have looked like a lake, except for the hedges and gate posts that defined the boundaries of farmland.

Further away, a church spire rose out of woodland. Bertie thought the scene would have inspired Turner, had he still been around, to paint another masterpiece. It was beautiful and *so* tranquil. The Rectory must be somewhere in those trees, he demised. The fragrant Melissande might be preparing breakfast: what a pleasant thought.

"That's it, then, Tom! Eighteen thousand, four 'undred and ninety two pounds only, since we've not had to spend more than one hour 'ere."

He handed back the last plastic card to Bertie who restored it to his wallet, and the wallet to the breast pocket of his tweed jacket.

"If we go back to the van, sir, I can give you a receipt. Then you can go and get warmed up by that fire. Nice and warm that was in there. In fact, this could be a very nice property, couldn't it, Tom?" He turned to his colleague.

"Yea, nice; but it needs a bit doin', don't it?"

"That's true. If you 'ad the money, it could be a bit like that other place – where they've got the lions and that."

"Longleat?" Suggested Bertie, as they walked back towards the walled garden.

"That's it! I took the kids over there: very nice!"

"How on earth am I ever going to pay you back?" Lady Veronica, clasping the mug of tea that Bertie had made. She still looked anxious despite the bailiffs having left to continue their distasteful duties.

"Let's not worry about that for the moment," soothed Bertie. "Let's just say how fortunate it has all turned out to be. If Reg's heart had not needed attention when it did, I might never have found such a delightful place and good company."

"And I might have been left in a bare house! It was indeed fortunate for The Manor and me; and of course for poor Haines – he might have *died*."

"Which reminds me: I would like to go and visit him, if I might borrow the car once more."

"That's very kind of you, Bertie. I would come too but I feel quite exhausted after that ordeal."

Bertie advised her to stay in the warm for the rest of the morning. He would bring back some kind of lunch and all would be well. He didn't say so, but he did not want her to be there while he discussed future solutions with Reg – since, apparently, no one else apart from the bank and the bailiffs knew the situation at Tytherton Kellaway Manor. The lovely Arabella was unlikely to contribute much to any such discussion but it was plain that someone needed to intervene to prevent the inevitable – if the demands in all the rest of those brown envelopes were to be met.

As he returned to the kitchen for the car keys Bertie noticed a dusty picture on the wall of the passage. Until this morning it had been too gloomy to show up, but a moment of sunshine brightened that part of the wall via a scullery window and an open door. He stopped to look.

It was an ancient map of the estate, dated 1777. A tiny image of The Manor House and surroundings was almost in the middle of the picture, while from it, he made out fields and woodland, paths and cottages extending as far as the church he had seen. In the other direction, it reached the edge of what was marked as Chippenham. This must have been a large estate, at that time.

Interested, he looked for and found the roads and paths he had followed from Chippenham. With pleasure he noted that Maud Heath's Causeway was included – with a small ink drawing of the many-arched bridge over the low ground.

"Fantastic!" Said Bertie: "and it must have already been there for three hundred years! What an amazing woman! She really left her mark."

"How did you know I was ready to come home?" Asked Reg, when Bertie finally arrived at the cardiac ward in Swindon. "They were only going to phone a few minutes ago. I said I thought you would probably pick me up if they asked."

"I wasn't coming to collect you, but it looks as though we can set off straight away," said Bertie, observing the packed bag and Reg dressed, waiting in the armchair by the freshly made bed.

"I've just got to wait for my pills," said Reg. "I don't expect they'll be long. They said I must take a letter to my doctor when I get home; then a lady come round and asked a whole load of questions about my house. She wanted to know if I had stairs; and whether anyone else was there. I thought she was a bit cheeky at first but she said I ought not to be on my own for a day or two. I took the liberty of saying you were there, Bertie. I hope you don't mind! You will be, won't you?"

"Of course I shall, Reg. I'm very comfortable in your spare room and the place is warm as toast. It's just what I need at the moment – a welcome change and I'll be happy to stay around for a while. In fact that's what we need to talk about. While we wait for the pharmacist, shall we pop down to the snack bar and see whether they have a coffee or something? I'll check with the nurse."

The nurse said they had plenty of time; the pharmacist wouldn't be back for another hour or so, but she advised them to be back by midday.

Reg was not feeling quite as strong as he thought he would, and held on to Bertie's arm on the way to the cafe, where they found a table for two and Bertie collected tea and biscuits.

"It's been another dramatic morning, Reg," said Bertie, once they had settled. He related the events, with the successful conclusion first, so as not to worry the old man.

"They went away again, so it's all quiet there now, but between you and me, Reg," said Bertie; "*someone* had to pay up on the spot, otherwise they might have made off with just about everything in the house, apart from a few essentials. Well, we managed it – with a little help of some credit cards."

"Do you mean you lent Lady Veronica all that money?" Reg looked dubious.

"Well, yes I did!"

Reg drew in air between his teeth and shook his head.

"I'm not sure that was wise, Bertie. I suspect you won't get it back. Her Ladyship's not good with money. It used to worry Mr John a lot. I think that's what gave him his final stroke – finished him off."

"You mean Lady Veronica's husband? What did he do?"

"He was the squire; tried to run the place but spent most of his time running around after Lady Veronica. She's a lovely lady but she led him a dance, I tell you!"

"Oh dear! What kind of dance?"

"Nothing wicked of course but she did like to enjoy life. She always wanted to be going up to parties in London. She must have spent a fortune on dresses and all that. I used to hear about it from the housemaid."

"When would that have been?"

"Back in the Fifties, when I was the chauffeur."

"My goodness, you've been here a long time!"

"From when I left school in 1943," Reg chuckled, "until now! Except for a couple of years when I went for National Service. Before that I was just a sort of boot boy and helped out at the stable. I got married in Coronation Year and me and Beth lived in the cottage up the hill for forty years, until I lost her. She had pneumonia and died rather sudden. Very sad it was."

"Did you have any family?"

"Children? No, sir, we weren't lucky in that department – but we had a very happy time together. She was a wonderful wife to me and I miss her every day."

"I'm so sorry to hear that; it must have been a very sad loss," said Bertie.

"Well that's when I moved into the Lodge. They wanted to let out our cottage to bring in some money. It was a bit of a wrench but I've settled in nicely over the years; and now it's just me and Her Ladyship – and Miss Arabella when she feels like it!"

"Didn't Lady Veronica have any children either?"

"No: we was all in the same boat! A bit of a shame, really."

"So Arabella will inherit all the estate, will she?"

"What's left of it!"

"Did they sell off all the land?"

"Most of it," grumbled Reg. "There's only about two hundred acres left and there's a mortgage on *that*."

"Do they grow stuff – corn, potatoes – that sort of thing?" Bertie knew very little about farming.

"You must be joking!" Reg laughed with frustration. "Did you notice any floods when you was walking from the station? You were on foot, weren't you?"

"I was – but apart from the marshy bit, where there's that amazing causeway, I didn't see much, over the hedges. Today, though, I was up at the Roman temple and you could see several fields under water. It looked like a lake."

"That's what I'm talking about," said Reg. "It's been like that in winter for the last two years: worse this year. It's killed off most of the grass and that was the last bit of money the farm made for Her Ladyship."

"How do you make money out of grass, then? Making hay?"

"I wish she could 'ave! But she don't have the machines and it costs a lot to get someone else to do it. No, in summer she let other farmers bring their animals – cows mostly – to eat it up. The farmers would pay for their keep. We didn't even have to keep an eye on 'em, the owners did that too. The money wasn't enough to run this place, but at least it kept the wolf from the door."

"But now you can't do that because it's under water."

"That's it; and the weather's got worse, this past year or two. I've never known nothing like it. Years ago, the occasional flood used to do the fields good, leaving mud and stuff from up river – it would make it extra green the next spring, but now the water hangs around for weeks and weeks – kills everything except sticklebacks!"

"It makes one think they ought to turn it into a boating pond," joked Bertie.

"That's about all its fit for – or a fishing lake!" Reg wasn't being funny. "And of course all Mr John's plans have gone out the window, now he's gone."

"What plans?" Bertie asked, curious.

"Oh – he was going to do a deal with some big building company to put a housing estate down there! I tell you, it caused a hell of a fuss around here. Made 'im very unpopular. It was in all the papers: he got a lot of nasty letters and comments – 'specially from the other landowners and people he used to think was 'is mates. I'm sure that was part of what killed 'im. They wouldn't 'ave it!"

"I'm not surprised," said Bertie, remembering the scene of verdant beauty he'd been looking at from the Temple Mound.

CHAPTER 6

There still being another twenty minutes before midday, Bertie fetched more tea and Reg continued his story.

"So what happened?" Asked Bertie.

"Nothing – to this day!

"So the whole idea was dropped, was it?"

"Well no – that's the funny thing," Reg perked up. "Would you believe – he got the go-ahead from the council! They was all ready to bring in the diggers – then he died. Lady Veronica couldn't cope with all that business, and after that, we had floods. No one's done nothing about it ever since. It's a dead loss: only dries out for a few weeks in the summer, then it's a lake again!"

"But a *housing* estate! I'm surprised he thought he could get away with that," said Bertie. "Green Belt and all that: and on a flood plain, of *all* places!"

"That's what Mr John's posh neighbours thought, but there was some plan or other forcing the council to build so many thousand houses somewhere in the district and it seemed like a good idea to tuck some of them away out of sight down here."

"So what happened?"

"Like I said – nothing. 'Er Ladyship and me are still 'ere – livin' off our pensions and everything's gone quiet."

"Mm," said Bertie, thinking.

"That's why I say, Bertie, I'm not sure it was a good idea, lending 'er that money, although it was very 'elpful of you. The poor old soul wouldn't 'ave 'ad nothing left in the 'ouse! But if you'll pardon my askin' – it's none of my business – but have you thought how you might get the money back?"

"Well I hadn't actually," said Bertie; "not yet."

"Mm," said Reg. "It's a lot of money."

"Mm," said Bertie.

"What a lovely day!"

Melissande saw Bertie before he saw her. She narrowly avoided spearing him as she emerged, dung-fork first, from the stable carrying a large dollop of horse manure. Carrying a stepladder, he was surprised by her yet again and came to an abrupt halt, averting an accident. He gathered his wits and smiled with pleasure.

"Isn't it? Beautiful! Such a change!"

The thought that Melissande *might* be around *had* been in his mind but he had hoped to meet her in a less hazardous setting – perhaps polishing harness in the tack room.

"We can't go on meeting like this," he said, laughing. "I shall have to tread much more carefully near the stables – you always seem to be lying in ambush!"

He regretted putting it *quite* like that when he saw the embarrassment his remark had caused. Melissande's face had reddened and she was looking uncomfortable.

"Oh dear! I didn't mean it like *that* of course," spluttered Bertie, trying to put things right.

"Of course not," said Melissande, feeling hot in the face and even more embarrassed. "I shall have to whistle or sing, or something – so you know I'm around. I don't want to scare you off!" Then after a moment's consideration. "And of course I don't mean it like *that* either! How embarrassing this conversation has become!"

They both began laughing and Bertie made it even funnier as he remembered what had happened the last time he was whistling.

"You'd better sing, rather than whistle," he said, between guffaws. "It might be Arabella approaching, and not me!"

Melissande obviously knew of Arabella's little weakness.

"Has she mentioned it? Told you off?" She asked, amused.

"That was the first thing she said to me: asking me not to. She said it might stop the horse."

"Oh I say, that's a good one!" Melissande laughed, feeling less self-conscious. There was something about this large gentleman that put her at ease.

She finished her journey with the loaded fork, dumping its contents neatly on the edge of the dung heap the other side of the stable yard before returning to stand by Bertie as he unfolded the steps under the lamp.

"If you are wondering why I have brought steps," he said; "it's because I thought I'd give the outside light a bit of a clean. The glass is so dirty!"

"I've been meaning to do it for ages," said Melissande, "but I haven't really got time to do any more than feed the horse and top up his water; then in the afternoon it's more important to give him some exercise, otherwise he'll get fat and lazy. Arabella wouldn't like *that*."

"Do you look after other peoples' horses as well?" Asked Bertie, as he climbed the steps clasping a damp rag. He wanted to keep her talking so he could get a better look at her and make better acquaintance. Apart from their close encounter in the dark, when his nose sensed her attractive scent and her voice had told him a lot about her background, he had no proper impression of her appearance.

The trouble was that if he looked down, he couldn't carry on with what he purported to be doing; and while he cleaned the glass of the outside light, he couldn't see her, standing below.

"I say: would you mind terribly hanging around for a minute? I could do with some help."

That did the trick – now she couldn't leave without being ungracious.

"Of course! What can I do: hold the steps?" She propped the fork against the wall and stepped forward to grasp the steps as he stood on them.

Bertie glimpsed down as she looked up for an answer.

In that fraction of a second Bertie's world stopped rotating. He nearly lost his balance. He had to drop his screwdriver and grab the lamp bracket attached to the wall, to save himself.

Melissande, to steady herself and prevent the steps toppling, took hold of the steps with both hands.

In that instant Bertie's life changed. Before, he had not seen Melissande's eyes or her expression; now he was bowled over by them, almost literally.

This third 'ambush' by Melissande was, like the first two, unintentional. All she did was look up to see what Bertie needed by way of help. She had no idea of the effect his first clear view of her face would have on him. Her first impression was that he was about to fall off the steps, and her instinctive reaction was to stop that happening by steadying them. Later, after a glass of port, Bertie speculated that she might even have saved his life.

Until then her eyes had been hidden by the brim of her blue bush hat and severe spectacles, but, as she turned her face upwards, Bertie saw them properly. A phrase from an old novel he'd read came to mind as he held on to the lamp bracket: 'what gorgeous peepers!'

They were large and bright blue with a dark band around the iris. There was a twinkle to go with their quick intelligence; and an unreserved readiness to be of assistance. Meeting his gaze she looked down instantly, grateful that she too had something to hang on to. She held the steps even more firmly, not for his safety but to prevent her knees from giving way.

Blushing even more hotly, and feeling angry for it, she couldn't allow his equally blue eyes to intrude for another second. She felt as though she were being consumed by curiosity and interest – almost as though she were not properly dressed. She had glimpsed his delighted reaction and impatient desire to know all about her.

She had never learned how to cope with such looks except by escaping them. Normally she would then make herself scarce, but on this occasion she could not, without endangering the perpetrator. Anyway, it was something else that stopped her from removing herself from this man's presence.

She couldn't pin it down, but on reflection she decided it was because she rather enjoyed being near him: he was somehow so warm – and charming. That fact that her knees nearly let her down, was, however, disturbing and most unusual. Perhaps she had rushed her breakfast or was sickening for a cold, but, looking up at those penetrating eyes, the broad shoulders and tallness, emphasised by the stepladder, had made her feel most odd.

From the top of the stepladder, looking down, what had captivated Bertie was her innocent eagerness, such as he had observed in children expecting something nice to happen. He was equally smitten.

Only weeks later at a meeting with council officers and the Parish Council when Melissande was sitting, with her father, listening to their response to The Great Plan, did Bertie get time to study more details of her face. He had to do it surreptitiously, lest she blush but, relaxed and concentrating on the matter in hand, her cheeks didn't have that touch of rose that appeared when she was labouring in the stable yard. With the bright window behind him, she couldn't see he was staring at her.

Her nose was just the way he liked a girl's nose to be: straight and perfectly proportioned, with discreet nostrils. She had a slightly prominent upper lip, giving an air of determined dignity, while the generous lower one seemed to promise a most rewarding kiss, if the opportunity ever arose.

Despite the complications being thrown up by TGP, as she and Bertie had named it, her expression was calm. Any movement she made was unhurried, perhaps raising her hand to touch her lips or brush a wisp of hair behind her ear. The only quickness about her was in those eyes. Facing the bright light of the window, their pupils were tiny, showing up the blue of the irises but, as the officer pointed to the chart on display and back again to the document in his hand, Melissande's eyes followed the action instantaneously, before flicking back to see whether people looked impressed or negative.

Bertie could see that she was taking it all in and, from the affectionate glance she gave her father, guessed she had good answers ready to deploy when the time came.

During those weeks, Bertie had grown to envy the elderly parson such a glance. She would rarely look him – Bertie – in the eye, after that first startling thrill that almost knocked him off his stepladder.

Here indoors, in public, she wore no hat and her light brown hair, still retaining hints of blond from last summer's short sunny spell, was swept back from her forehead. There wasn't a sign of a frown or wrinkles and Bertie could see where she got her carefree expression because her father's was similar. As usual, his head was slightly inclined backwards as he observed the proceedings. It made him look patrician and gave an air of nobility tinged with cheerful amusement, thought Bertie. Like Melissande, The Rector's chin was strong, with a faint dimple.

What Bertie also found so attractive was the way in which, in repose, Melissande's face showed no boredom, no petulance (unlike Arabella!) and the corners of her mouth were still the same as they must have been when she was born – ready to smile, show distress or joy but giving no clue as to what might come next. She had kept that childlike spontaneity: the readiness to listen, please and participate.

When Bertie *was* fortunate enough to receive a smile from her, the smile was never excessive – not one of those toothpaste dazzlers delivered with a steely look, such as one might receive from slick city businesswomen about to clinch a deal. Melissande's smiles were bestowed on Bertie with reserved pleasantness, her eyes showing a welcome, and willingness to give him her full attention: curious to hear what he had to say.

The trouble was, Bertie rarely received any such smile. Melissande took great care to avoid any but formal discourse with him; and seemed to stay away as much as she could.

He had never been treated like this before by a woman over whom he had developed such an overwhelming crush. He didn't like to show-off or go over the top, bombarding a girl with bunches of flowers and suchlike, but nothing about him seemed to impress her. The result was that now, in her presence, he became tongue-tied: as shy as she was. He had even, on occasion, felt *himself* blushing.

For her part Melissande was also shocked by the 'second lamp incident'. Until that moment when she looked up into his face, Bertie had seemed to be simply 'rather a nice man who had suddenly turned up at The Manor' and whom she had literally bumped into.

Admittedly she had learned, during that first melee, that he used pleasing aftershave and did not smell of tobacco, perspiration or dogs; and, as he had extricated himself from her and her bicycle, she had noted that he was very well muscled and not an ounce overweight.

Admittedly, yes, he was a fine figure of a man but until now, Melissande had never taken much interest in men, except in a social and work-related way. She found most men, especially young ones, somehow 'distasteful'. This one, she found 'disturbing but attractive'.

"Her Ladyship's in a bit of a state," said Reg, as the two cleared the table after supper, one evening soon after Bertie had moved in.

"Did she come to visit?"

"No, I went up there: thought I'd see how it felt, getting out a bit. I can't sit here doing nothing!"

"Don't over-do, Reg. You don't want to be back in Swindon!"

"The doctors told me I could do a bit of exercise, once I felt like it: and today I did! Besides, the cat didn't turn up at her usual time and I thought I'd see what was what."

"Did you find her? The cat, I mean."

"I did – she was shut in the pantry, not at all pleased! She must have followed Her Ladyship in there and got left behind."

"So, what was Lady Veronica worried about?"

"Money – what else?" Said Reg. "She's not a bit happy about you coughing up so much to save her bacon and she was trying to work out how to pay you back. She's got no idea what to do and it upsets her. Mr John always sorted things out, even though it'd get worse all the time."

"It's not as though she hasn't got *anything* left, is it?" Bertie asked.

"Not far off it! She can't borrow any more: 'tis all mortgaged up to the hilt."

"Mm," said Bertie. "Do you have any ideas? Who does one talk to?"

"That's the problem," said Reg. "It's no good talking to Her Ladyship; she gets all in a twist. You can talk to Miss Arabella all you like and she doesn't seem to hear a word – just asks why you 'aven't moved the electric fence or something."

"Isn't there anyone who has a grasp of the situation?"

"Only me! And that Melissande. We talk about it sometimes, when she's in, doin' the 'orse. She knows just what's what because Her Ladyship has a good moan to 'er about it, and Miss Arabella complains all the time. It's a wonder the young lady keeps coming over 'ere – although I think she needs the money. She's about all Miss Arabella pays for, apart from the farrier and the horse-feed: tight as tight that niece is."

"I get the impression that The Rector's daughter is rather over-qualified to be a groom," suggested Bertie, trying to sound casual; "rather bright, I thought."

He wasn't going to mention that she was his favourite subject at present but Reg had already noted how often she was turning up in conversations and had twigged Bertie's interest.

"'Er is! She went off to college and got a degree. I asked her once, what she was doing, and she said 'economics and business studies' but I wasn't much the wiser. It sounds technical though. Nice girl: very good to her mother. She worked in Bath for eighteen months for some big company and then Mrs Blythe was took poorly and Melissande gave it all up to come 'ome and look after 'er. All that education wasted! She was at some posh school, too, with Miss Arabella, that's where they met. They're supposed to be friends but Miss Arabella doesn't treat her very nice – terrible selfish 'er is."

"Isn't there anyone else at all?" Bertie feared they weren't getting far in resolving the crisis facing Tytherton Kellaway Manor.

"Well there is that solicitor chap, Mr Penworthy, who used to come over when the guv'nor was still alive. I believe he used to look after things but I guess they stopped paying his bills; you never see him these days."

"Do you know where one could find him?" Asked Bertie. At least here might be someone who knew more of the family's legal position.

"Why on earth do you want Melissande there?" Arabella was not pleased, the following Saturday as she stood, dressed for the hunt, in the drawing-room doorway at The Manor.

"Because, my dear, I feel she understands my situation rather well; and I'm very fond of her – she makes me feel safe. To tell you the truth, I see more of her than I do of you, my own niece! She's so kind – always pops in to make sure I'm all right."

"But she's not family!" Arabella grasped her riding crop across her buttoned black jacket, raising her chin slightly to ease her high white collar and tie. "And that new man, Bertie, why do you want *him* to know all about our problems. He's only here until Haines gets back on his feet, isn't he? It's a bit like washing one's dirty linen and all that."

"Arabella, just for once, will you do as I ask?" Lady Veronica did her best to sound firm. "I'd like you to be here by tea-time, because we are having an important meeting and I have invited Melissande because I want her there. It's not as though you don't know each other very well – she's been about the only friend you've kept up with since leaving school – and she knows as much about us as you do! Her parents are some of our oldest friends. I owe Bertie a lot of money; and the solicitor, Mr Penworthy is coming and you will learn what it's all about this afternoon. I know you are in a hurry to get to the meet and I get quite flustered trying to explain things – so just do as you are asked."

"Very well, Aunt Veronica; but it all seems weird!" Arabella closed the door rather more firmly than she intended and hurried off to the stable.

It had taken a promise from Bertie and a bank reference before Mr Penworthy had agreed to attend the 'family meeting' that Lady Veronica Kelway wanted on that Saturday afternoon at The Manor. Bertie had traced him to his office overlooking the river at Chippenham and explained the situation faced by his new friends and acquaintances; and his own involvement, which Mr Penworthy agreed had been somewhat precipitous.

"Lady Veronica still owes us quite a large sum in fees," Mr Penworthy told Bertie at their first meeting. "We have refrained from pressing for payment in view of the long association between our two families but this has proved somewhat expensive for Penworthy & Penworthy."

Looking around the office, with its leather chairs, ornate chandelier and oak bookshelves laden with richly bound law-books going back a hundred years or more, Bertie got the impression that Penworthy & Penworthy had not been suffering *that* much from the Kelway Debt. He found 'the young Mr Penworthy' much less dusty and conservative than he had imagined, after listening to Reg's description. Perhaps Reg had only met the previous generation of this well-known local family. It had been encouraging to find someone who talked business in language with which Bertie was familiar. In any case, Penworthy & Penworthy held all the records for Kellaway Estates and would do so until accounts were settled, though if it came to the crunch, there was some doubt as to how much would be left to pay legal costs after mortgages and other debts had been settled.

"Well, you seem to have stepped in to keep the wolf from the door this time," said Mr Penworthy junior, "but unless someone takes radical action to reverse the fortunes of the Kelway family, I fear, Sir Bertrand, that The Estate and The Manor will move to different ownership."

"Oh please call me Bertie. I haven't been at all swanky in Wiltshire – it's not my county; and it's rather fun just being one of the workers," chuckled the baronet, who had been keeping quiet about his title.

"I do beg your pardon, but having looked you up on The Internet to make sure of your bona fides, it seemed only fitting to use your title. I hope you'll excuse me?"

"Of course, old chap; no offence taken but try to avoid spreading it about: I'd rather maintain my cover for the moment – it gives me another perspective on life; but tell me, have you any ideas as to what might be done to turn things round at Tytherton Kellaway?"

"Well perhaps you know about the late Mr John Kelway's plans for a new village on his lower land?"

"I had heard, but it's going to sound pretty funny if they start talking about building it under water, especially after this winter. The place still looks like a boating lake!" He chortled. "Not much of a solution there – if you'll excuse the pun. At least it's not a salt solution, like some of the low land on the South Coast, what?"

Mr Penworthy did his best to smile and continued.

"At Saturday's meeting I suppose I should spell out the seriousness of the situation and then see what Lady Veronica and her friends come up with."

"Quite so, quite so," agreed Bertie. "Tip out the box and see what we can all find!"

The meeting itself turned out to be unique in the history of Tytherton Kellaway. There being no lord of the manor to preside, Mr Penworthy was allowed to take the chair. In an unprecedented change from Kelway tradition, 'staff' were allowed to be present, by way of 'the groom' and 'the gatehouse keeper temporary help' (Bertie). This was because holding such a meeting for Lady Veronica and Arabella was unlikely to have led to any financial solutions, whereas Melissande and Reg Haines were known to have comprehensive knowledge of the workings of The Manor, and Bertie – although unbeknown to anyone except Mr Penworthy, who had discovered in his research, that 'Sir Bertrand Lamotte, lately of that West End centre of influence, Ogle Associates' – was one of England's wealthiest bachelors.

Bertie had sworn Mr Penworthy to secrecy but this knowledge gave him, as chairman of today's meeting, the confidence to insist that Bertie's views were not pooh-poohed by Arabella, who seemed to have taken an instant dislike to him.

She had voiced her disapproval first to her aunt, who had to remind her that it was Bertie who had fought off the bailiffs with his credit cards. Arabella then tried to lobby Melissande, who by this time, despite her better self, found that Bertie refused to leave her thoughts as she mucked out the stable, prepared supper for her parents, or even as she sat in church for early morning Communion.

"It's not just the way he paid off the debt *immediately*, but he seems to have done it for no personal gain," she said, in his defence, when Arabella caught up with her, grooming the stallion.

"Huh!" Said Arabella. "I suspect he's just some City slicker, trying to pick up a prime bit of countryside for a bargain price. You can hear from his accent he's not just a chauffeur or footman from Town. I wouldn't be a bit surprised if he didn't start asking me out before long. You should see the way he looks at my arse! He's got his eye on that – and on my inheritance!"

"Arabella, I wish you wouldn't be so *crude*," said Melissande, offended by such talk. It was so alien to her background at The Rectory and she hadn't even heard such a word until the third year at Cheltenham Ladies.

She had never quite fitted in at boarding school. The other girls, including Arabella, used to stop talking about things like boys and sex when Melissande came into the room. It was done because they liked her and knew she found such talk distasteful. "She's not like us," they used to say, "but she's lovely anyway!"

Indeed, it was to Melissande that the other girls turned when they wanted some kindly advice. Arabella remembered, for example, the time when she herself had fallen under the spell of the new gym mistress. She had been smitten with an overwhelming crush on this athletic bundle of energy, who was usually seen with a whistle clasped between her teeth.

The fact that the new teacher seemed to ignore her completely was too much for Arabella to bear. She cried on Melissande's shoulder and poured out her anguish. Melissande's advice had proved very sound.

"If you want to get her attention, get into one of the teams – netball or lacrosse. Score plenty of goals and she'll eat out of your hand," she had said. Arabella took her advice, doubled her training and soon joined the first team in both games. She even developed a 'dodgy knee' which would 'give way' during a training session, requiring a little massage from the gym teacher. A few tears from 'the pain' were rewarded by a kindly arm around the shoulders, which satisfied her passion for days.

At Saturday afternoon's meeting it was Melissande who had come up with the suggestion that was to change the fortunes of all present. Arabella was the first to express her disbelief.

"You must be joking!" She exclaimed with a derisory laugh and snort. "You can't even see the pegs – it's all under water! How on earth will anyone ever want to live there?"

"I say, hang on," intervened Bertie. "Before you write it off, it's about all you've got left here – the land, the Manor House and permission to build a housing estate. I think we ought to hear Melissande's proposal, because although I don't want to sound avaricious, I *would* like to be reimbursed at some stage!"

"Absolutely," said Lady Veronica, supporting his view. "Melissande, do tell us what you have in mind, my dear: something like one of those villages in the Far East, all on stilts?"

CHAPTER 7

"Well actually, Lady Veronica – you're not *so* far away from what I had in mind! I've been racking my brains, the past few weeks, wondering what those poor people down on the Somerset Levels and along the Thames could do. They must have felt so helpless, watching the water rise in their living rooms and kitchens and I felt terribly sorry for them. At Church we've been organising collection of various things to send down to parishes in Bridgwater where people are taking refuge – you know – blankets and cushions. Then the other day, I heard someone on the radio talking about houses that floated!"

"How ridiculous," said Arabella. "Don't be so pathetic, Melissande: stick to your mucking out!" She laughed in such a patronising way that Bertie began to be annoyed, which was unusual for him.

"Not at all ridiculous, in my opinion," he said, frowning at Arabella. "They keep talking about 'major change in how we live' and then spend days arguing about whether we should dredge rivers or allow farmland to flood: nothing much new at all! Melissande may have something there! The mind boggles! My goodness yes, I can see it!" He swept his arm as though describing a vista of floating houses and moored launches.

"You're not being serious!" Arabella sounded even more scornful.

"Why not? Can you suggest something better?" Bertie delivered his rebuke with a charming smile: he didn't want to start a fight.

Arabella kept quiet: she *could* think of something *much* better but could *never* admit it, even to her tolerant friend and confidante, Melissande. It was to marry someone who was 'bloody rich'; get him to settle the debts, knock the place into shape and then get on with life, hunting, organising charity balls and going skiing in winter.

"May I suggest," said Mr Penworthy in the ensuing silence, "that we seek advice on what might be possible to bring this estate and property back 'into the black', as it were? Perhaps a management consultant or one of the major land agencies: I'm sure they offer such services."

"They need payin'!" Said Reg Haines scratching his chin. "Then it gets 'ard."

"That is indeed a problem," admitted Mr Penworthy; "although if they were invited to become part of a management team that would share the rewards later......?"

"Absolutely not!" Arabella was adamant. "Once they get their claws in, we'd finish up with less than we have now! There's got to be a different way of digging our way back out of the mire; and we've got to keep it in the *family*." She threw a hostile look in Bertie's direction.

Lady Veronica shook her head:

"My dear, we've been saying that for decades and your beloved uncle was about to rescue us, when he was so tragically taken."

"Yes – but to build a housing estate on a *flood* plain! Much as I loved him, Uncle John's idea was potty *then*, and even pottier now, with the weather becoming perfectly ghastly. It may be permanent too! We may discover that all we own is a lake with dying hedges poking out."

"Exactly," said Bertie. "That's why Melissande might have something, and I think you should investigate the whole idea. It might work! I'd certainly be prepared to put some effort into finding out more about it. Now that Reg is almost back in harness, I have nothing else pressing and it could be fun."

"You realise we can't afford any remuneration, Bertie!" said Lady Veronica; "which is why I wanted this meeting. It was to find ways of repaying what we already owe you – and it's terribly unfair to ask you to stay working for nothing – just to get yourself reimbursed! Oh dear, it's all so *desperate!*"

"Lady Veronica, don't worry on my account: I'm on a kind of sabbatical – and this is just what I need – something to stimulate the brain and give me a bit of interest. I find the whole situation absolutely fascinating! I don't *need* any remuneration – although as you say, it would be nice to be reimbursed at some stage: balance the books and all that."

"And what do *you* know about running a country estate?" Asked Arabella, unpleasantly.

"Not a great deal, I have to admit," said Bertie, "although I did spend several years living on one. I fear my interests have always been rather office-bound in London. However, it occurs to me that we have, at this very meeting, someone well qualified to carry out the kind of research you need." He cleared his throat before continuing.

"I understand, Melissande, that you have a degree in economics and business management? Feasibility studies and that sort of thing?"

Melissande was annoyed with herself for blushing yet again but there was nothing she could do about *that*.

"My friend Reg told me," continued Bertie, before she had time to reply.

"As if she had nothing better to do," interjected Arabella, concerned that her groom might spend less time on her equine duties.

"You haven't been near that kind of work for ages, have you?" She directed her question to Melissande.

"Well, a couple of years," replied Melissande, modestly; "but that's not to say that I don't still take an interest. From what I hear, my former colleagues have been having a hard time, what with the recession and bank problems. It might be good to do a little preliminary research – keep my brain in trim; and the idea *does* seem to be open to opportunities. There must be millions of people worrying whether they will be able to afford to insure their houses from now on, after the last few winters – especially this one."

"Such a bore," said Arabella. "I've given up watching the news: nothing but people in waders, moaning about 'The Government'."

"Sometimes, Arabella, you are singularly unsympathetic," said Lady Veronica. "We are fortunate that The Manor is built on higher ground, otherwise you might have found yourself in the same – I nearly said boat, but perhaps I should say waders."

"That's precisely it, Aunt Veronica. Our family built it up here on higher ground to make sure it *didn't* get flooded. Those people on the Somerset Levels must have *known* the risk they were taking — the place *keeps* getting inundated but they didn't sell up before it got really bad – now they're suffering the consequences. It would be the same here!"

"The poor things couldn't afford to live anywhere else – and many of them were born there. All this bad weather has taken everyone by surprise."

Mr Penworthy could see the discussion was getting nowhere.

"I think we should stick to how to resolve immediate problems facing Tytherton Kellaway Estate, rather than getting into the politics of a neighbouring county," he said. "May I ask – does anyone have any *other* practical proposals as to what might be done, apart from calling in an experienced land agent, or pursuing the idea of a new kind of 'water-resistant' housing estate? I regret that I have another appointment in half an hour and I feel we need to come to some kind of plan for action before we end this meeting."

"Well I don't think Miss Melissande's idea is as daft as all that," said Reg. "At least she and Bertie could take another look at it: 'cos otherwise 'er Ladyship might 'ave to sell up and move into Chippenham – so far as I can see, with all due respect, your Ladyship."

"I think it's up to Lady Veronica and Arabella to decide," said Bertie. "It's their property, after all."

"Well I've got to go," said Arabella, standing up. "I mustn't miss the five fifteen or I'll never get back in time for tonight's appointment. You decide, Aunt Veronica – but do let me know. I'll see you on Wednesday, Melissande: you'll order some more bran, won't you?"

"I'll do it Monday," said Melissande.

"Don't forget, will you?" Arabella picked up her handbag and departed, leaving an atmosphere of annoyance at her off-hand exit.

Bertie sat back in his chair, observing the scene. Apart from feeling ruffled at the way Arabella treated Melissande and the other matter of eighteen thousand pounds, he felt detached from the situation: an outside observer. Apart from the money it was nothing to do with *him*. The thought was consoling – he could walk away from all of it with a clear conscience.

Things certainly looked grim for Lady Veronica, but he himself could move on. Reg, now he had almost recovered, could care for Lady Veronica, the cat and the stallion, given a little help from Melissande; and Arabella would look after herself.

Tomorrow, he could write off his losses, pick up his haversack and head south to see what else might turn up. He had done his bit, stepping in when needed, now he could leave. Perhaps this had been the first trial of many on his quest? What other excitements might await him, further along the way?

It was, however, his biological side that prevailed over common sense. He persuaded himself it was romance rather than lust that dissuaded him from bailing out of Tytherton Kellaway so quickly. To his own surprise Arabella's bottom was no longer sufficiently alluring to make him wish to stay here. Having observed her objectionable behaviour, his better judgement over-ruled the urges of his primate self – and despite those delectable shapes, he thought he would find the rest of her too much like hard work.

Rather, it was a less carnal side of his being which felt drawn towards staying. He was strongly attracted to the compassionate and intelligent Melissande, even though she seemed to back away as soon as he looked at her.

Also, he was seeing life from a new perspective – that of 'the common man', rather than one of social standing and a fat bank balance. It was like that TV show where the boss glued on a moustache and went to sweep warehouses to see how the other half lived. Mr Penworthy, as requested, had not blown his cover, so here at Tytherton Kellaway Manor he was still just 'Bertie' who had drifted in and been helpful, rather than a high-powered baronet and businessman.

On balance, therefore, it was *not* yet time to take up his haversack and walk. It was congenial to have somewhere comfortable to live, in friendly and undemanding company. It was hard to resist the challenge of winning the affection of a fair maid; and intriguing, thinking about the prospects of a crazy scheme that might make another fortune – or not.

Leaving now would be nothing but another retreat like turning his back on Ogle Associates. That, he assured himself, had not been a 'running away' retreat, but a 'tactical withdrawal'. Such action, on this occasion, would not be appropriate.

Without any more hesitation or reflection, he found himself taking the next step into a new phase of involvement in this green and soggy estate – despite its crises – or perhaps because of them.

Arabella's sudden departure had disrupted the concentration of those remaining and apart from Bertie, lost in his own thoughts, the others were now dispersing their discomfiture by chatting about trivia, while Mr Penworthy looked anxiously at his watch. He was relieved when Bertie took a deep breath, sat up straight and brought the focus of the meeting back to the matter in hand.

"This idea of launching – that's the right word, isn't it? – a 'water-tight village on a flood plain', sounds really exciting," he said, brightly, raising everyone's spirits, "if a little risky".

His last proviso raised doubts but his companions remained mildly optimistic. This man's confidence was infectious. If *he* was prepared to clutch at a straw, then chances were that it wouldn't be a short one.

"Just think," he continued, "if you could get it to work *here*, the future could be very rewarding! There must be many other places facing the same situation. I read only a couple of days ago that five million homes in the UK could be flooded if the weather goes wrong; and who knows how much worse it could get! I can think of all kinds of people who would like to get involved in something where there was so much scope for growth."

"Do you really think so?" Lady Veronica sensed hope at last.

"I do," said Bertie; "and I'd be happy to give you a hand, Melissande – if you'd let me – in finding out more about it. Then we could meet again if it looks promising," he said, turning to Mr Penworthy.

"Excellent," said the latter. "What do you say to two weeks time?" He took out his diary. "Would that be all right with you, Lady Kelway? Mr Haines – and you, Sir... Mr Lamotte?"

"I think much would depend on whether Miss Blythe feels she has the time to undertake some research without disrupting her other responsibilities," said Bertie, conscious that Melissande was not being properly consulted.

Bertie's respect for her situation helped Melissande make up her mind. Most of the time people took her for granted. Her parents knew how much she loved and cared for them and assumed she must know it was mutual. The stallion and the cat considered her to be one of their servants, while Arabella knew she could push Melissande a long way before her friend jibbed.

In general, it was only Lady Veronica and Reg Haines who treated her with consideration. Most of the time this routine of service – along with worship in church on Sundays – added up to contentment for the devout and faithful Melissande. Here, though, was this large, gentlemanly stranger, who had turned up like a knight in shining armour at The Manor's moment of dire need, putting *her* needs first.

She had been finding his presence profoundly disturbing. She recalled that, apart from handshakes and polite kisses on the cheek, he was the first man she had touched since childhood, except her father, with whom she had always been affectionate. For some reason, while at university and then during her working life in London, she had missed out on events like college dances, hunt balls, late night parties and clubs. She didn't give off signals that appealed to lusty young men and had no urge to do so, but would excuse herself early on the grounds of having important presentations to finish, or choir practice next morning.

It wasn't that she had no friends but most of them were either children in the choir at the churches where she sang; or married couples, the men of whom found her attractive while the women trusted her not to be a threat. The past few nights, however, as she was getting ready for bed, Melissande had been paying herself more attention than usual in the bathroom mirror.

Colliding with Bertie, feeling his strength and breathing in his aroma had produced strange tightening of muscles and hair follicles that were new and exciting. As she viewed herself, she stroked her flanks and admired her lack of spare tyres or droopy anything. No spots or blemishes – except for some hair in places never shown in public. For convenience, she avoided sleeveless blouses or tops and as for wearing a bikini, the occasion hadn't occurred. The last seaside holiday she had had was when she was eleven on guide camp and her one-piece bathing suit had given her no qualms. Now, though, for some reason, she felt an urge to make everything as attractive as possible and she borrowed her father's shaving kit and the scissors he used to trim his sideboards, to remove any hair from some places and to trim it in others until, on re-inspection in the full-length glass, she felt really – and she hesitated before even thinking the word – 'sexy'; a new experience.

The very word made her shiver a little. It was not a subject that she ever allowed to become prominent in her head. It carried overtones of 'sin' and 'Ten Commandments', 'being coveted', 'fallen' or 'defiled', especially if anyone else were involved. The tickles and pleasurable feelings that she had accidentally discovered over the past few years, were personal and secret – not involving anyone else, so they couldn't be 'sinful'; but now, this great big male with his compelling looks and bright eyes, seemed to impinge on those private feelings, causing embarrassment, blushes and generating heat that made her want to take off some clothes – simply to cool down, of course.

So it was Bertie's consideration that made Melissande accept the proposed extra work. She had no idea, at this moment, how she would fit everything in, but she could not resist the prospect of delving into facts and figures for a project that might, eventually, rescue The Manor, bring more parishioners to her father's church, and of course, more contact (not physical of course) with Bertie Lamotte. They were all wholesome, moral reasons that gave her a growing enthusiasm to take on more responsibility.

She had stayed silent as all these thoughts flashed through her mind, and suddenly became aware that it was quiet. Everyone was looking at her and she remembered why. It was with great pleasure that she now responded. Forbidding herself from blushing, she said, with surprising briskness:

"I'd love to. I think the whole thing sounds most promising. Equally, if we find that our study reveals insurmountable barriers, then it will still have been worthwhile."

This reply brought satisfaction all round and Mr Penworthy was able to draw the meeting to a cheerful ending.

After he had left and Melissande had returned to the stable, Bertie made tea for Lady Veronica and Reg, and the three of them sat around the fire in the drawing room, enjoying the quiet as they contemplated the brainstorming of the past hour. It had been exhausting for the residents but stimulating and inspiring for Bertie, still in the first week of his great adventure.

"Tell you what," said Reg, breaking the silence; "I was reading the paper up there in 'ospital and I saw a bit that said they was thinkin' about paying farmers to let their fields go under water in the winter to take the strain off the towns. That could bring in a few bob too, couldn't it? I mean, if people had bought floating houses, they'd want to float now and again, wouldn't they? Give 'em something to tell their friends about! Otherwise, what's the point?"

"I say, you may have something there," said Bertie. "I'd been thinking that being able to float would be a kind of 'emergency only measure' – make you feel that even if it did flood, your carpets wouldn't be ruined. You are suggesting people might even *enjoy* a bit of a 'static cruise' for a week or two at a boring time of year!"

"Make a change, wouldn't it?" Reg chuckled. "Might even organise an annual duck shoot! Or a bit of coarse fishin'!" This suggestion brought amused laughter.

"We might even sell 'winter cottages for water sports' or 'Tytherton Barge holidays'!" Bertie added.

"Well yes! Why not?" Lady Veronica joined in. "Remarkable what the young get up to these days. I was amazed when Arabella told me some of her friends dashed off to Newquay after Christmas to go *surfing*. I ask you! In gales and freezing cold! They wear some kind of rubber clothing, I understand. It sounds most uncomfortable: imagine how chilly one must get!"

"You don't have much by way of Atlantic rollers in Tytherton Kellaway but at least they could water ski," said Bertie: more laughter.

"I've actually done a bit of winter surfing," he went on; "and my toes did go rather blue but it was great fun. We were about the only people in the country enjoying the foul weather. The stronger the gale, the better the waves; but I say, changing the subject, does anyone fancy a port?"

"I'm sure we all do," said Lady Veronica; "but there isn't any. It's no longer part of our shopping list, is it Haines?"

Reg shook his head and smiled.

"But it's still on mine and I happen to have bought a bottle, earlier," said Bertie. "It's in my coat pocket in the hall. Shall I get it?"

"Yes do! We can certainly find some glasses," said Lady Veronica. Within a couple of minutes they were all enjoying the sweetness and warmth in the throat delivered by the wine, fortified with brandy by its Portuguese vintners.

There ensued a companionable silence, while the three of them enjoyed the taste of the port, and watched firelight making the glasses in their hands flash dark red and orange from the dancing flame in the fireplace.

"You would have to do all the building in summer, wouldn't you?" Lady Veronica broke the quietness.

"That's a point," said Reg. "Trouble is, you never know if it's going to stop raining even then!"

"Have to dash in whenever it's dry enough, at least to get the roads and drains in place," said Bertie. "I wonder whether we'd need to build the roads on raised embankments?"

"I was wondering that, too," said Lady Veronica; "otherwise how would the people get out to do their shopping when the floods came? You'd need a boat!"

"Where would they keep a car?" Asked Reg. "You'd have to park somewhere up the hill a bit."

"Then they'd be stranded unless they had a dinghy. That could be dreadful, going shopping in a *dinghy* in February. Not very tempting! Just imagine taking the children to playschool or going to church!" Lady Veronica was beginning to think the whole idea might be too whimsical: not the solution to her financial problems; but the port was taking the edge off her concern. After all, she reassured herself, there was no harm in allowing the imagination to run riot and stretch its legs: it might lead to something feasible in the end.

"What kind of housing estate did your husband have in mind, Lady Veronica? Was it one of those with masses of houses all packed together?" Bertie asked.

"Well, I remember him saying that unless the estate could provide a large number of homes, they wouldn't get the necessary permission, but he couldn't bear the thought of making it a mass of little boxes all jammed in with no gardens. In the end, I think an artist friend made some drawings of various suggestions which included a number of luxurious houses on the lower land surrounded by grass and trees and then blocks of attractive flats overlooking the plain – so enough families could live there to meet Government requirements."

"It's beginning to sound like an obstacle race," said Bertie; "although making it a *floatable* estate might serve everyone's purpose. You, the landowner would get paid for letting it flood, making the luxury houses into holiday islands for part of the time, while giving large numbers of people in nice apartments a splendid view. They'd certainly get a changing landscape!"

"One of us is going to have to get up soon," said Reg. "It's time to feed the cat! Look, she's gone to the door. Now I'm here again she'll expect everything to get back to normal. I generally feeds 'er about now, down at my place."

"I'm a little peckish myself," said Bertie. "What about you Lady Veronica?"

"A few biscuits and cheese would be plenty for me but I can arrange that. You go back with Haines and the cat, I shall be perfectly all right."

"I was thinking that, it being Saturday night, I might persuade the car to take me to Chippenham to collect some chips. What do you think?"

"I'm sure that wouldn't do," said Lady Veronica, "after two glasses of port! We don't want you to get into trouble."

"You could phone up for some," said Reg. "They delivers out 'ere if you ask nicely. I've done it before."

After that, it was only the cat which had to make decisions. After eating its supper in The Lodge, would she prefer to return to the drawing room fire at The Manor, or take her place at the bottom of Bertie's bed, as she had for the past few nights? It was less trouble to do the latter.

CHAPTER 8

Arabella's 'appointment' that evening in London was, to her, important and strategic.

She had met this apparently boring but good-looking man at some do or other; and learned that he was 'someone to watch' because of his future prospects, and certainty of inheriting a great deal of money. He was being voted on to the board of some well-known City companies, and she determined to get closer to him – a lot closer.

She had ascertained that he was not gay, having asked a few of her contacts. She took this as a major advantage because what she had to offer was not what gay men found attractive. (In her experience they seemed to prefer women who gave them lots of sympathetic girlie love and accompanied them shopping.)

She knew this eligible bachelor would be at tonight's event, which was one to which she had been invited by a friend in public relations. She was to 'brighten the place up' at the launch of a new fund; 'make things a bit more congenial' and 'flash herself about a bit'.

All these activities were Arabella's specialities and she was able to command a useful fee for 'consultancy' simply by tarting herself up (elegantly, of course) and smiling a lot. For special people she had an endearing way of putting her hand on their arm to make a point.

Apart from her remarkably good figure and looks, she was skilful at using very little make-up to portray a picture of youthful innocence and clean outdoors, and her sensuous lower lip always seemed to want to be kissed. Arabella had also learned the secret of holding a man's attention by asking him to talk about himself.

She stood within easy hearing distance of the toast-master, resplendent in his red tails and white tie, as he called out names of fund managers, CEOs, chairmen (of both sexes) and well-known investors. There was even a junior minister from The Coalition's Treasury team, to whom Arabella offered a charming 'how do you do?' before excusing herself from his invasive attention.

"Mr Tristram Heath-Cohen of RSIG associates," called the red-coated gentleman, reading from the business card he had just been given.

Here was her man: Arabella stepped forward to make sure she was directly in his way as he headed towards the waitress holding a tray of champagne flutes. He couldn't help but see her, his attention captivated by her body movement as she changed tack, allowing him to pass. She flashed him her coyest of smiles.

"So sorry," she murmured, stepping to one side and leaving a waft of her Chanel in the air into which Tristram now moved.

"Not at all! I shouldn't have been in such a hurry for the drink," beamed Tristram. "Are you part of the launch?"

"Not really, just helping a friend – make people feel at home before they get down to business. Why not let *me* get you a drink? It'll give me an excuse to have one myself – one doesn't like to drink alone!"

This offer was accepted instantly and Tristram, waiting for Arabella to return, made a quick assessment of the gathering in which he recognised several familiar faces. These were chaps who had done well for themselves by smelling out a good thing in its early stages. Their presence bode well for whatever scheme was being presented.

Add Arabella's presence and it promised to be a good event. 'Fantastic!' he thought, as he observed Arabella's rear view. It reminded him of Pippa's at Kate's wedding to Will. 'Delicious', he nodded; today had potential. 'Most satisfactory', he concluded.

With the first sip of champagne, Tristram was ready to answer Arabella's interrogation. She had lowered her voice, both in pitch and volume, forcing him to move quite close to her, which he found congenial and he leaned towards her, getting an even better look at her complexion. This passed his 'fluff' test – it was smooth, even, and free from blemish – the face of a young girl – on a sophisticated and shapely woman. Better still, she was ready to make the running.

"So, tell me, what does 'RSIG' stand for," she demanded, with an innocent smile. "Do tell me about it!"

"Oh, it's the Risk Share Insurance Group," he said, adding, "we are a sort of second tier of back-up to brokers who need a bit more capital for special projects. With us they don't have to worry too much about being able to pay out if something hits the fan! What?" This last expletive, Arabella soon learned, indicated that he was being humorous: his version of 'a short self-deprecating laugh'.

"How interesting," said Arabella. "What kind of projects?"

"You know – tower blocks, the odd ship and a few art collections – just in case of war, earthquakes, floods and other Acts of God."

"Fascinating," said Arabella. "Have you ever had to pay up? Must be a painful business!"

"Painful's not the word! But not entirely without merit."

Tristram then extolled the benefits of an occasional disaster: how it brought warm feelings of relief to those who had been paying high premiums, and persuaded others to take out new protection.

"Best of all," he concluded; "it means we have very good reasons for raising our premiums – very regretfully, you understand! What?"

It was a pleasure to entertain this girl and Tristram had to drag himself away to concentrate on the matter in hand. In fact, Arabella turned out to be the best component of the launch. She was the only one to be successful in diverting his attention sufficiently to keep him from being bored. The new fund was not one which inflamed his interest – rather the opposite – being more in the line of extinguishing *any* kind of fire, since it concentrated on floods and leaks. These chaps seemed to be convinced there would be plenty of profit in managing the risk associated with Climate Change, which was very boring anyway.

For Tristram, the thing to do if the weather didn't suit you, was to go somewhere else; which he did frequently, visiting his apartment in Monaco whenever there was nothing pressing to do in London. It was not long before he had returned to her side, waiting until an elderly board member had finished making unsuccessful advances to this 'lovely young thing'.

From Arabella's point of view, Tristram was an easy conquest. From the moment she had executed her sexy swivel to show off her attributes, it was downhill all the way. Tristram soon lost interest in the launch, though he accepted the glossy brochure that Arabella fetched for him and slipped it into his crocodile-leather portfolio. He spent the rest of the proceedings chatting her up and answering her questions about his interests, achievements and family history.

He found she wasn't just some PR totty, but heir to an ancient Wiltshire family, which impressed him geographically. His own roots were in Yorkshire, which, since Eton, had made him feel slightly inferior to his chums from further South. They used to laugh when he said 'grass' as in 'crass', which he had picked up from his nanny.

By lunchtime, and after a couple more glasses of champagne, he could see that not only was Arabella 'jolly all-right', but she thought *he* was too, and seemed more than willing to devote the rest of her day, (and with luck, night), with him. He thought he'd better make it worth her while, so invited her for a quick whizz around the National Portrait Gallery – to see whether they could find any of her relatives hanging on the walls – followed by tea at the Ritz and then 'perhaps popping in to the flat to freshen up' before going out to supper somewhere cosy.

The freshening up proved the best bit so far, for all concerned. Arabella just happened to let Tristram see her wrapped in the huge towel that he'd supplied for her shower. She had not been in any hurry to hide away, but had continued to dry her shoulder, accidentally allowing the towel to reveal one of her pert breasts – just for a split second you know. It couldn't have been described as 'flaunting' but it did the trick. Tristram did as she hoped, took a step forward, his arms spread, intent on kissing her.

Predictably, the towel dropped away, the kiss took place with considerable energy – which had been building ever since they met – and not long after, Tristram's trousers joined the towel on the floor as Arabella's knowledge and skills of men's belts and zips were applied.

Early in the embrace she had felt in his back pocket and extracted a little packet in which she suspected she might find a necessary trio of contraceptives – and was proved right. This saved her from retrieving her own from her handbag. (She had not been a Girl Guide for nothing).

"Oh I say! You crafty minx! What have you found there?" Said Tristram.

"Not sure – but let's see if it fits," she replied, knowing exactly what needed liberating from restrictive underwear. It did and the next hour, while having many elements of freshness and variety, also left them replete and relaxed.

After a doze, legs entwined, on the king-size bed, they rose, dressed and proceeded to the nearest winebar for supper. A mutually most satisfying launch, they both concluded. They had, so far, only experienced the very best of each other – charm, beauty, skill and experience. Neither suspected the other's steely interior and self-centred focus although this was unlikely to deter either of them.

A few hours earlier, at The Rectory in Tytherton Kellaway, Melissande had been relating to her parents the latest instalment of the saga of The Manor and its estate. The Rector and his wife were fond of Lady Veronica and she was one of the few parishioners with whom they maintained a close personal friendship. Most people, though they would not be able to detect it, were kept just a fraction away from being 'close', not being given details of family affairs, results of doctor's visits or domestic issues.

Parishioners, as a whole, were treated more as 'our flock', to be shown care and kindness, and made welcome at The Rectory, where they would be invited to tea and occasionally to 'a sherry' (two at the most). They were visited when sick or 'having problems'; and they were warmly received at the Church Door on Sundays – both on entry and at departure: indeed it took almost as long, leaving church, as it did to listen to one of Canon Blythe's sermons, as he shook hands and exchanged kind remarks with each in turn.

The Canon and Mrs Blythe had been alarmed by the incident with the bailiffs. What a shocking thing to happen: poor Veronica! Under a vow of secrecy, they listened with relief to Melissande's revelation that a white knight called Bertie Lamotte had come up trumps and saved the day. That information, particularly the sum involved, would remain an unwritten Rectory Archive under strictest security.

Both her parents noted the change in Melissande when she talked about this new arrival at The Manor. There was a certain extra animation as she said how fortunate it had been, his turning up out of the blue at the precise moment that Mr Haines had been smitten by a heart attack; and that he seemed to be cultured and apparently well-off.

There was more, as The Rector and his wife were to learn. They shared Melissande's glee as she told them how she had collided with him in the dark, the evening after his arrival. (Only the barest outlines of the encounter and no mention of her strange reaction to it.) Then there was today's 'council of war' to which Melissande had, surprisingly, been invited.

"And you say that Arabella didn't even stay until the end of the meeting?" Asked Canon Blythe.

"Well, you know what she's like. After the first five minutes she was bored and I'm surprised she stayed as long as she did," said Melissande. Her parents smiled fondly. Arabella was a dear girl, but so different from her old school friend. They all knew she took Melissande for granted, but forgave it because the two girls had been such close friends for so long.

Canon and Mrs Blythe didn't know *half* of what Melissande knew about Arabella; and Melissande herself didn't know half of what Arabella had been getting up to since they left school. Her relationship with the Blythes and Tytherton Kellaway had remained clinically separate from Arabella's city life and although her behaviour during her rural visits was anything but unselfish and kind, the Blythes still loved and tolerated her. She exploited this connection to its limits.

Sometimes, even Melissande's mother would become exasperated at the way Arabella took advantage of Melissande's kindness and patience. For example, Arabella, until a few weeks ago, had owed Melissande hundreds of pounds back-payment for looking after the stallion.

"Sorry Melissande, I'm a bit skint this month," she would say.

The first time, the Blythe's sympathised, understanding what it was like to exist on a very small stipend, though Mrs Blythe felt more sorry for her daughter, having to muddle along with virtually no money for so long. Later, she became indignant at the way Arabella shrugged off her responsibility for paying her dues.

"About time too!" She had said, uncharitably, when Melissande came home rejoicing one evening, waving a cheque.

That was some time ago: today's events were new and intriguing.

"So what was the conclusion of your meeting?" Asked The Rector. "Did it matter that she walked out in the middle? She is, after all, the heiress."

"Not really. It became easier, actually," said Melissande. "We assumed she would go along with anything that might sustain the status quo. The only thing that seemed to worry her was that someone like Bertie might come along and snap up The Manor at a bargain price. She was very prickly about him and seemed to forget that, except for him, poor Lady Veronica might have had to go into sheltered accommodation. I don't know quite how it happened, but the meeting asked me to find out whether it might be possible to pick up the pieces of the housing project that Mr Kelway had begun."

"Oh dear! Not again! I thought that had died along with poor John," said The Rector.

"But Daddy, it might have been the making of this parish. It could have doubled the population and maybe the congregation too!"

"Not if it were anything like those new estates in Calne," said her father. "I'm afraid they've turned out to be quite a bunch of heathens. The vicar has had to install television cameras in the churchyard and pay for a security company to rush out to stop vandals."

"But that's three or four miles away, Daddy, and it's always been more urban. For centuries everyone there killed pigs and made bacon. They were bound to be, shall we say, more venal? Tytherton Kellaway is much more rural and would appeal to different people altogether, especially if the estate were to be imaginatively designed."

"It would certainly need a lot of imagination to build at present," said her mother. "The place is under water! I ask you!"

"Well I think that's why I have been asked to do some research to see what might be done, given the right investment."

"*You* dear?" Canon Blythe asked.

"Yes – well, you see – it was something I brought up. Everyone thought the same as you, that there was no point in pursuing the housing estate idea to rescue The Manor, but I said I'd heard a programme on radio about houses that didn't just sit there and wait to get flooded, but rose up and floated, like Noah's Ark."

"My dear, how ridiculous!" Mrs Blythe could sometimes be very sharp when responding to Melissande's enthusiastic outbursts. "Just imagine – all those houses floating off into one corner of the estate! And how could they stay connected to electricity and drains? What a suggestion!"

"Mummy, in the programme I heard, the houses only rose and fell with the water level. They stayed in place, sliding up and down on pillars."

"How frightful! So ugly!"

"No: they mentioned the name of an architect who was developing this kind of arrangement and I looked at his website at the time, and the pillars are discreetly built into the walls of the house, they hardly show and of course, you can build all kinds of different building, once you have some kind of raft on which to base it."

"I think it most unlikely that one would be able to put enough of such houses to fulfil the numbers on which the Council was insisting," said The Rector. "As I remember it, the whole reason for allowing it at all was to meet the quota of new dwellings being imposed by Government."

Melissande updated her parents with what she had heard at the meeting, and explained that she had been appointed to do a preliminary feasibility study.

"Do you know how, my dear?" Her fond father asked.

"That's what I spent three years at university learning about! It's what I was doing before I came home to live."

"I do remember, vaguely," he said. "But you never talked about floating houses!"

"Perhaps not, Daddy, but the basic questions are very much the same: how much might it cost? How much income could it generate? Is it legal? Would anyone like to join in – and of course, is there anyone enthusiastic enough to take the risk of having a go at it?"

"Well is it? And would they?" Mrs Blythe asked.

"That's what I'm going to try to find out," said Melissande.

"Well you sound quite keen," her mother replied. "Is this Bertie person involved?"

Melissande suddenly became busy, putting a log on the fire and collecting coffee cups. She headed for the kitchen before her mother noticed that the discussion had brought on a sudden hot flush. As soon as she was out of the room, Mrs Blythe leaned forward and remarked to her husband:

"She seems rather struck on this man Bertie, doesn't she, Edward? I wonder whether it will ever come to anything?"

"Give the poor girl a chance," said The Rector. "She's not twenty six yet and you seem to think she's on the shelf. Any man she mentions instantly becomes a son-in-law and father of your grand-children. He may be married, anyway."

"If that's the case I hope she finds out soon. You can see she's smitten. Did you notice how she was blushing just now?"

"No, I wasn't looking," said her husband. He was not as keen as Mrs Blythe to get Melissande married off. The present arrangement worked very well. Her mother's ailments meant that apart from running the Mother's Union and providing a shoulder for troubled parishioners to cry on, much of the responsibility for running The Rectory rested on Melissande, who seemed perfectly content for the moment. She enjoyed looking after the horse at The Manor and was a great support in the parish community. The arrival of a potential suitor might rock the boat. He chuckled to himself as this metaphor brought visions of himself trying to visit the sick in a canoe across the flooded fields at Tytherton Kellaway.

The following Monday, Clive Penworthy happened to be at the District Council for a meeting. It was to do with a forthcoming appeal and his client had asked for him to be present to see fair play. The chief planning officer had done something similar, inviting the Council's legal department to take notes so that no misinterpretations might arise at a later date.

The meeting proved to be brief, brusque and unpleasant, as Clive's client showed the frustration he felt by using language that, in a public place, could land him in police custody. The chief planning officer reminded him of this, and the man walked out, slamming the door. Mr Penworthy was unable to reason with him, outside in the passage, and the client left the building growling "call me tomorrow! I'll see them in Hell!"

Mr Penworthy thought *that* would be an unlikely outcome, but resolved to make the phone call next day, and returned to apologise to the chief planning officer for his client's behaviour.

"I'm used to it! I'm always surprised at how rude some of these developers can be," he said. "You would expect them to be friendly and persuasive but so many of them come in here, telling me how to do my job so that they can double their money. Just having so much of it makes them think it gives them the right to do what they like: and what they like is spending as little as possible and amassing as much as possible!"

Mr Penworthy sympathised. The client was equally off-hand and rude to him too, but he had observed this early on in the relationship, and had added ten per cent to his normal hourly rate to compensate for this discomfort of being treated badly. While the client was ranting, the clock was ticking and his bill was going to please both Mr Penworthy's accountant and the tax man. This seemed to be the right moment to raise Tytherton Kellaway Manor.

"Changing the subject," he said, cheerfully, "I wonder if you remember that scheme for building houses over at Tytherton Kellaway. It must be a couple of years ago now, and went all quiet when the landowner died – Mr John Kelway."

"Funnily enough, it was discussed only this morning at one of the meetings here," said the chief planning officer. "I was called in because Government's been pressing The Council to implement their District Housing Plan. They're afraid of another housing bubble because too few people are getting on with any building. Prices have already begun to rise again, and banks are getting braver, given all the incentives and kicks they're receiving from Whitehall. The Councillors wanted to know whether the scheme had died, along with Mr Kelway. I was going to make some enquiries in the next few days. Do you know something about it? I haven't got the file out yet."

"From what I gather," said Mr Penworthy, "there's still a year or two left before the planning permission expires and I've just come from a meeting of family members where they were discussing how they might carry things forward. Quite a coincidence!"

"Well I never! Have you got anything I could tell the committee? They want to see something happening."

"Not yet – apart from the fact that most of the sight is underwater. It has happened every year since the scheme was devised and until now, has proved to be somewhat of a disincentive. However, someone's now come up with an idea that might make the district famous!"

"Oh God! Not one of those!"

The chief planning officer's last appearance in the media had been when an enraged landowner had held him at gunpoint for three hours last summer, when his application to open a permanent funfair on top of a hill overlooking a local beauty spot, was refused.

That evening on 'Points West', Mr Penworthy had watched the undignified flight of the officer when a police marksman had winged the landowner in the leg, causing him to drop his twelve-bore. However welcome the safety of a water-filled ditch had been at the time, in retrospect the planning officer often remembered it with shame. The suggestion that another such episode might occur worried him.

"Don't worry," reassured Mr Penworthy; "it could really put this Council on the map as being progressive and environmentally very friendly. I can't say anything about it yet, but I can assure you, if it works out, I wouldn't be surprised if there weren't some MBE's handed out afterwards. It's really quite a radical development and would be most satisfactory all round."

"Whatever it is, there are bound to be objectors," complained the chief planning officer. "There always are! Put up a wind turbine and celebrities pop up all over the place moaning that it makes drafts over their sunbeds or gets tangled up in their kites. Put in a culvert and someone says it will kill off the crayfish. It's a wonder anything ever gets done!"

"Don't despair," said Mr Penworthy. "This one shouldn't give you too much trouble; and I'll put you in the picture as soon as I'm allowed to. They're making some further enquiries before considering how to take things forward."

The last phrase was one that Mr Penworthy had been using frequently, since he heard it at a conference several months earlier. It carried overtones of movement, action and progress. So much more expressive than 'considering what to do', or 'whether to do it or not'; also it was less pompous than 'how to proceed'.

CHAPTER 9

"Mel!" The call went out from the stable yard. Arabella was pacing up and down, watched by the stallion, hoping it meant he would get an outing. His tiny mind also associated Arabella's presence with those occasional trips where he was loaded into a horse-box and taken to mount a willing mare, despite receiving the occasional nasty kick when the timing wasn't quite right.

"MELISSAAANDE!" Arabella's voice really did carry when she was impatient. Normally at this time, Melissande should be here mucking out, but for some reason she was missing. Arabella pushed the stallion back from the door and looked into the stable. The straw had been freshly replaced and there was clean water in the bucket, so Melissande must be about somewhere.

"Are you calling?"

"Bloody right I am! Where have you been?" Arabella hated being kept waiting.

"I was just looking for motor-bikes down the lane. Bertie said he'd heard one. I went to see if anyone was still around; I want to catch those scramblers who've been messing it up. There wasn't a sign! Do you want something?"

"I do, actually; but is this Bertie man still hanging about? I thought he'd have left by now."

"He hasn't; and a good job too!"

"How's that?"

"Well Mr Haines still isn't fully better; and without some help at The Manor, your poor aunt wouldn't survive for very long. He's been going in to keep the fires going, cutting wood, doing the shopping and doing lots of odd jobs; and he's also been helping me with the feasibility study."

"Whatever's *that* about?"

"It's what we were all talking about at the meeting, the other Saturday. You'd left just as it was decided. I'm digging out facts and figures about building on flood plains."

"Oh God! I'd forgotten all that!" Arabella's nose turned up at the memory of the tedious meeting. "You're not really spending time on *that* are you?"

"I am actually – and enjoying it: finding out all sorts of interesting things."

"What about the stable – and the horse? I don't want things to slip, you know."

"Arabella, have I ever allowed them to lack attention? Be fair: and by the way, I need some more funds. Anyway, I'm enjoying doing some research; it's what I was trained for."

"If you wanted more work you should have said so: we could have looked at it!" Arabella was becoming peevish.

"Well I don't like to complain – you know that. This has only been a friendly arrangement: I'm not here to get rich!"

"But if you're sliding off to look in libraries and doing other stuff you are bound to have less time here – or helping your mother. You shouldn't be skimping on your responsibilities. Who's paying for all this research stuff? *We* certainly can't afford such a thing!"

"Bertie."

"*Him* again! What *is* he up to?"

"Nothing sinister, as far as I can see. He's already 'invested' eighteen thousand pounds. Both your Aunt and Mr Penworthy agreed he should be repaid. The only way was to revive the housing estate scheme. Bertie was prepared to pay for a feasibility study and suggested I might be the right person to do it."

"Not if it means you're going to neglect things here! Your poor mother! And what about the work I pay you for?"

"I need a word with you about that, as I said, because I shall be going away for a couple of weeks, soon, and I was going to suggest we agree on dates when you can take time off to cover things at this end."

Melissande had not intended to raise the subject until Arabella was in a good mood but her friend's bullying had niggled her sufficiently to make her bite back. They did occasionally have little spats, when Melissande eventually got her own way by being more stubborn, choosing grounds of reason and morality. If Melissande began saying things like 'that's illegal', 'immoral', or 'unworthy of you', Arabella knew she was on a loser.

"Hell! You're always going on holiday!"

"There's no need to swear, Arabella! It's not worthy of you and you don't want to appear coarse, do you? Even grooms are entitled to time off, you know, and actually, I haven't taken any holiday for more than six months. I can show you on the calendar if you like: I'm due for nearly three weeks actually; and now we're on the subject, you owe me a hundred and fifteen pounds for the past four weeks."

This salvo had the necessary effect. Arabella knew it was time to negotiate if she were to avoid a difficult rift with her longest-standing chum.

"When are you going, then? And where?" She asked sulkily.

"Not sure yet – but somewhere that I can find amphibious houses to look at: find out how much they cost and see what's available. It might be some research establishment in England or maybe Holland."

"They're not *really* going ahead with that crackpot idea, are they? I thought Penworthy and Auntie would soon get over it, if I let them. I suppose it was Bertie what's-his-name who kept the thing going, was it?"

"No, it was your Aunt Veronica herself. She's very worried about being so much in debt and wants to get The Manor back on a firm financial footing before she 'goes to St Peter's reception', as she puts it. She's doing it for *you* as much as anyone – unless there's someone else out there who might inherit all this."

Melissande went past her friend and began sweeping outside the stable door with a yard broom while continuing to reinforce her case:

"I could see she wasn't best pleased when you marched out. She's afraid you'll let the whole place go out of the family if you don't 'engage' a bit more."

"Well I had an important appointment that evening," said Arabella; remembering with satisfaction the merging of minds and bodies that had continued into the next day. Her pout changed to a reminiscent smile as she recalled some of the action.

"On a *Saturday* evening? It doesn't sound like work," commented Melissande.

"Well you could say it was mixing work with pleasure, as far as The Manor is concerned," said Arabella. "I've met someone who definitely needs cultivating. He's got oodles of money ... (and a gorgeous body)..... He might be just what we need to keep The Manor afloat!" She managed to edit the sentence before it left her lips: living, desirable bodies were not discussed with her friend. The pun about The Manor floating was accidental and Arabella didn't see its significance until after she'd uttered it. She giggled at her own cleverness, and the atmosphere relaxed as Melissande learned the truth about 'the appointment'. They reverted to being close confidantes although Arabella wouldn't dare tell Melissande about the 'going to bed' part. On the other hand she didn't mind her knowing she fancied someone.

"*Now* we know what made you take yourself off! It had to be something in trousers!"

Melissande laughed as she put down the broom and pointed to the clean horse-blanket she had just fetched from The Manor, having soaked it overnight in the scullery. It had been quite an effort to wash and rinse, and in the end, she had jammed it into the spin drier and was about to hang it up on a line in the tack room when she had found the irate Arabella calling her name.

"Here, give me a hand with this," she said, handing one end of the blanket to Arabella. "Let's get it over this line. It will never dry outside in this weather. What's he called?"

"Tristram. He's only just turned up. His parents live in the West Indies, but he was at school in England and university in America. He was chilling out in St Lucia until recently but they've told him he's got to start some kind of work, so he's come back to London and hangs out with his old mates. Someone told me he's just collected a trust set up by his grandparents."

"Is he nice?"

"It depends what you call 'nice'. He's very good looking: built like an athlete."

Here, Arabella stopped herself saying 'and well endowed', which she knew would not come into Melissande's category of 'nice'. After the hesitation she continued: "he's got a very flashy car; is mad about sailing and has been known to play polo. He's been very polite and charming to me so far, and we get on well. How does that sound?"

"Promising! Do you think you'll keep him?" Melissande's experience was that Arabella soon tired of boyfriends, being easily diverted by 'something better'."

"Don't know – but it's a possibility. I'll be old and wrinkly soon and then it won't be so easy. Anyway," she said; "you've given me an idea. If you go away, I might ask him down for a bit of riding. We could get everything ready for the Hunt event. I'm supposed to be running it. I was planning to come down for that week, hoping you might help but you are obviously far too busy now. I suppose I could come down a few days earlier."

"And Tristram would be much more fun than me! Wouldn't he?" Melissande enjoyed having the occasional dig at her conceited friend.

"Well – yes!" They both laughed.

"If you're planning to use the lane as part of the trek, you'd better take a look – the motor-bike has turned it into a quagmire."

"Oh shit!"

"Ara*bella*! Please! Mud will do!"

Later, at the Council offices in Chippenham, Bertie was in a meeting with the Chief Planning Officer. Clive Penworthy had met the official at a function a week before, when the officer enquired about Tytherton Kellaway Manor.

"I've got someone coming to see me about the proposed housing estate there," the official said. He knew Mr Penworthy well, having been involved in several previous planning matters, most of which had ended to their mutual satisfaction.

"You used to act for them – but I thought it had all been dropped when the old man died. Now there's someone called Bertrand Lamotte wanting a meeting. Do you know anything about him?"

"I do: and strictly between you and me, he's actually Sir Bertrand Lamotte, baronet, but he's keeping quiet about that, at present."

"Whatever for? Nothing to be ashamed of, is it?"

"Not sure really, but he wants to stay incognito – I suspect it's because he's amused at the way Arabella Kelway – the next 'lady of The Manor' – treats people. She can be quite brusque, if I put it kindly. He's acting as handy-man chauffeur while their usual man is recovering from a heart attack."

"Extraordinary! Is he 'all right'? From what he said, it sounded as though he's acting on their behalf. Do you think he's genuine?"

"Oh I'm sure it is!" Mr Penworthy had looked Bertie up in *Who's Who 2014.* He wasn't going to reveal more about Bertie's financial stake but he knew the officer would accept his endorsement.

"They'd better get on with it, if they want to proceed," said the Chief Planning Officer. "I don't think we could give permission again, once the current one has expired. I had a look – it's only got two years to run and the weather's changed since that one was approved! The place seems to be almost permanently under water now! I'm not sure how my predecessor allowed it to go through: it was dodgy even then as regards flooding: and it doesn't seem to have stopped raining since!"

"Talking of that, just look at those clouds outside," said Clive Penworthy. "It's pretty black, and those trees aren't very safe." He pointed across the parkland beyond the council offices at trees being bowed by powerful gusts of wind. "This morning's forecast was talking about Force Nine – and to expect 'structural damage'."

"Don't! We can't afford it! We're cutting enough without fallen trees!"

Bertie's bona fide having been informally established, the meeting had then been arranged. On his way home Mr Penworthy had to use a diversion, due to a large fallen oak, blocking his usual route.

The storm did not abate that day – or for several days. When it wasn't blowing a gale, it was chucking down rain in stair-rods. The centre of low pressure seemed intent on hovering over that part of Wiltshire, day after day.

"I don't remember ever being asked to offer prayers to *stop* it raining," remarked The Rector over lunch, later in the week. "It's usually *for* rain; not that we've ever been very successful in getting The Lord to co-operate, although it always seems to make farmers and gardeners feel better."

"Have you emptied that bucket in the attic room?" Mrs Blythe asked Melissande. "We must get the Diocese to get that leak fixed. I keep meaning to remind you, Edward; please will you make another note of it?"

"Of course, my love; but we haven't had *quite* such a problem before, have we?"

"Well it doesn't usually rain enough to fill the bucket, but this time it's incessant. Look at it now – it's *pouring!*"

"It reminds me of when we were doing our National Service in the Far East," said The Rector. "It used to rain like this in the jungle; but at least we don't have leaches grabbing our ankles in Tytherton. They were revolting!"

"Daddy, not at mealtimes, please!" Melissande was squeamish about such matters, despite having to remove the occasional tick from the silky skin beneath the tail of the stallion. That procedure could be done without nausea, in the ambience of the stable, with the offending tick being crushed outside on the concrete yard by Melissande's irate heel – but was not a subject for lunchtime.

She didn't like killing most things but ticks and other parasites, being freeloaders, offended her sense of justice and fairness, especially since they carried unpleasant diseases. Ticks needed killing.

"You might have to take the long way round to The Manor," said her father, changing the subject slightly; "although I don't expect Maud Heath's causeway is flooded yet, is it? I can't remember it not being passable."

"It was almost over my wellies at the turn-off to the lane this morning and all the mud's been churned up as far as the drive. Someone on a wretched scrambler motor-cycle must have been racing up and down again. You can hardly move and I almost lost a boot."

"Can't you stop him?"

"It's a public right of way. I've been trying to catch him in the act, to ask him to go somewhere else but I keep missing him. For some reason he always seems to choose *there*; I haven't seen him anywhere else."

"Perhaps it's because it looks deserted and the noise doesn't carry – it *is* a bit like a tunnel," Mrs Blythe commented.

"Maybe he hasn't got a licence – or insurance! If I *see* the bike I'll take its number and ask the police. He's making it almost impassable."

"If this rain goes on much longer I shall need a boat to get around the parish," said The Rector.

"You will anyway, if this housing scheme goes ahead," laughed Melissande. "At least for part of the time."

"They're not really going to build houses on those meadows are they? They really will need a boat to go and rescue residents every winter. And who would be foolish enough to buy a place down there anyway?"

"That's what I'm working on," said Melissande. "We're looking at making the houses amphibious – so that if the floods come up, the houses will too."

"Good gracious! Won't the owners get seasick?"

"No, Daddy, the houses will slide up and down on pillars. I expect they'd move a little, but not rock about."

"But wouldn't the people be stranded on little 'house islands'? How would they get to work, or go shopping – or come to church?"

"That's the sort of thing I've got to find out," said Melissande. "We're going to have another meeting after that, to see whether it might be possible to make a go of it, pay off the debts and save The Manor."

"It's going to need a great deal more money to build all those houses, isn't it? Who's going to risk their savings on marshy meadows? Just remember how difficult it was raising funds even to repair the church roof." The Rector recalled previous efforts.

"Bertie thinks it might turn out to be quite lucrative," said Melissande. "He says that if I can find viable solutions to 'living with floods' there must be plenty of other places with similar problems – The Somerset Levels, for a start: all those villages there."

"That's true," said The Rector; "and I suppose there are famous precedents. I seem to remember that they said the same about the wet ground around Singapore, a couple of hundred years ago; and the Romans did a good job for the Via Apia to cross the Pontine Marshes, three centuries before Saint Paul might have used them." He nodded wisely to himself, concluding that humanity had long since learned how to thwart some of Mother Nature's plans for her Earth. That, however, was not to say that humans always got their way – as 'natural disasters' so often demonstrated. His mind drifted to higher things but was brought back to more mundane issues by his wife

"This Bertie is a most mysterious person, isn't he?" Mrs Blythe remarked. She had noted how frequently his name had come up at mealtimes at The Rectory and how Melissande had blushed when that occurred. She sensed an opportunity to direct a few more pertinent questions about someone who might possibly, in the future, 'join the family'.

Melissande's single status was something that worried her. She feared her daughter might finish up a frustrated old maid – and felt guilty about it, especially since she was growing increasingly dependent on her.

"He's quite well off, isn't he?" Her mother tried to sound casual.

Melissande had told her parents, in confidence, about the emergency loan coughed up by Bertie to pacify the bailiffs, so this wasn't new ground. Melissande suspected that other embarrassing questions might follow.

"The chiropodist's coming today, isn't she, Mummy?"

By the time Bertie met the Chief Planning Officer, the meadows at Tytherton Kellaway were under five feet of water, and the water was lapping against the top of the highest brick arch of Maud Heath's Causeway. Even all this did not deter Bertie's enthusiasm.

"With a bit of luck," he suggested to the officer, "the Department of the Environment people will pull out all the stops after serious flooding like this, to make sure the rivers are dredged and suchlike. They'll *have* to now: both the Prime Minister *and* The Opposition have promised they would – otherwise everyone will vote UKIP and we'll all be kippered!"

He snorted at his own joke; then remembered he must be sounding like Arabella. The post-joke snort was something he had to abandon.

"I feel sure Government will release quite large sums for flood prevention, as well as declaring disaster areas to help insurance claims," he said, confidently.

"Yes, they might – but they're hardly going to allow projects like Tytherton Meadows to go ahead, are they? I certainly couldn't recommend it, even though the Council is desperate to find somewhere to build so many homes."

"That's the point!" said Bertie; "if we can come up with a viable scheme that not only keeps residents warm and dry but also allows deep flooding for certain periods – it's exactly what they're looking for! If they're going to be paying farmers to accommodate flood water, keeping it out of towns during the monsoons, it will pay the extra cost of making our houses 'rise to the occasion'." (He stopped himself again from snorting.) "The thing is, we must get in there first, before someone else has the same idea!"

The Chief Planning Officer had begun life as a civil engineer and the concept being put forward by this resourceful gentleman appealed to his creative self. Years of working under financial constraint, however, brought doubts 'flooding' into his mind.

"I see what you mean – and it's an ingenious solution – but it's going to cost a *fortune*, isn't it?"

The way the Chief Planning Officer said 'fortune' resonated for Bertie. Exactly! What had he set out to do, a month or so ago? Seek his fortune! His resolve took another step forward and upwards. 'Government', 'bureaucracy'; 'raising money', 'Climate Change' and 'rules' were the dragons and perils that confronted today's adventurers; and he sensed that he was just about to vanquish an important one. If he could get the support of this official – who could help put his case when the time came – it would be victory on a grand scale.

"Absolutely! A fortune!" said Bertie, endorsing the officer's conclusion. "It will be bloody expensive from all sorts of angles. I don't think it's difficult technically, because we've got all kinds of things that float, including concrete – remember those portable docks they dragged over The Channel for the invasion of France in 1944. A much bigger problem will be convincing people that it *is indeed* a solution! Once you've done that, it will be easy to raise the money. If you start talking about amphibious houses, or 'homes over the water' people imagine Indonesian villages and tropical islands. Only folk in sarongs and turbans live like that!"

"Unless you go to Venice," contributed the Chief Planning Officer. "That's been pretty successful!" He was now finding himself involved in enjoying a little imaginative freedom.

"Absolutely! But they're in trouble now – sinking below the waves! I've been there – trotting along planks balanced on bricks, to keep my feet dry – it's horrendous, watching those marvellous old buildings beginning to get washed away. But you're right – that would be a good starting point for our argument – one step further than Venice – palaces that don't sink!"

"I don't know about palaces – but certainly some quality residences begin to sound possible, even in a flood plain like Tytherton Kellaway," moderated the Chief Planning Officer. "It's a beautiful setting, just right for up-market houses; and I believe there are two blocks of modern apartments included in the plan for adjoining, higher land, aren't there?"

"There are indeed; and the artist who visualised them made 'a good view' an important part of his design, although it was before this persistent flooding. I've been having all kinds of inspirations about ox-bow lakes, beds of willow, lagoons, summer grazing and charming houses – plenty to please the eye. Those flats are going to be snapped up by discerning people commuting to London."

Their conversation was interrupted by a particularly strong gust of wind that rattled the building. The window was awash with rain and the noise was forcing them to raise their voices.

"This weather is *terrible*! Just look at those trees!" Bertie pointed; and even as they watched, one of the tallest, a cedar of Lebanon, snapped off at the top and a large part of it fell to the ground. "I've never seen anything like it, have you? There will be trees down all over the place: you're going to have all kinds of disruption!"

"I'm afraid we are: and from what the scientists are telling us, it's going to get like this more often in the future. The trouble is, politicians and the media won't believe it's going to get worse."

"A few more storms like this and they'll begin to get the message!"

"You're right. Then they might begin to vote some more money to help people adapt to the new weather patterns."

"That's what I've been thinking," said Bertie. "It's going to make it easier to raise money in The City – if Government makes it more attractive to invest in schemes like ours!"

"I don't think that's a good idea," said Melissande, leaning on her broom, having swept mucky puddles into the stable yard drain. Arabella had saddled up the stallion and was leading him out.

"You look like an ancient Chinese warrior," she said, with a laugh. "All those water-proofs. You'd better use the mounting block or you'll never get into the saddle!"

"Ha ha! Very funny!" Arabella was determined to show Melissande that not only would she stay reasonably dry but she was still agile and fit. She put her left foot in the stirrup and with a mighty effort, attempted to leap on to the horse's back. She made it: not, however, without alarming the stallion, who pranced around backwards as she accidentally hauled one side of the rein.

Melissande went into action bravely, dropping the broom and grabbing the stallion's head, hanging on to stop the disastrous motion. The suddenness of the halt nearly threw Arabella but by now she was holding on to the pommel with both hands and stayed put, safe but irate.

"You could have held him in the first place," she hissed, "instead of just standing there being insulting."

"I was just saying I didn't think it was a good idea to go out in this weather and with all these floods around. When you enter water, it may look shallow but you don't know what ground has been washed away and you may just go down a hole. It's not *safe*, Arabella. I was trying to reason with you but you are so impatient you wouldn't wait! I'm *asking* you – if you insist on going out – to stay up here behind The Manor: don't go down the lane or down towards the lower ground – it's been under water for *days*."

"But I've got to see what's happened to our event course," said Arabella. "We might have to re-arrange the whole thing and there are only a few days left before everyone turns up."

"Goodness knows where you're going to park all the horseboxes. There isn't a dry field anywhere down that way." Melissande pointed.

"I know what I'm doing," said Arabella, haughtily; and now, back in control of the situation, with both feet in the stirrups and reins secure in her hands, she set off – towards the lane.

Melissande picked up the broom and finished her sweeping.

CHAPTER 10

Melissande thought the sensible thing would be to go to Holland to get some idea of what amphibious houses might look like, what they cost and what was involved when you came to build them. Her research kept coming back to the small town of Maasbommel, where there was a row of such houses next to a river which, during frequent floods, would normally have drowned all of them, if they did not 'rise to the occasion'.

Going to Holland and spending time there was not going to be cheap and Melissande was wondering how she might approach Bertie about it. To ask for even *more* money when Tytherton Manor already owed him £18,000, seemed a bit much.

Not wishing to seem exploitative, she decided to do as much research as she could using The Internet, perhaps firing off emails to the sales staff of companies offering different types of 'flood-conquering' dwellings. It would provide ball-park figures as to possible costs and returns.

She was meticulous, too, about keeping accurate records of the time she spent on the project: the phone-calls made and the extra electricity consumed by keeping one of the spare attic rooms at The Rectory warm during her research hours. This was what she and Bertie had agreed. While setting things up, they had also negotiated the rate for her fees. Unusually, it was Bertie who had to press the prospective employee to accept what he considered a reasonable rate for her work. Melissande felt it was too much.

They were sitting in the kitchen at The Rectory, where Bertie had called in to put his business proposition to her as part-time researcher, picking up the pieces of the late John Kelway's 'great plan' for a housing estate on his riverside pastures.

"That's awfully high!" She had said when he first suggested a figure. "Fifty pounds an hour? I'm not a solicitor, you know! I don't need anything like as much as that!"

"If we're going to put some credible figures together," he replied, "we need a portfolio of background information that bankers and investors can check out and find to be solid. It's no good quoting guesswork – we need concrete quotes, realistic time scales, projected market trends and consideration of all the factors that could affect the success or failure of our two hundred acres of flood plain. If anyone discovered that the basic work had been done by someone for peanuts, they're not even going to bother to check it out. I think you should set up a small consultancy, give it a title, register it as a company, and give the whole thing a commercial air – then people will take it seriously. You've got the qualifications, haven't you?"

"Yes of course, but that doesn't mean I should over-charge you. After all, you're doing it almost as a favour for Lady Veronica."

"No I'm absolutely not! I don't know where you got *that* idea. OK, in a moment of crazy public spiritedness I got rid of the bailiffs, because her plight made me remember my mother and what it might be like if she found herself in a similar situation – but when you came up with such a bright idea for getting Tytherton Kellaway Manor back into the black, I got hooked on it. It's a great plan with tremendous possibilities, not just here but around the world!"

"Anyone would think we were a bunch of tycoons planning a million-pound project!" said Melissande, laughing; "not a groom and a handy-man scratching about for a rescue package; or even a Rector's daughter and a city escapee day-dreaming."

"Ah," said Bertie, solemnly. "I think I have some explaining to do if I'm going to persuade you to accept a proper fee for your work, but I'm going to have to ask you to keep it to yourself. I won't bore you with all the details – you'll be able to look them up on the net, but I'd be obliged if we could keep my background confidential, at least for the moment. It's such fun being ordinary, for a change – seeing the other side of people like Arabella! I suppose I should own up, really, because until a couple of weeks ago, I *was* a bit of a tycoon. I've always kept a low profile, because most of my work was being done for well-known figures and companies and if anything went wrong, I didn't want my involvement to spoil my reputation, if you see what I mean!"

"That's rather sneaky of you!" Melissande felt she knew Bertie well enough by now to say what she felt about things.

After all, they had been working together several times, changing light-bulbs, mucking out and helping old folk go to the loo – very practical situations.

"Not 'sneaky' – commercial!"

"So what *did* you do in your previous life?"

When Melissande heard about Bertie's connections with the cities of London and Westminster, and the clients for whom he had been acting, things began to fall into place, although he didn't think it necessary to let her into the secret of his social identity. There was something so romantic at pretending to be a modern version of a knight in disguise, wanting to woo a fair maiden.

"So you worked for Ogle! I used to come across them in my former existence but we would never have met because I hardly left the back office. You were one of those smoothies, always in and out of Number Ten! I suppose you've got a pass to get into Parliament and get coffee in Old Scotland Yard?"

"I used to – but I handed them all in when I resigned. I'm just an ordinary nobody these days, as far as the world's concerned."

"But now you're talking about big money again – and offering me the kind of fee I used to pay the top freelances."

"If we're going to get people to treat our great plan seriously, that's what we've got to do! I know I shall have to come out of hiding if it all comes to anything, but until we need to drum up large sums of loot to spend on our bouncy castles, you can be our public face!"

"That's not my image at all; leading a 'great plan'." Melissande was about to back out of the whole thing. "I've been enjoying a more domestic existence with no one breathing down my neck – except Arabella and her horse!"

They laughed, but it needed more persuasion on Bertie's part before Melissande finally agreed to sign up.

"Don't worry: there's no need for anyone to breathe down your neck." He paused, censoring the next phrase that came to mind, which was: 'although I'd love to kiss it, given half a chance'. He told himself: 'Focus, Bertie' and managed to keep it respectable by saying: "and I wouldn't put pressure on you". Having got a grip on his carnal temptations, he continued:

"If it looks at all viable, we'll need to set up a development company and I promise you'll be on The Board; and I'll make sure we have equal shares of the equity. I have to say I've been impressed by your approach to life!"

Having blurted that out, Bertie suddenly felt shy. He hadn't meant to be so open about the admiration that had been propelling him in her direction. Her response was equally coy. She blushed and turned away, brushing a hand across her face, scooping up stray hairs before re-setting the scrunchie on her ponytail.

"Tell you what," said Bertie, trying to regain his aplomb and pretending not to notice her discomfort: "if you're agreeable, I'll get one of my old colleagues to do me a favour and design a logo and letterhead for you, so you've at least got something on which to write an invoice. If it all comes to anything, I'm sure some of the others will do the necessary, helping set up the company and all that. They'll be half expecting me to turn up with some mad scheme or another before long – we've all been friends too long!"

Melissande took the opportunity to get up from the table and put the kettle on. It was time for elevenses and her parents would be expecting it – her father busy with his sermon in the study, and her mother writing letters in the drawing room, a rug round her knees to protect against The Rectory drafts that made it so expensive to keep warm.

"Well, what do you think?" Asked Bertie, hopefully. "Have we a deal?"

"If you are sure you're not over-rating my capabilities, then I must say it's very tempting!"

By now, both had overcome their hesitancy. Bertie was pleased he had been able to let her know his feelings for her, while Melissande's morale continued to rise, at receiving such a compliment; and the prospect of further contact with this person, who became more interesting every time she met him.

"Let's shake on it!" Said Bertie, wanting to feel her hand in his. The emotion was mutual and the handshake took rather longer than might have been expected, each enjoying the other's touch. Bertie noticed that, despite all Melissande's manual work, her hand wasn't leathery or wrinkled with red knuckles: it was smooth, slender and very white. He glanced at her nails and saw they were neatly trimmed and finished with clear varnish. This added to her attraction: he hated long, gaudy nails.

Melissande, for her part, enjoyed her hand feeling so safe, enclosed in Bertie's large paw. She couldn't help but look at it because she was avoiding his eyes, after the way they had, several times, affected her legs. He too had clean nails and his hand, though large, was elegant with long fingers.

They were rescued by the kettle, which was beginning to jump about on the Aga. At the same moment, Melissande's mother came in.

"Any chance of a cup of coffee, darling," she said, as she opened the door. "Oh – sorry – I didn't know you had a visitor!"

"Not a visitor, Mrs Blythe – just 'a fellow worker' popping in to talk shop, you know," said Bertie, standing up, respectfully.

Most encouraging, thought Mrs Blythe. Such a nice young man: I do hope she won't fend him off like she has all the others. She made a hasty retreat.

The rain stopped at last. For the first time in days, Bertie woke to the sound of birds singing and a shaft of sunlight bringing out all the colours of Reg's tiny spare bedroom. He almost expected bees to fly in (through the slightly open window he always kept during the night), to check the flowers on the curtains for nectar. By the time he was washed, shaved and dressed – and had taken tea into Reg, even the gutters and shrubs had stopped their musical dripping and the puddles around The Lodge had begun to disperse.

After porridge and toast with Reg, by now in the warm kitchen in dressing gown and slippers, Bertie put on his tweed jacket and cap, stepped into his wellies, which had stood by the Rayburn all night, adjusting the straps to keep the knees of his trousers comfortably loose, giving the look of plus-fours.

"I'll go and see to everything," he said, heading towards the back door.

"Good on yer!" Called Reg. "A couple more days and I'll take over again – I'm pretty well better, I reckon."

"Better do what the doctor says, Reg. He's told you 'light duties' for another week, didn't he?"

"He don't know nothing about it! I'm fit's a fiddle. All these exercises!" He had been attending physiotherapy sessions in a hall in Chippenham where other 'heart patients' were also being put through their paces by two charming nurses.

"Give it a few more days and you'll be better than you were before!" Said Bertie. "Anyway, I've got used to my routine now, dropping you off for an hour while I do the shopping. You'll be ready when I get back won't you?"

"You're almost as big a bully as that Arabella!" Complained Reg. "She's about, mind you. I heard her car arrive last night. She was getting wheel spin in all that mud."

"I'll keep a weather eye out: she's probably gone riding already. You know what she's like: can't stay still for a minute."

"Ah! And wants everyone else to be the same, runnin' around after 'er!"

"That too! Bye for now, Reg. See you later." Bertie stepped out into the bright morning light, such a change from the windy gloom and pelting rain of so many days.

He was half way to the stable when, coming from the direction of the drive and lane, he heard the angry high pitched revving of a motorbike. It sounded like someone racing over a trials course. Bertie wondered whether Melissande had managed to catch the culprit in the act yet. She had been annoyed about the way in which the lane had been churned up. However, Bertie was not going to let this noisy intrusion interfere with his morning routine – of checking Her Ladyship, the fire in the drawing room and its supply of logs, followed by a cursory look at the stallion in the stable – if Arabella had not already taken him out. As far as Bertie was concerned the motor-bike intruder could get away with it one more time.

This was not to be, however, because the high-pitched two-stroke cacophony suddenly stopped, to be replaced by a dual scream – a horse whinnying in terror and a woman in distress. The effect on Bertie was electric. Without even thinking, he changed direction and half flew down the drive towards the wooded entrance to the lane. The first indication of what might have happened was the riderless stallion galloping towards him from the other direction. It dashed past, heading towards The Manor. Bertie ignored it, except noting that it didn't seem to be injured and would doubtless stop, once it reached the security of the stable yard.

What was worrying him was the condition of Arabella, who must have been the one screaming and might be lying injured in the muddy lane.

He soon found her – certainly in the mud: covered in it. She had regained the sitting position and was obviously not sufficiently hurt to prevent her from delivering a torrent of abuse towards a leather-clad man in a crash helmet, trying to extricate himself from a steaming scrambler bike several yards away – wallowing in a sea of stirred mud, fallen leaves and rotting twigs.

"You *stupid, inconsiderate* BASTARD!" She shrieked. "You are a fucking menace! Who gave you permission to even bring that machine on to my land! God knows what you've done to my horse! I'm going to sue you for every penny you've ever heard of, you *complete prat!*"

Bertie's first feeling was one of relief. No one killed or badly injured. Not even the stallion, which had been moving very freely past him, as it headed for home. Arabella was plainly in fine fettle and full of aggression. The man, however, seemed to be having trouble getting himself from under the bike.

Bertie, quite naturally, went over to help him, lifting the machine off the man, allowing it to fall the other way, back into the mud. The man leapt to his feet.

"Don't chuck my bike about you c---," he growled, without an ounce of gratitude. "That cost a bomb!"

"I *beg* your pardon?" Bertie was not used to be addressed in this way – especially from someone to whom he had extended such ready assistance.

"Can't you understand fucking English?" said the man, placing his gauntlets each side of his head to lift off the mud-covered crash helmet that was hindering his vision and hearing.

"I understand English rather better than you might imagine," replied Bertie, now giving the man his very fullest attention while feeling his heart-rate build rapidly as adrenalin surged through him.

"Well tell that cow to keep her fucking horse off the road! Why can't she stay in the fucking fields?"

"This happens to be her land, my friend; she can go where she likes and I ask you to refrain from using such foul language in front of a lady."

"Lady? My arse! 'Ave you heard what she's calling me?"

"The way you have been trespassing on her property, causing her to be thrown from her horse, would seem to be ample cause for her to be very cross and I can easily forgive her from using strong language. The very least you can do is apologise and remove yourself before we call the police."

"And you can piss off, you great poof, before I put you where you belong, on the fucking deck!"

The man stepped forward and without a moment's reconsideration, punched Bertie in the face with his muddy leather glove. The blow nearly took Bertie off his feet but in the split second that he saw the fist heading in his direction he braced his body and took half a step back, as he'd learned in the gym at school. The cold mud on his cheek and the force of the punch, however, shook him badly and changed any restraint he might have had, into retaliatory aggression. In an instant his right hand came up into the defence position and his other delivered a straight left to the side of the man's jaw, now unprotected by the crash helmet, which his opponent dropped into the quagmire. The owner quickly followed, falling beside it, knocked out cold, wet and muddy by Bertie's experienced martial arts technique.

Bertie stood back, ready to repeat the treatment if the intruder rose again to challenge him. It crossed his mind that if the position had been reversed, and he himself had been lying inert in this mess, the man's boot would by now be about to arrive as a powerful kick in the ribs. He was grateful that was not the case. So was Arabella, still sitting in the mud observing the action.

"Hit him again before he has another go," she shouted, with venom.

"I think it's more to the point if I take the number of his motor-cycle," he replied, reaching for the notebook and pencil he always kept in the breast pocket of his jacket.

"Melissande has been on his trail for several days now. She will be very pleased that we now have found out what's been mucking up the lane."

"Get his name too!" I'm going to sue the bastard!"

"I'll certainly try," said Bertie, "but I don't think that will be forthcoming. He seems to be very surly."

Bertie was right. The man, rising from his humiliation, told him to 'F off'; turned his back and went to salvage his precious motorbike. After several frustrated attempts at kick-starting it, he gave up and, with difficulty (because of the state of the lane, caused by him during the preceding week), pushed the machine off towards the main road.

Bertie went to help Arabella to her feet, while trying to avoid getting his clothes any more soiled.

"Thank you," she said. "Did you see the stallion?"

"I did, heading towards home – he looked all right," said Bertie.

"No thanks to that idiot," Arabella snarled. "Is your eye damaged?"

"Now you come to mention it," said Bertie, somewhat surprised at her enquiring after his health, which until now, had not concerned her; "it is rather painful. I suspect it's going to turn rather an unpleasant colour if I don't urgently apply some steak."

They made their bedraggled way back to The Manor, where Bertie washed his hands and face in the outhouse before beginning his morning chores and Arabella took herself off for a bath and a change of clothes. Bertie's eye was now hurting, though he could still see perfectly well, which was a relief. It was an injury he had experienced before at Eton, where he had achieved high rating at Karate and other such gentlemanly pursuits.

Bertie was relieved that Lady Veronica did not seem to notice the swelling and redness around his face, and retreated back to The Gate Lodge, where Reg gave him sympathy and helped him apply some stewing steak to the affected eye. Later, they washed the steak and put it in the pressure cooker along with an onion and some carrots. By evening, however, the surroundings of eye had turned black and the white of the eye had turned red.

"I really am quite a sight," Bertie told himself that night, as he cleaned his teeth in front of the bathroom mirror.

Arabella was a little stiff from her fall in the lane. She complained to Melissande and Bertie about it when the three met up next day in the stable yard.

"I don't know how he got that far up the lane behind me before I heard anything," she said. "The overhanging trees must muffle the sound and I suppose the horse's feet were making quite a squelch in all that mud. He took us completely by surprise and the stallion reared up, tipping me off backwards! I suppose I was lucky to land in the mud rather than on a hard road. It broke my fall but my clothes are worse than after hunting on a foul day. The best thing was when you floored him, Bertie. I would have, if I'd been big enough. In fact I'd have killed him!"

"I hope you wouldn't," said Melissande. "I'm glad it was a mud bath, rather than a blood bath. We'd have had to come and visit you in prison for ever more! And your horse would have got fat with not being ridden."

"But at least the lane wouldn't be mucked up! Can we sue him?"

"You'd have to ask Mr Penworthy," said Bertie.

Melissande wanted retribution.

"I'm going to report him to the police, now that I've got the number of his bike. At least we can find out whether he's got insurance and a licence. I don't think he should be allowed to get away with it; especially since he gave you that black eye, Bertie. That's grievous bodily harm at the very least! You could get him charged."

"And I'd be your witness: it would be an open and closed case!" said Arabella.

"I don't think it's worth the aggravation and I don't think he'll want to come back for a while, do you?"

Arabella laughed, re-enacting the punch that Bertie had thrown. "He'd better not or he'll get another one of your Japanese wallops!"

It was after this incident that Bertie noted a slight change in Arabella's attitude towards him. She even managed to flirt a little, while retaining her haughty air. Bertie's eye, however, was still purple and blue with greeny yellow borders, the next time they met, a week later to talk about TGP.

By then, Melissande was ready with her preliminary findings, the result of much surfing and several phone-calls. She had caught up with Bertie's broad-brush impressions of 'the amphibious village' and traced ideas and concepts back to their sources.

"The best place to get hold of some facts and figures for such a project is Holland," she told the 'TGP Board', as Bertie now described it.

Setting up the meeting, Bertie had commissioned Mr Penworthy to be there; Lady Veronica didn't have much option because Reg Haines had made up the fire in the drawing room at The Manor and it was far too comfortable to go anywhere else. So when he, Bertie, Mr Penworthy and Melissande descended on her, with a tray of tea *and* some fairy cakes (that Melissande had made that morning), suggesting they might discuss the subject of the flooded meadows, it was all too good to refuse.

When they had sat down, joining her around the fire, her first concern was Bertie's black eye.

"Oh dear, Bertie," she asked, looking worried, "whatever happened to you – did you walk into something, or was it the stallion?"

Bertie laughed it off.

"Nothing really, Lady Veronica – just a spot of bother. I'm sure Arabella will fill you in on the details but I'm fine, I promise you. It just looks worse than it is and one doesn't like to use make-up to hide one's misfortunes."

"How intriguing! Perhaps Arabella will be around later. The Hunt event starts next weekend and I'm sure she's not ready yet."

"Fingers crossed," said Melissande, "Arabella and her new beau should be here soon. From what she told me, he might be just what we need because he's just come into money – although officially we don't know anything about that, if you see what I mean!"

"I shall be absolutely discreet, my dear," said Lady Veronica. "I know *northing!*" She put on a funny foreign accent and the meeting got off to a good-natured start.

"What have you found out, Melissande?" Asked Bertie, taking the lead.

"A lot of people are *talking* about 'floating houses' but no one seems to be *doing* anything. All the academics and engineers have been writing papers and books about it for the past five or six years but I couldn't find a single project except the original one in Holland where they've actually *built* a row of amphibious houses."

"Have you managed to get hold of any those books?" Asked Bertie.

"I haven't yet – because all across The Internet, people have put the prices up to silly levels. Second hand copies of the books I'd like to look at are selling for seventy or eighty pounds! Their original cost might have been only a tenner but there must have been a sudden jump in demand and the websites have picked it up and are all cashing in. I've had to depend on newspaper and BBC reports."

"Better get a move on, then," said Reg Haines. "Sounds like other people are thinkin' the same as you."

"You're right, Reg," said Bertie. "Somehow or another we need to speed up – get all the information we can and then produce something we can show people."

"What do you suggest?" Asked Mr Penworthy.

CHAPTER 11

"Listen to this, Bertie! No wonder it's bloody wet!" said Reg as he lowered the Sunday paper that Bertie had bought that morning.

"Enough to make you emigrate!" He chuckled.

'As much of Europe recovers from the severest winter in several centuries, scientists say average annual flood losses could be almost five times greater by mid-century.'

"Are you going to, then?"

"What?" Asked Reg.

"Go to Australia?"

"I think I'll stay 'ere, Bertie. Not sure I can be bothered to pack everything up at my age! Anyway, I think we may be on to a good thing with these floating 'ouses, if it's goin' to get five times worse and floods twice as often!"

"When's that going to happen, then?"

"It says here *'within the next 30 years'*!"

"Who's saying that?"

"Some Dutchman – and an Austrian, although I wouldn't 'ave thought they had much by way of flood plains – all mountains, ain't it? They're saying most of it's coming from what we're doing – concreting the world over – changing the weather and all that. The floods'll wash it all away again – cost a bomb! I'm glad I won't be around to see it: need bloody water wings!"

"I think your Dutchman's right, though. Now's the time to get moving – all these storms! We can't go on like this, getting flooded – roofs blowing away every year. It's a real opportunity for us, though!"

"Bertie – I believe you might be right, but it'll be a Hell of a job!"

"What we need is a lot of money as soon as we can get it; plus people who are prepared to back this particular horse."

"Sea 'orse, more like! Give us a drop more tea, Bertie."

As he reached for the milk jug, Bertie thought it might be a good time to broach a proposal to his doughty companion.

"Reg, how are you feeling?"

"I'm about all right, thanks. The old ticker's working more steady. I do get a twinge now and again, but the cardio-whatsit told me to expect that. That bit of plumbing 'e put in is still stretching things, but 'e said don't worry – so I'm not!"

"If I went off for a bit, could you take over, back here?" Bertie poured Reg's second cup.

"I reckon: yeah, why not? There isn't all *that* much to do and I'll manage, if I take my time. I'll keep an eye on Her Ladyship, and Miss Arabella can look after the logs – she's bringing some young chap and she'll get him to do it for sure! You know what she's like!"

"I hope she won't put him off by making him some kind of servant," said Bertie. "If he's a possible investor she's got to be nice to him."

"I suspect she might be doing that in *other* ways, if you see what I mean," said Reg, chuckling.

"Mm," said Bertie, pausing for a moment to visualise the possibilities; "mm ... ... but I don't want to go away thinking I've left you in the lurch."

"No, no, boy, I'll be fine. Lady Veronica and Mel will back me up; and *they* won't be gettin' into fights down the lane, coming back with a shiner! My goodness, it's still a good colour! You've got to stop worrying about me, Bertie – I'm as fit as you, an' better lookin', at the minute!"

Bertie touched his swollen eye, forcing a smile.

"The thing is, Melissande needs to go to Holland to see what they've been doing – that means she would be away too."

"Is that where you're going, Holland?"

"That's where I'm starting, yes!"

"With Melissande?"

"Well yes – I think two heads might be better than one." Bertie tried to look casual.

"Mm," said Reg, nodding sagely. "I suppose Spring *is* just around the corner."

Later, Bertie called at The Rectory. He knocked quietly at the back door, not wishing to disturb The Rector; and as he passed the church he'd caught a glimpse of a windswept Melissande taking a basket of washing in from the back garden. She came to the door, expecting the postman. Seeing Bertie was a mixed surprise. Her heart missed a beat in celebration – she couldn't prevent that – but it was disconcerting that she had put on an awful old pullover and jeans, not expecting visitors, and her hair was all over the place. This was compounded when he explained his mission.

"Do you mean *you're* coming too?" Melissande was quite shocked, as she made coffee for them.

"Well yes," said Bertie. He was somewhat taken aback by her attitude. "We're both 'board members' and I think it's important that I, too, get properly briefed, don't you?"

Melissande's stomach had gone into a knot. The thought of travelling and 'going around' with Bertie for several days was alarming. What about hotels? Would he want to share a room? 'No – of course he couldn't: I'd refuse,' she told herself.

"You'd better sit down," she said, playing for time to think up answers to questions that she suspected might shortly be asked. "Pass me those cups." She pointed to the dresser.

She removed the washing from the kitchen table, gathered her wits and caught up with herself as she bustled round. This done, feeling calmer and less conscious of her scruffy appearance, she resumed her search for reasons why Bertie should *not* accompany her to Holland, as she pushed a plate of biscuits across the kitchen table.

"But what about everything here? Who's going to look after Lady Veronica? And poor Mr Haines? Surely he can't manage?"

"He says he can, and I believe him. Arabella's bringing this young man down to help with her Hunt event and Reg is sure she will soon rope him in. I'm sure things will be fine at this end, but what about your parents? Have you made some arrangements?"

Melissande had. When the dates for her absence had been decided, she suggested that her mother's sister came to stay for a while, as she did from time to time. Being younger by a decade, she was in much better health, and, being bossy by nature, would manage The Rectory very ably, although The Rector, by the third day, would be looking forward to Melissande's return.

"Aunt Gwen will run it like clockwork. Poor Daddy finds her trying, but he'll have to manage: he wouldn't want to hinder my career. But won't it be rather extravagant, both of us going? All that extra cost – I mean, two people travelling – and double the hotel bills."

It was a clumsy way of putting it but she *had* to be sure Bertie wasn't plotting some kind of seductive 'dirty weekend' of the type she'd read about with a mixture of excited curiosity and distaste. Books she'd picked up at the jumble sale – and guiltily read – had caused her to say The Confession in church the following Sunday with extra vehemence.

Her excuse for reading such trash was that she had only been 'doing her bit' by spending at least *something* towards a good cause and in haste, not knowing what kind of books they might be. She knew she shouldn't have continued turning the pages, as soon as it became apparent that they were 'smutty' – but she hadn't been able to bring herself to miss the graphic love scenes half way through the well-thumbed paperbacks. Descriptions of such passion resulted in disturbing physical responses that Melissande could only conclude as 'sinful'. The books were the kind of things her outrageous friend Arabella often described as 'naughty but nice', while putting on a Cockney accent. Such comments usually ended a conversation as Melissande quickly changed the subject. Nevertheless, the temptation to think carnal thoughts would often lurk in the back of her mind for the rest of the day, especially if she and Arabella had to witness the stallion perform one of his reproductive feats.

It took a moment or two before Bertie got the message that Melissande was worried about his motives. Having deduced what she was getting at, he replied as coherently as he could, while smothering a desire to laugh and feeling suddenly that 'it was rather warm in here'. He hid his face by taking off his sweater.

"Please don't ... er... get me wrong, Melissande; I'm fully aware of the extra costs involved – two single rooms, double air-fares and all that but I feel it's justifiable investment if we're going to make a proper go of it. I hope you didn't think I had some ulterior motive?"

He almost snorted because it was half meant to be funny, but stopped himself. He did, however, look embarrassed, as did Melissande. To disguise her discomfort she got up and turned once more to the Aga, moving the large aluminium kettle to the hot side. Lifting the cover made her cheeks burn but at least gave them an excuse for being that colour.

"More coffee?"

"How kind! Yes please, Melissande. Do you want *me* to make the travel arrangements, or shall you?"

"Oh, I'll do it! I used to have some good connections for that kind of thing, I'll look in my address book and see if they're still in business. There's an excellent agent in Hanover Square. We became quite good friends."

"Splendid, thank you; meanwhile I'll start making a list of investors we might approach once we've got some convincing figures and pictures to talk about."

It was quiet for a while in The Rectory kitchen, as Melissande busied herself, at the same time making mental lists of what she would pack and whether her office clothes would still fit. She went out into the pantry for some more milk.

Bertie, having recovered his cool, waited comfortably in the carver chair at the end of the table, day-dreaming. He was still on his own when the other door opened and Mrs Blythe's head appeared.

"Oh! I was looking for Melissande," she said, pleasantly surprised to find Bertie, yet again, in her kitchen.

Bertie stood up hastily.

"Oh good morning, Mrs Blythe. She's just nipped out to the pantry. We were talking about our research trip to Holland."

"How nice to see you, Bertie! She's been looking forward to her trip, but I wanted to tell her that Arabella's here, with a friend. They're looking for her. I'll see them into the drawing room; let her know, would you?"

"Of course Mrs Blythe. I'll be off in a minute, anyway."

When Melissande returned, Bertie passed on the news and immediately made for the back door.

"They won't want to meet plebs like me at this stage!" He said. "The poor chap will have to be let down gently if we're going to recruit him as a shareholder. I'll leave it to you women-folk. See you later: I've got some jobs back at The Manor!"

Without giving Melissande time to comment, he was gone – not a minute too early, because Arabella could be heard, putting on her best 'yah' accent, as she introduced someone to her father in the hall.

"Dear Bertie," said Lady Veronica; "I'm so glad you came in. We have a minor crisis. Poor Haines does find the stairs a bit much at present but we need to get Arabella's visitor's room ready. I daren't attempt it myself and have been wondering what we can do."

"Can't Arabella do a little towards being the gracious host?"

"I'm sure she would, in the ultimate, but it wouldn't make for a good atmosphere for her to find she had to make beds! It's something I've always tried to do since she was little, coming here for half-term and so on. She used to travel down with Melissande and John used to pick them up at the station – such fun!"

"I think you spoiled her!"

"I'm sure we did but she's the nearest we got to having a daughter and she *has* been very affectionate and kind, on occasions."

"I see the cat's here. Has she deserted Reg?"

"No, she's only just arrived – it's her usual time – when the drawing room has warmed up to her liking – watch!"

The cat rubbed against Bertie's leg and then tip-toed purposely off across the hall, pushing open the drawing room door an inch or two.

"Arabella's over at The Rectory," said Bertie. "She had this chap with her, so I slipped out the back door. I know my place!"

Lady Veronica and Mrs Blythe, only the day before, had discussed Bertie's increasing presence at The Rectory. They knew it was 'business' but both wished to be careful not to discourage him. Mrs Blythe was a little concerned that 'we don't know much about him'; fearing that he might be some fugitive, hiding from the fraud squad. Lady Veronica, by now devoted to this young man who had appeared from nowhere in her moment of need, pooh-poohed such a thought, though it was one she had harboured occasionally in the early hours of the morning when trying to decide whether a cup of tea might be worth all the trouble.

"He's been perfectly sweet to Haines – and me too! I don't know what we would have done without him. The cat has taken to him as well, and she's usually a very good judge of character. I thought Arabella was taking an interest at first but she seems to find him irritating. He does tend to whistle when he's concentrating on what he's doing and she finds that rather trying."

Lady Veronica knew she could share such gossip with Mrs Blythe because they were old friends and were able to discuss the shortcomings of family members.

"Melissande has been amused at the way he teases Arabella," said Mrs Blythe, warming to the subject. "She's told me about a few incidences. He tends to drop hints that she might be a little more helpful and considerate during her visits and she finds that infuriating. I think it's her conscience, although she puts it down to 'staff being impudent'."

"But of course, Bertie isn't 'staff'! He's more like a gallant knight coming to the rescue! Did you hear about our visit from the bailiffs?" Lady Veronica lowered her voice.

"No?" Mrs Blythe did lie, from time to time, when it was the Christian thing to do, but she took the precaution of crossing her fingers, because Melissande *had* given her a full briefing about the financial plight of Tytherton Kellaway Manor. It would have been upsetting for Lady Veronica to think that her private affairs were being discussed in detail at The Rectory.

Lady Veronica went on to relate how she nearly lost all her furniture. Having confessed her shame she felt a lot better, and she hoped it restored Bertie's reputation as a rescuer rather than refugee. Today, as if to prove her point, she was depending on him to make up the spare-room bed for Arabella's guest.

"I can't remember the young man's name," she told Bertie, later. "I think it might be 'Christian' or something like that. Very good-looking – about the same height as you and very well spoken. They only came in for a minute and Arabella showed him his room. He took his case up but then they went straight out. She wants to salvage as much of the Hunt event trail as she can. They're going to have to divert several parts of it and she said something about the churchyard. That's why they went over to The Rectory. I'm not sure how The Rector might feel about ponies and horses traipsing between the graves."

"I don't mind making a bed," said Bertie. "Living on my own, I've been doing it every day and my mother brought me up to clean sheets on Mondays! Is the linen handy?"

They found Reg, tidying up in the kitchen and Bertie was pleased to see the old man's cheeks a better colour, his stance more sprightly.

"You're looking well," he said, cheerfully. Perhaps their chat at breakfast had bucked the old boy up.

"I'm feeling pretty good, thank you Bertie," replied Reg, putting away knives and forks in the kitchen table drawer. "They certainly done a good job up at Swindon, fixing me up. It's stopped twingeing now, and I've got a lot more energy. I reckon I'm all ready to carry on as usual."

"Bertie's kindly agreed to make up the spare-room bed," said Lady Veronica, returning from the scullery, which they now used as a utility room, with an armful of sheets and pillow cases.

"Good on yer, Bertie! I don't fancy them stairs!"

There was a surprise waiting for Bertie when he entered the spare bedroom. He recognised the battered suitcase the moment he saw it. He owned one just the same: which he used to take to school every term. He turned it over to read the name printed on the side.

"Well I'll be damned," he chuckled. "Don't tell me she's got her claws into Batty! She'll have her work cut out, that's for sure! Especially if his old man has died!"

Tristram Heath-Cohen, nick-named 'Batty' because of the risky pranks he thought up, had a father who was tight as they come, paying his son's school fees only to keep him away from home as long as possible without going completely to the dogs. Tristram was due to inherit a good whack, one way and another, from the estates in St Lucia and oodles in the bank.

Here was a fellow with both feet *very* firmly attached to the ground who knew *exactly* what he wanted, Of course it might not be him at all – it might be someone who picked up a suitcase at a jumble sale. Bertie couldn't wait to find out, but from Lady Veronica's description, it *did* sound like the same chap. He made up the bed, military style, as he'd learned during cadet camp at school, opened the window to make the room a little less musty, and returned to his duties.

Melissande had asked him to repair a hinge on the tack room door. It was an easy job – simply needing longer screws. One day soon the door-post would need replacing, not having been painted for so long: it was rotting progressively from the bottom upwards.

Bertie nearly swallowed the screw he had been holding in his lips while trying to hold the door still with one hand and the screwdriver in the other, when Tristram slapped him on the back.

"Bertie! You sly fellow! Fancy finding you here, of all places!"

He had followed Arabella into the stable yard and had recognised the backview the moment Arabella had told him en route that 'the handyman's' name was 'Bertie La-something-or-other'

"Lamotte! It has to be! Sorry dear chap, did I make you drop something?"

"Bloody typical! I might have known it would be you, sneaking up from behind, blast you, Batty! Long time! How are you?"

Arabella was frozen to the spot. She couldn't believe what she was witnessing. Here was the eligible bachelor she'd enticed down to her country home, meeting one of the staff as though they were long lost brothers. Either Tristram wasn't quite the man she had hoped, or Bertie *definitely* wasn't. She was soon to find out. Tristram, seeing her dilemma, explained.

"Bertie and I were at school together for about four years! We were great mates, weren't we?" He put an arm around Bertie's shoulder. "I used to go to Suffolk to stay with him and his mother during the summer holidays. My folks were overseas."

"And Batty used to kick the wind out of me in martial arts. He's a dreadful man, Arabella. If I'd known, I'd have warned you!"

"It looks as though someone else has taken over my role, knocking you about," commented Tristram, pointing to Bertie's black eye.

"Very funny! I walked into a stable door, so back off, Cohen!"

Arabella needed a rapid change of attitude towards the man she had come to identify as 'Haines' stand-in'. She joined in the ensuing laughter with as much enthusiasm as she could muster.

"Well I never! I say, Bertie, you are a dark horse! Why didn't you say something earlier?" As she said it, various incidents, and her behaviour towards him, flashed through her mind. How humiliating! Never mind – better make the best of it and hope it would blow over.

"Extraordinary," she continued, without waiting for Bertie's reply. "Tell you what, let's all go out for a drink this evening. We can make up a foursome, I'll get Melissande lined up. You won't mind will you, Bertie?"

"Not at all - I'd be delighted!"

In the event, Melissande was in two minds as to whether to join them or not. It was supposed to be choir practice that night and she never missed *that*. It was only her mother who finally persuaded her that just once, it would not matter, but it would do her good to go out and 'have a good time', for a change.

"After all," said Mrs Blythe, "from what Arabella tells me, this gentleman may be just the kind of person you need to take part in your 'great project' for the Manor meadows. Apparently he's rather well off! I really do think you ought to go and support the home team, darling." Secretly she felt it might be an opportunity for Melissande to spend a little leisure time with Bertie, instead of only meeting 'at work'.

"I expect we'll talk shop anyway – Bertie and I are deep into floating houses and stuff, and Arabella is only just beginning to catch on. With a potential investor she'll *have* to support it, so apart from bags of reminiscing between the men, I suspect it will be rather a staid evening, but if you think the organist won't mind too much, I'd better go."

Actually, Melissande wanted to go for several reasons. It was a chance to make herself look nice when Bertie was around. It wasn't something she had wished to do for anyone else and she was slightly surprised at herself, but, just this once, she was prepared to allow her biological prompting to have its way. It would be amusing, too, to see how Arabella now reacted to Bertie. 'Batty', certainly looked like the kind of person who would not be cowed by her friend's brash and imperious manner. Arabella might have met her match!

In the event, the evening was anything but mundane. After a couple of drinks in the saloon bar of the nicest pub in Chippenham, they put on their raincoats and ventured out into the pouring rain to move to the restaurant they'd booked for dinner.

"We can cut through the covered arcade," said Melissande. "It will give us a chance to shake our coats before going the last hundred yards.

It was as they stopped to do that, when a group of young men came in for the same purpose, taking off their crash helmets and shaking their gauntlets. They were cursing the weather and being generally noisy. One of them looked across at the foursome and took a second look, before drawing his mates' attention to them.

"That's the spare prick who chucked my bike down!" He announced. "How's your eye, pig-face?" This last remark was delivered with a sneer, and the confidence of being in a group with superior numbers.

"And that cow fell off 'er 'orse, then blamed me! Still got muddy knickers darling?"

There was general laughter and the speaker felt brave enough to move towards the peaceable group taking brief shelter from the rain.

Bertie realised the man was going to take his revenge, now that he had back-up forces. He handed his shoulder-bag to Melissande, and said:

"Melissande, you and Arabella had better go on to the restaurant. Tris and I are going to have to see to these fellows. Terribly sorry!" He turned to Tristram. "This is the one who gave me a shiner – he hits first and wonders why one returns the gesture."

He had hardly finished his instant briefing, when the his old assailant charged, grabbing Bertie by the lapels. This turned out to be a mistake because on this occasion, Bertie did not adhere to the rules of the martial arts and performed a most ungentlemanly action. With a neat nod, he brought his forehead down sharply on to the man's nose. This was certainly effective. The man staggered back and clasped his face, roaring with pain and anger.

At that his mates piled in but the two old school friends were ready, taking up the stance of ancient Oriental warriors. The aggressors were met with precisely directed punches and kicks of devastating velocity. Those who came back for more found themselves propelled into the air as their impetus was used and enhanced by these two experienced unarmed combat veterans.

The whole event was being watched on closed circuit television at the police station and within minutes, two vanloads of police arrived – one at each end of the arcade. Arabella and Melissande, who had not had time to absent themselves before the assault, were the only two not apprehended and carted off to the police station. By the time the two girls arrived, Bertie and Tristram were coming out.

"What a relief," said Melissande. "We thought you were going to be locked up! How awful! Are you all right?"

"We're fine, thanks," said Bertie. "The sergeant saw the whole thing. He watched those fellows attack us and when I said I was worried about leaving you two unprotected, he took our names and addresses, and sent us away. He was jolly decent about the whole thing: said not to worry, he had it all on film, and no one had been badly hurt. He didn't think the other lot would bring any charges and from what he'd seen, they wouldn't bother us again for a while. He wanted to know what club we were in!"

"We told him it had been years ago, at school," said Tristram, "although I'm not at all fit these days. It was a good job the scrap didn't last long. Are we too late for supper?"

Melissande had taken the precaution of phoning the restaurant, hoping for the best, and warning the proprietor 'we might be rather late'. It didn't matter, because due to the foul weather no one else had booked; he was happy to wait. As she walked beside Bertie, following Arabella and Tristram, she observed that they seemed to know each other rather better than she'd expected. Arabella was holding on to Tristram's arm in such an intimate way. Melissande had a strong urge to take Bertie's arm too, but shied away from such an idea as being provocative and immoral. She did, though, feel a warm glow of gratitude and yes, admiration, for this fine man who had fought for her honour. Lust, however, must not be allowed to spoil the evening, she told herself. She pulled herself up a little straighter and walked in step with Bertie behind the other two, who seemed no longer aware they weren't on their own.

Arabella, for her part, doubted Tristram's claim that 'he wouldn't have lasted long' in such a battle. She knew better about his durability and stamina. This evening, too, had already been quite a thrill: not at all boring. She pressed herself closer to the strong arm.

CHAPTER 12

The two horses came to a halt. Arabella wasn't at all sure how to proceed. Normally after a few days of flooding, there was an isthmus where one could cross the low point in the field but now the muddy, speeding water of the Avon on its way to Bristol and the sea, mingled with the calmer waters of Tytherton Kellaway Manor's submerged summer pastures.

"Oh *Shih Tzu!*" She reverted to the polite version of her most frequently mouthed expletive. The stallion's ears went back: he knew there was no small dog about to snap at his heels but was familiar with his rider's tantrums. He began dancing nervously.

"What's up?" Asked Tristram. "Lost the trail in the water?"

"Yes! And it's cut off the last way through here. I'd planned the route to go round the edge of our farm, never thinking this field ever got flooded this badly and now look at it!"

"How deep do you think it is? Couldn't we ford it?"

"We might be able to – but there's only a couple of days before everyone else will need to and some of the ponies are a bit near the ground: they'd be washed away. Health and Safety would have a field day!"

"What do you think we ought to do?" Tristram was enjoying this, seeing Arabella getting slightly worked up. He admired a girl with a 'bit of spirit'. It made things more fun, as he'd discovered the day she had been rude to one of the staff at the National Portrait Gallery.

As she forced the stallion backwards and forwards, looking for somewhere to cross the water, he was reminded of her tantrum that day. An official had tried to tell them this section was now closing. Arabella would not accept this and gave the poor man a tongue-lashing, accompanied by aggressive body language and foot stamping, which ensured another fifteen triumphant minutes in which to make a leisurely search for some distant ancestor.

Seeing Arabella so irate made him want to crush and subdue her; and that night he'd been able to try it – only to discover that she wasn't averse to such treatment, given the right setting and circumstance.

Here on horseback, as she fumed against the River Avon, was not the moment for him to restrain her. He had to make do with watching, as Arabella, in her irritation repeatedly jerked the reins, aggravating the stallion even further.

"Stand!" She shouted, taking out more of her anger on the horse. She looked across at Tristram, found him smiling and became crosser. So he thought it funny, did he? Without further hesitation, she directed the stallion as best she could towards the floodwater, dug in her heels and gave him a sharp thwack on the rump with her crop.

"Come on! It can't be *that* bad!"

Horse and rider plunged ahead. Arabella had expected it to be no more than knee deep at most and it was only a matter of yards to the other side; the grass, no distance away on the other side, looked temptingly close. What Arabella had forgotten, however, was that at this point, due to occasional flooding in previous centuries and recent passage of large quantities of water, there was a ditch, now hidden below the murky surface.

The horse, under pressure from his irate rider, plunged ahead expecting, like her, to walk across to the grass opposite. Instead, its front legs descended into deep, cold water.

The stallion had, earlier in the season, received physiotherapy in an expensive equestrian centre in Gloucestershire, which included swimming. The depth of the water, therefore, did not faze him. He kept his head up and swam in the desired direction. The shock of being suddenly plunged into very cold water, did, however, cause Arabella to forget she was on a horse and instead of holding on and going with him, she let go of the reins, threw her arms in the air, lost her stirrups and shrieked, before treading water, wondering whether to go back to the dry land she had so recently left, or swim in the horse's wake, to the other side.

The water reached her body very quickly through her clothes and the temperature was so low it almost took her breath away, prompting her to give up the horse and seek safety, back with Tristram. She blamed the horse.

"Bloody animal," she said with trembling jaw, as she emerged from the water, dripping from everything except the hard hat and looking a picture of bedraggled fury.

Tristram's gallantry now came to the fore. He slipped down from his borrowed gelding – a fine seventeen-hand grey – and offered a hand to Arabella, assisting her squelch from the murky water.

"Here," he said. "Have my jacket."

Arabella shivered while he took off his coat and helped her on with it.

"Look," he said. "You can't hang about soaking wet; you'll catch a death! Jump up on this one, canter home and get yourself into a hot bath as quick as you can. I'll walk back and get Bertie: then we can both go round and catch the stallion from the other side, if he hasn't found his own way back. I suspect he's already nearly in the stable yard by now. I can't see him, can you?"

Arabella did catch a cold. The stallion did *not* make its way home and it was left to Tristram to tell Arabella that the lusty animal had been found on a neighbouring smallholding, mating with a donkey named Doris. They interrupted the connubials and were about to leave when Doris's irate owner approached them, wishing to take details of the stallion and where they might be contacted in case of any 'unforeseen circumstances', such as the jenny picking up some kind of disease from the intruder.

Tristram, in response to this implied criticism, replied by demanding Doris's details and her owner's address, because, he said: "normally there's a considerable fee to be negotiated for a service by a stallion of this quality".

The route for the Hunt's fund-raising cross-country trail, needed to be modified, with participants taking a diversion that included leading their horses over Maud Heath's Causeway. This called for more volunteers wearing day-glow waistcoats to ensure that riders *did* actually dismount before mounting the narrow raised path. Some preferred to risk using what had become a ford on the road.

On the day, the event was a great success. More than thirty horses, ponies and their riders took part, picking their way around the dry perimeters of the farm and local lanes, emerging eventually from the muddy lane, up the drive, to The Manor. There, the hunt provided refreshments for participants as they checked in at the end of their trek.

Without Melissande or Bertie being there to make the stable yard more presentable, the place was not looking its best. The trestles carrying bottles of fizzy pop and beer for the grown-ups stood in a mucky environment and the raffle prizes were arrayed precariously on a couple of straw bales in an empty stable, to keep them dry in case of further rain. A table covered with a blanket would have made them look more valuable but Arabella had done her hasty best.

Her Ladyship and Reg Haines helped out, with Reg taking his turn selling the drinks, and Lady Veronica, the raffle tickets. She managed to do this for an hour, before collaring Arabella to take over.

"So sorry, dear," she said, "but I really must go back to the fireside, this cold air is making my joints quite seize up."

Arabella sold a few tickets, between sneezing and blowing her nose and then found someone else to take her place, lending them a rug to put round their knees.

Reg enjoyed every minute of his two-hour shift, despite his cold feet. He found he was more popular than he imagined. Most of the people knew him and he was gratified to hear how many asked 'are you better now?' Business was quite brisk, as competitors checked in, having finished their trail; and the yard echoed with horsey talk and 'yah'. Reg overheard one or two of the local county set commenting on the state of The Manor; remarks such as 'gone down rather, since the old boy died, hasn't it?', and 'I wonder how much longer she can keep it going,'. Someone even suggested that Arabella was 'a waste of space' who ought to be doing more to save the remains of her inheritance. Reg pretended not to have heard, but to be engrossed in arranging the bottles on his trestle but there was nothing wrong with his hearing. In any case, he was inclined to agree with them.

Tristram amused him when it was time to hand over drink sales.

"I think we should be charging more!"

"Give it a try," said Reg. "See if they stop buying!"

"I shall," said Tristram, and people paid up without flinching; sales boomed. His commercial nose had been right and the day's takings rose to a total of six hundred and seventy-two pounds.

That evening, Reg gave Lady Veronica her night-cap and made up the fire soon after nine before traipsing home through the drizzle, carrying the cat.

"I do feel rather tired," Lady Veronica told Arabella, who had produced her best cordon-bleu supper for the three of them (although Reg had had to get his own at the Lodge); "so I'll turn in now. Thank you for such delicious food, my dears, and goodnight."

During the rest of the evening, spent mostly lying on the floor in front of the fire on the threadbare Afghan rug and cushions from the armchairs, was when Tristram caught Arabella's cold, without minding at all.

At one stage, resting between their horizontal athletics, Tristram, running his fingers through Arabella's hair said:

"I wonder how Bertie's getting on, travelling with Melissande."

"Nothing like this," said Arabella, her head resting on his chest. "She's a bit straight-laced, you know!"

"She seems very respectable – nice-looking too," commented Tristram. "Perhaps she'll finish up as the next Lady Lamotte.

"What do you mean? Don't tell me he's got a title!"

"Oh yes! Didn't you know? What a dark horse he is! He's a baronet."

"Then what the Hell's he doing, hanging around here doing odd jobs?" Arabella's feline contentment was draining away.

"I've no idea – haven't had time to ask him properly but he said he was fed up with Westminster and Mayfair and was talking about 'seeking his fortune'. I don't know quite what all *that* was about – he's got pots already."

"He's not going to find much fortune at The Rectory – they're as poor as church mice!"

"Perhaps it was *you* who caught his eye? You are rather gorgeous." He stroked her hair back in a loving gesture.

The praise pleased her and she rewarded Tristram with an appropriate snuggle.

"Hoping to do some property development, more like," she said, now uneasy, "and get hold of some cheap land". She was beginning to think she might have missed an opportunity.

"He's no need to do that *here*," said Tristram, "especially on something as wet as this! He's a big landowner; got several thousand acres of Suffolk to play with."

"Why doesn't he run it?"

"Because his mother does. His father was in the navy but died young and she's still a hands-on farmer – masterful! Made a fortune in the seventies. Bertie found it boring and went straight into banking and politics after school; then lobbying and PR: made a mint! Now he seems to have pulled out of all that too: weird! Never mind about him, Bella, how about finding me a blanket? Or warm me up with your lovely body."

Arabella resumed the actions of eternal love and devotion, while berating herself for not having done more to learn about Bertie's background before making assumptions. She might have gained herself a title, not to mention deep pockets.

For the moment, Tristram would have to do: she'd better cultivate him further, before she lost her bloom. He did, after all, have plenty to offer and seemed fairly predictable; definitely not gay – and not married, although she'd better check that out: messy divorces were to be avoided. What she wanted was a good-looking man with the right bank balance who would commit himself to her and give her at least one baby. That had been her mission for some years but each year it became more urgent as she approached what she feared might be her sell-by date.

"I wonder how Batty's getting on with Arabella," said Bertie, as he, Melissande and his mother sat around another log fire at Framlingham Hall in Suffolk. Lady Lamotte had had it lit especially for them, although it wasn't necessary, the central heating being ample for the whole house, but a fire in the hearth was more homely.

Bertie had suggested calling in for a night, en route for Holland. They could go by train to Saxmundham where his mother could pick them up. Next morning they'd drive on to Harwich for the early ferry.

"I'll pick up the car at home. I don't keep it in London: people keep bashing into you and it's rather a special toy."

Melissande had been quite surprised when booking the ferry, at the dimensions of the car. She had not come across an Aston Martin, except in fashion magazines, which Arabella sometimes passed on to her. It made her smile. She couldn't visualise herself draped over the bonnet, like the glamorous creatures which these sleek motors seemed to attract.

"It's rather large, isn't it?" She had asked Bertie.

"Well I do have rather long legs."

She didn't say anything, but having Googled it, she discovered the purchase price and was shocked at the extravagance. It had made her even more wary of this otherwise personable and good-looking man although now, his mother's brusque and friendly demeanour made her feel very much at home.

The house wasn't what she expected either. It turned out *not* to be the Framlingham Hall built inside the ruins of the magnificent Framlingham Castle, but a large Elizabethan house built on an ancient site, surrounded by the remains of a water-filled moat, a few miles out of town.

The Lamotte home was not extravagantly furnished or showy in any way – neither was it as threadbare as her father's Rectory, but comfortable and conservative in decor and atmosphere. Such surroundings restored some of Melissande's first impression of her new business partner. Coming from a background like this and having such a nice mother must surely have given Bertie the right start in life, despite his authoritarian father; Bertie had mentioned being whacked when he was young.

"The Old Man failed to instil as much discipline as he might have wished," Bertie had said as they chatted about their respective families on the train, earlier.

Watching Bertie now, she could see the likeness between him and the portrait over the fireplace labelled 'Rear Admiral Sir Edward Lamotte. She was still thinking about this when she became aware that her companions were waiting for some kind of comment about Batty and Arabella.

"I expect they will be tired, after the fund-raising day," she suggested; "all those horses, mud and refreshments. She will have kept him busy, that's for sure!"

"Batty, tired? Not likely - endless energy! But I'm not sure how he will react to receiving orders. He's a bit of a lad, but from what I've seen of Arabella, he'll have to tow the line at Tytherton Kellaway," Bertie added. "I know she's your oldest friend but she does tend to be rather 'controlling', don't you think?"

"Oh, I don't take any notice of that," laughed Melissande. "She's quite muddled-headed under all that posing. She knows she won't get her own way all the time with me and we get on well."

"She sounds fascinating," commented Lady Lamotte. "Have they known each other long?"

"She's only been mentioning him recently – they met at some function in London. If he's anything like her other admirers, he won't last long! She soon gets bored. They have to tick all the boxes before they stand a chance of staying in favour. She often talks about the perfect blueprint but never seems to find a good example."

"I can't wait to hear more about her. I know Tristram so well – ever since he was a teenager. I'm very fond of him, even though he can be very wilful. He and Bertie have always got on. He used to come down for the holidays because his parents were in the West Indies for months at a time. It was quite sad – all he got was a few postcards. He treated us like family. At the time I was almost a 'single mother' because Edward was always at sea."

"Tristram's folk had sugar estates," Bertie explained, "but they were too tight to fly him out for the holidays – it was cheaper to send him here. I didn't mind because we used to get up to all kinds of things around the farms – shooting, mostly."

"I used to have the horrors when I saw you boys going off with the guns but your father insisted that you wouldn't come to any harm – and you didn't!"

"I always wondered why he got called Batty," said Lady Lamotte. "It seemed rather unfair."

"When he first came to Eton he got teased about his 'up-North' accent. He soon learned to sound more like everyone else, but for a while he diverted attention by doing crazy things to make people laugh. People said he was completely batty – and it stuck, but he was anything but mad – he knew just what he was doing and became quite popular. Even some of the masters called him 'Batty Heath-Cohen'. I hung around with him because it was amusing and we became known as Batty and Bertie."

"He was devoted to me – like another son, but I've always found him very single minded when he wants something. You were much easier to manage, Bertie!"

"I'm not sure how to take that, Mummy! But I see what you mean about Tristram; he thinks the world of you. He preferred coming here to going to Yorkshire and was purposely objectionable to his parents to make sure it happened. He's still very good at getting his own way but I hope Arabella doesn't frighten him off! I don't think she realises how useful he might be for our great plan at Tytherton Kellaway."

"Why's that, then?" asked Melissande.

"Hadn't I mentioned it? He's an insurance underwriter – hard as nails – and his firm specialises in flood risk. How about that? I don't know if she's even mentioned to him what we have in mind for The Manor: she's probably been so full of the hunt event."

"She didn't seem to be very keen on 'the great plan' at that meeting we had," said Melissande.

"This is getting more and more interesting," said Lady Lamotte. "I can't wait to hear all about it but I must go out and see if the sheep are all right. We're in the middle of lambing and I like to make sure everyone's happy before I go to bed. They expect me at about this time."

"Mummy do you have to? Fred's still here, isn't he? You say he's a wonderful shepherd and perfectly able to cope."

"I've got two veterinary students too, but it's good for morale if I show up: makes them feel part of the estate and that we're all part of a team."

"You sound like those people I'm trying to get away from!" Bertie teased.

"I'm your mother, Bertie, and you should be grateful for all my hard work – I just hope you are more interested in the farm by the time I stand down. I'm doing all this for you, darling! Isn't that what they say?" She turned to Melissande. "Officially he's in charge already, since he inherited the title, but I know he has more fun in the City – or used to – and I've always enjoyed being involved with the farms, unlike his father, so the arrangement suits both of us; doesn't it, Bertie?"

As the evening went on, Melissande learned a lot more about the Lamottes. By the time she went to bed, she and Lady Lamotte had become firm friends. She felt at ease here. For a start it was much warmer than The Rectory and having an en-suite bedroom was a great luxury – except that she was alarmed to find there was another door leading from the bathroom. She quickly engaged the brass bolt, ensuring that no one could interrupt her privacy. What a thought! It might even have been Bertie! Such an idea speeded her pulse and led to sinful fantasies of the kind she tried to resist at this time of day. Even her usual remedy of kneeling beside the bed to say her prayers was unsuccessful. The words still went through but it was like driving – automatic and competent but nothing to do with what she was thinking.

Bertie, in his old bedroom, surrounded by memorabilia of childhood, teenage successes and yearnings, did not feel like bed. The room was presided over by a balding teddy bear carefully balanced on the mantelpiece, legs dangling, and one grubby arm tucked behind a martial arts trophy, to keep him secure.

'Ted' had listened to many of Bertie's complaints over the years. His mother had often been amused, listening at his door after lights out, hearing her little boy telling Ted 'it's not fair!' or 'I had too much ice cream – now I feel sick'. What she didn't hear, was the advice that Ted gave Bertie, although Bertie heard every growl and remembered its content. Tonight he reverted to his old dialogue.

"Ted, it's too early to go to bed! I'm not tired. I feel like clubbing!"

"You've got a big day tomorrow – get some sleep and stop thinking about that girl," growled Ted.

"You have to admit she is rather lovely?"

"How could I? You haven't brought her in here yet!"

"Ted, what an unthinkable suggestion!"

"You've brought other girls in here – and I've had to watch all kinds of antics. Remember that Spanish vet?"

"Teddy – that was when I was young and wild. I'm respectable now – anyway, Melissande would never speak to me again if she even suspected that I wanted to."

"Your mother doesn't mind!"

"Mummy's always been broad-minded. I remember her telling a friend about it one day, when she didn't know I was listening. She said she'd rather know where I was, and whom I was with, than worry about me being out somewhere driving like crazy or snorting coke."

"Well? See what you're missing! Beautiful face – if you took off those specs, perfect figure even if her clothes are a bit dowdy – great legs!"

"How do you know? You just said you'd never seen her!"

"I can read your mind, Bertie! You should have asked your mother to put her in the next room, then you might just have managed to barge in on her in the bath!"

"Well that's where you're wrong, Ted. I especially asked for her to have the room looking out over the lawn, well away from this side; Mummy understood. I don't want to scare the girl."

"You didn't mind scaring the others!" Ted laughed in a growly way.

"Shut up – or I'll put you in the drawer. I've got an early start: ought to get some shut-eye!"

"Isn't that what I told you?" Ted liked to have the last growl.

CHAPTER 13

It had been years since Melissande had been to sea. As the ferry left Harwich and butted its way into the waves of the North Sea she was full of excitement despite not sleeping well the night before. Perhaps the room had been too warm? Even the bedrooms were heated at the Lamotte home – unlike The Rectory, where bed-socks were the order of the night.

Maybe she had too much on her mind? True, she had double-checked all their travel arrangements before turning in and that may have been a mistake, because it reminded her of the purpose of this trip – to gather facts and figures on which to base a feasibility study. There were so many factors to be taken into account, any of which, if ignored, presenting impossible risks to the enterprise. Her mind began checking off those already noted, focussing on every factor that might affect the bottom line.

She knew she needed to get statistics about frequency of flooding – although predictions being announced almost daily by scientists warned that within the next year or two Wiltshire could expect summer droughts and winter monsoons. Historical data was hardly relevant any more if new weather patterns like those causing havoc recently were to become the norm. Was this a major risk – or an opportunity? It might make a compelling sales theme: 'Don't sink: invest and stay afloat with TGP!"

The political risks seemed less likely to become opportunities. With Tories and UKIP competing for the votes of Little Englanders to leave the European Union – without losing its advantages of course – what investor was going to risk their money? The nearest geographical targets for safe flood-plain development were Holland, Belgium, France and Italy – (what if Venice were to sink out of sight?) – but authorities in those countries might prefer to work with other EU members, rather than ex-members from an island fortress about to 'go it alone'.

She told herself to stop fussing – nothing had yet been decided. Her research could discover that TGP might never be a runner in the current economic situation: but what had she forgotten? There was bound to be something. She hoped it wouldn't be in their travel arrangements. There should be no problem about finding their destinations because Bertie's car could do that on its own, with satnav. There *shouldn't* be any problem about hotels either, because she had made the bookings herself.

In theory, therefore, there was nothing related to TGP to keep her awake, but as soon as she began to feel sleepy, another side of her life began its clamour. The dreams invading her churning mind were not the kind one might expect to meet in a nicely brought-up daughter of The Rectory. Unwanted images of Bertie kept interrupting.

Eventually Melissande's tiredness overcame the worry and she had drifted off to a troubled sleep in which she dreamed of fleeing Bertie's outstretched clipboard while losing her wellies in slimy mud, to the jibes of pony club riders squelching past, laughing at her.

When the alarm had gone off at six, it was pitch dark except for the crack under the door but it was a relief to be rescued by the reality of the comfortable bed, warm bedroom and the prospect of today's journey – in such a fantastic car; a short sea voyage, then being driven across Holland by – oh dear – the same man whose image seemed to have kept her awake half the night.

The way to stop these intrusive thoughts was action: no good lying here thinking up new hazards. She got out of bed telling herself to stop wittering. In the shower she could see her reflection in the glass door. She wished she looked as good when dressed! The physical work as part-time groom at The Manor and daily toil as her mother's carer in The Rectory certainly kept her body in good shape. She had worked off the slight enlargement of her bottom gained from the sedentary jobs after university. Now, her rear profile, she observed, was actually not much different to when she was fourteen. Vanity! She turned off the shower and speeded up the whole process of getting ready to brave breakfast. She hoped Lady Lamotte would be there before Bertie. After all the dreams she had endured over-night, the very sight of him would make her blush and feel antagonistic: unfair on him, she admitted, because in real life he might *not* be such an evil creature. At least there would be someone else to talk to if his mother were there.

As she dried her hair she couldn't help wondering whether it was getting too long: too hippy dippy? Perhaps not; it was still strong, thick and shiny – one of her best visible attributes: pity she didn't have something really nice to wear with it, and some expensive scent to dab on her wrists. More vanity – almost depravity! Get thee behind me! Well, maybe not quite yet! Concentrate on the job in hand! Had she done everything, got everything? Passports, route, addresses, phone numbers, mobile roving?

After so much self-questioning she felt sinful and tired; worse, she lacked confidence, and the clothes she had brought didn't help. They were fine for the village, even if she might be considered to be one of those 'nice young women destined to stay at home and care for her parents'. Tytherton Kellaway's Sunday best did not confer a young executive analyst with the panache and shine that might allow her to ask cheeky questions about costs and benefits.

Her trouble was lack of funds! Perhaps in a month or two, if Arabella paid up and Bertie continued to pay her a salary, things might improve. She might even get her eyes fixed and stop having to wear these unbecoming spectacles. The only thing she *could* do, this morning, was make sure her hair was at its best. She gave it an extra good brushing and by breakfast time, it was magnificent. As an act of bravado she left it falling around her shoulders, Princess Kate style, before making her appearance.

Lady Lamotte said exactly the right thing as soon as Melissande presented herself in the dining room.

"You look charming, my dear! Good morning!"

"Oh! Thank you! Good morning! What a lovely day!"

Things went on improving. Bertie, when he appeared, was obviously taken with her less prim appearance. He even remarked on her hair looking 'amazing', which while boosting her morale by several more points, did trigger a blush. This added to her charm, in Bertie's eyes: she was a real original. As they tucked into the devilled kidneys and fried potato cakes, he wondered how he might liberate such a pure princess from her inhibitions. He remembered what the teddy bear had told him, as he left this morning.

"Behave yourself, Bertie! Don't forget she's still a filly – let her come to you, my boy!"

He suspected that Ted, as usual, was right – although dropping the odd compliment about her hair couldn't go amiss. Just look at the delicious confusion it had caused. What a treat! One of these days something would happen again to enable physical contact beyond a peck on the cheek or a handshake. What a delightful prospect! That first encounter in the dark stable yard had been memorable but never repeated.

On reflection later, as they drove towards the port, he decided the rest of breakfast had been most enjoyable. It was ages since he had brought a girl home, and today's visit had not been for Melissande 'to meet my mother'. This was a business trip and they just happened to be passing, yet somehow he felt keen that his mother liked his new colleague. His mother had been her least controversial, going out of her way to make Melissande feel at home.

She had spared asking him about the strange colours around his eye. He was grateful for that, because it was not the first time he'd gone home the worse for wear. It had, during his father's time, led to some hurtful interrogations, which tended to spoil the atmosphere.

Safely on board the ferry, heading out to sea, under way in his quest for new ideas and prospects, a beautiful girl in sight – even if she were still inaccessible behind the brambles and castle walls of religion and conscience – this was beginning to feel more like seeking his fortune in the good old-fashioned sense. Bertie indulged in a little cheerful whistling.

For her part, the stiff east wind, Bertie's cheerful mood and the rising waves were all having positive effects on Melissande. They blew and rocked away the guilt about those dreams, and lifted the tired hangover – not that she deserved any because last night's aperitif and two glasses of wine had done little more than add a charming touch of colour to her cheeks and a little more sparkle to her eyes. Bertie had wished she would take off her tortoiseshell Specsavers frames so he could read better what her eyes were saying. She didn't know this and kept them on so that she could study his face closely, watching for any hint of insincerity. Gradually she was beginning to feel more confident in him and found herself in an unprecedented mood of contentment.

It was an extra large wave that answered Bertie's prayer for 'something to happen'. He was closely behind Melissande when they were about to mount a companionway to a higher deck, when the ferry gave a lurch that caught her off balance. Her hand missed the starboard handrail and her arm swung back, giving Bertie's head quite a thump as she tried to regain her balance. It was her elbow that made contact – right on her funny bone, giving her unpleasant tingles along her little finger. She ignored this in her concern over Bertie's head. It wasn't nearly as bad as she feared, because her elbow had glanced off the top of his forehead, hurting her more than him.

Bertie, seeing those big eyes fill with tears, took advantage of the situation and quickly covered his face with his hands, pretending to be quite the wounded sailor. Her natural reaction was to pull his hands away so she could assess the damage and begin first aid. Bertie loved the feel of her warm hands tugging at his, trying, gently, to uncover his eyes. It made his hair stand on end, as though he'd received an electric shock: bliss!

"I'm *so* sorry, Bertie," she blurted, almost in tears with remorse and agitation. She was castigating herself inwardly: how *was* it that she kept doing stupid things when he was around?

At this moment, the ship joined in again by giving another sudden lift as its bow mounted the next of three large waves. To save themselves from falling over, Bertie and Melissande had to hang on to something – whatever was nearest – which in this case, was each other. It not only had the desired effect of saving a tumble but enabled Bertie, quick off the mark as usual, to cash in by unobtrusively pressing Melissande to himself as though to protect her, while laughing at the situation.

It was the laughter that made Melissande see how silly they must have looked, and instead of pushing him off as soon as decently possible without seeming ungrateful while offering polite thanks to regain her dignity, she got the giggles and forgot all that. She leaned against him for a magic moment, holding rather tighter than she would normally have dreamed of doing. It turned into a hug and Melissande wasn't sure how long she should allow it to go on, but the feeling of Bertie's chin being pressed against her hair and the accompanying waft of after-shave was so intoxicating she was unable to decide.

This was a major advance as far as Bertie was concerned. It must not be spoiled by allowing himself to be deemed as 'going too far'. With skill and self-restraint, in order to consolidate his progress, he disentangled himself in a gentlemanly way, so as not to give the slightest suspicion that he was longing to seize her and kiss that delicious mouth and revel in her entrancing scent.

"Don't worry! You didn't hurt me at all – I was only playing!"

"You wretch! I thought I'd blinded you or given you another black eye," she protested, still shaking with laughter and trying to control her rebellious legs, which once again were giving notice of letting her down. She forced herself to stand back from him.

"Come on: let's see if we can find the bridge – it's such a lovely day and this air is so bracing!" She set off up the companionway at quite a pace, hoping Bertie would join in her childish adventure. He did, loving every second.

By the time the ferry docked they had enjoyed a brisk exploration of as much of the ship as passengers were allowed, and finished up in the bright warmth of the restaurant, for cappuccino and croissants. As they drove from the port, Melissande stayed quiet so that Bertie could concentrate on driving on the right.

It was a companionable silence, interrupted only by the Aston Martin's satnav giving instructions to bring them to the right road for Maasbommel and Petten.

"It's flat as a pancake, isn't it?" Commented Melissande, once they were on the motorway, heading East out of Rotterdam. "And so many straight lines!"

"It is – compared with most of England," said Bertie, "but have you been further North? Up beyond Amsterdam – where they've taken land from the sea – it *really is* flat there!"

"I haven't been anywhere, much," confessed Melissande; "except a few school trips and then when I was working, to a couple of capital cities – including Amsterdam. That was the most recent."

"What were you doing there?"

"It was a conference. I went over with colleagues from the company when I was working in Bath. I didn't see much of the city even then."

"That's a pity! What happened?"

"It was all rather sordid. I finished up on my own in the hotel every evening."

"Why was that?" Bertie sensed an opportunity to probe a little deeper into Melissande's privacy.

"I'm sure you don't want to hear all about it. The others took themselves off to a part of town that I'd heard about where it seemed 'unsuitable' for me to go."

Bertie guessed immediately where that must have been, but decided to pursue the subject, after giving Melissande a few minutes to mull things over. He looked over at her, sitting in the passenger seat, determinedly watching the succession of ploughed fields interspersed with endless water-filled ditches and occasional bright green oblong of wheat beginning its spring flush.

"Unsuitable how?" He asked, keeping his distance from the lorry in front.

"The red light district was not somewhere that I wished to visit. Nor did I want to go and dabble in drugs; and I suppose I was trying to set an example, too."

"An example of what?"

"Well – that one could be happy without resorting to debauchery and loss of control."

"Dear dear! You do sound straight-laced! Would you deny them a bit of the highlife? I bet they were only being curious." Bertie knew this was pushing his luck but he wanted to see her response.

"That kind of curiosity can lead to all kinds of disaster. It's not the kind of thing they would have wanted their wives or parents to know about; being 'abroad' seemed to give them licence to misbehave."

"I suspect it wouldn't worry Arabella," said Bertie.

"That was part of it! We used to have long arguments about things like that. I'd always been brought up to believe that the human body was sacred – not something to be bought and sold for what would otherwise be considered as abuse. I always felt she was allowing herself to be libertine – dangerously so, although she wasn't on that trip."

"So you stayed in the hotel, feeling righteous, while they went to see what was on offer?" Bertie was now being purposely provocative.

"I did: but not feeling righteous, as you put it – more scared, if I'm truthful."

"A bit of the 'lead us not into temptation' nerves, was it?"

Melissande needed time to consider how she should answer. She hid some of her shyness by reorganising her hair, pushing it back from her ears on both sides, leaning forwards and flicking it back so that it fell further down her back, before daring to sit comfortably and look at him. She *wanted* to tell him about it but was finding it hard. Her emotions wavered between recklessness and caution. Could she venture into the subjects that troubled her so much without feeling she was being ravished? She was attracted to Bertie but feared he might turn into the usual kind of seductive groper who made her skin crawl?

Certainly it would be foolish of him to 'try anything' while he was driving: that made her a little bolder and human instinct, accompanied by increased heartbeat, began to win ground against her intellect and upbringing.

Whatever it was, convinced her that this was not foolhardy but a measured retreat. Allowing him nearer was not without consideration: she *had* known him for several weeks and there *had been* occasions when he had every opportunity to invade her privacy and even her body – like today on the boat when she had failed to resist to the strange weakness that his presence inflicted on her when she thought she'd hurt him. She knew she should have stepped back from their emergency embrace immediately, but she had allowed herself to just flop there – letting him hold her up – just for a few self-indulgent seconds and he had *not* taken advantage.

The funny thing was that afterwards, she had not suffered any remorse or distaste. It had been glorious! Perhaps she might trust her intuition again? Bravado triumphed. For the first time she unlocked her privacy and allowed *a man* into an inner sanctum of her thought. She wanted to trust him; and the only way to be able to do so was to take the risk.

He was still waiting for an answer, although the atmosphere between them was relaxed enough for this not to spoil the moment as they sped along the dual carriageway, the deep hum of the Aston Martin providing enough sound to fill in the pauses. She did not detect any impatience on his part, which was reassuring.

She considered how she should answer his question. Had she stayed in her room, (admittedly lonely and sad), because she was afraid, or because she wanted to 'show her light to lighten the gentiles'?

It was time for confession.

"I suppose that's true – I wanted to go with them but I was terrified at what I might find! And what it might do to me: it was the kind of thing I knew nothing about. With having no brothers or sisters or even close cousins, Arabella was about the only person I talked to in depth and she always said I was 'disadvantaged' by having such religious parents. She would never go into any detail in case I told them what she'd said. I grew up believing that certain things should only be done between married people – and that when I got married I'd find out."

"Mm," said Bertie and said nothing for a while; then: "Keep your eye open for Junction 34, will you? We turn off there."

Melissande said she would; and waited for him to comment on what she had just told him, only to be disconcerted by his lack of any reference to it. Surely she was due a response? After all, she had 'bared her soul' to him and all he had done was remark on their route.

Didn't he realise what this had cost her, sacrificing her self-respect? She began to panic and wish she had never mentioned such things.

Bertie rescued her just in time before her mind went into overdrive with indignation, remorse and shame; and in such a casual tone – as though she had said nothing remarkable.

"Tell me, though – do you still believe the same?"

"About what?"

"About – well – what we were talking about! Marriage and stuff. Didn't you ever want to explore the subject – surf the web and all that? I thought most teenagers did, these days."

"Well of course in those days we didn't have The Internet at school, and the only time I began to venture into cyberspace was with Arabella when I went for the occasional weekend at her parents' place. We could hardly start looking for 'naughty' things there, because it was before the time when everyone had their own computer in their bedroom. Theirs was in her father's study and they always kept the door open, in case we got up to mischief! I was very devout at the time and wouldn't have allowed myself to take part in any such surfing, anyway."

"Have you made up for it since? You've got a laptop – and your own room at The Rectory." He laughed.

Melissande laughed too, admitting perhaps that this might have happened but without saying so. She was not going to say anything about what she had discovered because she still felt bad about it, having watched all kinds of antics between couples during her enquiries into the facts of life. They had had the same effect on her that Bertie was now having. Her body would react in a way that was exciting yet alarming – taking over from what was right and proper and giving her a melting instability.

Somehow, however, when Bertie hinted at such things it didn't seem grubby and demeaning but adventurous and exciting.

She had a strong inclination to continue this line of conversation and now took some initiative herself. She wanted to know more about him: why should *he* be the only interrogator?

"What about *you*? Have you been to Amsterdam before?"

Bertie had, and sampled many of its delights. With Tristram and a small group of mates from school they had gone, one half term, on a 'fact-finding mission' to Holland after convincing their parents it was part of an EU module from College. Dare he talk about it with Melissande? He didn't want her to think he was some kind of debauched ogre poised to snatch her virtue.

"Only briefly," he said, presenting a straight bat. Melissande, having stepped over the first threshold into the world of transparency, was not satisfied, and bowled him another fast ball.

"That doesn't tell me much! Did you visit the parts of the city I've just admitted I avoided?"

Now it was time for Bertie to squirm a little. Without veering from his steady course on the road, he shuffled his bottom and flexed his shoulders, as if to refresh his circulation.

"I'm sure you won't want to hear about all that," he said, now on the back foot.

"But I *would*," persisted Melissande. "Go on – tell me about it! It's your turn – I've owned up and I won't say anything to your mother!"

That made him laugh but she was not going to relent. If she were to be so unrestrained he should be too: it was only fair; and at this moment she was proud of herself for having overcome her shyness. By making him laugh about the threat of 'telling tales when they got home' she had succeeded in forcing him, in turn, to take risks.

'What the Hell!', thought Bertie. 'I'll tell her! If it puts her off me, that's her hard luck; and it might even move things on a bit!'

He cleared his throat and spilled beans that he had never mentioned to anyone except other members of that assault party of seven or so years ago. True, he and Tristram had laughed about it a few times since but it had not been his proudest hour, despite losing his virginity without disgrace or failure.

Melissande listened with awe, as Bertie described scenes he'd witnessed and places he and his friends had visited. She asked about the girls and women involved and tried to get him to assess what kind of people they were and why they might have given themselves to becoming sex workers. Coming at it from this angle made it easier to for Bertie to become less cagey, as he tried to describe individuals whom he'd found memorable.

"Wasn't there just *one* who made an impression?" she asked innocently, guessing that he had done more than look. There was: and once he got started with a description of a young Latvian, Melissande edged him towards admission after admission – yes, he had spent some time alone with her and paid handsomely for that privilege; and yes he had been scared out of his wits.

Eventually Melissande extracted from Bertie his account of how he overcame 'first night nerves', and whether he had taken necessary precautions; how long they had spent together and whether he had enjoyed it. That led to his final admission that, no, he hadn't really enjoyed the act itself, but rather the achievement of leaping such a huge hurdle of his teenage existence. He had never told any of his mates, but he now confessed how timidity had reduced his virility: it had all been over very quickly.

In the following pause, Bertie realised that Melissande had extracted from him information that no one else in the world knew – except for the Latvian, who had probably forgotten anyway.

Somehow he didn't mind her knowing, though he might regret it later, if their relationship developed the way he found himself hoping. It felt safe enough for him to start casting a few questions over the pool, in the hope she might rise to the lure.

"You are so canny! I've never told anyone else all that – I don't know what's got into me!"

"I think it's nice that you can trust me enough," she said, rewarding him with a touch on the arm.

"How about you, then?" He ventured.

"What?"

"Haven't you had some lurid experiences?"

"Nothing like *that*!" she said, hastily. "I think I've had a very sheltered existence! There's always been so much to do – and I've devoted myself to church things, mostly."

Bertie, at that point, gave up his quest and went on to learn about exciting events like Sunday-school outings, The Royal School of Church Music and summer guide camps. That didn't last long because neither found it riveting and the conversation soon reverted to Bertie's past, although he censored a lot of it.

CHAPTER 14

Fuelled by such conversation, the time flew, and it was the shortest 'long journey' that either could remember. As Melissande plied Bertie with question after subtle question, extracting as many details as she could, finding it easy to forgive each youthful transgression that he hesitantly revealed, sometimes to his own discomfort. His incentive to continue was that the more he told her, the less she seemed to hold him at arm's length, although her interrogation did become more probing. She gave no hint of shock or blame at his replies, rather, accepting him – he hoped – sins and all.

Despite this, Bertie was a little worried, having reviewed what he'd been saying. His lack of discretion might ruin his chances of any kind of future with this one-off pure charmer. He'd had girlfriends before who, like Melissande, wanted to know more of his past, but after acknowledging ex-lovers, they had been rubbed in his face during subsequent tiffs and unpleasantness. Indeed, he had promised himself: 'never tell a girl anything which might be brought up and used in evidence against you'. Yet here he was, revealing all – and in more detail than ever before. Whatever was happening to him? He must be losing his grip! He expressed his concern:

"I say, you're not going to hold all this against me, are you?" Her response was instant.

"Let's have a pact," she said. "That anything, outside business, that we discuss in the confessional of the Aston Martin is sacred between us, not to be regurgitated in anger at some future date, to each other or to anyone else – ever!"

"Done! And thank you – I do feel I've been very indiscrete in telling you. A moment ago I suddenly felt very vulnerable – like that junior minister resigning last Spring when the papers accused him of buying some Brazilian's bottom. Do you remember? The BBC editors ranked it as the most important thing in the *whole world*! It led news bulletins for days! Ruined him!"

"Well *you're* not hoping to become Prime Minister, are you? You can forget *that,* now I've got all the dirt on you." Melissande was bubbling with laughter.

"You, madam, are a minx! You have extracted gory details from me while I'm otherwise preoccupied, keeping us safe from Dutch lunatics in their big cars; and now you're threatening me with a damaged career! Fie on you, heartless, cruel woman!"

"Don't worry, I'll be merciful – as long as you honour our Aston Martin pledge. Actually – I haven't quite finished."

"Oh *no*!"

Bertie waited for the next barrage of information requests. He was apprehensive at being hit while his defences were down, while enjoying having someone to whom he was now powerfully attracted, rummage in his most private history. Her expression of interest and warmth towards him felt as though she were opening her arms for an embrace.

It was by no means a one-sided probe: in Melissande's terms, *her* defences were down too, and her questions were revealing what *she* needed to talk about – delicate, sensitive things she had never discussed with anyone else. In her lack of knowledge, she was a timid but intrepid explorer.

Bertie had a vision of himself being a rock-pool at low tide, while a sweet and innocent young girl hopped from rock to rock around him, looking deep into his trapped water – turning over any stone that looked promising – noting any creatures that caught her inquisitive eye.

Melissande was in no hurry. She wanted to frame her questions in a way that wouldn't cause this 'great big person', whom she now realised was lonely and hungry for affection, to shy away and clam up. Into her mind, too, came the image of exploring sea life, dangling a tasty morsel left from the picnic over pale waving tentacles of a sea anemone, hoping to see it take the bait, rather than withdraw into itself and turn into a pink jujube, pretending to be part of the scenery.

She edged forward with her next question.

"But after your previous trip to Holland – did things improve?"

"School, you mean? I suppose I became a bit more cocky, knowing I'd got a secret reputation, the same as my mates, although I kept quiet about the disappointing side of things."

"That's what I was asking about! Did you try again?"

"Well no, not in the same way."

"Were you 'abstinent'?"

Bertie began to feel rather warm and avoided the issue for a few extra seconds by fiddling with the temperature controls in the car, before passing a couple of fingers across his forehead to remove the moisture he could feel there.

This was all getting a bit near the bone. He was, however, aware that Melissande was leaning towards him with an eager smile. How could he resist? By asking all this she was allowing him even closer, wasn't she? Or would she write him off, having discovered the truth? In for a penny, in for a pound: she wanted an honest answer and was going to get it.

"No."

"Go on – what happened?"

Melissande's question took him back to that summer when he thought he had been in love, discovering a magic combination of affection, trust and passion – and the physical expression of it. He wanted to share the memory.

"At university a girl was in the same digs and we got friendly. It sort of developed and we finished up in her room after a party."

After what she'd just been told, Melissande's imagination quickly filled in the details, and, resenting this 'other woman' who had got there first, she wanted to know more.

"Was it better, that time?"

"Bliss!"

"And what happened afterwards? Did you stay together?"

"No – I found that she had done the rounds of the digs and I was last on the list!" Bertie laughed – although at the time it had been no laughing matter and had nearly caused him to miss the double first that eventually rewarded his previous diligence.

"Did you feel bad about it?"

"You bet I did! I'd been a complete prat, thinking it was just me she liked and then finding out that she wasn't a bit interested in *me* – only in gratification."

"*That* I can understand but it wasn't what I was asking. Didn't you feel bad, wicked – sinful – as though you had demeaned yourself?"

"No – not at all! I just felt I'd been used."

"Hadn't you been taught it was wrong? Having seen your home and met your mother I would have thought yours was a respectable and proper background. You used to be a regular church-goer and all that."

"I would have felt awful if I was in my early teens, but being at boarding school had washed such scruples away – along with the myths about 'self-abuse' that banned perfectly natural behaviour as being wicked and dangerous. We boys got larking about after lights out and things accidentally got touched, tickled and grabbed, with predictable results. None of us suffered any ill effects and it didn't feel '*wrong*' despite everything that had been drummed into us. In fact it helped us sort ourselves out. Some of us – not including me – discovered that we weren't interested in girls and 'came out' – and by that time being gay was allowed in our society – not like when my father was alive when you could go to prison for it or get drummed out of the navy."

"And it didn't put *you* off girls?"

"Not a bit – that's why we went to Amsterdam; but I've been awfully frank with you. After *this* you won't want to associate with such a dissolute chap and I do so enjoy your company. All those sins: shall I be forgiven?" His self-conscious laugh was an effort, not at all convincing, and it was a relief when Melissande replied without hesitation.

"Of course you will! It's me who was egging you on! It's my own fault if I don't like what I've dug up – but to be honest, I've never had the chance to talk like this before, especially to a *man*. It's been great to be able to talk so openly: Arabella won't, for reasons I've told you; and I'm sure my parents wouldn't have even heard of most of it."

"That's what you think! You don't become a parson unless you know a bit about the ways of the world. They specialise in sin during their training! They deal in remorse: it's a commodity. Part of their power is obtained by making people feel guilty!"

"That's rather unkind, isn't it?"

"Dodgy, too – flaunting my prejudices in front of a Rector's daughter who is fast taking me a helpless prisoner!"

"Don't worry – I feel the same much of the time. I've heard too many fatuous and infuriating sermons – not from my father,

I should hasten to add: I like his sermons, they're short and practical – but I can't take most of the religious hierarchy seriously any more. It's not just in my own faith or denomination, but I resent people whose power leads them to disappear up themselves until they think they're infallible. You should see my father after a meeting of the parochial church council – he comes home distraught at the unpleasantness and venom as zealots try to destroy each other. They want to control him, me, the parish and everyone else! The world is full of popes, all infallible – and goodness knows – when *female* popes become more numerous – they'll be even more lethal!"

"Wow! I didn't know I was travelling with an anarchist!" Bertie was tickled. "You would have done well in my profession."

"That's something else," said Melissande, finding she had started another hare. "No one seems to know much about you, and this past day or two has been such a revelation! It turns out you're a baronet, rich as Croesus; lost your virginity to a Latvian; are disarmingly charming – and did 'something in the City'. I've been wondering what *that* was. Nothing riddled with sin, I hope?" This last question was accompanied by a forgiving giggle.

"That all depends on your point of view. Some people accuse us of perverting democracy – others pay well for such services."

"Physical, political or mental?" Melissande was getting cheeky.

"The latter two – yes. Trying to ensure that certain arguments are presented in the most persuasive way, to the most influential people."

"Delivered with gifts?"

"Not by the outfit I worked for! I see you are not only anarchistic but also cynical! I'm surprised: I thought you were sweet and innocent."

"Sorry – I don't mean to be horrid but you *did* have a go at the church just now – my last question just sneaked out. I wanted to scratch you back! I've been wondering, though, what job you did that was so lucrative, yet drove you to run away from it. You have to admit it's mysterious."

"That's something for another journey, but suffice to say I could have been described as a 'lobbying spin-doctor and PR-man'. Then I found I'd had enough of it – and decided to do something completely different. That's what I was attempting to do when I got sucked into Tytherton Kellaway, and look where that has led!"

Bertie felt himself relax. Between them there was a growing intimacy that was not so suspicious and guarded. He was beginning to experience a warmth and acceptance radiating from this person. He chuckled and summed up his new situation.

"Here I am, travelling with The Inquisition to look at houses you can't sink. I've escaped from the frying pan into the fire! Like Croesus but floods didn't save Croesus either – he still burned to death on the pyre, didn't he? Once he was well alight they couldn't extinguish the flames – even after the Gods dropped a cloudburst on him. He was let down by the people in charge on earth *and* 'the management above'! The poor chap didn't stand a chance. I might have just scuppered mine by letting you into all my lurid secrets!"

"Don't worry. I won't set you on fire. I've found this journey most memorable."

"Life changing?"

"I wouldn't go as far as that – but it's given me lots to think about," said Melissande, half to herself. She *wanted* to say 'endearing' but couldn't bring herself to. She began mumbling something about 'being revealing' but thought better of it.

"What was that?" Asked Bertie.

"Oh, nothing! I suppose I'm envious, in a way." Melissande's hands clasped each other anxiously. She was now looking straight ahead.

"What of?" Bertie felt he was now off the hook as the tables were turning. Maybe he'd get to know a little more about his rare companion.

"Of you not feeling you'd been indulging in something wrong – against all your upbringing."

"I didn't! As far as I was concerned I wasn't hurting anyone or damaging myself – but fulfilling a human need."

"But in our society we try to pass on patterns of behaviour to our children that generation after generation have found to bring eventual happiness even though they may mean a certain amount of self-denial and discipline – moving away from our animal instincts."

"Like what?" Asked Bertie.

"Like the Ten Commandments – OK – and like not going to bed together before you are married. I can see why *that* was taboo – because you'd finish up with a lot of unwanted babies and spread all kinds of nasty diseases. A girl would get pregnant far too young and finish up burdened with all the responsibilities and hard work before she'd had time to learn about life and cope with its problems."

"I think that depended on the kind of society in which you lived," said Bertie. "In the South Sea islands, Captain Cook's sailors were delighted to find people making love any time they wanted – and not even hiding to do it. Babies were welcomed, if they happened, and were gathered up into the larger family – which, if I remember from tales I've heard, was run by the women. The priests were more interested in food than sex! Adult males and females were not allowed to eat together on pain of death, although they could have sex ad lib; and some foods were taboo! It was the European sailors who spoiled all that by introducing alien diseases and breaking the rules."

"I had heard about the disease part – a sort of veiled warning about what happens to 'wicked girls'; and I read somewhere that, on those islands, if a peasant boy made a royal princess pregnant both he and the baby would be killed – although if a prince made a common girl a mother, that was OK!"

Bertie laughed: "There we are! Back to the twenty first century – it's all about food and class! We do seem to have come a long way with our chat: but you *will* keep all this to yourself? It's not something I ever want people to know about me – ruin my image!"

"It's a deal! Now, where are we going? You haven't missed the turning, have you?"

"No but if you listened to the satnav she says it's the next exit." Bertie took the right hand lane, still hoping that Melissande, despite her pledge not to set him on fire, might change her mind and light his blue touch paper to start a blaze.

To feel this way about her was most unexpected because to look at, she wasn't at all his type but she'd certainly got under his skin – and he was enjoying her presence. It was time to get back to more immediate matters.

"Where was it we are staying? I remember the hotel was called 'the Mucky Moorhen', although I suspect my Dutch pronunciation might not be accurate."

Melissande reached for her briefcase and pulled out the 'travel' file.

"It's the Hotel Moeke Mooren, and it's in the village of Blauwe Sluis which means 'blue sluice', according to my research, although you Suffolk people might call it 'blue dyke'."

"Yes – I'm always confused when people talk about 'dykes' when they mean 'ditches': not sure where the confusion arose," said Bertie; "but a sluice sounds like something to carry water. Is it far from Maasbommel? That's where the amphib houses are, isn't it?"

"Only a few minutes in the car, but I chose that hotel because it's right by the water, overlooking lakes and peninsulas – sort of holiday zone. It looked great and isn't too expensive. I thought it would put us in the right frame of mind for what TGP might feel like if we ever went ahead with it."

"I wonder if they've got the same kind of problems as Tytherton Kellaway – periodic flooding and all that," Bertie wondered.

"It doesn't seem to. It looks permanent. A few years ago I wouldn't have seen *any* similarity. Those fields belonging to the Manor were simply 'meadows down by the Avon' and when Mr Kelway made his plans for houses it wasn't considered to be a 'flood plain'."

"The pictures I've seen of the amphib houses at Maasbommel looked as though they lined up along a river bank – not as I'd visualised on Manor meadows."

"They are – on the river Maas – but I've been reading that the Dutch give their rivers much more room to overflow and these houses *would* flood if they were fixed. The raised banks aren't right next to the river, but set back so that the river can rise to the top of its usual channel and then spread over a much wider zone, which becomes an enlarged river until the level drops again. The houses just rise above it all!"

"Well – that's what we're after! We need to be able to cope with seasonal flooding as a routine event!"

"The interesting thing is that the lake that our hotel overlooks is permanently connected to the river Maas, rather as the Manor meadows are connected to the Avon at the moment, after all that rain."

"Do you mean where Arabella went swimming the other day?" Bertie still found this amusing.

"Poor girl – she caught a rotten cold – you shouldn't laugh. It could happen to you, Bertie. I expect it will, before you're finished with this project!"

"Well I hope by now I've learned that one needs to be cautious when entering puddles near where *you* live."

"The difference is that at Tytherton, the water is likely to come and go with the weather, but at Maasbommel and Blauwe Sluis it stays there all the time – just rises and falls. There are boats everywhere. It must be wonderful for sailing. The lake is permanently connected to the river." Melissande had done her research.

"I was wondering about that for the TGP: whether we could dig some parts up – make it a permanent backwater," suggested Bertie.

"That's a long way from a housing development. Government wants houses, not a marina. You'd have a battle on your hands. My brief is to keep things simple, isn't it?"

"You're right, Melissande: it was just a thought. The two unique selling points are that the houses don't suffer when the land floods; and when the land does flood, the landowners are paid to hold the water there until the river can take it without drowning houses and people downstream. What we need is a sluice – not 'Kellaway Straits'."

At Tytherton Kellaway church that Sunday, the rain pelting down outside as it had for days, The Rector announced the hymn. The sparse congregation stood and sang, in a half-hearted way:

'Eternal Father strong to save;
Whose arm hath bound the restless wave;
Who bidd'st the mighty ocean deep,
Its own appointed limits keep.
Oh, hear us when we cry to Thee,
For those in peril on the sea!'

As the verses dragged on, Canon Blythe hardly liked to admit, even to himself, that he had included this maritime lament because he was worried about Melissande crossing the North Sea with such an enigmatic stranger. Despite the good things in which Bertie had been engaged since his recent arrival in the parish, little was known about him.

Melissande had led such a sheltered background. He had hoped that going away to university and working away from home for a while might have made her more street wise, but she seemed to go through life blinkered to its dangers. Perhaps he should have warned her more about the perils and hazards? There it was again 'peril'! Truly, there was so much to threaten innocence in this day and age.

"Edward, did you have that hymn because of Melissande?" His wife asked, back at The Rectory before lunch. "Or was it the flooding? I would have thought *that* was nearly over by now, the forecast's better."

Canon Blythe was tempted to fib, not admitting his real reason for such a choice, but resisted it, using a politician's answer.

"My dear Caroline, why should I worry about Melissande and her ferry trip? I'm sure she's quite capable of looking after herself. It's not her first time away from home."

This confirmed Mrs Blythe's analysis of the choice of hymn – Melissande's safety was high on his list of concerns. Her own reaction to hearing that her daughter was going to Holland with such a nice young man had been one of excitement. She needed to reassure The Rector.

"You are quite right, Edward: we needn't be concerned for her safety, Mr Lamotte has proved to be a great help over at The Manor and I'm sure he'll look after her properly on this trip of theirs. You never know – she might have met someone she takes to: it really is about time she found herself a young man, don't you think?"

"I suppose it's selfish of me *not* to," said The Rector. "But I wish we knew a bit more about him, though I have to agree he does seem to be a gentleman."

Their conversation was interrupted as Caroline Blythe's sister bustled in with a tray of aperitifs – sherry and a small bowl of salted cashew nuts.

"Gwen – how extravagant!" Said Mrs Blythe. "What a treat! You do spoil us!"

"A treat indeed!" The Rector added with enthusiasm. While he found his sister in law 'trying' and somewhat overbearing, her visits often brought small bonuses like this, which he appreciated.

"We were just talking about Melissande and her trip to Holland. Edward was hoping that the young man she went with is as dependable as he seems. Melissande hasn't encountered predatory men and they are so often well disguised, aren't they?"

This was not a subject that her younger sister knew much about, because predatory men tended to avoid her formidable appearance, looking as she did, like the archetypal headmistress, hair drawn back into a severe bun and half-glasses half-way down her nose. One investigative glance from her and they fled. On this occasion, however, she was pleased that he should have been mentioned because, just this once, she had some delicious gossip to share – and it was about *him*."

"It's funny you should mention this young man, because after church I was chatting to Lady Veronica – it had stopped raining for just a minute or two and we were enjoying the smells of daffodils in the graveyard. She told me something very interesting about Melissande's travelling companion."

"Do you mean," asked The Rector, "about how he turned up out of the blue and saved poor Mr Haines?"

"She did tell me that, but something much more dramatic, which perhaps you didn't know about him."

"Oh do tell, Gwendoline!" Caroline Blythe only used her sister's first name when she wanted to please her.

"Your 'Bertie' is actually Sir Bertrand Lamotte, baronet! Now isn't that a surprise?"

"It is indeed!" Said Canon Blythe. "My goodness, The Manor is moving up in the world – having a baronet as a handyman! And from what I gather, for no charge!"

"I can't say I'm entirely surprised," said Caroline, "I felt there was something .... noble about him. His manners are impeccable; and his bearing is really quite regal."

"You do seem rather smitten, Caroline!" Gwen's acid side was now showing as she bestowed a stern look, with pursed lips.

"Don't be ridiculous, Gwen! I'm just commenting on my observations. He has been a regular visitor during the last week or two and I must say he has impressed me, but to be smitten, dear, is quite another thing."

"What's more," Gwen resumed her newscast, enjoying the limelight, "he owns a large estate in Suffolk, which is run by his mother, and until recently he was a high flyer in what they call 'the Westminster Village', keeping company with all kinds of national figures."

That last revelation caused The Rector instant anxiety.

"Then what on earth is he doing in Tytherton Kellaway?" He asked, his worries returning in spades. "Was he disgraced or something?"

"From what I gathered, in our brief conversation, he had set out on a walking holiday of some kind and quite by chance, found Mr Haines having a heart attack. After that, something about there being no one to look after Mr Haines' cat – which ended up with him moving into the Gate Lodge, where he's been ever since. Most extraordinary!"

CHAPTER 15

"Shall we go and take a peek at the amphib houses straight away? There's still time before supper and I could do with some exercise, couldn't you?"

"That's fine by me," she said. "When you're ready."

Bertie's impatience surprised Melissande – he was usually so laid back and this was the first time she had seen him so animated since he had sprung into action in sorting out the yobs that night in Chippenham.

What a difference between now, and then: here, now, the tranquillity was palpable. Perhaps it was the lack of any wind, except an occasional breath, causing lakeside reeds to sigh as they made themselves comfortable. The sun shone a path across the oily calm water and it was almost warm enough for Bertie to take off his jacket.

"Well chosen, Melissande! This is the kind of hotel I like – the quiet is almost too loud!"

They were enjoying a cup of Holland's version of tea on the terrace of the hotel, having checked into their rooms.

"Does this place float? It doesn't feel as though it's moving."

"I don't think so;" said Melissande, "this part is on stilts. We seem to be out over the water – what a marvellous view!"

"You see those moorings?" Bertie pointed to where a long, double-decker tourist boat was moored. The streamlined white craft was tied up to a jetty accessed by a gangplank from the shore. "That quay floats – you can see the high post at each end, keeping it in place as it goes up and down. That's the way our amphib houses would be."

"They seem to be expecting a huge difference in water level!" Said Melissande, observing the tall piles. "It's like being in a tidal estuary."

"Except we're miles from the sea. I expect it's for when the rivers flood. Over the centuries the Dutch must have learned how to carry on as normal despite the water."

"It's a pity farmers in other places can't afford to do the same kind of thing – they still get washed away almost annually – places like Bangladesh."

"It's going to get worse, too! We can expect loads of other countries to find out the hard way – that's why it's such an opportunity, if we can get our act together."

"It does seem unfair – us talking about spending millions on amphibs when we've got so many other sites where we *could* build houses!" Melissande's conscience was being activated by memories of sermons from visiting preachers and missionaries.

"Well you've got to start somewhere! I've no doubt those folk will work out all kinds of ways to survive, but before we get into a philosophical argument about whether we really *should* be devoting ourselves to lucrative paths – let's take a quick trip round to Maasbommel? I can't wait!"

Melissande had to admit she was equally impatient and in no time they were back in the car, heading for the village the other side of the lake, next to the Maas.

Disappointment dampened Bertie's enthusiasm.

"Oh dear! They look like the old Nissen huts on wartime airfields around Suffolk," he complained. "Those rounded roofs – I wonder if that's a necessary part of the design – I hope not! All in a line, too – they look awful!"

"I think it's just modern architecture," said Melissande. "We'll have to ask Professor Veerman tomorrow."

"We are lucky to get him," said Bertie. "He must be very busy. I remember him being the Dutch Minister of Agriculture – and saw him in Brussels loads of times."

"His name kept cropping up every time I looked for information about flood plains in Holland, floating houses, the environment – you name it! He's chairman or consultant to almost everything around land or water in the Netherlands. You are right - he must be a *very* busy man!"

"I'm looking forward to meeting him," said Bertie: "quite an unusual combination: academic, businessman and politician – so I'd better be careful what I say about those curvy roofs – but I don't like them!"

"It's not what I had in mind as being a 'desirable residence' for Tytherton Kellaway but I think we could make them a bit more attractive to the kind of buyer who can afford it," said Melissande.

"You make them sound expensive – is that based on your research?" Bertie sounded anxious.

"No – don't worry, I did see *some* prices but it's mostly me guessing, but if you think about it, all their connections to services will have to be flexible and if you take sewage as one example, it's not going to be simply a cheap plastic pipe you bury underground. It's got to be bendy and *that's* much more complex and costly. Another thing – sewage won't run uphill! You'll need pumps to shift it."

"I see what you mean. It's bound to cost more until we can get the numbers up. The first few will have to be loss-leaders, treated as investment, otherwise we won't be able to sell them!"

"With a bit of luck we might get subsidies to help get things moving; and you should be able to negotiate a special price from the manufacturers," said Melissande. "It's in their interests too, to create some interest. They should be able to work out better ways of doing things and patent them. As I understand it, our Great Plan needs to put a development package together so we could go to – for instance – the authorities in New Orleans where they're still struggling after Hurricane Katrina. The Americans are already getting ahead on this kind of thing so we shall need to be very competitive."

"We've got some pretty ingenious building research people in the UK and they ought to be able to come up with some unique solutions – but the rest of it seems pretty straight forward, doesn't it? Concrete floating base with a wooden house on top – we might even find a substitute for the concrete – something like a reverse swimming pool, using a liner to keep the water out, instead of in! Just surfing the net I've already found houses built on steel floats, polystyrene blocks, wooden rafts – the lot. We're coming in late to this business but even that has the advantage of other peoples' ideas!"

"Now you're getting technical! I'll stick to whether we can make any money out of it!"

"That's a change of tune," quipped Bertie. "A minute ago you were being all guilt and charity!"

He had almost said something about being 'half nun, half tycoon' but curbed his satire, not wishing to spoil the moment.

"Do you think we could talk to some of the inhabitants?" He said, changing the subject.

"Why not? There's someone cleaning windows in the third house along – do you think she speaks English?"

"Everybody seems to, around here," said Bertie confidently; "or German, and I can manage that."

"You'll have to translate, because I can't!"

The resident welcomed them with a smile and saved Bertie the translating by returning their greeting in perfect English. She said it would be good to take a few minutes break for a chat about the house.

"We've got used to it," she said. "We have visitors from all over the world coming to look. What would you like to know first? Let me guess. Have we floated yet? The answer is no – and we hope we don't need to but at least we know we *can* and that's why we spent so much on this house. My husband and I want to feel safe. There were bad floods where we used to live and we had to be evacuated twice. I was scared every time it rained but here it's OK. The people who built this house don't expect it to lift off its concrete base more than once every twelve years or so, even with climate change."

Melissande wanted to know whether one had to be careful about heavy furniture being all on one side of the house and was reassured by the amused house owner that although that remained to be seen, it had been one of *her* first questions, too. The developer claimed stability was no problem – not like a houseboat or car ferry. The conversation ranged far and wide and they were invited in for coffee and a quick tour of the house. The rest of the family were at the sports centre and the woman was glad of company. They exchanged email addresses and pledged to keep in touch.

It was at supper an hour later that Bertie's mobile rattled in his breast pocket. He put down his soup spoon to see who it might be.

"It's Batty. I wonder what *he* wants. He's never called me after hours."

"Better ask him!" Melissande looked around to see whether they might be annoying anyone, but noted someone else two tables away smiling into a tiny handset, no one seeming to mind.

Bertie answered and listened for what seemed like ages.

"Hang on, I'll ask her." He turned to Melissande.

"Can you spend an extra few days on this trip?"

Her mind went into top gear. What about The Rectory? Could Aunt Gwen stay longer? Melissande remembered that her mother's last remark as they left was something along the lines of 'Gwen says she can stay on for an extra week if necessary because her friend won't be back until the end of the month'. At the time Melissande suspected the two sisters had decided Bertie might be a candidate for 'her young man' and been plotting to that end. It would have been her mother's idea but one which now gave Melissande a shot of adrenalin.

"I expect so – as long as it's OK with Arabella about the horses. I can ring home. What's he got in mind?"

"I'll explain over main course," said Bertie. "Tris, you there? She says probably 'yes' but we'll confirm later. OK – bye".

Melissande detected a mischievous twinkle in Bertie's eye as they resumed their soup.

"It's your friend Arabella, up to something," he said. "She's been working on Tristram to get us to go somewhere else, with them, to see houses threatened by periodic flooding."

"That's a surprise: is she taking an interest now? There must be an ulterior motive!"

"You've got it! Guess where she's suggesting."

"I don't know – Alabama?" She laughed.

"No, that's too much like work: try Venice!"

"That's a different kettle of fish! Oops! Not the right expression, but you know what I mean. Surely that's not relevant to what we've got in mind?"

"Batty thinks it might be: like how they deal with electricity, fresh water and other services; and how they carry out maintenance surrounded by water."

"That's a bit thin, isn't it? We could see all that here!"

"I know but it could be fun. It might be the last chance of a break for quite some while if we want to get this thing off the ground."

"Don't you mean 'off the bottom'?" Melissande had caught the frivolity: perhaps it was the aperitif – only a rare treat at The Rectory.

"Whose bottom, Arabella's?"

"Bertie! How can you be so vulgar?" Melissande was genuinely taken aback by his crudity. He had turned her little play on words instantly into the realm of lust: and why should his mind turn to Arabella so readily – though her friend *did* seem to dress to draw attention to this shapely part of her anatomy – those jodhpurs?

"I do beg your pardon, Mel; I apologise. I'd better explain. Tristram told me they'd had a tiff, and for the last few days Arabella has been rather icy. He's trying to get back into her good books, suggesting a trip, and she has just agreed but wants *us* to go too."

Melissande's ambivalence at Bertie's smutty remark gave way to suspicion as to Arabella's motives. She knew her friend's interest in building houses was minimal – there had to be some other reason for wanting to go on a jaunt with 'her groom' ('old school friend, you know!'). An intimation of motive entered Melissande's usually forgiving mind and with it, a growing sense of indignation.

Arabella might be 'after' Bertie! Not satisfied with having (probably) seduced Tristram for his looks, money and high profile in London, she had now discovered that Bertie not only had all of that but also a *title*. It was quite likely she was out to latch on to *him* while dumping Tristram. She knew Arabella of old! Melissande's hackles rose but her conscience chided her. So what if that *was* Arabella's scheme?

Trying to be reasonable she told herself: 'Bertie and I aren't involved in any way other than business. I'm employed by him to do research and that's all. If he's stupid enough to fall for it, then she's welcome to him! Why should I worry how Arabella organises her love life?'

With emotion making her stiffen Melissande had to admit that the very thought of Arabella getting off with Bertie made her angry. It prompted a host of uncharacteristic feelings, mostly antagonism. 'What's wrong with me?' She struggled to regain her relaxed and tranquil state.

"Don't you like the soup? Gone cold?" Bertie asked, observing that Melissande had become statuesque, spoon frozen above the plate and a distant look in her eyes.

"Oh no, it's fine! Sorry! I was just working out what needed doing if we were going to change our travel plans," she ad-libbed.

Oh dear! Now she was *lying*, too! What was happening to her? The truth was she had switched into cat mode – wanting to scratch, spit at, and see off her best friend!

She needed time to think but couldn't mention her true feelings without landing herself in an even more awkward position. She must not encourage Bertie into any 'aggressive male behaviour' towards her by letting him know how she felt about him. Better go along with Arabella's plot and see what to do when the time came. She took a firm grip on her irrational animal instincts and suppressed them.

"I'm sure it will be fine. I'll phone Aunt Gwen and take her up on her offer to stay on for a while. Did Tristram give any dates?"

Oh God! Now she was going to Venice – somewhere she'd *always* wanted to see – but with three people whose lives had been so entirely different from her own. She feared this could be a journey into the paths of the unrighteous, or, at very least, severe temptation, but she longed to ride in a gondola – with Bertie – despite the way his very presence made her lose her bearings; or was it *because* of that? Better concentrate on eating!

After another glass of wine she calmed down and the rest of the evening passed in a happy blur. They agreed on an early night, planning to meet for breakfast at seven thirty.

The weather next morning was still good: a warm spring day. The leaves on the trees opposite Maasbommel Church were beginning to open, a pale bright green. It was here that they were to meet the man for whom they had so many questions.

A car pulled up beside them. The window wound down.

"Good morning – you must be Miss Blythe?"

"Professor Veerman?"

"Yes, let me park."

As he walked back towards them, Melissande was reminded of an early-retired golfer, casually dressed, and a neat thatch of greying hair protecting his head from the nip in the air.

"Hello: everyone calls me Cees – like 'suit-case' – please!"

"I'm Melissande, and this is Bertrand Lamotte."

"Bertie will do!" corrected Bertie,

"So, Bertie and Melissande, I know you want to look at the new houses so why don't we walk as we talk? As you can see this is the older part of the town and they are by the river, so we can head that way. As we go, tell me how I can help you."

"We're trying to catch up on 'how to live with regular flooding'," said Bertie; "and you in the Netherlands have an enormous lead!"

"A case of necessity," said the professor. "As you can see, Holland is mostly sky and water, so we have to spend a lot of time and money on creating more land for ourselves, then protecting it against the tides and weather."

He went on to relate how, over the centuries, other countries further inland had improved their drainage systems, which emptied rainfall into the massive rivers that made their way westwards into Holland and the North Sea, making them overflow increasingly often. The prospect of weather patterns changing made the risks even greater.

"Since the year 2000, the cost of floods in the European Union averaged nearly five billion Euros a year," he told them. "In the summer floods of 2013, they were more than twelve billion Euros in only nine of the member states in central and eastern Europe. That's an awful lot of money! It's getting worse and annual losses could increase five-fold by 2050, according to university research in Holland and Austria. I believe in England, you have been having some problems too!" Professor Veerman laughed. "We have been watching your Somerset Levels on television news, but of course it's no joke!"

"It's needed *your* pumps from Holland to bail us out!" Said Bertie. "And that's the kind of situation we want to avoid on a project we're evaluating."

He outlined TGP and was encouraged by the professor's response.

"It sounds like a good idea," commented the professor; "because the United Kingdom is going to experience more flooding in unexpected places. People will be forced to change their housing or move! I read that disasters like those of 2013 occur on average every sixteen years at present, but by 2050, this will have increased to once every ten years. House-owners will find it very expensive or impossible to get insurance."

"That's why we feel there's such an opportunity."

Bertie related how the idea had sprung from attempts to salvage the scheme at Tytherton Kellaway.

"I'm just an outsider who happened to get involved," he said. "Melissande lives there and what we're doing now is trying to see whether the numbers could stack up. That's why we asked to meet you."

"And when Miss Melissande contacted me with your request I looked *you* up on Google and saw that you must know many of my political acquaintances; also that you own land in Eastern England. To be honest, you looked interesting – and I always like meeting new contacts, so here I am!"

As requested, he had drawn up suggestions of people to visit and places in Holland where relevant things were happening. He had sent out emails of introduction. Bertie was impressed with both Melissande's preparations and Professor Veerman's response. Afterwards, at the hotel, he asked her:

"Why didn't you tell me you had been so busy? I had no idea this was going to be so good!"

Melissande blushed.

"I was going to tell you about it in the car on the way over – but somehow we got distracted to ..... other things!"

At Tytherton Kellaway, trouble was brewing. The woman who owned the donkey that had given itself to Arabella's stallion had been angered by the attitude of the horse's owner and the provocative way in which Tristram had dismissed the intrusion.

These people had lost control of their horse, which had broken into her paddock and violated poor Doris. To make it worse, this arrogant man had had the gall to suggest that she might be indebted for this unrequested insemination.

All this came to a head when, several weeks later, Doris's owner, Danielle Marchmont, called the vet because her donkey seemed to be bloated and some unusual discharge had been observed from beneath its tail. Had the poor animal indeed picked up some unpleasant microbe from the violator?

"The jenny is pregnant, Miss Marchmont," said the vet, handing her an invoice. "You know, of course, that her gestation period is a year – I'd say there's about nine months to go. Better de-worm her in a month or two – give me a call – one has to be careful about it – don't want to harm the foetus and all that."

More expense! Danielle was seething. Why should she have to pay for all this?

"It's going to be a mule!" She told him. "Will that give problems?"

"It can't be a mule," said the vet, smiling in a supercilious way.

"It certainly can," retorted Danielle. "I saw the stallion 'doing it'!"

"In that case, if it resulted in pregnancy – which plainly, *something* has, the offspring will be a 'hinny'."

"Well, whatever it's called, I didn't ask for it, or want it."

"Ah, well, these things happen!" The vet said, washing his hands. "Must dash!"

The injustice of the situation preyed on Danielle's mind. The smart-arse vet hadn't helped, highlighting her ignorance. She was determined to get both revenge and recompense. She began her investigations as soon as she reached her caravan. She suspected the stallion was connected to the recent horse event that had been held at The Manor, because she had seen a number of riders with numbered labels on their backs. She discussed it with her new companion, Trevor Bunt, who had recently moved in to her dilapidated residence to 'share her life'. He had appeared one day from Bristol, looking for his son, Travis, whom he thought was lodging with some drop-outs locally.

For his age, (about fifty eight), Trevor was still pretty good, although he had let himself go to seed a little. Danielle couldn't complain, because she too, though not quite as old, was no beauty, being over-thin; and her smoking, she had to admit, had spoiled her complexion, giving it a waxy tinge and heavy lines.

Her upper lip did have a haddock hue, when observed in certain lights.

Trevor was glad of a home and she put up with him despite his 'rough edges'. He made her feel young again by treating her courteously and making her laugh. It had begun when they met at the pub. The next night he had escorted her home and even kissed her hand before departing from the bottom of the caravan's aluminium steps. The third night she had invited him in and they had discovered that it wasn't too late to indulge in the pleasures of the flesh. Both of them were rejuvenated.

The pace of their relationship steadied after a couple of nights and Danielle began to find other positive aspects of his presence because he was good with his hands and technically adroit. What sealed his invitation to co-habit was his volunteering to remove the green algae that disfigured so much of the caravan, giving it that decayed appearance.

He had taken a broom, bucket of soapy water and a step ladder that he had managed to 'find' on an allotment in Chippenham – and scrubbed away Mother Nature's external decoration from the thin roof and walls, completing his task by closing all the windows and throwing several more buckets of water over to rinse away the green mess. The home looked ten times better. Danielle's only worry was that, looking so bright, it might catch the sun more and draw the notice of interfering people who objected to her not having permission to keep it there or live in it.

She had had trouble from busy-bodies at the Council and received various warning letters but fortunately staff shortage had prevented any more from happening – until recently, when another 'final demand' had arrived, even suggesting a date by which she and the caravan must have departed.

Danielle's mission for justice for Doris produced some very satisfactory results. It began when she and Trevor were enjoying puffs from a roller between them as they recovered from their twice weekly intimate moment under the lumpy duvet.

"I'm sure I've seen that stallion in the paddock by the river," she said, blowing out smoke, after they had discussed the forthcoming birth of Hinny, the name already given to the foetus. Each animal – hen, duck and guinea-pig on her establishment were given names despite finishing up on the plate (except Doris, because this was not France), when they were large enough or had stopped laying. She thought Hinny rather an attractive name, often used to address girls and children 'up North', and she had the impression that it was a term of endearment. The half-donkey half horse might be the result of an intrusive visit by an alien creature but that was not *its* fault and the colt, foal or whatever deserved the love and care she bestowed on all the residents of her little domain.

"The field that's flooded?" Asked Trevor.

"One of them! Practically the whole place has been under water for weeks, like last year. I'm lucky here, just that little bit higher. I considered that when I bought this little holding, not that there'd *been* any flooding in those days; but it's lovely down here, isn't it Trevor – all those trees and green fields."

"And mud and barbed wire," joked Trevor. "I like the old baths you've got for drinking troughs; and your two old cars give the place a touch of 'motor museum'." He intended to restore them, in due course; rust was the current problem.

"Oh shut up, Trevor," she gave him a nudge with her bony elbow. "I'm being serious; anyway, you've made a great start, tarting things up. We might even get a bob or two for those old cars – everyone's looking for something to up-cycle, these days."

"That's what you've done for me, Danny," said Trevor, touching her tenderly.

"I wish you'd use the pumice stone on your hands, dear. Your hands aren't 'alf scratchy! You could nick some of my hand cream – keep 'em nice."

"What were you going to say about that stallion?" Trevor had seen the animal and admired its attributes, as well as those of its female rider. Danielle had pointed it out with an accusing finger as she and her new escort were out for a stroll along Maud Heath's Causeway, one Saturday after lunch.

"I'm going to find out if it does belong at the Manor and I'm going to get them to pay for some of the costs they've given me through their negligence in controlling that animal."

"It's difficult to control a stallion when you've fallen off, isn't it?" Chuckled Trevor. "Didn't you say it still had its saddle on while it was, er... seeing to.... Doris?"

"Yes I did! And it didn't seem to affect him at all, otherwise Doris wouldn't be pregnant, costing me a small fortune. That vet's a blood sucker in more ways than one!"

"Well I might have some good news for you, Danielle, my darling," said Trevor, in triumphant tones. "I happen to have been chatting with someone down the pub I used to know when I lived in Bristol."

"Go on then! Tell all!"

"I was saying how your caravan hadn't even got wet feet but the fields next door had been under water for some time, and he said that a couple of years ago it was those same fields what first brought him up here. He was booked in to stay bed and breakfast for two weeks while he did a job there. He drives a digger and his firm was going to do all the ground work for a housing development there."

"Oh I remember! I signed a petition to stop them spoiling the countryside. It all went quiet for a bit, then all these pegs started to turn up and I heard that work was going to start – but it never did. I thought that was the end of it."

"No – what happened was, the bloke owning the fields died."

"That must have been Lady Muck's husband – he was only a 'mister'. Poor old thing, I've heard she's had the bailiffs in, can't pay her bills. At least *I* can with my little part time job."

"Well: you know when my Travis got beaten up that night in town?"

"I expect he asked for it!" Danielle knew more about Trevor's son than she let on. Her part-time job was working with social services 'looking after the interests of teenage girls' in the district.

Her psychology degree and post-grad MA in Social Work had never, for some reason, led to her promotion and progress in Social Services. She put this down to her own individuality not being acceptable to entrenched reactionary civil service insiders. Her superiors might have drawn attention to her dreadlocks, beads, grubby clothes and smouldering roller at the corner of her mouth, added to which, her revolutionary attitude to discipline and time-keeping had never helped achieve her ambitions. Her part-time job was due to desperate under-staffing locally and the high number of girls becoming teenage mothers while in care locally. *Someone* had to be recruited to make lists of names and 'last known addresses' and send out warning letters to other authorities in case there were repercussions. It was an impossible job, trying to 'save' these girls but one or two had managed to be returned to Bristol or Slough.

"I suspect you're right; he'd had a few, but the cops didn't do anything about it because the bloke that bashed him up was some toff staying at your Manor! Anyway – my mate from Bristol says they're talking about sending him up here again on the same job; asking how long it would take. I wouldn't be a bit surprised if they wasn't going to have another go at that housing estate."

"But that's crazy! It's all under water!"

"You noticed!"

"It's not *my* manor, Trevor. I can't even call this my address but you're right: it's criminal, trying to build there. I wonder if people know?"

CHAPTER 16

"Let me carry that," said Bertie, taking the bulging briefcase from Melissande.

"Handle with care! It may be only paper but it's valuable," she said, handing it over gratefully. It was the first time she had been parted from the heavy bag since they'd left Holland and Melissande felt an inch taller, relieved of its pull on her arm.

She had trailed along behind Bertie, carrying it, as he presented tickets and passports until they passed through into the luxury world of First Class Travel – but until now she would not be parted from all the treasures she had been collecting – architects drawings, photos, price lists, maps and weather charts. They were going to be meat for her forthcoming weeks of study and calculation.

Safely aboard the water taxi, they had a chance to watch the world go by. Melissande was surprised to find how choppy the water in the Grand Canal was.

"It's like being at sea!" she commented. "Is it always like this?" She assumed Bertie had been here more than once. She was right.

"Only when the wind blows – and launches start showing off – which they both do rather often!"

The buildings each side of the Grand Canal were exactly like the paintings Melissande remembered since childhood. Modern launches foaming past and the occasional lattice of metal scaffolding on some of the tall palaces were the only signs of the Twenty-first Century.

Bertie suggested that, since it wasn't raining and they were in good time, they could do some sight-seeing on the way to the hotel, which the taxi skipper was only too pleased to provide.

"You're not sea-sick are you?" Bertie enquired.

"I'm not – but Arabella can't go near a boat without feeling squiffy. She would take a helicopter to get to the hotel if she could! I wonder whether they've arrived yet."

All Melissande's antennae were ready to pick up news of 'the enemy' – not that she hated Arabella; it was just that she was damned if she was going to let the self-centred so-and-so make off with Bertie.

Quite *why* she felt so defensive still defeated her. She concluded that Bertie must be her 'weak spot'.

The sun came out during their mini-tour and everything sparkled. The strong breeze was putting white tops on top of the waves and watery turmoil caused by all the myriad vessels carrying people and goods around the city. As they left the Grand Canal to enter the basin of St Mark the great white abbey of St Georgio Maggiore, balanced on the surface of the water the other side of the bay was like a Canaletto come alive, surrounded by the movement of the boats and water – with scudding clouds as a backdrop for its tall, pink brick tower and white cap.

Melissande was thrilled at the sheer scale and grandeur of these ancient buildings and their exposed setting, which might have been way out at sea. How on earth had the monks and engineers, hundreds of years ago, managed to erect such magnificent and long-lasting structures?

"It's truly fantastic," she said to Bertie, and without thinking, put her hand on his arm in her excitement as she pointed across the bay. It was the act of a child sharing the moment with a trusted friend, unconscious and unrestrained.

For Bertie, it was the first time he felt he was being allowed so close to her. His instinct was to place his hand over hers and press it but he dared not, in case she realised what she was doing. Instead, he froze, hoping it might be the first move on her part to allow them to share more than work. He would not allow himself even to look at her, but he felt an infusion of vigour and fresh life such as he had not experienced for years.

This was a moment that neither of them would ever forget: she, remembering well-known images coming to life; he, recalling her eager touch as she shared her delight.

Luckily for Bertie, something else caught Melissande's attention before she became aware of what she was doing. She needed both hands to support herself as she turned to look at yet another familiar landmark.

"It's truly extraordinary," she said, her face alight with wonder. "I can't believe how *big* everything is – and how far away St George's Abbey is from the rest of Venice. I'd never really thought about it but I suppose I was expecting it to be on the same sort of scale as the Palace of Westminster with County Hall across the bridge – but it's more like looking out across the Solent!"

The salty wind blew away the earnestness of the past few days – concerning weather patterns and the construction of water courses, sluices and concrete piles. The spray from the bow of the taxi took Melissande back to seaside trips with the Sunday school and all the associated fun. Bertie, too, was bubbling with enjoyment, longing to throw his arms around Melissande and whirl her around to make her scream with laughter. He resisted such impulses.

'It would not be sensible," he told himself sternly. "To demonstrate such exuberance, especially in a small boat. It could end in disaster, as well as frightening the girl away for ever. Behave, Bertie!'

He took his own advice and as the taxi drew up at the jetty by the Hotel Ca'Sagredo, overlooking the Grand Canal, restricted himself to offering his hand to help her disembark, revelling in her ladylike grip as she steadied herself to step ashore. He was beaming up at her just at the moment she looked down to thank him and Bertie was rewarded by a new kind of smile.

Melissande had taken off her specs, which had become covered in spray and put them in her shoulder bag. It was the first time Bertie had seen her this carefree: happy in sunshine and relaxed in his male presence. He realised how beautiful he found her: those perfect blue eyes, so full of trust and happiness.

He took a mental snapshot: the long, fair hair she was gathering from her face as the wind teased it from its neatness; the perfect proportions of her mouth and nose; the pale, smooth skin, long natural eyelashes and open expression.

In his eyes, at that instant, she was transfigured into someone so lovely it filled him with passion, reminiscent of his early teens when he used to get bowled over by emotions that turned his life upside down. Then, it might happen at a hunt ball or birthday party; but this was a moment of enchantment: no sudden crush.

To him, over the past weeks, she had become unique, special – essential – and now it dawned on him that all he wanted was to be with her *all* the time. His hair tingled and he felt his whole body change. It was at this moment that he realised he was madly, permanently, hopelessly in love with this precious person.

This was new and alarming: at the flip of a mental switch all his familiar life targets and patterns became pale grey, dimmed by this bold, colourful state of focus on Melissande and what he might be, with her.

"Come *on* then, Bertie!" Melissande was offering him a hand in return, now that she was safely ashore. She was laughing at the way he was standing there with a dazed smile.

Checking in, Melissande noted with relief that she and Bertie had single rooms. It would be unthinkable to follow the example of their companions. She had heard them discussing the suite Tristram had booked. It was also reassuring to read a note she found pushed under the door of her room as she went in. Arabella and Tristram were already installed. Perhaps Bella was not, after all, scheming to entrap Bertie. She re-read the note, scribbled on a sheet of hotel stationery.

We're on the floor above - tel No 452. Don't ring until after 5pm. We're resting ☺ after the journey. Tris suggests we meet about 7 for a drink and dinner – OK? XX Bella.

Good: because, before they went to their respective rooms, Melissande and Bertie had agreed to a similar rendezvous; so Melissande took her time and treated herself to a long luxurious bath, adding some of the scented oil and potions provided.

By the time she and Arabella spoke, arranging where to find each other in the sumptuous entrance hall, Melissande had completed her toilette and was ready to put on the new dress and shoes she had bought before setting off for the trip. At the time, it had been her mother who prompted this extravagance.

"You never know, dear," she had said. "Meeting these business people, you may have a dinner or function when you want to dress up a bit. It can't be all work, can it?"

She knew it was part of her mother's ongoing campaign for grand-children. She had never said so, but would drop hints about other people's families: 'what lovely grand-children' or relate how a friend's daughter had just had a second child.

A light touch of make-up and a hint of lipstick and Melissande was ready to meet any challenge, social or competitive, that an evening with her three wild companions might present. She practised a few steps in her high heels: it had been a year or two since she wore them for presentations and interviews and it felt good to be taller, with one's body moving more ... sensuously. That was odd! Before, it had been a necessary 'evil', dressing up to look sexy but tonight a new Melissande had emerged in this bathroom with all its mirrors. Tweezers and cream, deodorants and moisturisers had released this body of hers from every unsightly hair or any blemish she could discover as she stretched and posed and pretended to be a glamour model. As she emerged, a new woman, into her bedroom, she gave herself a knowing, and amused look. This was fun!

The old Melissande was excited but mildly offended by the way the new one was behaving, especially at such a brazen display of her body, although even she had to admire it. When it came to trying on the dress it was an easy decision not to wear that piece of underwear that normally prevented any provocative bounce or display of physical arousal. She didn't need it because her breasts were just like those of a mannequin – no droop – and the word 'pert' came, unwarranted, to her lips, making her smile broaden. She enjoyed applying a little scented moisturiser to make them perfect.

The only other garment invisible to the public was, for her, unusually skimpy; bought on impulse just before she left, her feeble excuse being that it took less room in her case. The material of the dress itself did allow this daring approach because it had enough 'body' to save her from looking naked – not like those 'clingy little black numbers' that show-cased every nook and cranny. Looking over her shoulder when fully dressed they received her approval because she couldn't see any sign of them and her rear view reminded her of Pippa at Kate and William's wedding – but with fewer buttons: good!

'This is very unlike me,' she said to herself; 'but I'm enjoying every minute!'

For once, she did not want to be in the background, supporting someone else or 'contributing to a good cause'. She had an urge to draw attention to herself, stand out, be charming and the centre of attention – at least, Bertie's attention. 'Most unlike me!', she repeated. Somehow being here, in these amazing surroundings, so far from parents, the parish and all her day-to-day responsibilities, was releasing a dare-devil independence she didn't know she had. 'I'm becoming quite shameless'.

It felt so good she even helped herself to a small gin and tonic. She would have preferred tea but this was quicker and simpler and might prevent her feeling self-conscious. She'd heard about 'Dutch courage' and shortly after the second sip she understood what it meant because it quelled the niggling fear that she might not have the nerve to brave the raised eyebrows of her companions, who by now must be wondering what had happened to her.

As she entered the lift, which was lined with mirrors, and began her descent, Melissande's spirits and confidence were high and she indulged in a little more self-appreciation in the reflections all around her. She was eight minutes late: never mind. 'Do I look worried?' The walls said no.

Bertie minded. He was sitting with Tristram and Arabella, listening to them chatter but being impatient for Melissande to be beside him. Arabella's pushy behaviour was irritating. She was trying to appear enthusiastic and knowledgeable about Venice's relationship with water, but any idiot – except Arabella – could see that Mother Nature was defeating its citizens' attempts to keep dry feet.

"We should have brought our wellies," said Arabella in conclusion, with a minor snort. "This is wetter than the Manor Lane."

Tristram seemed to find it amusing. He must be besotted with her. Why wasn't Melissande here? Bertie needed her serene presence; when she was around people weren't silly. Where was she? He looked at his watch once more.

Over a cup of tea, and fatter than usual home-rolled fags in their mobile home by the River Avon, Danielle and Trevor were plotting.

"I think a letter to the local paper would make a good start," said Danielle. "Along the lines of 'a reminder that the threat to our countryside, tourism and environment, caused by reckless building development on a flood-plain, still exists close to our town' and that 'it seems, despite recent unprecedented disruption and saturation, no one seems to be questioning it.' What do you think Trev?"

"Sounds good to me. That should get 'em going!"

"Just think: all those poor people – cheated into spending their life-savings, taking on the burden of expensive mortgages; thinking they're going to get the house of their dreams and finishing up with ruined furniture, stinking carpets and sandbags in every doorway. It's criminal, that's what it is!"

"You're right, Danielle! Shall I nip out and get some chips?"

"Yea; and pick up a Wiltshire Times: see if there's a Chippenham News as well. Next week we'll give BBC Wiltshire a call – if they don't see our letter in the paper and come to us first. It's disgusting, those people being allowed to do that! We've got to put a stop on it! You can see the kind of people they are – look what happened to our poor Doris!"

"That's right, love. Pass my hat, will you? 'Ave you got a tenner? I'm cleaned right out. I won't be long."

Bertie's attention was fixed on the lift entrance. Tristram and Bella were still enjoying each other's company and discussing the menu. Bertie was worried that Melissande, in her shyness, might feel out of place in such surroundings, especially as he and his companions were dressed to kill. He had wanted to look his best for her, and the others were turned out like pictures from Tatler. Yesterday she had been 'The Rector's Daughter' in her academic researcher role, confidently questioning architects and engineers but tonight was different. How would she fit in to an evening in a five-star Venetian Hotel?

At first he didn't recognise the woman leaving the lift. Watching each time its doors opened, and dismissing arrival after arrival as 'not her', Bertie's first impression of the tall, elegant woman now emerging was that, once again, it was not Melissande. Very attractive – lovely walk – super figure and WOW! It *was* her! He leapt to his feet. Tristram automatically followed suit. Arabella turned to look and her eyes opened more widely. Her friend had been transformed.

"Mel you look stunning!" she said, a picture of surprise.

Arabella had never, *ever*, said that to her before and despite all her resolve, Melissande could feel her cheeks going red. She looked down at the small evening purse that went with the dress and smiled with embarrassed pride.

"Thanks, Bella!"

This vision of beauty and modest shyness was too much for Bertie to resist. He stepped forward and, taking her hands in his, kissed her warmly on both cheeks before ushering her to the spare armchair next to his.

"She's right, you know," he said in a voice low enough not to be generally heard. "You are an absolute picture!"

"You'll have to read the menu for me," said Melissande with a laugh. "I can't see a thing without my specs but I thought they'd spoil the image. Do I *really* look OK?"

"I am almost speechless," said Bertie, "you look *so* good! Irresistible! Are you hungry?"

She was, and it was not long before the four of them were enjoying a series of small courses of exotic foods, each accompanied by a wine chosen after discussion between Bertie and Tristram, (showing off their knowledge of oenology). Melissande felt obliged to taste each new colour and vintage, confident that, since she was also *eating*, she would not feel squiffy. If she became aware of any side-effects she would decline the next sample.

As the meal progressed, however, she didn't notice that the lights had become slightly less bright and the activity of the waiters less hurried. The last bottle of a sweet white that came with the pudding, seemed to empty without anyone doing much and Melissande still felt comfortably relaxed but perfectly sober.

The arrival of two extra members of the band that had been playing soft music throughout the meal did catch her attention, especially when the drummer struck up a faster rhythm and they began serenading the diners with a piece that she'd heard several times on the radio recently. Several couples rose from their tables and moved to the centre of the restaurant in front of the band. She hadn't noticed the dance floor until now but, with lights dimmed, couples were gathering under a revolving globe of tiny coloured mirrors which sprinkled shafts of light over their flowing movement. Tristram and Arabella looked at each other and without a word, stood up and made their way to join in.

"How about a whirl?" Bertie took Melissande's hand. He couldn't wait to hold her in his arms.

She hesitated for a moment, considering the risks and exposure but decided there were enough people gliding around for her to blend in without being conspicuous.

"I'd love to," she said – and meant it.

Standing up – oops – she was aware that her balance was not as it should be. She felt light headed and had to hold on to Bertie's arm as they manoeuvred between the tables towards the coppice of dancers.

On arrival, Bertie's wish was fulfilled. He raised her right hand and they moved together, ready to dance. For a few seconds they stood, waiting for the right moment to start. At first there was an inch or two's space between them but Bertie gently pulled her to him, as she was longing for him to do, and, as his unbuttoned jacket opened slightly their bodies touched, torso to torso, with only Bertie's dress shirt and the single layer of Melissande's dress keeping them apart.

Both became aware of the warmth of the other's body and its poise. She sent a stern message to her legs not to give way.

Melissande, during her teens, had learned to dance at church socials and attended classes by the lady at the youth club. One thing she was good at was allowing herself to follow a partner's steps and momentum. This now came automatically as she gave herself to Bertie's lead.

Bertie, for his part, had also taken lessons, both at school and privately because he wanted to cut a bit of a dash with the ladies. After university, when he was having to entertain clients, their wives (and daughters), this had proved an advantage: he was an excellent dancer and was delighted to discover that Melissande followed so well she might have been part of him.

"This is bliss," said Bertie, very close to her ear.

Without thinking, she pressed her forehead against his cheek in agreement and kept it there as they performed a graceful turn, pressing against each other and feeling as though they were about to float off into heaven. As the dance continued, the physical contact, mingling and brushing of their limbs, had its effect on Bertie's natural instincts. To hide this, he allowed a little more distance between them, but Melissande had noticed. She found it thrilling and dangerous and closed the gap to regain the contact that had made her catch her breath as adrenalin coursed through her.

She knew he must have recognised the permission she was giving, but she didn't care and the exhilaration this caused made her feel as though she was going to pass out. Bertie felt her relax in his arms, as she rested her head on him, giving him once more the chance to inhale her own special fragrance, reminding him of that night in the stable yard. He gently kissed her ear and began humming the music to which they were moving in perfect synchrony.

Melissande knew she had let herself go further with this man than with anyone else, ever. It surprised both of them. Bertie was bowled over by the way she was being so uninhibited. He had never dreamed that she could have this in her, although in the last few days he had been wondering how he might win her confidence to be able to embrace her like this as the music slowed and dancers barely moved.

When Bertie saw she had recognised his body's response and even given it encouragement, he wondered whether he had completely misjudged her. Maybe she was a dark horse with hidden secrets.

With other beautiful women on occasions like this, there had been a foregone conclusion that they would finish up either at his place or hers but Melissande had never given any hint that this might be the outcome. For him this didn't matter; he didn't mind that *she* set the pace of their relationship; if necessary he was prepared to wait indefinitely for her to give herself to him, the way she seemed to be doing now.

As the music came to an end, Bertie wanted to be alone with her, away from the other two, who were obviously enjoying each other's antics and might want to do stupid things like asking the band to play an eightsome reel or conga.

"Let's get a breath of sea air," he suggested to Melissande as they reluctantly broke apart. He needed to be sure he wasn't allowing his wishful thinking to misinterpret the messages he thought he was receiving. For once in his life a woman, other than his mother, had become precious to him. Melissande was inside his protection and care, like part of him – not outside to be enjoyed and discarded. He must cool it – talk – understand, before making any further advances.

"That door, over there," pointed Melissande and led the way, not dropping his hand.

It led to a magnificent marble staircase and the two looked at each other and smiled as they descended like king and queen, acknowledging the applause of imaginary, grateful subjects. They soon found the terrace at water level and stood, looking out across the Grand Canal. Amongst the empty tables and arrays of pot plants, they were alone.

"It's a bit chilly," said Bertie.

"We can go inside in a minute – but let's just get the feel of Venice at night," said Melissande.

The wind had dropped and the waters of the canal had a gloss that reflected all the myriad lights from palaces, passing boats and lamps illuminating bridges and walkways.

"Can I snuggle up?" She stepped close. "You're right, it's not warm."

"Be my guest," said Bertie. "Delighted to be of service!" He held open his jacket and Melissande moved in, putting an arm around him to share his warmth. He held her close but was concerned to feel her shaking. Was this tears?

"Are you all right?" He asked anxiously.

"I'm fine," she chuckled. "Shivering a bit – I haven't got much on and you're right – it's cold! But I was just thinking what frauds we are, pretending this might have something to do with Tytherton Kellaway's housing development!"

Bertie, relieved, thought for a moment and then, plucking up his courage – for he had never said this to a woman before – he began a hesitant declaration.

"Perhaps not: these buildings certainly don't float, but I'm beginning to believe that even if you find the figures don't add up for TGP, it ..... doesn't matter; I shall still want to be around – floods or no floods: it's you I'm really interested in, Melissande."

She looked up at him, his face illuminated by the reflected light of Venice's nightlife. She wanted to see that his face endorsed his words. In the split second in which she had time to focus before he kissed her softly on the mouth, she recognised sincerity and hope. Then both closed their eyes as the whole world centred on their caressing lips, preventing more words – almost stopping them from breathing as they tasted each other's affection.

Melissande needed to draw breath – it was almost overwhelming. This was her very first such kiss! So often, watching a film or television programme she had been embarrassed by such activity, finding it distasteful. She would look away, wondering why it had to be included so often. Now though, she wanted to do it again, and for it to last for ever! She had to hold on to him to stay upright, her arms feeling the muscles of his broad shoulders as he took the weight of her body against him. Freeing herself for a moment she took a huge intake of sea air and sighed.

"Bertie – I've never kissed anyone before – not like that!" She wanted to tell him this was a first and she wasn't always like this – for him to know its significance and that she wasn't a 'loose woman'.

"I say! Oh dear! I hope you didn't mind!" He was now in full retreat, fearing that he had blotted his copybook.

"I don't *think* I did – shall we try it again?"

"Oh Melissande – you are such.... such a *darling*!" Bertie was completely besotted and barely in control. Such was his relief that no offence had been taken, that his enthusiasm overcame his restraint and he kissed her again passionately: only to discover that his ardour was being returned – and it wasn't like kissing someone who was simply 'wanting to get on with it' but who, with each tiny movement of tongue and each change of position was telling him 'I want you – I'm yours!' Her hands were pressing hard against his back.

All evidence of primness, reserve or disapproval had blown away. Here in his arms, sharing his fascination and desire, was a woman, a girl, like none other he had ever embraced.

"Let's go upstairs," she whispered. "Your room or mine?" This time it was accompanied by an audible giggle.

"Are you sure?" Bertie was trying to be honourable.

"Yes: it's cold; and no, I've never done it before, so hurry up before I change my mind."

"What will the others say?"

"I'm sure you can work that out for yourself, Bertie! They've got nothing to complain about."

Melissande could hardly believe what she was saying. Could it be that the wine sampling had undermined her better self?

CHAPTER 17

At The Rectory in Tytherton Kellaway, all was not well. Gwen had just returned from shopping. Normally it was Canon Blythe who did this, but today he was conducting yet another funeral. As he told the archdeacon the next day: "I'm losing a lot of parishioners to this severe bronchitis that has sent so many of the elderly to their next abode, hopefully with The Lord."

Both he and Gwen were worried that his frail wife might be thus afflicted. When Caroline offered to accompany Gwen to the shops it was vetoed.

"You must keep in the warm," Gwen had declared. "I'll pop down to town for what we need; and I'll add lemon and honey to my list."

"Perhaps you could pick up a *Gazette and Herald*, dear," said Mrs Blythe. "There should be a report of last week's Mother's Union coffee morning." She actually liked to read her stars in the *Swindon Advertiser* but didn't like to ask Gwen to bring that, in case she asked why.

"Oh good gracious!" It was Caroline Blythe's tone of voice that made Gwen stop in her tracks as she unloaded the shopping and put things away.

"What is it, dear?" Gwen was not used to any kind of outburst from her elder sister, usually so meek.

"Have you seen this?" Caroline pointed to the large black headline:

FLOOD PLAIN MADNESS
New development despite river hazard

"Read it out, dear, my glasses are in my coat pocket."

"It's all about Veronica's meadows at The Manor – and how they're going ahead with building those houses. I thought it was all forgotten when John died, but apparently Arabella's reviving the whole thing, despite all the terrible flooding we've had this year and last. What a foolish girl!"

"Didn't you tell me that Melissande was doing some research about a project involving The Manor and its estate?"

"I thought it was to do with the old house itself – but I find it hard to believe they would build houses in those meadows after all that's happened – they are still under water, aren't they?"

"It's beginning to dry up now, but yes, when I went for a walk yesterday it still looked like a fishing lake."

"Come to think of it, Melissande did say that she and that nice man, Bertie, were going to look at some new houses in Holland. Perhaps that had something to do with it? Wait! They're even quoting Arabella, here: listen:"

"The plans, approved some years ago, for a large residential development at Tytherton Kellaway will become reality in the next few months," a family member of the owner of the estate, told the Gazette and Herald.

"No details yet but we'll see how things go," said Miss Arabella Kelway, niece to Lady Veronica Kelway and the late Mr John Kelway, who passed away in 2011, aged 83, before he had been able to commence operations on the site. Miss Kelway declined to answer any questions about the risk of flooding to any new properties there. "I leave that to the engineers," she said. "But I'm quite sure we wouldn't be doing this if it weren't perfectly safe."

It is understood that the family is seeking investors for the project.

The present permission for development of these low-lying meadows expires in 2016 and at least one local resident, Miss Danielle Marchmont, is concerned that this is what she describes as a flagrant case of 'building houses on a flood plain', a practice that has proved so costly to so many home-owners in recent years.

"This permission should be revoked before more people are ruined," Miss Marchmont, a social worker, told our reporter. She says she intends to rally support from local residents to petition the District Council and if necessary bring national attention to what she describes as 'dangerous activity by outside speculators.

"They have to be outsiders," says Miss Marchmont, "I can't believe that local people would even consider spoiling such a beautiful piece of countryside by turning it into a housing estate, especially since it is known to flood. The whole idea is scandalous."

"How frightful," said Caroline. "Surely Melissande would never involve herself in anything like that!"

"I'm sure she would not," said Gwendoline. "We shall have to ask her when she gets back. There has to be a reasonable explanation: she's such a sensible girl. I think it's quite likely this Marchmont woman has the wrong end of the stick, or a grudge against the Kelways. Some people just love to stir up trouble, don't they?"

"I fear you are right, Gwen. We'd better keep the newspaper so she can see what's being said."

The paper was not only being read at The Rectory: Reg Haines saved his copy for Bertie. "That's going to make trouble," he told the cat, curled up, purring on his lap.

Substitute the word 'trouble' with 'litigation' and exactly the same thought came to Mr Clive Penworthy's mind as he perused the latest headlines. From his point of view it would mean more work, perhaps tipping the decision towards taking on an extra pair of hands, which had been a matter for much discussion with his partners recently. Of course as a firm, they would need to handle this very carefully, wishing to give their clients at Tytherton Kelway Manor the necessary legal support, while not damaging their good name amongst Chippenham and district residents, because conveyancing, probate, divorce and civil disputes for local residents were bread and butter for their firm. One didn't want to become unpopular for being 'in the pocket of city slickers'.

"Sorry to disturb you, Cat," said Reg, who didn't look at the gazette until the evening as he sat by the fire, cradling the animal.

"You can stay here while I check on Her Ladyship." The cat settled down again on the warm seat and Reg took the paper up to the big house to discuss the news with Lady Veronica before he helped her upstairs, as he did every night at about this time.

They enjoyed a chat, last thing, talking about the weather, leaky roofs and any gossip that had come Reg's way. Arabella was often the subject of their conversation, as one or other of them shared that day's example of her off-hand behaviour. When she was away, as now, the atmosphere was more tranquil although the newspaper report gave them plenty to talk about.

"We could tell them we're going to stretch our legs," said Melissande as she and Bertie made their way back up to the restaurant and its dance floor.

"That wouldn't be so far from the whole truth, would it? I know you don't like fibs," said Bertie, amused. He was trying to appear confident and calm despite the severe butterflies in his stomach. He was so nervous at the prospect of what they had in mind that his knees were actually shaking.

"And then I could say, casually, that I'm tired and would probably turn in," Melissande added, with a smile that turned Bertie's pulse up by another notch.

"The journey certainly took its toll on me, too," agreed Bertie. "I'd be happy to endorse that statement."

They nodded approval to each other of their deception and excused themselves from the group after one more dance, a slow waltz during which their heartbeats and breathing were anything but slow and Melissande was experiencing very unusual sensations, making her wonder what was going on.

Bertie suggested that her room would be better, because *he* would then be the one who had to travel unaccompanied back to his own, later. He knew, too, that women liked to have all their own 'things' by them – powder puffs, toothpaste and so forth.

"I'll just nip up to my room and see there aren't any urgent messages," he said. Neither he nor Melissande could think of anyone who might be trying to contact him but both understood that they needed moments alone in which to prepare for this momentous occasion.

"You'll let me in, won't you, when I come back – I'll give a secret 'Archers' knock' – you know, 'dum-di dum-di dum-di dum'." He tapped the air.

Melissande laughed at this elaborate plan.

"Perhaps we'd better agree a password, too" she suggested, enjoying the game.

"How about 'amphibian'?"

"I can remember that!"

The reasons Bertie needed to go to his room were twofold. His abdomen was in such turmoil he needed time in the loo, followed by appropriate ablutions and a touch of deodorant; he also needed to collect the emergency 'packet of three' that was permanently secreted in a small pocket of his suitcase.

In her room, Melissande underwent much the same process, slipping out of her dress and spending a while in the en-suite, emerging washed and fragrant, wearing the silk dressing gown provided by the hotel. The routine movement of brushing her hair, until it shone, relieved some of her nervousness. She had just finished checking her diary to make sure that no lunar-linked event was due, when there was a 'dum-di dum' on the door, which made her laugh again, so when she opened the door, Bertie was confronted with a happy, sparkling smile.

He had knocked very softly – discreetly – and was wondering whether it had been loud enough, when Melissande appeared, her hair streaming over her shoulders and wearing a shining white gown that left little to the imagination. The vision was enchanting and he stopped, speechless.

It flashed through his mind that, even after years of casual bedroom encounters, this was all new: he was, once again a terrified boy about to attempt something forbidden and mind-blowing.

Melissande saw his consternation. She took his arm, drawing him into the room.

"What's the password?" She giggled.

It broke the tension and Bertie started functioning again.

"Oh God – I forget!" His body sagged and his shoulders descended a couple of centimetres as he gave up, turned to close the door, (which he did quietly) only to be pulled back to face this glorious creature, whose transformation had caught him so completely off balance.

Afterwards, Melissande put it down to the influence of the wine-tasting having given her such brazen confidence and careless regard for her propriety, but she simply didn't care that, in taking Bertie's hands in hers to lead him over to the wide bed, she let go of the front of the dressing gown, which drifted open, revealing the skimpiest and most portable underwear. His swift arrival had caught her before she'd taken off her spectacles, (so necessary when reading her diary). They looked so incongruous that Bertie, overcoming his desire to take her in his arms, said:

"Take off your glasses, Miss Smith!"

"Oh, Sir Bertrand!" Melissande must have seen the same film. She held up both hands in mock horror, revealing once again her miniscule apparel, smooth pale skin and statuesque form. He took the specs gently from her nose, carefully placing them on the bedside table.

When he turned once more to face her he was thunderstruck at just how shapely and desirable she was. Again it was Melissande who made the next move, breaking the spell that had frozen him.

Lying in his arms later she talked about it.

"I thought you were going to run away! One of us had to do something!"

What she *had* done was to take one wing of his bow tie and given it a tug, releasing the knot; pulled it completely away and dropped it on the floor. Next, she got to work with both hands, undoing the buttons of his shirt from the top, downwards. Bertie responded, slipping out of his jacket, letting it join the tie. Melissande reached the last two buttons and went on to tackle the cufflinks, freeing his shirt and vest, pulling them over his head to reveal a torso that reminded her of Michelangelo's David but decorated with a discreet area of curly hair that darkened the centre of his chest and tapered down towards his navel; below that, a smooth belly disappeared into his trousers.

Bertie undid his belt as Melissande lightly brushed the soft hair on his chest.

"I like this," she said, "I hope you don't mind if I stroke it?"

"Be my guest," he said, relishing the thought of being able to do the same to what still remained concealed of her own body.

By now, his trousers had slipped down to his ankles and Bertie was at a disadvantage: he couldn't move his feet.

Melissande saw her moment, and placed her hands firmly on each side of his muscular chest, pushing him backwards. He could do nothing but topple, holding on to her in a vain attempt to save himself.

The bed caught the back of his knees and the pair of them landed on it with mirth and no damage.

Melissande released herself from the iron embrace that had failed to keep him on his feet, and knelt at the end of the bed, removing his shoes and socks. Taking hold of each trouser leg she commanded.

"Lift your bottom!"

Bertie obeyed, taking the weight off long enough for her to give the trousers a tug, gather them up and toss them to his other clothes.

"Now it's fair," she said, allowing the glossy gown to slide off her shoulders on to the floor. Glancing at the bulge still covered by Bertie's remaining underwear she wondered what it might be like when released – but nothing daunted, she joined him on the bed and without hesitation, resumed the sensuous kissing.

It was then that Bertie's confidence returned. He lay on his back, pulling her gently on top of him. She liked the idea and collaborated, lithely extending her length over his. This enabled him to reach behind her to undo the catch to release the lacy bra that was denying access to those delicious little breasts. This he accomplished with surprising ease, deciding the hook must have been designed by a man with such action in mind. He allowed her to continue the kiss. He had little option, because Melissande now had her hands holding his face, pressing his head to the pillow as she devoted her attention to his lips. She wanted to consume him.

All her apprehension and revulsion of such activity had blown away. It belonged to yesterday and the other world, of 'purity and demure chastity' – yet it felt right and wholesome, not sinful. She couldn't believe how wonderful it was, giving her body to this powerful, oh-so-warm and pliant lover beneath her.

Everything in her upbringing had implanted in her that these mysteries must not be revealed – even discussed – until 'being married' sometime in the future.

Secret sensations and urges, so long resisted and suppressed as 'inappropriate' were rampaging, their bonds discarded like the clothes on the carpet as they began to make love in the world's most romantic city – with its mythical dwellings, streets of water and monuments to heaven.

She was free, unafraid and committed to this person and his magnificent body. The accumulation of reasons for trusting his sincerity and truthfulness, built over the past few weeks, now assured total confidence in his intentions, giving her this unprecedented permission to merge with him, become one body, one unit of humanity. This is what she wanted, what her body demanded.

Later, when satiated, she might acknowledge this as the primate response to a suitable mate, but at this moment its excitement, joy, urgency and irresistible need was unstoppable. She felt his hands slide down her back, his fingers exploring each muscle and electrifying her skin. She wanted to eat him! She wanted more: more of everything –
NOW!

Bertie, for his part, was having trouble thinking at all. This girl had changed beyond recognition in just one evening. Previously he had treasured each stolen touch of her hand, or peck on the cheek. Now, she was on top of him fierce with intensity, sharing with him the smoothness and heat of her body, every part of her pressing against him, seeking yet closer contact without anything – no thread of cloth or molecule of air – between them.

He was finding it so difficult to concentrate, her kiss enchanting him with alternate tenderness and urgent searches. One moment he could feel her tongue dancing against his, the next, her mouth tracing the outline of his own, while her hair cascaded around his face and ears.

His hands and finger tips were collecting delightful messages from her silken back, so strong and long, finally encountering an elasticated cord below her waist.

It took a moment or two before Bertie recognised what it was. Identification dawned: 'Well I'm blowed! The Rector's daughter is wearing a thong!'

"What's this?" he freed his mouth to ask, while giving the cord a flick. He had touched beyond it and instead of soft cloth, had found yet more delicious skin and sloping buttock that became even more exciting.

"It's the first time I've ever tried one," came the reply. "The girl in the shop said I ought to, because ordinary knickers might spoil the line of the dress. I wasn't very keen because I thought it might not be .... comfortable."

"And is it?"

"Oh yes! I'd forgotten about it until you asked." She returned to her kissing, allowing Bertie to work out what to do next. He presumed that its removal must be similar to that of other such garments, with the extra pleasure of feeling the shape, each side, of these firm and delectable orbs, so easy to caress and stroke, or grip and pull to himself. A combination of all these movements accompanied the descent of the thong to Melissande's active knees and calves. Her feet took over, one tweaking the little garment from the other, and flicking it away.

"Melissande, are you sure you want this?" Bertie had to ask.

"Quite sure! As long as you don't make me pregnant – not yet, anyway!" Her reply was prompt, as though she'd been waiting for him to ask.

"But after all we talked about in the car ...... won't you regret it. I shouldn't have given you so much wine. I feel responsible."

"If you like, I'll get off and stand on one leg with my eyes closed, to prove I'm sober and have all my facilities."

"You certainly have the most perfect 'facilities'," said Bertie, as Melissande changed her position, sitting up, her bottom resting just above his knees. She shook her hair back over her shoulders, raising her arms to bunch it together behind her head, drawing yet more attention to her projecting small breasts and their untouched little nipples. She looked down, saw what he was studying and took his hands, placing one on each. He needed no further direction, but with the light touch of a feather, allowed his fingers to run over every contour, curve and hardening tip. Meanwhile, Melissande was feeling and examining that part of him the like of which she had never seen before, even on a statue – especially in this condition. It was so different from that little thumb resting on Old Testament David's marble plumbs.

"Do go gently," advised Bertie, "it might go off!"
"Would that be the end of it all? So quick?"
"Well, for a little while. It takes time to have another go."
"So we could take our time?" Melissande wanted to know all about it and, considering its size, she was wondering how she might accommodate such a thing, even after her little barrier had been broken – a process which she had long feared. A little extra time might be a good idea; so she ignored his request and continued caressing this novelty.

Bertie understood, and gave way to her wishes. To make it even better he took her hand away from its activity and pressed it to his mouth, delivering with his tongue the natural liquid that makes skin move against skin so easily.

"What a good idea! That answers another thing I wanted to know," said Melissande. "That's allowed is it?"

"My darling Mel, everything's allowed, as long as it's done in love and respect. You can achieve the same effect by doing this." He reached forward and gently searched amongst the neat stripe of pubic hair she had left during her preparation and 'bikini line depilation', making her catch her breath with excitement and shock as his finger softly parted the entrance, collecting the wetness that had increased so much in the last few minutes, making her wonder whether her diary might be wrong. He transferred this to where it was needed and lay back for her to continue a process which was causing his whole body to tense, every follicle tightening as though he was going to sneeze and a rising ... rising .... inevitable ... explosive energy, gathering beyond all resistance.

Melissande was fascinated – to see the dignified Bertie, normally so courteous and considerate, in this state of what appeared to be pain and tension. And what she was holding, hot and slippery, fitted so nicely into her hands that perhaps it would fit elsewhere without too much difficulty. 'Of course it will,' she told herself; 'otherwise how could the human race continue'.

Her own feelings of desire were beginning to detract from her scientific observations and she too, wanted to 'get on with it'. That's how Bertie must be feeling too, she observed, increasing the speed of her hands just a little.

That did it! The part of Bertie she was handling began to pulsate and his whole body went rigid as he gasped and raised his hips to her. She stopped her movement and held him tightly, feeling a new arrival of very wet, warm deposit over her fingers.

"Wonderful!" Gasped Bertie. "Mm! Lovely!" He chuckled, relaxing and collapsing beneath her. "Don't let it get too near your 'you-know-what', it could make you pregnant," he warned. "Better get a flannel – or my hankie. It's full of little chaps with one purpose in mind – to find their way to your egg and it only takes one!"

"I did biology at school, too, and I know that," said Melissande, amused, but backing off a little towards his knees. "And I know about the 'morning after' pill, too, so there!" She laughed. "I'm not quite as innocent as you may think: even though I've had to break all kinds of barriers to get this far. I hope you realise I wouldn't be doing this with anyone else – and never have!"

"Well it's been bliss, so far, and I know I'm truly honoured by your attention and imaginative approach. I feel just the same as you. I've never experienced something like this before – you are so special. I have a strong urge to say something I've never say to anyone."

"What's that then?" She knew, but she wanted to hear it. She dismounted and, curling up her legs, propped herself beside him, a real life version of the Copenhagen mermaid, her free hand wandering amongst the hairs on his chest.

Bertie sat up, turned towards her and, looking directly into her eyes, held his breath for a second before blurting out: "Melissande Blythe, I'm in love with you! I love you, more than I've loved anyone or anything! There! I've said it – and I'm not sorry – it's been hovering in my head for weeks and I've never dared let it out: it's such a dangerous thing to say – you might tell me to 'get lost' – or you might be upset and scared. I've wanted to say it but didn't dare."

"Oh Bertie! Are you sure?"

"After what's just happened, in the moments after such a climax – such a starburst – a chap is left in the cold light of day. That's when he knows his true feelings: he might reach for a cigarette, or decide he's late for a meeting, or suddenly feel ashamed of himself – but I'm ecstatic to tell you that, even with the lid off, I'm absolutely, completely, utterly, crazily potty about you, Melissande – I love you, MY Melissande – if you'll have me! "

"Bertie! What are you saying? I thought we were just 'making love' and trying things out. I haven't had my turn yet! I may find it awful and you know what you were arguing in the car – that it was risky to commit yourself before you even knew if your love-making would work. I don't know what to say!"

It was the faintest hint of a smile on Melissande's lips that gave Bertie a lifeline. For a moment he had been stunned by her response to his declaration. For a split second she was enjoying the shock on his face, wondering whether she was testing him just that little too far. In the next millisecond he spotted a twinkle in her eyes as they narrowed by a fraction and her mischief dawned on him.

"Melissande! How could you? After my working myself up to say the most difficult thing in the whole of my life and you pull my ... leg! You little.....!"

"Go on – say it – monkey! Well, aren't we both? But, yes, I *think* I *do* love you but we'll have to see what *you* can do!"

CHAPTER 18

At that moment, in their suite on the floor above, Tristram and Arabella had just decided to share a bath together. Tired but sober they filled the ornate and spacious tub in the mirror-lined bathroom with foaming waters.

"I wonder what happened to the other two?" Said Tristram.

"I expect Melissande went to bed and Bertie might well have finished up on his own. Maybe he'll go out and look for a bit of nightlife: he looks like a lusty sort of man."

"Arabella, he's not a bit like me, you know! I admit to being a late-night bird but he's always disappeared early on these occasions, usually because he's got some kind of presentation or meeting early next morning."

"Well he hasn't, here! This is only a jolly, isn't it? Even for him?"

"It might be for you and me – perhaps Melissande too, but Bertie's actually a very serious cove. I think he's looking to Venice to give him some inspiration for this crazy project he's getting into."

"Well he's hardly going to want to include a cathedral – even a chapel, is he?"

"I think it's more to do with how people manage to live in a world where practically everything has to be carried by boat – both in and out. He mentioned sewage earlier today and wants to meet up with the municipal people to talk about that."

"I'll suggest we go and look at some art while he's doing that – it's not one of my favourite subjects! Let's not talk about it right now – come on – you get in and make sure the water's not too hot."

Tristram braved the bubbles and was soon luxuriating, watching Arabella step daintily into the other end of the bath. He was admiring her long limbs and delectable shape. Such a poppet! All services provided – and so far, she had not impinged on his way of life. He was appreciating the way she kept herself separate from him, not invading his presence or attempting to control his thinking. When making love, she was satisfying her own needs as much as he was, but afterwards she wasn't clingy or possessive. Like now, she was more or less ignoring him, far more interested in her own thoughts and needs.

When comfortably installed, she moved her foot against his knee, under the water.

"Ah! There you are: I've found one leg. I guess the other's there somewhere."

"It is, I promise."

They made no further move to seek more contact but settled down to a relaxing soak in the fragrant warmth and supporting water. Their lust expended to repletion during the long afternoon's frolics in the next room, each had now retreated into their own life. Tristram's mind naturally turned to the making of money.

"Actually, I don't think Bertie's scheme is such a bad one," he said, balancing some bubbles on his finger. "It's not going to be cheap, though. We shall have to raise a fair bit of capital."

"I thought he was going to do this with his own?"

"Bella – he may be rich, but he's not *made* of money. I'm sure he won't want to risk the lot on such a novel idea."

"It's not *that* new is it? Look at Venice, for a start! That's been around for some time; and they've just been in Holland looking at something there. "

"*You* know that and *I* know that, but the public perception in Britain is that you mustn't build housing estates on flood plains any more. They've all been watching poor souls peeling up stinking carpets and buggered television sets. It's going to take some hard selling to get something like this off the ground."

"Or water!" Arabella's snort reminded him of so many other girls with whom he'd shared baths. "Are you going to put any money into it?" She asked casually, raising an eyebrow.

"Who says I've got any? Have you been checking me out?" Tristram's head moved to one side as though he were listening for an intruder. His eyes did not leave hers as they peered at each over, over the foam. His guard was not down.

This was a pretty hard-nosed creature, despite her great looks and nice accent. She definitely had class and in the not-so-distant future would be the proud owner of the land on which this ambitious project was being planned; not to mention a dilapidated but charming old manor and outbuildings set in the most delightful countryside within easy reach of London. Just the sort of woman he'd been looking for to give him a bit more status without too much control. As long as she had her horses and 'yah' friends she'd be happy and he could get on with his life, enjoy her body, produce a few heirs – and have fun. Things could be great.

Better not let her know what he had in mind! She had obviously done her research and might try to pin him down: better see how things went, first.

"No of course I haven't," she lied without a qualm, "but God, you look serious! What's bugging you? Auntie's meadows"

"Well – that sort of thing, you know! Just trying to work out how to go about it. I wish I could find out what Bertie *really* has in mind. He does keep stuff close to his chest. I'd like to make sure that you and I get a fair share of what might turn out to be a goldmine."

At this remark, Arabella began to perk up. Perhaps Tristram and Bertie weren't such bosom buddies after all: maybe their loyalties were financial rather than human? People after her own heart: total freedom at all costs – and that means having money: lots of it.

"I must say I've been concerned about his involvement. He turned up, out of the blue, and has got my aunt eating out of his hand; acted as district nurse to her and Haines, and installed himself as Haines's lodger – all within a matter of days. It feels rather as though I've been pushed to one side."

Tristram smiled to himself. Yes – she must have been pissed off when she discovered that Bertie was far more than he seemed. He could just imagine her behaviour towards him when he was only a casual labourer. She reminded him of his mother – another controlling woman who knew exactly what she wanted and how to get it – so he had experience of how to survive and prosper with someone like that.

"If you take my advice you'll make bloody sure your legal people tie things up tight when it comes to your ownership rights – but don't put him off – he's a pretty smart operator and a bloody hard worker. I'd trust him with anything; and he's clever, too. It would be better to go along with him on this: he's got a nose for 'a good thing' and you'd be better off being part of his potty scheme than just his landlord – or landlady, in your case!"

"Do you really think so?"

"I do! And he could use your skills too, if you're any good at marketing. We're likely to come up against it if some idiot starts bleating about 'the countryside' or something like that. There's always someone who can't bear anything changing the view."

"How about you, then? Where do you come in – apart from being old mates?"

"Well, accommodating risk of things getting flooded is part of my speciality – it could be relevant. He needs backers, too, and I do happen to have a few quid stashed away – now you mention it; although I suspect you did know that, didn't you?"

"Of course I didn't – how could I?"

"You're a bright girl – with great assets! I'm sure you'd find a way." He rubbed his foot against the inside of her knee, making waves in the bath.

Arabella knew when she had been rumbled and liked it. Here was a man with whom she could negotiate, get what she wanted and who had similar views on the good life.

"Well I did happen to hear you owned a flat in Monaco."

"And that my folks live in the Caribbean? I bet you did!"

"It's my job to know these things – I looked you up before that launch where we met. I looked *everyone* up. You don't mind, do you? You should be pleased that I thought you were worthy of my attention! I'm a single heiress – good looks, fun to be with and all that! I've proved it haven't I?" She extended her foot, seeking to nudge him higher up the thigh.

"Some heiress! A bloody great mortgage and an underwater farm! But I'll give you the rest of it – you're not bad company! Nice body: very nice!"

At this, Arabella decided that aggression would be the best way to deal with his impertinence. She rose up out of the froth, and was attempting to invade his end of the bath but slipped, falling on top of him with a soapy splash, slopping water over the marble floor.

"Oh I say!" Tristram laughed and blew foam away from his face, "this is fun! I thought you'd had enough for the moment but an underwater frolic might be novel!" He seized her roughly and growled. "I'll be your sea monster, if you like! You can be my mermaid!"

"You think I'm fishy?"

"Not in the slightest, my little pet – but before we embark on our little maritime charade, I'd like to make just one suggestion – before we forget. How about you chatting Bertie up and making a fuss of him to winkle out what he really has in mind for your inheritance. I'd hate to think he was pulling a fast one."

"Come to that – what about *your* intentions?" Arabella was now groping around under the water to find and strengthen his resolve.

"If you go on doing that, my immediate intentions will be to Roger you most severely!"

"Irresistible!"

Before they dropped off to sleep, Arabella and Tristram had agreed a strategy.

"What do you want me to find out?" Asked Arabella.

"From your point of view, I'd like to know whether he intends to get a slice of your real estate – or whether he really is trying to put a development package together which he can apply anywhere. You know – identify the site, get permission, raise the money and put out the contracts to get the work done – then market the finished properties. It would turn the whole thing around – from being 'blighted land, subject to flooding' to being the very latest fad, 'floating around with the elite – away from the plebs.'"

"You mean – he might *not* be trying to pick up my aunt's estate for a song and keep it?"

"That's what you need to know, because if that's what he's trying to do: and it could be tempting – a very desirable spot, beautiful views, green and peaceful and all that. You could stop him: make him change his options and then reap the benefits for yourself. He doesn't need more *land*. He only works because he enjoys it – it's just a matter of nudging him in one direction or the other. Once you find out his vision, you can begin working on it. Maybe you could ask Melissande: see what she can find out – they seem to be getting pretty thick."

"Huh! She won't know anything! Much as I love her, she's such a simple soul – what you see is what you get: I can't see her getting to Sir Bertrand Lamotte's inner thoughts! She does what she's asked, goes to church, looks after 'Mummy' and is generally very good-natured. She's being paid to draw up facts and figures and that's what she will do. She'd be horrified if she knew what we'd been up to tonight – or come to think of it, the other nights in London – you really are rather good at horizontal jogging!"

"Not again, Bella! I want to go to sleep – perhaps we can try one on land again in the morning. No – I think you are going to have to work on Bertie yourself – chat him up a bit, let him get you on your own and see whether he's tempted by your gorgeous body and sexy movements."

"Won't you mind?"

"Why should I? It's all in a good cause!"

"Even if I go to bed with him?"

"Bella!"

"Some men don't talk until they've got their trousers down."

"Are you serious?"

"I might be!"

"Well, I suppose he *is* my best mate – and we have shared 'experiences' before!"

"See? I bet you've never told anyone else that!"

"OK – and I've got no pyjamas on! You'd better keep that to yourself."

"I'm discreet, if nothing else!"

"That's a bloody good job. Perhaps we'd make quite a team?"

"What do you mean by that?"

"Can't talk any more – very sleepy."

Arabella did not drop straight off – but examined her own options. Here she was being encouraged to flirt with, and seduce if necessary, another potential suitor – one with a title and rosy financial future. She could even offer to help Melissande with her research: just the occasional errand? Mel might be glad of a hand.

Hotel staff had to spend some time clearing up sodden bathmats and towels in that particular suite next morning but its design saved the rooms below from wet patches on the ceiling. The architect had included the possibility of such romps and had given the en-suite bathroom extra drainage to cover such eventualities.

Reg Haines was not pleased. It was a wet and blowy morning; he had only just got back to the Gate Lodge after making sure that Her Ladyship was properly launched into the new day. The fire in the drawing room would keep going for a couple of hours, fender in place. Then this young man appeared at the door.

Afterwards, Reg thought he should have sent him away but he'd taken pity and asked him to step inside, out of the rain and wind, which was trying to snatch the door out of his hand.

"What can I do for you, then?" He'd asked.

"I'm from the local paper," said the young man, giving himself a shake and taking off his dripping baseball cap. "I wonder if I might ask you a few questions about Tytherton Kellaway Manor?"

"You can ask – but I might not be able to give you proper answers. I only work here. Take off that coat and sit down a minute. I'll go on with what I was doing, if you don't mind. The cat's not been fed and she'll start getting uppity if I don't see to her. What is it you want to know?"

Reg was playing a straight bat – he suspected this was a follow-up to those inflammatory headlines he'd been reading. Moving about, opening the odd tin and pottering between questions would give him time to think and work out how to get rid of this intruder. The logical thing would have been to send the boy up to talk to Lady Veronica but he didn't want her upset or flustered. It wouldn't do her heart any good; his own, by contrast, seemed to be pumping well enough, and the pills he took daily by the handful had allowed him to make quite a come-back, one way and another. The best thing he could do was divert things towards someone like Arabella – she would know how to deal with it.

"My Editor's interested in the housing project that was approved a few years back, on those fields down by the river."

"How's that then?"

"Well, some local people are suggesting that since it's been flooded for the past two winters, it might be better to review the plans – build somewhere else."

"Is that so? Well I suppose everyone's entitled to their opinion."

"Have you heard whether anything's being planned? Are the stories right about surveyors putting in pegs?"

"Oh, I don't get out much on to the farm, my friend. You'd have to ask Miss Arabella about that. She's often out and about on her horse."

"You mean Lady Kelway's niece?"

"There you are – you know about everyone already! She's the one you should talk to. Lady Veronica's a bit frail, you see: she just leads a quiet time these days; not at all well, though I hope you wouldn't report such a thing – I'm just telling you so you'd know. It wouldn't do her any good to be asked questions, thinking what she said might be printed out for everyone to read. I'm sure you understand."

"Oh yes, of course, Mr ...?" He had taken out his notebook and was about to write.

"You don't want to know me – I'm just part of the furniture! You need to talk to Miss Kelway – but she's away abroad at the minute. I'm not sure when she will be back, but I can give you her phone number in London – that's where she works. She only comes down now and again."

Well at least that was something, thought the reporter. He could squelch his way back to the office and keep trying the number. His Editor would understand – he hoped. There must be other stories to follow. This old boy obviously knew more than he was letting on. Perhaps he could call another time, now they'd got to know each other. It wouldn't be difficult to ask around for his name and role at The Manor.

In Venice, Melissande was thinking it was about time she appeared in the dining room.

Breakfast would soon be over and she was distinctly peckish. The thought of a warm croissant and black cherry jam was very beguiling. So, however, was lying in this large bed, even though Bertie was no longer there with her. Shock horror! What a thought! What *would* her parents have thought?

On reflection, she suspected that her mother, without displaying a hint of it, might *not* be so disapproving. Recently she had been dropping hints about Bertie being 'such a nice young man'.

'Maybe it's *me* who's been the prude all this time,' thought Melissande. 'All my friends have been very nice about it but, apart from Arabella, I've never had any idea about what they'd all been up to. They might have been doing what Bertie and I were doing half the night. If so, I didn't know what I was missing: I *do* now, and I wish I'd started earlier!'

She took hold of the pillow on which Bertie's head had been resting until half an hour ago, when he'd slipped out, silently gathered up his clothes, crept into the bathroom, dressed and left her room, thinking she was asleep. Hugging the pillow to her naked body she breathed in the last traces of Bertie's scent, a mixture of pheromones, enhanced with after-shave and a touch of delicious armpit. The aroma had developed during the course of the night, during which the temperature under the single sheet had on occasions risen high enough to make them both perspire profusely.

At the time, the wetness between them made things all the more sensuous and unifying as their bodies slid, clung, pressed against and finally pushed together in exhilarating copulation.

The thought had flashed through her mind that at some stage they would have to pause and attend to contraception, but her desire over-ruled any doubts about whether Bertie might infect her with something dreadful – or that she might become pregnant. Her body and mind had decided that she could trust him absolutely and must give herself to him without delay. Let the future take care of itself! This, she realised, was what she had wanted without knowing it, for a very long time.

When she felt his weight on top of her and looked up at the great head and wide shoulders, she had a moment of fear, but his expression of eager tenderness reassured her that he was thinking about *her* and it might not be as painful as she'd heard. She could feel his hardness probing against her, somewhere down there, and she widened her legs to help him find the way. She felt him stop as soon as he knew where he was, and very,

very softly began, pressing and withdrawing the tip, feeling his way without penetrating but sharing and spreading the lubrication that seemed to appear from nowhere.

She wrapped her arms around his back, pulling him down on herself, his chest flattening her breasts and his weight making her take breaths in little gasps. She raised her head to reach his mouth with her tongue seeking his. At the same moment as kissing her deeply, he yielded to that powerful need to be one with her, by pushing past her hymen with a firm but slow movement of his hips. He would have stopped if she had cried out or tensed but her response was positive as she raised herself against him, her passion as hungry as his.

There was a moment of sharp soreness and then the most amazing feeling of him being further and further inside her. It wasn't frightening or unpleasant but what she now knew she had been waiting for. She wanted him all the way into her. When there was no more space between his groin and hers he stopped pressing and paused to allow her to get used to this presence.

"Bertie – stay like that. It's all right, it didn't hurt – I just want you inside me like that for ever!"

"My darling Melissande – it's where I want to be: and I can tell you without any problem that I love you desperately, and I've never felt like this before."

He took some of the weight off her chest by raising himself a fraction with his elbows and she took a deep breath, smiling up at him as he looked down to assess her expression and response to what came next. He allowed her what she had asked for and stayed, their lower halves fixed tightly together and the coolness of their perspiring breasts refreshing their energy.

Then he raised his hips by a tiny amount, making Melissande contract with surprise – an automatic reflex to keep him there – giving herself yet another new sensation as his hard erection moved inside her. But he changed direction again, pressing down once more, refilling the available space, reaching somewhere deep inside her that was unbelievably pleasurable. He repeated his previous movement, withdrawing a little further this time and she enhanced it by lowering her bottom against the bed. Next time he pressed down, she rose to meet him and slowly, they developed a rhythm, speeding up until it was barely tolerable: and then he pulled too high and she dropped too low and they disconnected.

She felt him, wet against her thigh and couldn't bear him not being inside her. She reached down and took hold of the slippery, rigid thing and guided it back to where she wanted it so badly. Bertie needed no encouragement, but thrust into her fast and strong, waiting until they both felt secure again. Now she felt his pouch and gonads against the top of her legs and the very thought of them reminded her of Michelangelo's David and Arabella's stallion, firing her to resume precipitous activity. She raised herself and spread her knees even wider apart, levelling her pelvis to him, opening herself completely to his invasion. She felt his rough pubic hair against her belly and wriggled to savour its touch, allowing her body to move faster and faster, with a rising, unstoppable tension that electrified her groin, her legs, her breasts, her head and then, with an explosion of light, stars, gasps, snatched breaths and cries of delight followed by cascades of joy, she froze, as did Bertie, except for his penis and her vagina, which pulsated, pumped and gripped in waves as their exudations mingled and mixed.

Bertie thought he would never stop but gradually, as the delicious seizures drained him of every last drop he had to offer, he came back to earth. He opened his eyes and saw that despite her blissful smile, tears were running down Melissande's face.

"What is it, Melissande, my dearest? Have I hurt you?"

"Oh no! Anything but! It's just so marvellous and I want to cry with happiness. Bertie thank you! That was the most amazing thing I've ever done – and the first time I've ever had such a FANTASTIC feeling! I can hardly breathe – please don't move now. Just let things stay like that. It's so good!"

"You may not believe it but I feel the same: as though I've arrived for the first time. I can see what the old madrigals meant by 'dying' – and now I'm in Heaven."

When the Latvian maids finally gained access to Melissande's room, as she descended for a late breakfast, they found traces of what had been going on, despite Melissande's attempts to clean it up with her flannel and towel.

"She had a visitor!" Said one.

"First time, too!" Said her colleague as they scooped up the bedclothes and began to remake the bed.

At breakfast they couldn't join their companions because Tristram had come down first, choosing a table for two. Bertie, arriving next, had to go to the only other available place some distance away by the window, overlooking the Grand Canal. That suited him fine: he hoped Melissande might join him.

By the second cup of coffee his wish was granted and he stood to welcome her, drawing some attention to the little ceremony of her arrival. Some elderly tourists assumed the young couple must be on their honeymoon.

Once installed and having made her choices from the breakfast menu, Melissande felt she was ready for anything as she buttered the piece of crisp new roll she'd broken off to keep her hunger at bay.

"Did you sleep well?" Bertie asked politely, without a hint of a knowing look.

"Straight through! So comfortable, thank you, Bertie. Did you?"

"I did, thank you – yes it was most comfortable." He then lowered his voice. "I've just realised that we omitted one thing in our 'discussions' last night. The matter of provision of prophylaxis for participants."

"It did occur to me too," admitted Melissande, "but at the time its importance didn't seem relevant."

"That's the danger at the early stages of a project. One tends to miss an important matter when becoming enthusiastic over another aspect of a grand plan. Then it becomes necessary to make remedial arrangements afterwards. Is that what you are thinking?"

"It was, actually. I've looked up the Italian for my requirements and will pop out to buy the necessary before we begin our technical investigations. That's if you think it's necessary."

"I was thinking that, perhaps on this occasion, it might be desirable to allow things to take their natural course – a risk that I'd be happy to take."

"How strange! That's just what I was thinking."

Bertie felt an affectionate rub of Melissande's foot against his, under the table.

CHAPTER 19

The conclusion of Melissande's feasibility study, after weeks of consultations with engineers, insurers, suppliers, contractors and financiers was that changes would have to be made to the plans if they were to meet Mr Kelway's original proposal of providing a set number of dwellings to fulfil regional targets while ensuring that the inhabitants should not sink beneath the seasonal flooding by the River Avon.

John Kelway had foreseen 'ordinary buildings', with desirable middle-class residences laid out in avenues, cul-de-sacs and small squares. His goals had been unambitious but tasteful. Had they been implemented, many of those residences would by now be deserted, at huge cost to insurance companies and property owners.

Melissande pointed out they would also be unsaleable – a situation that faced flooded households in neighbouring Somerset already. Revised budgets and designs to accommodate the new climate patterns were now essential.

Bertie hadn't seen his secret lover make a presentation before and was impressed by her poise and panache. Had he attended the Sunday-school classes she'd been leading since being confirmed at fifteen, he would not have been surprised. She knew how to make things interesting and keep people's attention. Her gift for public speaking had been inherited from her father, whose sermons were a great relief to people like Bertie, who had been obliged to endure listening to all kinds of drivel at his mother's favourite church.

"I won't bore you with *all* the details," she told the gathered board of TGP briskly, as they met in the dining room at Tytherton Kellaway Manor. Her hint of humour got things off to a good start.

"You can study them later if you wish, but let's get to the conclusions straight away!"

That gave everyone hope and curiosity, making them pay attention. The only creature ignoring her was the cat, comfortably snoozing on Reg's lap.

"My conclusion is that what we've come to know as 'The Great Plan', could be great! It's a classic case of a crisis creating opportunities. My task was to assess the possibilities for adding value to what had apparently become a liability – and to predict the risks involved. Well – here we go! See if you agree with my findings."

She then presented a short series of slides, illustrated with images, first with the meadows deep under water, then an artist's impression of what the new concept might look like – in all seasons. It was as though she was selling a new house to each person in the room, zooming in to various designs at rest on their base platforms or floating serenely with a motor-boat on its hourly run, picking up residents on their way to or from the raised car park to the east of The Manor.

"You may remember that Mr Kelway, with his interest in sport, had included a football pitch in his plans, which included a simple running track around it."

To win approval of the changes in design, several advisors had suggested that this feature should remain, as being 'socially desirable', especially as Government was seeking ways of 'rolling out the fatties' from their path towards diabetes and other afflictions leading to early and expensive demise.

There followed a series of images of athletics, football, ice-skating, water skiing and a grand village fete. The site was recognisable in each, because of the trees, spectator stand and impressive scoring screen. In some, the action area was lush green, in others, picturesque with the reflections of the sky, trees and lights in the waters that covered it.

"Organisers would adapt events to the state of the sports zone," she explained. "This would require imaginative preparation – perhaps on the lines of pentathlon activities to suit the prevailing conditions. It would keep participants on their toes, flippers, skates or water-skis!"

"I can see cricket umpires having a bit of a job," interrupted Reg. "Having to decide if it was time to change the sport!" His chuckle was endorsed by smiles and movement amongst Melissande's audience. She paused for a moment as the board settled down again to hear more of what was promising to be an entertaining talk.

"I'm not suggesting that all these things would happen at the outset but it would be up to the community to learn how to live with unpredictable outdoor conditions and enjoy them appropriately. I have assumed we should build in these options."

"It sounds expensive!" Tristram sounded a note of caution.

"Absolutely!" Agreed Melissande. "My brief, though, said 'be bold'."

Bertie nodded energetically. Melissande, despite herself, blushed with pleasure at his support and resumed her narrative. She wasn't giving them a sales pitch, but taking a BBC approach of 'on the one hand', and 'on the other', balancing costs, benefits and risks. Her findings showed clearly that the extra cost of making houses amphibious would necessitate the finished products to be up-market and attractive to well-heeled buyers.

"Paying as much as that, the advice from estate agents is that we couldn't expect buyers to want rows of floating semis," she said.

"I don't think those houses at Maasbommel would sell here. My sources say that each house must have sufficient space to allow privacy and individuality. To accommodate the required number of homes it would mean including higher density apartments on the ground which doesn't flood. These flats would be of the very highest standard, built to blend with the countryside, and designed by someone with the future in mind. The beautiful surroundings and novelty of a trendy, ultra-modern suburb with easy commuting to Paddington suggest they would sell at a price to achieve a satisfactory return on investment."

Melissande finished her presentation and resumed her place next to Bertie. For a few moments, no one spoke. Lady Veronica, sitting at the other end of the long table, seemed relaxed, not having followed much of what was being discussed but enjoying the presence of people taking up the strands of her late husband's dream. Mr Penworthy, in the chair, was waiting for someone else to start a discussion. His main concern, for the moment, was the reputation of his firm. While he wanted to see

TGP succeed financially, (enabling his fees at last to be paid), he was hoping that it could be done without public furore.

It was Tristram who spoke first.

"Well before I say my piece, may I thank you, Lady Veronica – and Arabella, for inviting us here today for our meeting – and for allowing me to join the board of The Great Plan. It's always exciting to be in on something so new and promising; and while Bertie and I represent the harsh world of business, I am very aware that this is your home and your community – as it is for Melissande and her parents; and of course Mr Haines, who performs such noble duty at The Manor. If things went wrong, Bertie and I could move on and seek other pastures, but *you* are the ones with much more at stake, and it's an honour to be given so much trust by you, the owners and local residents."

Tristram looked around to see how his speech was being received. Lady Veronica was smiling graciously, and Arabella had her business face on: intense attention fixed on the speaker. Reg was stroking the cat's head but looking content at being included. Mr Penworthy was busy making notes: he wanted a full record of decisions agreed, which he could quote on future occasions as they formalised a proper constitution and set up a company.

"I must congratulate Melissande for her excellent presentation," continued Tristram; "which demonstrated the comprehensive research she must have carried out. She has led us, step by step, to a conclusion – at least for me – that here we have a most promising prospect for a profitable, modern, and ecologically sound project. I would like to propose that we create a company with appropriate officers; and that we go ahead to bring this project to reality. Naturally, as with any such project, we shall meet, and are indeed already meeting, opposition. We are fortunate, therefore, to have my old chum Bertie, around, to deal with that. It's an art that has brought him great success at the heart of Government." He turned and put a hand on Bertie's shoulder.

"I believe it's a stroke of luck for Tytherton Kellaway Manor and its residents, that has led him to be sitting with us here, now," he continued. "He has already demonstrated his commitment by investing a considerable sum towards keeping the project 'afloat' – as it were – and we couldn't want for a better batsman to face all kinds of aggressive bowlers such as have already joined the opposing team. I do hope you'll excuse my sporting parallels!"

"Get on with it, Tris – this isn't a Tory Party Conference!" Bertie's impatience was delivered with a smile and good humour but it brought him a nudge from Melissande's knee and the hint of a frown from her when he caught her eye. She knew this 'decorative approach' was for Lady Veronica and Arabella. The latter had been treating the whole thing as an unnecessary disruption of her riding and Melissande could see that Tristram was trying to win her over. Reg Haines chipped in again.

"He's right, though! If Bertie hadn't come along when he did, I might not have been sitting here now, holding the cat! Him turnin' up was more than a stroke of luck for *me*; and since we're among friends I can say it was lucky for The Manor too. He was a star, that day when he got rid of them bailiffs. If he can do the same with that Marchmont woman and her donkey it could save us all a lot o' bother!"

Reg's informality allowed Arabella to become more herself.

"We can blame my blasted horse for getting *her* going!" She snorted, "though really, she ought to be grateful!"

Lady Veronica, too, now felt included – the discussion having moved away from 'feasibility', which she knew little about. She had been very disturbed by the flurry of newspaper and radio coverage of what seemed to be a growing public opposition to Dear John's plan, the only remaining chance of saving The Manor from penury.

She felt that the issues raised by the wretched Danielle Marchmont were essentially those for which, as owner of the land and member of the county's elite, she was qualified to have some opinion.

"I can quite see why *that* neighbour has a grudge against us; and you will have to compensate her in some way, Arabella."

From the expressions on the faces around the table, Lady Veronica was pleased to see that her suggestions were getting approval. She had made a useful contribution.

"The other thing she and other protesters must understand," said Tristram, "is that we won't be destroying the landscape or making Chippenham a suburb of Bristol. We shall be adding a desirable new area in which to live, attracting moneyed residents and bringing opportunities for employment – and of course more trade for the local shops and businesses. As the first project of its kind in this country it could bring tourists, who in turn will be looking for hotels and over-night accommodation. Everyone will benefit."

He paused and pointed to his old friend.

"This is where your expertise will come in handy, Bertie. Putting the word about to the right people, what? Getting the local press on side and all that, mm?"

"I certainly do have some ideas for that side of things," admitted Bertie. "But we shouldn't underestimate the appeal that Miss Marchmont's complaints may have to the public. We need to tell people the whole story and demonstrate that The Great Plan is not elitist but a valid way of living with situations that face all of us. I think we have to sell the idea that this is a demonstration of how society may have to live, if it wants to avoid catastrophes like those in the Somerset Levels and other places last winter. It's a step into the future but we're going to need backers – and that's where *you* come in, Batty. It's going to cost a packet!"

"That's true," said Tristram. "But new solutions always tend to start off expensive. Take air travel! Before World War Two it was only the very rich who flew to London to Paris – now it's everyone – unless they use The Tunnel and see what *that* costs; and who could afford to carry around the first mobile phones, the size of bricks, looking cool? Not many! Now practically all school kids and grandparents have them."

"We've all come up in the world a fair bit," said Reg. "One of these days, I might even get myself a package holiday, if I can get someone to take over here for a week next winter. I really fancy a bit of sunshine, – cheer me up: something to look forward to."

"I might even come with you," laughed Lady Veronica. "I'm sure no one else could keep the drawing room fire going the way you do and it would be bleak here without it."

"That would get the locals talking, wouldn't it? You and me goin' off together," Laughed Reg.

"Oh God! Just imagine!" Said Arabella.

"I'm not sure about a mobile phone, though," said Reg. "I like my phone to be on the end of a piece of wire – then I know where it's going!"

"Do you not think we ought to talk about drawing up some formalities?" Mr Penworthy, seeing his valuable time slipping away as the meeting drifted into trivialities.

"You are right," agreed Bertie; "and we must find someone to bring all these ideas together and produce a ground plan. I've got hazy ideas of where the amphibs might be and where the luxury flats could be higher and drier but not over-prominent. I agree with Melissande's point about people not wanting rows of floating semis like those in Holland. We need a bit of individuality – to appeal to owners, and people who care about the countryside too."

"How about some kind of competition?" Suggested Melissande. "There are some very talented people around here – at Wiltshire College for a start! Then there's Bath University and all the independent design and architects firms. I can imagine it would be the kind of thing that would have wide appeal."

"It would also make the whole thing more protracted, wouldn't it?" Suggested Mr Penworthy. "Everyone would want to be heard and then canvass their own ideas. Wouldn't it be better to persuade the current protesters to back down – keep them happy in some way? Then we could get on with it and complete the project."

"What's the hurry?" Asked Reg. "Better to spend a bit of time getting everyone on board – most of them, anyway. They've got to *live* 'ere."

"For you and me, Mr Haines, I think time is limited!" said Lady Veronica. "Mother Nature will want to recycle *us* before long, and if there's any urgency it's that I'd like to see my debts paid off before I leave this earth; and I'm sure you would like to see the future of Tytherton Kellaway Manor secure."

"I would indeed, milady; but as long as it sets off right, I don't have to be in at the finish!" Reg chuckled. "It may not take all that long! A couple of years, perhaps, and I daresay both of us can last *that* long – even a couple more!"

"I can see this as being an effective way of silencing the opposition," said Bertie. "By welcoming public participation and explaining properly what we have in mind, we could hope things ran more smoothly. Melissande has a very good point. It's certainly an approach that I would support: the kind of advice I'd give a Member of Parliament or someone seeking public approval. I would be happy to devote time to putting that side of things together."

"Arabella could help you," said Tristram. "Just up her street, isn't it Bella? Public relations and all that?"

The prompt way in which Arabella responded, rang warning bells in Melissande's head.

"What a good idea! Yes, I'd love to: get involved and all that. After all, it's very much in my own interest, and Auntie's, isn't it? Just let me know when you need a hand, Bertie."

The discussion returned to the general appearance and design of the estate. Bertie thought that once a rough layout had been drawn up with the aid of a civil engineer – possibly someone with experience of yachting marinas – each individual house could be built to suit the buyer's wishes.

"If we got residents involved right from the start, they could finance the architects and artists to come up with plans for their own future home – which could be entered into the competition."

"If houses are going to float some of the time, they'd have to be very light, wouldn't they?" Arabella was now taking interest.

"You're right, Bella," said Melissande; "most amphibs we've looked at are made of wood or recycled plastic, built on to concrete floatable cellars; and even they don't *have* to be made of concrete if you're a purist wanting to save energy. But there's nothing wrong with a building being light, according to the experts. It can still be warm, cool, dry and comfortable – and stable so it won't blow away."

"It shouldn't blow away on that low ground!" Reg commented.

"According to the scientists, it might! Even on sheltered land we might have to include features that protect the houses against hurricanes," said Melissande.

"Are you sure?" Tristram was not convinced.

"While I was looking up 'future weather trends' I came across an article in *Nature*, which said that many places, where you wouldn't expect violent storms will become increasingly at risk from tropical cyclones – like hurricanes in the Caribbean and typhoons in the South China Sea. They are creeping further north, and south, every year, threatening to create havoc in unsuspecting coastal areas."

"But we're miles from the sea!" Said Arabella.

"Pardon me – but we're not!" Melissande knew her facts. "Bristol's only just down the road and it's one of our major seaports! A proper hurricane can be very wide and hit large areas of a small island like Britain – look what happened in 1987! Even last autumn it was nearly as bad."

"That was *freak* weather," Arabella wasn't giving up yet.

"Not according to *Nature*. Listen: I've got it here." Melissande quickly opened her report and went to the appropriate section.

"It says that 'scientific records show that on average, the storms have been migrating towards the North and South Poles at the rate of thirty three miles a decade in the northern hemisphere, and nearly forty miles in the south'."

"So how can you stop a wooden house blowing away?" Arabella was in retreat.

"I've been looking at that, too," said Melissande. "I don't think you could make a wooden house strong enough to behave like Dorothy's in the Wizard of Oz – flying around in one piece – but in the West Indies they've got roofs designed by aeronautical engineers, which allow the wind to blow through them and around them in a way that doesn't give them lift, but makes them sit tight. I expect that sort of thing will be brought into building regulations in this country, before long."

"You can't have roofs whizzing about landing on people!" Bertie added, jovially. "I'm sure Melissande's right, there's nothing wrong with lightweight houses: they're very 'green' too, if you use wood or recycled plastics, you're tying up carbon for decades!"

Reg decided it was time to start winding things up; his back was aching and they didn't seem to be getting anywhere. Transferring the cat to his seat he stood, stiffly, and told the meeting he was going to make a cup of tea.

"When I bring the tray in, I hope you'll have got things lined up for what needs doing next," he said. "I can't stay here all evening and Melissande's got to feed the horse."

Mr Penworthy thought that was an excellent idea and brought the meeting to as fast a conclusion as he could manage, guiding everyone to agree on a series of decisions that would enable him to refine and formalise what had, in principle, been agreed. Since he was keeping the minutes he was able to iron out various points of disagreement that could be resolved before the next meeting. As he put on his coat, picked up his leather briefcase and umbrella to return to Chippenham, his only worry, nagging at the back of his mind, was his firm's reputation amongst the local community on which he and his colleagues depended. He was extra sensitive at present because of the arrival of competition.

Another young solicitor had put up her plate in the main street – admittedly not very prominent or appealing to new clients, because the brass plaque and electronic door-release security system only presented callers with the vision of a rising staircase between the Oxfam Shop and the butcher's. The two-room flat, converted into offices above the former, carried a faint aroma of second-hand clothes, wafted up from below. One couldn't open the window even during the summer because of traffic noise. The aspiring lawyer lived in hopes of moving to a more salubrious property as soon as her clientele made it possible. She was not sure whether she should specialise in any particular area of the law but would see where Chippenham's population led her – perhaps towards domestic conflict; maybe property or probate; even criminal matters. With a bit of luck her first few briefs might include a bit of everything, giving her the feel of the place. The legacy she had recently inherited should last a few years.

Mr Penworthy had met this personable young woman at a recent civic function and was well aware of her potential threat. At a time like this he did not want to blot his Chippenham copybook by being painted as 'a Lackey of City Property Speculators Intent on Destroying Our Green Environment'.

He was not to know that it would be Melissande who would inadvertently rescue him from the peril of such a slur, as she surfed the net one evening looking for *Amphib 21 Ltd's* first sub-contractor or employee.

At the Gate Lodge, Bertie, having helped clear up after supper, said: "I'm popping over to The Rectory – got a few things to discuss with Melissande. She should be back by now."

Reg smiled to himself; he suspected there was more than business involved.

Arabella and Tristram out for a stroll, now it had stopped raining, caught sight of Bertie, disappearing down the muddy lane. Tristram quickly over-ruled Arabella's suggestion that they should hail him to share their sunset stroll.

"Oh give it a break, Bella," he said. "We'd only talk shop and I was hoping to have you to myself for a bit: let's keep out of sight!" He pulled her behind one of the two large cedar trees, whose trunks were wide enough to conceal all kinds of deception, and kissed her with more passion than she had experienced from him before. It certainly stirred all kinds of lusty feelings in her horse-riding body and made her doubt the benefit of swapping this young buck for the other, titled version. For the moment at least she would enjoy Tristram's libido (and wealth). Her instinct told her that she might find life with Bertie rather monogamous and limiting, while with Tristram she could enjoy what either of them might fancy at the time, giving each other latitude to 'lead their own lives' while maintaining the formal arrangements of matrimony. The whole matter needed more time for analysis before she made her choice. For the moment, therefore, she responded to Tristram with equal energy, finding that being pinned against the trunk of an ancient tree could be most gratifying. She was glad she hadn't changed from the skirt and skimpy pants she'd worn for the meeting earlier. Her contraception was, of course, right up to date – no problem there. Despite the knobbly bark behind her it was a delightful new experience.

Bertie was unaware that his appearance had led to Arabella being ravished (by consent and with enthusiastic participation) against a tree and strode off towards The Rectory, noting, as he came to the end of the lane, that it had not been churned up recently by motorcycle scramblers. He managed to reach the road without getting his boots dirty, which pleased him. His heart was light at the thought of seeing Melissande on her own.

It seemed ages since his life had been turned upside down by their nights of romantic revelation in Venice. He could not remember ever being so happy and his legs seemed to work on their own, covering the ground with long steps in a rhythm that began to play a march in his head. The tune was familiar but goodness knows why his subconscious chose that one – perhaps a blackbird had implanted the first few notes as it serenaded the thick foliage above the lane. Ah yes! The RAF march – no wonder: he felt as though he were flying back towards base after a raid – to the arms of the one from whom he never, ever, wanted to be parted.

Sitting next to her, their knees allowing the occasional surreptitious touch, while pretending to maintain the 'employer/employee' formality, had been tantalising and perhaps silly – but it was what she had made him promise on their last day in Venice,

She had been seated on her towel in front of the dressing table, naked, while he, equally un-attired but dry after their communal shower, enjoyed drying her long hair with a surprisingly quiet electric drier.

"Bertie, I don't want Arabella to know about us," she said.

"Don't you think she'd approve?"

"She's in no position *not* to!" Melissande sounded indignant. "It's not *that*, but I'm afraid she might bray it out to the world – she can be *so* indiscreet – and I want it to be our secret, just until I've got used to the shock and all the amazing sensations you've given me. I can't believe it's happened; or that it's real." She reached backwards to caress the calf of his leg. "I'd heard of 'falling in love' and all that, but never imagined that it could be anything like this – falling off a precipice with no parachute!"

Bertie gave his word, promising complete discretion and secrecy about their relationship, until she was ready.

Her hair now dry, Bertie was still standing close behind her moving slightly from side to side. She knew at once what it must be, pressing against her back. She knew exactly what must come next and her body was already responding to the prospect. She watched him in the mirror, smiling as his hands rested on her shoulders and he nodded confirmation of his pledge. Slowly she turned to face him and grasp what had been caressing her back, lowering her head to seal the agreement with her lips and tongue. Bertie let his fingers lift her hair, watching in the mirror as it flowed down her back. Her head rose and fell, just an inch or two. Bliss!

So far, Arabella and Tristram had given no sign that they suspected what had been going on between the two newly-beloveds. If anything, the opposite impression had been given as the two avoided each other in public, which encouraged Arabella's 'plan B', since it appeared that Bertie was not at all attracted to her old school friend – quite understandable – just look at the girl in her dowdy tweeds and serious spectacles: she wasn't any modern man's totty. Bertie was worth a go!

CHAPTER 20

"I think our Travis might have got a job lined up at last," Trevor Bunt was telling Danielle as they enjoyed a Chinese out of polystyrene diners one evening. "I'm not sure what it is because he won't tell me, but he's got an interview on Wednesday. When he went to sign on the other day the Job Centre told him they thought this job fitted him like a glove but the cheeky clerk there told him he ought to 'do himself up a bit'! I ask you – who do they think they are?"

"You told me he was quite friendly with one of them down there," said Danielle.

"Well he'd need to be – else I'd put in a complaint. I think it's takin' liberties, saying stuff like that to a young man – qualified like he is."

"To be honest, I expect they're just trying to help – he's been going there for quite a while," suggested Danielle. "What kind of job is it? A building site? I've heard things are picking up a bit."

"He wouldn't say. He was going to the interview to see what the people was like but he didn't like the sound of it. That's all."

"That's not like Travis, is it? I thought he could always tell you things?"

"Not everything! I didn't find out about that last punch up he'd had until the copper come round, did I?"

"Well no, that's true; but it wasn't his fault, was it?"

"No, course not! He changed a lot, after college; it was a good job he went there."

"A bit near though, wasn't it? I thought you said it would be better if he went somewhere further off, to lose that bunch of mates," said Danielle. "I mean, Lackham's only just down the road. Nice buildin's and all that but not what you'd call 'going away to college'."

"I *did* want him out of the county, after all that fuss about the bikes, but it shook him up, getting knocked about in the shopping centre: gave 'im a fright when his tutor heard about it and had a word."

"What's it to do with *him*?"

"Well – Travis always got on well with 'im. When I met 'im that time at the end of term, he told me Travis was doing well but needed to steady up. He'd come back drunk a couple of times and it was getting serious. I told the teacher Travis thought the world of him, and asked him to keep the boy in line 'cos he wouldn't listen to me! He said he would."

"Oh, right." That seemed acceptable.

"Well, after that, I met the same teacher in Chippenham and we stopped for a chat. He said he'd advised Travis that if he wanted to get employment around here, after the course, he must get himself a better reputation, 'cos countryside jobs generally meant dealing with the public."

"I never thought 'Countryside Management' sounded like him," said Danielle, collecting the debris of the takeaway as Trevor rolled them a cigarette each. "He only knows about labouring – and fighting."

"That's unfair, Danny! But I suppose, if I'm honest, that's what I thought too: not up his street, until they told me it included stuff like fishing and nature – he always *did* like that when he was little, before his mother went off. He's been learning about maps and that, too; and the law. I was very pleased when he passed – surprised too, to tell the truth!"

"He hasn't done much since." Danielle was not keen on Trevor's son.

"Well no, they haven't had much to offer him, since he got his B-Tec. I guess it must be something outdoors anyway. We'll see! I live in hopes."

"It was a good job he bent his scrambler: a lucky right-off!"

"I think he was getting fed up with it, anyway. He was in with the wrong lot – those mates of his were most of the trouble." Trevor scratched his chin.

"Mm," said Danielle.

It was The Rector who answered the door. This was the time of day when people turned up about weddings or christenings; or parishioners dropped by, hoping for sponsorship in marathons or shaving off moustaches. Normally it was Melissande who dealt with these visitors, because this was Canon Blythe's customary time to go out visiting: the sick in hospital, newcomers to the parish and neighbouring clergy.

Recently, Melissande had found it good exercise, trotting up and down stairs, because she had installed herself in her 'office', two floors up, where she used a table as a desk and fixed up her computer. She left the doors open to hear the bell.

Her father, being at home on this occasion, thought he would save her the descent and, feeling virtuous, called up the stairs: "I'll go!"

It took him a moment or two to recognise Bertie, who explained, shyly, that he had one or two matters regarding Melissande's report, which he'd hoped to discuss with her before a meeting tomorrow.

"I do hope it's not disturbing you, Canon Blythe," he said, removing his hat as he was invited in.

"No of course not," said The Rector, a little off balance. He had never before had to deal with young men appearing at the door to visit his daughter and wasn't sure whether to be protective, defensive, benevolent, formal or fatherly. Melissande had reached an age when young male visitors might become in-laws, even if not formally. Men coming to The Rectory were usually here to discuss other people's daughters – not his own. He knew just how to sweep them into his study and ask all the right questions, putting the visitors at ease with confident assurance, making them feel they were in good hands.

In this new situation he panicked and did what first came to mind. He directed Bertie upstairs.

"It's on the second floor; you'll find Melissande at her desk in the first room to the right," he said, wondering immediately whether it was the right decision. He soon learned it wasn't.

"You should have warned her first," his wife told him when he returned to her side in the sitting room, picking up the *Church Times* and settling back in his chair.

"My dear Caroline, how could I? He was right there with me!"

"She might have her hair in curlers for all you know, Edward. A woman needs notice: *really* my dear!"

"Well from what he said, she was probably expecting him," said The Canon in self defence.

"Oh! Now that's *interesting*." Mrs Blythe nodded and smiled broadly. "Such a charming young man, didn't you think?"

"Well, yes, he was polite."

"She *has* been mentioning him rather often."

"Well she's supposed to be working for him, isn't she?"

"Yes, but it's the *way* she talks about him. I've noticed a certain warmth when he turns up in conversation. It would be so nice if she were to find a beau, especially a baronet, wouldn't it?"

The Rector found the thought of his daughter becoming intimate with a man, 'noble' or not, somewhat distasteful. Men tended to be so untrustworthy these days and Melissande was the apple of his eye.

Melissande knew it must be Bertie coming up the stairs. She had heard the bell, thought it might be him and quickly grabbed her scent, dabbing a little on her neck and wrists, then glanced in the mirror to make sure she looked her best before resuming her seat in front the computer screen.

"Knock knock," said Bertie, approaching.

"Come in – I'm decent!"

"I should hope so, on the second floor of The Rectory," said Bertie, filling the doorway as he stepped into her domain for the first time.

Melissande stood up and the two faced each other for a second, not sure what to do but it was she who made the first move. She stepped up to him, put her arms around his neck and kissed him in just the way she had kissed him so often in Venice.

"It's been ages!" She said when they came up for breath.

"I know, I've missed you too – and it was so tantalising, sitting next to you all afternoon, only being able to bump knees and play footsie. It's a good job we didn't make each other laugh. It *was* a good meeting, though: your report was great!"

"Thank you Bertie!" Melissande disentangled herself and sat down at the computer. "There are a couple of things I want to talk about before I close the door."

"Are you sure you should?"

"What? Tell you? Of course I should! I think I've found someone to start on the field work."

"I was talking about shutting the door." Bertie laughed. "Won't your parents be suspicious?"

"They might, but my mother thinks you are 'very nice' and to be encouraged. She'll make sure my father's kept occupied if he's not going out; and we're OK for at least an hour and half; they never come up here anyway, it's too steep."

Bertie looked around the room. At one time it must have been a servant's bedroom. He walked over to its attic window, gaining a view of the houses near the church, and noting that from here, the Manor meadows, just visible through the trees, resembled a lake.

"I see the floods haven't gone down much," he said.

"Daddy says it's hardly stopped raining since we went away," Melissande replied. "That's good, in a way," she went on; "reinforces our case to try something different. The timing's good, too, with all the politicians trying to out-do each other, promising more homes before there's another property bubble. Have you *really* got stuff you want to discuss or can we 'enjoy each other's company' for a bit? The bed in here's not squeaky – I tried it!"

"Melissande! I'm shocked! Since when has a Rector's daughter been so brazen?"

"Shut the door Bertie," said Melissande loudly. "It's really getting chilly; I'll put on the heater." She pointed, jabbing her finger towards the door, whispering: "Out of earshot, out of mind! Just in case Daddy's lingering at the bottom of the stairs."

Bertie did as he was told, and sat in the armchair that Melissande had placed next to what had become her desk. As a 'staff bedsit' the room had converted easily into a small office and she had arranged cushions along the bed to make it more like a chaise longue. The ceiling sloped down towards the eaves of the roof and Bertie had found that he had to bow a little unless he stayed in the middle of the room or by the window, which had its own little stone-tiled roof, as did the other attic next door, giving The Rectory its characteristic English Baroque air.

"This is a perfect spot for clear thinking!" He commented.

"I used to come up here to do my homework – in summer," said Melissande. "And it's where I wrote the final draft of my thesis, so the very floorboards are loaded with my great thought-waves."

"It must have been them that inspired you when you were writing your feasibility study – it was great! Even Lady Veronica and Arabella perked up."

"Thank you Bertie – but you paid rather more than I deserve!"

"It was worth every penny! The side benefits were the best I've ever had!"

"So you make a practice of seducing your researchers, do you? Just like they do in Parliament! You cad! How could you?"

"How couldn't I? It was mostly down to you! I was most restrained, wasn't I?"

"Not at all – you 'groomed me' and wheedled your way into my affection and became irresistible. I was an innocent virgin before I met you. But I'm so glad I did."

She accepted the invitation he offered as he spread his arms wide – leaving her desk to sit on his lap, kissing him as he held her, his hands exploring her back and neck, seeking their smoothness and shape. He wanted to know her by heart, all over.

"Stop a minute!" She said, before things went further. "There *were* a couple of things I wanted to tell you. I think I've found someone who fits the job description. They phoned me up from the Job Centre and we can interview him on Friday. I suggested we do it at The Manor."

"That's good. We're nearly ready for our first employee!"

"Second – what about me? Don't I count," Melissande tweaked his nose.

"You're a consultant! Much more important: and now you're on the board. I'm glad you've managed to find at least one candidate; I wasn't sure whether we'd find someone who doesn't mind getting his feet muddy as well as being able to draw plans and knock in pegs."

"Well they've come up with a local man who did Countryside Management at Wiltshire College. He's been on their books since he qualified and they've suggested you try him for a couple of months."

"Sounds interesting! What was the other thing?"

"There are two, actually. They're both in my report but I didn't mention them this afternoon in my presentation. One was about the advantage of Tristram being into underwriting and investment. I suggested he could follow up that side of it."

"He could indeed!"

"Our amphib houses are going to cost about twenty per cent more than the equivalent 'rooted' house, but we should be able to get special insurance rates for them. That will make them attractive and help us break even sooner – just a few years. Also, you could lobby politicians for incentive grants to help get the scheme 'afloat'! It's going to save them millions in rescue and relief."

"I'd thought of that last one – I could certainly do some lobbying on that – and Tristram is well up with the insurance. We saw it in your report and talked about it, he and I. You did a super job. Anything else before we clock-off and get down to nicer things?"

"Only that it occurred to me that we might include some kind of corner shop in the apartment complex – and even a delis? They could be next to the residents' car park."

"That's a good idea too – we can get the designers to add that in. Now I'm taking my watch off – and that means it's time to relax. I'm also taking off your specs." He did so, reaching over to place them on her desk.

Melissande shifted on his lap, lying back on him, her head resting on his shoulder. They both looked at the sunset and Bertie absent-mindedly slipped his hand inside her blouse seeking a breast. In silence they watched the sky darken, by which time he wanted to feel the other too, and undid not only the last button on the blouse but also, taking his time, her belt and zip. He was now seeking warm, soft places. She enjoyed this for a while but was becoming hungry to consummate the rising passion and love she felt for this large but gentle man over whom she was draped. The chair cramped her style: she couldn't reach the parts of him she wanted to touch and hold, so she stood up, took his hand and pulled him to his feet.

They embraced and he eased the top of her jeans down over her neat, round bottom. She helped them on their way with a wriggle, treading her way out of them. She checked to see whether the right things were happening to Bertie where they counted, and was able to confirm this in no uncertain way: something needed letting out, urgently.

This was quickly achieved, because Melissande, in her room at the Hotel Ca'Sagredo by The Grand Canal, had learned about men's belts and how to undo them. The pants did not drop but had to be eased off – like her jeans, sensuously and with care. She spent a few moments, busying her fingers around what now stood free: not scary any more, she thought, but immensely desirable: just what she wanted.

"Turn round," said Bertie. She did, and he released the simple catch, allowing her bra to tumble loose from her arms. "Let's try a twerk!"

It was something they'd both observed on television news – a memorable occasion (before they'd ever met) - in what was, the next day, reported as a 'shock horror' scandal in the newspapers when a dancer had celebrated winning some award by performing such a movement on live TV. Melissande had never dared discuss it with anyone until their daring talks in the car on the Dutch motorway, when she had mentioned it as an example of hypocrisy on the part of the press, revelling in forbidden fruit while denouncing it. Melissande, at the time, found the revelation surreptitiously exciting, producing physical responses that had to be immediately subdued; but it had stayed at the back of her mind, simmering.

In the current situation, with them both unclothed and standing as they were, with his skin against hers, all the way down, she knew exactly what to do. She bent over as if to touch her toes but rested her hands on the edge of the bed.

As she stood, she took one arm off the side of the bed, reached back between her parted legs and helped that part of Bertie that couldn't see where it was going, to find her moist self. She pressed it to her, moving it from side to side to share her dew with his rigid member. He leaned over her, running his hands up her spine, massaging any aches or stiffness away while savouring the texture and feel of her skin. She felt her hair stand on end in anticipation.

He was able to reach around her to fondle both breasts at once, from behind, while pressing his penis against her active hand, which guided it into her warmth and tightness. She then gave the cheeky wiggle of her protruding bottom, while pressing backwards. He slid into her until they couldn't be closer, or further locked together.

"We're like forks in a drawer," he murmured. "What a great fit!"

He then ran one hand down over her flat belly and sought the little spot that he now knew gave her so much excitement, and she froze as he found it and – so gently that she wasn't sure whether his finger was still there – began a delicious circling movement that made her breathless with pleasure and passion.

By now, both were almost beside themselves, ready to explode; and Bertie gripped her pelvis with his large hands and pulling her against himself, drove back and forward into her as she corkscrewed back to him.

Melissande could see only her hair as it hung and swung past her face; and Bertie's eyes were closed as they reached their climax simultaneously, their bodies expending the last ounce of energy with wave after wave of rapture until they stood, regaining their composure, a motionless sculpture: tribute to requited love and desire,.

Melissande slipped from under him, lay on to the bed and beckoned. He obeyed and they made the most of his remaining arousal to be once again, deeply connected. She wrapped her legs around his back, and he rested his head beside hers as he crouched above her, supporting his weight on his elbows to save crushing her except where it mattered, groin to groin.

"That was quite something!" Sighed Melissande. "It's christened my office!"

"And I can see why twerking's popular in modern dance!" Remarked Bertie. "It's a step we might practice – but not perhaps at the Hunt Ball."

The rain poured all the way back to The Manor, where the human residents were asleep as Bertie, at ten past ten, torch in one hand, umbrella in the other, reached the Gate Lodge. He had been humming, all the way back from The Rectory. 'I'm singin' in the rain, mm-mm-ming ....in the rain' was going round and round in his head. He felt so happy. Both he and Melissande had been suppressing joyous laughter as they dressed at The Rectory. They felt like naughty children, hearing her father's mild agitation downstairs as he 'accidentally' shut the kitchen door rather loudly and called 'I'll be there in a minute, my dear', to her mother.

The Rector had been hovering for the past fifteen minutes, between the kitchen and his study, passing the bottom of the stairs and wondering whether he should say anything about it 'being rather late', or 'I'd like to lock up soon'. He had been much relieved when he heard the attic door open and Bertie's businesslike tread, slowly descending.

"Thank you very much – a most useful session," he heard Bertie tell Melissande very distinctly, not guessing that its clarity was especially for him. This was answered by a cheerful reply.

"I'm glad you approve," she called; "and I'll change that paragraph and those totals. See you tomorrow?"

"Yes, all being well. Perhaps you could come with me to see the planners?"

"Of course; what time?"

"I'm due there at eleven."

"I'll be there – goodnight!" Melissande closed the attic door firmly – there was no doubt she was going back to work.

"I hope I haven't kept you up?" Said Bertie, as he met The Rector in the front hall.

"Oh no, not at all," lied The Rector. "I was just about to make some cocoa for my wife, and then we shall be retiring. You're just in time for me to lock you out." The last remark was delivered with a friendly laugh indicating that this was his little joke and no offence had been taken.

If he had seen his daughter earlier, collecting her discarded garments from around her office he might not have been so benevolent – although his wife might have been secretly delighted, if a little shocked.

Bertie was about to let himself into the Gate Lodge as quietly as he could, when he was aware that something was happening in the stable yard. He could hear hooves on cobbles, which alerted him instantly, because the only horse present should have been Arabella's stallion and it should be safely in its stall, standing on clean straw. He returned the key to his pocket and made his way quietly up the path towards the stables. Surely it couldn't be Arabella, at this time of night. He knew she was impulsive and headstrong but going riding in the dark would be a bit much for even her.

As he approached the sounds changed, becoming louder and accompanied by metallic crashes, the sliding and striking of iron horseshoes against cobble stones and the clatter of things being knocked over. Something or someone was causing a horse a great deal of aggravation. Bertie went straight to the outside light switch. 'A good job there's a new bulb', he thought.

As the yard lit up the fast-moving tableaux told Bertie exactly what was happening, although he had to jump out of the way of a mass of flying hooves and a horse's gyrating body as the stallion thrashed about the yard, a metal bucket hooked firmly over its head. Blood was running down one of its front legs and, in its state of desperation, the animal was colliding with anything and everything as it backed away from the metal pressing on its muzzle.

It was essential that Bertie put an end to this bedlam before the stallion injured himself more seriously. Bravely, he chased round, keeping 'the right end' of the animal to avoid the vicious kicking and iron shoes sparking on cobbles, and managed to grab the bottom of the bucket with one hand, its handle with the other.

He could see what was needed, the handle having slipped back over the horse's ears as it tried to reach the last few grains at the bottom. When the horse had lifted its head, the bucket must have come with it – driving the animal demented. Bertie flicked the handle forwards just as the horse once more pulled backwards releasing its head.

Regaining its vision, the stallion charged round the yard seeking to make good its escape. Bertie was left holding the bucket, which he lobbed into the tack room out of the way. After two circuits, the stallion stopped, its nostrils wide and its eyes staring, still terrified. It stood stamping and shaking its head.

As calmly as he could, Bertie collected a halter and, talking to the stallion to get its attention and recognition, approached as casually as he could, so as not to provoke another crisis. Patting the animal on its shoulder, he said all the soothing things he could think of before sliding the halter over its nose and head, knotting it and gently but firmly pulling the horse towards its stable. He walked it over to the hay rack and tied the halter to the ring in the wall.

"Now we can look at your injuries," he told the stallion, running his hand comfortingly along its neck and withers. It must have collided with something sharp, because although nothing seemed broken, it plainly needed a few stitches.

What Bertie did *not* know, was that Lady Veronica had also been roused by the noise in the stable yard and had gone to her bedroom window to see whether she could detect anything between a gap in the curtains. She had been standing there when Bertie switched on the yard light and had watched the whole drama. As he led the now subdued stallion into the stable, she clapped with pleasure and admiration at his courageous action. This was indeed the kind of man The Manor needed. Wouldn't it be fortuitous if he and Arabella felt some mutual attraction. She had noted recently that Arabella was treating Bertie with more respect and was keeping her fingers crossed for the family succession. This Tristram person, despite his good looks and deep pockets had not struck her as being 'quite the right quality'.

Lady Veronica was asleep before the vet arrived, having been dragged out of his bed by Bertie's calling the number pinned up in the tack room. The stallion was duly repaired and Bertie was left with instructions as to further treatment.

"Give us a call," said the vet, "if you feel any heat around the leg when you change the dressing. Better safe than sorry: hang on to his head while I give him a shot of antibiotic, would you?"

Bertie eventually got back to the Gate Lodge, hung his wet coat and hat on the back of a kitchen chair, near the boiler in the Lodge kitchen. The cat opened its eyes but didn't bother to greet him, and Reg slept through it all.

As Bertie turned his bedside light out, he reflected that this had been another notable day out of the three hundred and sixty-six that he was devoting to the future: love, passion, and adventure - like braving both The Rector *and* Arabella's stallion.

"Eat your heart out, Dick Whittington!" He chuckled as he pulled up the eiderdown.

CHAPTER 21

"It's Tristram, for you", Reg told Bertie a few days later. Bertie got up from the breakfast table and went into the tiny hall to take the call.

"Hello Tristram – it's me! Can't you sleep?"

"I'm not up yet – wanted to catch you before you went off paddling." Tristram sounded bullish. "It's been quite something," he said. "I mentioned our project to a couple of chaps and they caught on straight away. They said they'd been looking for something different to spice things up. The mortgage market has been rubbish: these new stupid rules. We might be on to a good thing. How long before we can launch?"

"Any time soon," said Bertie. "Melissande's tidying up some of the sums she's been projecting and we've been getting some quotes before signing contracts. Give it about a month and we'll be there. I'd say end of May would be a good moment: what do you think?"

"Should give people time to make up their minds and get things tied up before they take off for the summer," said Tristram. "My office has done all the necessaries – the company's registered and we're all legal; Penworthy's done his stuff."

"What's our final name? Don't want to tread on any toes!"

"We settled on what Melissande suggested: *'Amphib 21 Limited'*."

"Says what it ought, doesn't it? Fine by me!" Said Bertie; "let me ask Reg, he's sitting just through the door here."

Tristram was slighting miffed at having to wait, but knew better than to show it: Bertie had his little quirks. What did it matter what the old man thought?

"Like I said before: as long as folk don't think it's some kind of motorboat," said Reg. "Or it might be something to do with the last war – Normandy landings and all that – p'raps not a bad thing? There's been a lot on telly, seventy years isn't it?"

Tristram had an answer ready when Bertie relayed the remark.

"We thought of that," he said. "The logo is a simplified modern house in a blue squiggle – the picture tells all! Wait 'til you see it!"

"What's the 'twenty one'?" Reg had forgotten.

"Twenty First Century: not something set up by Queen Victoria!" Said Bertie.

"I remember now," said Reg. "I'd better write that down. It's the first time I've been on the board of anything – can't think why you want *me*!"

"Because of your common sense, Reg; but I'd better listen to Tristram: I'm sure he's got more to say." He took his hand from covering the mouthpiece of the phone.

"When you've quite finished, down there in the swamps," said Tristram, with as good humour as he could muster.

"You're right: sorry! We'd better get together to work out how we sell the idea, don't you think?" Suggested Bertie, aware that his old friend was getting touchy. "Perhaps we'd better come up to Town? Get things set up?" The thought of taking Melissande to London for a couple of days had flashed into his head: delightful!"

"Suit yourself, old boy. I've got nothing much on: I could come down if you like – I know Arabella'll be there at the weekend. She wants to award you a medal for saving the day with her horse – she's been highly chuffed about it. Her aunt gave her chapter and verse. If you come up here I'm sure she'll organise some celebration."

"I bet they over-blew my part in the affair," said Bertie, modestly.

"Not according to Bella! She's waxing lyrical!"

"Well let's make it early next week – I'll see what Mel's got in her diary and we can book rooms at The Club."

"I thought you'd given London up for good: you haven't been near the place!"

"Well I haven't been sitting on my arse like you! I've been getting a life – muddy boots and all that! Wild horses etcetera!"

"Becoming a real bumpkin, what?"

"Naff off Batty!"

"You too Bert!"

They put their phones down with a smile. Tristram had to reach across the drowsy body of Arabella to do so.

"You weren't far wrong about having 'not much on'," she commented, as she gave him a slap on his bare bottom.

"Are you getting provocative? Two can play at that game!" Tristram leaned down and pretended to bite her ear. He and his lithe companion then got mixed up in a romp that ended the usual way, entangled and exhausted, reaching for their nicotine inhalators.

To interview the company's first employee it had been agreed that Lady Veronica, representing family (because Arabella was 'busy in London'), Bertie, Melissande and Mr Penworthy should be 'the panel'.

Melissande, as Finance Director, had authorised the young man to pay for a taxi to reach The Manor. This had raised some concern. When told about it Clive Penworthy had asked: "surely he ought to have his own transport?".

"He's been out of work since he left college and due to an accident in which his motorcycle was written off, he's been dependent on public transport for the past two months," the Job Centre had informed them. "He has been unable to find a bus which passes The Manor."

"Doesn't show much initiative, does it?" Bertie said, as the panel took their places. "You'd have thought he could have got someone to give him a lift – borrow a pushbike or even walk!"

"What counts is whether he can do what he's asked," said Lady Veronica, sagely. "Too much initiative isn't always a good thing. Let's see what he's like."

The Job Centre, for its part, had found it difficult to persuade Travis to attend the interview.

"I'm not sure I fancy going there," he told his advisor. "I was assaulted by someone connected with that lot."

"You ought to give it a go, Mr Bunt," said the advisor. "We don't want you to get the reputation of refusing opportunities, do we? I strongly advise you not to miss this one; it could have repercussions on your benefits."

Travis told his father the Job Centre 'had 'im by the balls'.

"Well, they're not going to eat you, are they," said his dad. "What sort of job is it anyway?"

"Something to do with 'land development'. Only for a couple of months and it's mostly outdoors, they said."

"There you are, then. You might like it! Give it a go – do yourself up nice – get your 'air cut."

"That's good, coming from you, Dad! Your ponytail doesn't go with a bald top: you can't talk."

"I'm not applying for a job, am I? It's you, Travis – you need it. You gotta do *something*."

Danielle took a bit more convincing. When Trevor told her about Travis's pending interview she put two and two together and instantly made four.

"It's bound to be for that daft housing scheme," she said, as Trevor unwrapped the chips.

"He'll need waders then, won't he?" Laughed Trevor. "It's still under water – they'll never be able to start."

"It's going to make *me* look silly if your boy's going to work for the other side – with me trying to make sure it doesn't happen," she retorted.

"I've been thinking about that, too," said Trevor. "You remember you said you didn't want this van to shine too much 'cos the Council's being funny about it?"

"Of course I do! It's all wrong I can't live here. I'm not hurting anyone and we blend in nicely."

"We did when it was all green, but since I cleaned it the bright cream does stand out a bit," said Trevor. "If you kick up too much fuss, someone will catch on and start having a go at you! It'd be much more to the point havin' someone working for the other side – get in wiv 'em."

"I hadn't thought of that," said Danielle, reconsidering. She decided to encourage Travis to go and attend the interview as being 'a good thing', offering to wash and iron his best shirt for the occasion.

It was, nevertheless, a shock to Travis when Reg showed him into the dining room at The Manor, seeing as chairman the man who had punched him in the shopping mall that time; and next to him, the starchy cow with the glasses who'd been with him.

Bertie, however, didn't recognise his former foe, dressed up for the occasion. He did, however, observe the way Travis reacted as he caught his eye.

Bertie thought he would try to put him at ease by asking a few sympathetic questions.

"The taxi knew where to find us, then?"

"Oh yeah; no trouble." Travis shuffled, not knowing whether to cross his legs or let them sprawl. Finally he remembered to sit up straight as advised by Danielle, who had checked him out before he embarked on this venture.

"I understood you had a motor-cycle?" Asked Bertie. "A pity it wasn't able to bring you today."

"No, I come off it: not much good after that: a write-off, like."

It was Travis's voice that rang a bell. Bertie had heard it before and the accent was familiar.

"Haven't we met? I'm sure I know your voice."

Travis coughed, holding his hand up to his mouth. This was a situation that called for maximum good manners. He was finding himself in an awkward spot within the first few seconds of his interview. He decided his identity would have to come out sometime, so it would be better to get it over with.

"Well, like: I did come up the lane this way a few times – on the bike – and we might have met then."

It all came back: that voice, the accent – the way a muddy fist had delivered him a black eye. He recalled, too, the satisfaction that followed, seeing the deliverer lying on his back beside the motorbike, cooling off in the mud.

"Oh yes! I do remember now. It wasn't a very amicable introduction, as I recall."

"No, well.....".

"And we did exchange a few blows on another occasion too, didn't we?" Bertie was enjoying the memory of the second encounter, during which he himself suffered no damage except sore knuckles."

"Well, yeah......"

Travis put his knees together, as Danielle had suggested during her coaching, and refreshed his 'sitting up straight'. This interview was making him feel distinctly queasy.

Bertie noted the change in attitude. No longer the foul-mouthed yob – this was someone eating humble pie, obviously trying to hold himself together. At least Bertie knew the boy was vigorous and strong. To be fair – and since no one else had applied for the job – Bertie decided he should try to help Travis show the panel why he deserved at least a fair shot at it.

"Let's start again, then, shall we, Mr Bunt? These are all different circumstances – and I note, from the state of our lane, that you no longer go in for scrambling."

"No, I've given up all that," said Travis, subdued. "I finished college now: got better things ... you know ."

It was a characteristic – he didn't finish sentences but nodded, hoping to be understood.

Bertie asked about Travis's interest in wildlife, the countryside, and his recent courses at Wiltshire College and the atmosphere began to relax. Lady Veronica began to 'quite take to him', as being a rough diamond. She asked about his family life, discovering he was from a one-parent family, no longer having a mother and this touched her – never having had a much-wanted son. He had a certain honesty about him and inside the big frame was probably quite a timid creature seeking a niche in life.

It appeared that Travis had acquired just the kind of skills needed at this stage of *Amphib 21*'s development. Melissande was the one who asked the technical questions, having learned the terms and language used in surveying and civil engineering during her intensive research for the project. She was impressed by his grasp of the subject. What sealed it for her was when she questioned him about the concept of amphibious houses.

"What do you think of the idea of having houses that don't just stay put and go under water, but float up above the flood?"

"Good idea!" Said Travis. "I've heard about that: they done it in 'olland; we had a video in our 'climate change' module."

Bertie asked the final question.

"If we were to offer you this role, how do you think you'd come to work, since there's no public transport except later in the day."

"I've thought about that," said Travis, now feeling he had a chance of doing something quite interesting and lucrative. "My dad's girlfriend's got a pushbike. She says I can borrow it." He was pleased to notice Lady Veronica nodding approval.

By the time he left Travis learned he would be appointed for a six-week trial period at a wage a lot more tempting than Jobseeker's Allowance.

"Who's going to give our man his orders every day?" Asked Lady Veronica, after Travis's appointment had been agreed and he'd gone on his way. Her Ladyship may not have been sensible with money in the past but setting the staff about its duty each day had been something she'd learned from her mother. With Reg it was hardly necessary; the cat made its own demands and the drawing-room fire likewise, but she didn't like the idea of people not knowing what was required of them.

"I think Melissande should," said Bertie. "She's dealing with the practical end of things until now." He turned to her. "You'll be writing to him, offering him the job, won't you?"

"Yes, if you like. I'd better tell the Jobcentre, too, hadn't I?"

"I expect they'll want to know," said Reg. "What do you want him to do first then, boss?" he added with a twinkle.

Melissande couldn't help the blush but rather liked being asked.

"I'd like him to make a detailed map of what's there now. We shall want to save as much of the landscape as possible: like hedges and especially the larger trees. After all this flooding I expect some of them will die off but the rest of them will probably have preservation orders. The design for where the water comes in and leaves is going to depend on what's there already. The less earth we have to move, the better the bottom line! I'd say we could do with a contour map, too. It's all quite level until you get towards this side. The architects will have to make more precise measurements but having a detailed plan will give everyone a better idea of where houses, roads and services might go."

"You are right," said Bertie. "It will test his initiative – I guess he could do worse than start with Google Earth, then go round taking photos and noting what's what. We can use it to brief the creative team to make everything fit together – houses, flats, car parking – all that kind of thing."

"Where do we get 'a creative team'?" Asked Lady Veronica. "It sounds like football!"

"It is rather, Lady V'," said Bertie. "I've got loads of contacts who can fit the bill – some of the best people around and they'd love to do something useful instead of just trying to flog things nobody wants. We'll need surveyors and civil engineers, too."

"Only one of each, I hope!" Mr Penworthy was thinking of the costs.

"Well, if we're going to launch at the end of May, we'll have to get our skates on," said Bertie. "Don't worry, the building contractors have their own folk to do that sort of thing – all we've got to do is produce the outline."

"Will you have several builders all working at the same time? I imagine that could be rather chaotic," commented Lady Veronica. She was remembering some of the discussions she'd had with her dear late husband when he had reached a similar position with his plans.

"I think it would be better to go with one of the big contractors like Barratts or Wimpeys, don't you?" said Melissande. "They must have experience of managing things like this."

"I thought everyone could build something they fancied," said Reg. "You were talking about a competition to see who could come up with the nicest house, bobbin' up and down on the waves."

"I don't see why that shouldn't still be the case. The contractor will be able to follow individual plans to suit the buyers, even though it does cost more. We want loads of variety but with everything working – like drains, water and electricity."

"So how do you choose your 'big builder'?" Asked Lady Veronica.

"I think we should have our launch, to show off what we have in mind, and then see who comes forward," said Melissande. "I'm going to have to go now, because Arabella will be here any minute and I don't want her to find the stables looking mucky; I must check on my invalid, too."

"I thought he was better. Isn't he?" Bertie remarked.

"The vet's stopped coming and he's getting quite stroppy. I think he'll soon be ready for a canter."

"As long as she keeps him away from that blasted donkey!" Said Bertie.

"If we're taking on that boy Travis, the donkey's going to be part of the family!" Said Reg. "Its owner is his father's girlfriend. They live in that caravan, so I heard."

"You see? That's the kind of thing we need to know," said Lady Veronica. "Your local knowledge makes you a really useful company director, Mr Haines. I remember seeing her picture in the local paper, creating a palaver about our project! We shall have to be circumspect in that direction."

Arabella decided to drive down to the Manor at the weekend. It would give her the chance to take Bertie out for a meal or even a trip somewhere. Aunt Veronica wouldn't mind if she invited him back to the house so she too could express her appreciation for his courageous intervention over the stallion, which, Melissande told her, was now well on his way to recovery having been patched up by the vet.

Arabella thought she would have Bertie to herself, once Melissande had finished her morning chores. She had no idea of what was going on between her stable-maid and the general labourer-cum-baronet. Whether it would have made any difference to her strategy if she *had* known, is another matter. Arabella was a great believer in everything being fair in love, business and war. She wasn't sure quite how one defined 'love' (though she understood the other two). Certainly she found Tristram very good in bed, which everyone described as 'love-making'; but was it enough? It wasn't that she didn't enjoy his company, too, but maybe he was too much like herself to make long-term commitment attractive. He would probably start playing away, once he'd got over the initial fun of the honeymoon: but so would she, if she were honest with herself; once she'd managed to produce some kind of heir.

Both potential husbands were well off, good-looking and full of life but Bertie was the better bet – especially with the added attribute of a title. He'd be more likely to keep the home fires burning in Suffolk while she could continue her 'career', keeping an eye on Tytherton Kellaway and conducting 'freelance PR' based on the London flat. She might even be able to continue a fun relationship with Tristram, too, as long as they were discreet.

Discretion, however, was a strong point in Bertie and Melissande's relationship, hence Arabella still being in the dark. While she was packing her sexiest lingerie and seamless jodhpurs, checking reserves of 'the pill' and all necessities for Bertie's seduction, she was unaware that she might be encroaching on her loyal friend's territory.

As far as Bella was concerned, Melissande was only interested in Bertie because he was paying her for some paperwork. She was ignorant of the trysts, two or three times a week in the attic office at The Rectory. As she sat with Tristram in the stalls of a theatre in the West End that night, she had no suspicion that Bertie and Melissande were engaged in sexual acts that were giving them untold joy and satisfaction.

At The Rectory the happy couple finally fell apart, trying to get their breath back. They were blissfully happy. It wasn't simply the physical release of the lust they felt for each other but the ever-growing bond of permanence: wanting to be with each other all the time; not necessarily having sex, talking or working but knowing the other was there, silent or not, in good health and contented.

Bertie had never been happier and was telling Melissande about it, once his heartbeat had slowed as they lay comfortably enmeshed in each other's arms and legs.

"You are such bliss!" He told her. "And so full of surprises!"

"What do you mean?"

"Well, when I met you, it could never have entered my mind that you might be such a fantastic lover. You gave off vibes which said 'I'm not like that!' I thought you were a typical Sunday school teacher – likely to finish up with a dog collar and cassock, like your father."

"I think I might have done – once I'd come to terms with all the terminology."

"What do you mean?"

"Well – I can't swallow all this 'Creator God' business, as though one's addressing some happy grandad."

Bertie was in agreement.

"I suppose," he said, "it all depends what you mean by 'God', doesn't it? I find it completely potty, the way they witter on about 'God loving you'. I'd never be accepted as a vicar. I don't see how anyone can if they are intellectually honest with themselves. At school we had to say the creed all the time and it felt like perjury every time."

"I agree – it is, if you haven't worked out what 'God' means. Generations of men have muddled their way through what they call 'theology', wangling it so they become authorities on the subject and gain power over everyone else!"

"Doesn't it make you attack your Dad?" Bertie chuckling at Melissande's vehemence.

"It did when I was fourteen. Poor Daddy, I used to give him a hard time! I grew out of it."

"You might even have followed his footsteps!"

"Well yes, until I met you. He presented me with his own conclusions and I found them – and still find them – convincing. He says forget all the guff and go straight to what that carpenter used to say because it's as valid now as ever it was. Jesus was brilliant, even when he was only about twelve – and he defined 'God' as being 'love'. He said it – told everyone and they didn't understand – it was too simple."

"So can you substitute 'love' every time someone says 'God'?"

"It works if you do! You can't beat Jesus' logical plan for peace or survival of humanity: it's fantastic!"

" I hope it's not me who has ruined your career by leading you into 'sin'. You'd make a great priest: even a bishop!"

"Not ruined! You've released me from all kinds of prejudices that I never realised I had! I can't believe how wonderfully free and bursting with life I now feel. The sex thing had been like an iron curtain. It blocked so many ways forward: I always had to hold back from close relationships and keep myself sterile by not being able to embrace anyone freely without guilt." She kissed his encircling arm.

"It's not my parents' fault," she said. "That was the way they were brought up. When I was little, I remember my mother remarking how 'disgusting' it was, people snogging in public. I was taught that anything below the belt – and above it, once I developed breasts – was 'out of bounds', forbidden territory which mustn't be touched until you were married and that any pleasure, accidentally – or worse, on purpose – derived from those areas was sinful."

Melissande's hand was now absent-mindedly feeling for that part of Bertie's anatomy that had so recently been giving them both so much pleasure.

"I say – be careful, or you'll get everything going again," he said. "But what I'd like to know is, how could it be possible for you to have changed from being so virginal to becoming red hot in bed! You've picked it all up remarkably quickly!"

"It's because once I'd been given a sensible analysis of the issues involved everything became legitimate! My natural urges and desires, if expressed in 'love' – by which I mean 'doing as I would be done by and more' – couldn't possibly be sinful. My carpenter guru's guidelines are what define us human primates as different from our ape cousins. All those sexy things I enjoy doing to you and all those super-duper things you do with me all become legitimate, desirable, positive, right and proper! I can suck your toes (after a bath, of course) or any other bits I fancy and you can do the same to me but as long as we are considerate and are prepared to justify the consequences, even unexpected ones, I'm not being 'sinful' or negative."

"But you are so uninhibited! I thought *I* was a rascal but you've taught me all kinds of fun I never knew about."

"I suppose it was because I was like an arrow loaded on to a bow-string – held back by the two fingers of conscience and external discipline. Your logic and approach to me tickled the bowman under the armpits, making him release the arrow, which has soared into the sky. All that energy, a bit of imagination and the removal of restraint and, as you say – it's been great, hasn't it?"

"And you *are* taking the pill, aren't you? I mean, once we got going....."

"Oh Lord yes! It would be sad and wrong to create a new life unless we both agreed beforehand, wouldn't it?"

"Yes of course: and, by the way, which lord are you calling on? I'm only a baronet!"

"Never mind – you'll do; but I'm hoping you might want to create another one at some stage, and with a bit of luck it will be with me as its mother – but I wouldn't dream of telling you." Melissande giggled.

CHAPTER 22

Arabella's journey down the M4 was not quite as nightmarish as the last time, when the rain and wind had forced the nose-to-tail London-to-Bristol traffic to a crawl. Today it was not raining. For the first time for weeks the windscreen wipers rested; nevertheless, she took the slightly longer route home by coming off at Junction 15 to get away from the relentless concentration of being part of a moving belt of traffic in which no part may touch any of the others on pain of expense and bad temper. She would weave her away across the Marlborough Downs, going past reminders of ancient Britain like Avebury and Tilbury Hill.

She didn't mind having to creep along behind a large tractor, the eight shining shares of its plough reflecting every movement until it turned off into a walled farmyard. The slower pace was helping her wind down after London's clamour; giving her time to consider how she was going to win Bertie's affection.

Arriving at Tytherton Kellaway, she parked, took her suitcase to her room and went to greet her aunt, installed by the fire in the drawing room.

"Just in time for a sherry, Arabella," said Lady Veronica. "Would you like to pour one? It will save me getting up. Haines has just gone home. We've had such an interesting meeting this afternoon – about my dear John's scheme. It really is going to happen at last. We're going to be busy as bees!"

"I hope I didn't miss anything important," said Arabella. She knew perfectly well what the meeting had been about, because Melissande had briefed her by telephone and it had been boring but Arabella wanted to show her aunt she was interested and taking an active part.

The fact that it would bring her into Bertie's company more often was, of course, immaterial.

"I think we managed quite well, although you might have found it somewhat trying. We interviewed a young man to work for us."

"Why's that then? I don't usually find young men a problem."

"Well it turned out to be the one who made such a mess of our lane with his motor-bike; although I hasten to add that after another accident since then it no longer works, so he came by taxi."

"What a cheek, coming back here!"

"He had to, according to Melissande. Otherwise he might have lost his job-seeker's allowance. In any case, he seems to be a reformed character."

"Perhaps Bertie knocked some sense into him!"

"That's not something I know about," said Lady Veronica, "but we have decided to take him on, as long as you and your friend, whose name I forget at the moment, agree to it."

"You mean Tristram?"

"That's the one! Have you seen him lately?"

Arabella didn't enlarge on Bertie's smiting of the wretched Bunt – if Aunt Veronica didn't know, so be it, and she wanted to play down Tristram's importance in her life – at least for the moment.

"I saw Tristram this morning, actually. I expect he'll agree: you must have thought that man was worth hiring."

"We did: he has been on a countryside course at Lackham and seemed keen to come and work here. After interviewing him, Bertie did mention something about an altercation on some previous occasion; and something about a donkey too, which I didn't quite catch. My hearing is nearly as bad as my memory nowadays! But how are you, Arabella?"

"I'm fine, thanks, Auntie. I'll just go and dust myself down – after I've got you your drink – because I want to see Bertie to thank him for rescuing my horse."

"Such a to-do! It gave me quite a fright. I watched the whole thing from my window; I was *so* impressed. He really was gallant. Such a fine man!"

"That's what I've been thinking," said Arabella, encouraging this train of thought. She served the sherry and went to her room, where she decided what to wear for the next part of her assault plan. She had brought a pair of the skinniest jeans and accompanying thong, to avoid any lines across the perfect curves of her bottom. Having put them on, she stood by the mirror and looked at them over her shoulder. She thought that, to a man like Bertie, they would be eminently pattable and she imagined his warm hand resting there. The thought made her quite lusty. She had already planned what to do on the top half. It was warm enough to do without her bra and the combination of a short top that just covered her breasts, unless she reached high, when a spectator could catch sight of two firm and self-supporting but full white globes, (but not quite their rosy pink centres of interest).

To go with this risqué garment, she had packed an embroidered waistcoat she had bought in Switzerland last winter, with just such a spring event in mind. To complete her 'sexy country look' she thought a pony tail would give her that healthy outdoor appeal that Bertie would surely find irresistible. A touch of make-up........ and scent...... there!

The only decision remaining was how many buttons to leave undone. There were only three and leaving all of them open might appear slovenly. Two, however, might allow a curious male tantalising glimpses of what was so skimpily covered. She undid the second one. Ready for the fray, she collected her bag and a carrier bag, labelled 'Harrods', with silk cord handles. This contained a bottle of Veuve Cliquot champagne in its golden box.

If only the bloody mobiles would work, here at The Manor. She wanted Bertie on his own and it was pointless trying to call him unless both of them were on higher ground like the folly on its knoll. How ridiculous – in this modern age – having to retreat to a mock Roman temple to make one's mobile work. She would try texting. If that brought no response, she'd have to go down to the Gate Lodge. She collected a couple of champagne flutes from the kitchen and slipped them into the top of her Harrods carrier, each wrapped in a paper napkin to stop them clinking. Then, having slipped her feet into ankle boots, she paused to send her invitation.

She had obtained Bertie's number from Tristram, who thought she was still on her intelligence mission concerning Bertie's intentions. As far as he was concerned it was quite a good wheeze which his old pal would doubtless enjoy.

No reply – even after ten minutes and two cigarettes. Oh well, nothing to it but to go down to the Gate Lodge and dig him out.

Bertie and Reg were watching TV news when they heard a knock on the door. Bertie, got up and went to see who it might be.

What a sight greeted him. Wreathed in smiles, the friendliest Arabella he'd yet seen; and a cleavage that really was most eye-catching. A chap's eyes couldn't help but be drawn towards the pale white skin so rarely displayed, for tonight, even more was on show than usual. A gold chain disappeared enticingly into a soft valley, making Bertie wonder what might be dangling on the end.

"I say! What a treat for sore eyes," he exclaimed. "Hello Bella! Do come in!" He stood back and held the door wide open.

"No I won't thanks," she replied, somewhat breathless. She knew this shortness of breath was seductive, having used the technique before. "I just wanted to ask if you could spare a minute to come up to show me what's being done for the poor stallion."

"Certainly," he said. "Just give me a couple of seconds to get a jacket: you go ahead, I'll follow."

"OK – two minutes then – I'll go on up." Arabella turned quickly, making sure that he was still looking. She wanted him to get a good view of her rear as she walked away.

He did: and remembered that this same spectacle was what had beguiled him into following the horse's hoof-prints into a hidden lane and what had become one of his life's most exciting and happy episodes. He took a jacket, hurrying to follow her so he could enjoy the vision of what his subconscious was calling 'this perfect arse' while his conscience and sense of fairness added 'but no nicer than Melissande's'.

Taking long strides he set off in pursuit, disguising any urgency by whistling 'Waltzing Matilda', a tune that Australia had implanted on his internal player during youthful surfing visits.

As you will remember, whistling had a strange effect on Arabella, which she did not welcome, but she couldn't say anything until they neared the stable. She stopped walking and waited for him to catch up. She had to actually, to prevent herself having a 'little accident'. She forced herself to smile, although her teeth felt gritted.

"Bertie, dear, please stop whistling – it upsets the stallion."

"Oh sorry!" Said Bertie, remembering her previous predicament and not allowing himself to chuckle or make any facetious remark. He was on best behaviour, partly out of loyalty to Melissande, whose friend this was, and partly because he wanted Arabella's full support with TGP – having learned how effective she had been with other campaigns in the past few years. He was quite surprised he had not come across her sooner, having consulted a few friends in the PR/lobbying profession – perhaps she had been engaged by a different sector of the market. This in itself could be a benefit – spreading the word beyond his usual circle.

Arabella managed to trip over a protruding cobble stone, shortly after resuming her progress towards the stable, and fortunately staggered backwards into the polite arms of the man behind her. She allowed him to set her back on her feet, looking up at him with grateful eyes wide open with admiration. She put her hand on his arm and took the last few steps into the stable yard leaning affectionately on his assistance.

"How silly of me!" She simpered.

Bertie detached himself to have both hands free as he opened the stallion's stable door, taking hold of the halter that Melissande had left on the animal for easy catching during his recovery.

"Steady old boy!" Said Bertie. "Just want to have a look – no injections or anything, don't worry!" The stallion knew him well by now, and was reassured by his tone of voice. He also recognised Arabella, of whom he was not so fond, having experienced her little tantrums when he took fright at something scary like a piece of waste paper on the path. She usually expressed herself to him with her riding crop. He hated being struck with it around the head, which she had done, and this had not endeared him to his owner.

Arabella went down on one knee and took a cursory examination of the bandage below the stallion's knee, placing her hand above and then below the dressing.

"It feels cool enough now," she remarked, knowledgeably.

"Melissande seems pleased with his progress," agreed Bertie.

"That's great!" Arabella turned towards Bertie, making sure he got a good view down her top. "Now let's leave him to settle for the night; I've prepared a little something in the tack room. Come on – follow me," she said, mysteriously.

Entering the tack room, Bertie was taken aback to see three neat hay bales arranged like a smiley face on the floor. On the middle one, was a round tray on which were a bottle of champagne, dewy with cold, and two glasses.

She had placed a horse blanket, neatly folded, on each of the accompanying bales to make comfortable seats.

"Goodness!" Said Bertie, "someone's planning a party!"

"It's for you, Bertie," gushed Arabella, putting her hand on his arm again and managing to lean against him before turning once more to display her magnificent rear before depositing it on one of the bale seats. "Do sit down. This is my little thank you for being such a brick the other night. Aunt Veronica told me all about it!"

"I'm sure she must have exaggerated," muttered Bertie. "It was nothing, really; I just happened to be around to steady him up."

"That's not what I heard. Go on, Bertie, open the bottle. We must drink your health, and you can tell me about this fellow you interviewed. Is he really the one you beat up that night? Unbelievable! They say he's reformed!"

This was what Bertie had been hoping – for Arabella to show some interest in TGP. As well as paying off what The Manor owed him it was to her own benefit to get the place back on its feet financially. He told her about Travis's interview, playing down the young man's previous reputation and emphasising his recent qualification.

"I think he gulped a bit when he saw me," laughed Bertie, "but he soon got over it. We'll see how he gets on with the first assignment. We've asked him to map all the existing features one could recognise on the chosen meadows – trees and ditches and so on."

"That's going to be difficult until the flood's gone down, isn't it?" Asked Arabella.

"That's what he said, but we asked how he felt about using a plastic rowing boat. The idea appealed to him and he actually smiled and said he loved boats and it would be great!"

"I suppose we ought to make sure that each house has a punt of some sort – so they can collect the morning paper. It might become quite a fashion accessory!"Arabella was becoming creative.

"We'll tell our design team not to forget the complications of becoming temporarily cut off from the road," said Bertie. "We might also need to provide a boatman to do the rounds – say once an hour during flooded periods to carry people and goods. You could include it as part of the service charge. The boatman could keep the grass cut when it's dry."

"What would happen to their cars? You can't just let them sink or float off when The Avon decides to move in, can you?"

Arabella was now showing that she had indeed been considering how the scheme might work.

"You are right," said Bertie. "I think part of our ground-boatman's duties would be to make sure that cars are moved to the higher and drier car park, further up the slope near the Roman Temple."

"That makes sense. We could use that for other activities during the dry season, too."

"Good thinking!" Applauded Bertie, beginning to feel mellow as Arabella poured him a second glass. "Pity we don't have any peanuts!"

"Ah, but we do," said Arabella, producing a packet of nibbles from the carrier bag by her bale. Knowing Bertie was keen to tell her more about plans for the amphibious community, Arabella asked more questions in her best, most intelligent way.

What with the rapid-action alcohol working on his brain, and the change of attitude of his former haughty employer, Bertie was enjoying his unexpected sojourn with this highly desirable young creature. She was hardly recognisable, (except from behind), as the same person who had not previously deigned to show him much civility. He said to himself: 'she's really quite something!' as his eyes once more caught sight of momentary display of a neat navel when Arabella raised her glass to emphasise a point she was making; and a little more when she raised both arms to indicate 'grand events' that might be possible.

She was giving this animated display of ideas to make most use of the little garment she had put on for the occasion. Her gestures exposed just enough to be seductive but not vulgar.

Bertie told himself he was not lusting after her but simply appreciating her attributes, so ably displayed. His heart and mind were comfortably the property of his beloved Melissande – although Arabella, he hoped, was still in the dark about it. Mel had been adamant that she didn't want Bella to know, because it was, for the moment, their secret.

Melissande had told him: "I'd be so embarrassed if she found out we'd been to bed together. She'd make all kinds of lewd remarks and it would be awful!"

What neither Bertie nor Arabella knew, was that Lady Veronica, following the drama the other night with the stallion, was now extra-observant of what was going on beyond her bedroom window. She had just noticed lights on at the stable. In the interests of security, she thought she'd better alert Arabella, who she knew was visiting Reg and Bertie.

She picked up her ancient but still functional telephone by her bed and dialled Reg's number. It took some time to answer but a sleepy Reg finally got there.

"Yes? 'Ello!" He did not sound best pleased.

"Oh, Mr Haines – I'm so sorry to bother you so late, but I'm worried: there are lights on in the stable yard again and I thought I'd better tell Arabella and Bertie. Do you think I might speak to them?"

"I'd say yes, but they're not 'ere, your ladyship. They went out about an hour ago."

"Oh – in that case I'm terribly sorry to have dragged you to the phone. Please excuse me." She said good night and put the telephone down. They must have gone for a walk. But *something* was going on in the stable yard and it might be a burglar or horse thief. She couldn't *see* anything happening from where she was, but who could tell?

There was little she could do in any case, being old and feeble, but Lady Veronica felt she couldn't simply leave things as they were. It was her responsibility as Lady of the Manor to ensure that matters were attended to. Then it came to her: she would telephone Melissande. She would know what to do.

Fifteen minutes later, Melissande having hurried across to the Manor, approached the stable yard quietly, not wishing to confront intruders, arrived at the tack room just as Arabella had her arms around Bertie's neck, kissing him passionately on the mouth, pressing her body against his, one foot cocked off the ground like a Hollywood heroine.

To Melissande, the whole horror of the situation was like a still from a movie. The empty bottle and glasses, the cosy seats, the embrace; the scanty garb of her school-mate as she locked on to the only man to whom Melissande had ever given herself.

It was like being shot in the head: shocking, impossible, unbearable, intolerable! She gave a gasping sob, turned and fled.

The two heads engaged in the kiss turned just in time to see the dismay on Melissande's face as she put both hands to her mouth and disappeared into the darkness.

"Oh shit!" Said Arabella, releasing Bertie from her assault. Melissande's arriving just when Bella was going in for the kill had ruined the whole evening! And why the Hell did she then have to make such a fuss? Anyone would think Melissande had caught someone shagging her husband! What did it matter to her? She was a stable maid at The Manor – and OK, was doing some work for Bertie but whether Arabella wanted to enjoy Bertie's body or not was nothing to do with Melissande!

For Bertie, as for Melissande, things could not have been worse. It had happened so suddenly. Before Arabella had pounced on him, he had just been saying how nice it was of her to arrange this little 'thank-you' party – though quite unnecessary, anyone would have done the same to rescue a distressed horse – and had stood up to begin making his way back to the Gate Lodge and bed. Arabella had risen too, and lunged forward, throwing her arms around his neck, planting one almighty mouth-open kiss right on him, taking him completely off balance. He had been forced to grab her to save himself falling backwards over the bale.

Just at that very instant he had heard Melissande's cry of anguish and shock, followed by the vision of her stricken face before she had gone, without a word, away from a scene of what must have looked like sordid treachery.

"What ever's got into her?" Said Arabella, furious at the interruption that had spoiled her carefully organised advance.

Bertie, slightly befuddled by more than half of the contents of the champagne bottle, felt as though his guts had dropped out. He had never felt worse. Despite the slowness of his reaction he knew that this must have destroyed Melissande – mistakenly and so unjustly!

He had had no idea that Arabella was going to leap on him like that, otherwise he would never have allowed it. In the old days, before he met Melissande, he'd have welcomed such a blatant invitation to get his hands on that delectable backside but that was all over and done. He had no desire or need to accept offers such as had just been made. Indeed, the kiss was not pleasant, tasting of cigarette; and the crude way she was hanging on his neck and pushing herself against him was a real turn-off – and now for *this* to happen. Poor Melissande!

It was a total disaster and he had to act fast, but without Arabella finding out that Melissande was his only true love.

"You'll have to excuse me, Arabella. I must go – an early start in the morning, you know." Then he added, almost as a passing remark: "Poor Melissande – I wonder what's the matter?"

"God knows! She can be odd at times – don't take any notice. I never do!"

Lady Veronica was relieved when she heard Arabella shut the kitchen door, rather loudly, a few minutes later. She called downstairs:

"Bella – is that you? What's been happening? I was so worried. Did Melissande find you?"

"Absolutely nothing, Auntie," Arabella called back. "And yes, she did, but flounced off as though I had some dreadful plague. Bertie was there too. I was just thanking him for saving my horse the other day. Go back to bed, Auntie – there's nothing amiss!"

Arabella said all that with the best grace she could muster, although afterwards, under her breath she muttered: 'except bloody Melissande wrecked my chances of landing a decent fish!'

It was only at breakfast next morning she discovered it was her dear Aunt who had put the cat amongst the pigeons.

Poor Melissande was distraught. She was beside herself with the anger and revulsion at seeing how she was betrayed by this vile man. All the warnings she'd had since childhood about 'promiscuous men' and 'immorality' came flooding back, making her feel worse.

That she should have been such a fool to fall for all his grooming – for that's what it must have been – all that sweet talk, all those loving gestures – all false; designed to satisfy that evil man's desire to conquer her body and take her virginity. She had debased herself by being so deceived, abandoning all her personal standards. She was now overcome with grief, guilt, anger and hatred.

For the first time ever she considered killing herself. This would escape these frightful emotions and give her peace. How had she best do it? As she walked blindly back towards The Rectory various methods crossed her mind as it sifted through the memories of newspaper reports and their tragic stories of unrequited love and depression.

Perhaps it was the walking that helped burn off some of the mental agony warping her mind. The essential Melissande arose from deep inside and berated her for considering suicide. 'How could you inflict such pain on those who love you? What about your poor parents? How could you be so selfish?'

As if to express her anguish, the weather joined in, making things worse. Wind suddenly tore into the surrounding hedges and trees, and large drops of rain began hitting her face as they splattered their cold wetness against her. A flash of lightning and simultaneous explosion of thunder literally made her hair tingle and broke the tension that was driving her forward, every nerve jangling, towards the sanctuary of her bedroom.

The shocking bright explosion of Nature's rage took the last of her strength away and she collapsed to the ground, clawing at it in fear and distress, wanting to be dead and away from everything. She didn't care about *anything*: she had been abused, betrayed, destroyed.

More flashes, tearing wind, pouring rain and falling leaves, the crashes of thunder less immediate as the storm moved off towards Swindon, left a shaking, distraught, young woman lying on the ground by Maude Heath's Causeway, sobbing, not knowing what to do to assuage her unbearable loss and degradation. She curled up and wept, not caring what happened to her. This was the end.

CHAPTER 23

If Bertie was to respect Melissande's wishes about their secret, he couldn't dash off to follow her like some lovelorn teenager; Arabella would smell a rat straight away.

He had to hide his emotions and not show any reaction to Mel's dramatic and heart-breaking departure. It had torn his soul to hear her distress and realise that she turned up with disastrous timing, but it was paramount he 'act natural' to prevent Bella finding out *why* Melissande had been so distraught.

It seemed to take Arabella an age to gather up the empty glasses – leaving the champagne bottle on a window-sill for someone else to transport to the bottle bank: (Arabella never went *there*.)

Bertie humped the bales back to their stack in the fodder store, and then Arabella spent an age re-folding the horse blankets before putting them back on the shelf above the saddles.

Bertie, in his agitation, began to whistle 'Waltzing Matilda', softly in a half-toned rendition.

"For God's sake, Bertie – shut up!"

What a different Bella from ten minutes ago! Bertie stopped his tune in mid phrase. The thought of Bella wetting herself might normally have been amusing – so easy to nudge her off her plinth – just whistle and off she would tumble, crossing her legs. Now, though, he didn't even get mild fun from her weakness – all he wanted was to find poor Melissande – make sure she was all right and then plead his defence.

In the end, Arabella, with barely a nod, said: "Goodnight," and stumped off towards the Manor. Bertie's last impression was the sullen way her bottom seemed to flounce with each grumpy step. 'Bloody funny, some women', he muttered to himself. 'One minute they're all over you – and the next they're buggering off in a paddy!' He supposed she was annoyed that Melissande had caught her trying to get him up against the wall.

'I wasn't going to fall for it anyway – her breath smelled awful!' He told himself. She did have a magnificent rear, but these days even that was unimportant, his loyalty was to only one. His concern was much more for his beloved, out in the pouring rain and fierce gale.

He left the outside light on, and taking his key-ring torch from his pocket, set off quickly in the direction in which Melissande had gone, those agonising minutes before.

In the cleaned-up caravan, still illegally sited in the field by the river, overlooking TGP's soggy meadow, Danielle Marchmont and Trevor Bunt were arguing about UKIP. Both had decided to vote for this party, which seemed to sympathise with all the issues that impinged on their life: unnecessary planning rules, foreign cheap labour keeping Travis out of a job; rich politicians taking liberties, and the high price of fags entirely due to Brussels being ridiculous. Their argument was about how best they might serve the new party.

"You ought to stand," said Trevor. "You'd show a few of these Tories and their wishy-washy mates a few fings."

"I can't, can I? I haven't even got a proper address, you gump!"

"You could use my old mum's."

"She'd *love* that wouldn't she?"

There was one person Trevor's mum could not stand, and it was Danielle (whom she called 'that stuck-up bitch' at every mention). Danielle was not the sort of person she'd like to see on Trevor's arm after a football match: she was common as muck but 'so far up herself she sees backwards'.

"No – it would be better if I offered to drop leaflets and go canvassing," said Danielle. "I'm going to keep my head down until this caravan loses its shine a bit. It shows up like a bloody beacon after all your washing and polish."

"It was *your* idea!"

"I'd forgotten what it used to look like!"

"Well, don't blame me, then."

"I'm not. I'm just stating a fact: it's too bright to be inconspicuous."

"You an' your long words!"

"Just because some of us are educated, Trevor Bunt – there's no need for envy. Give us a drop more of that hooch.

We ought to drink one for your Travis – he thinks he got that job, doesn't he?"

"He does: and I'm glad – except he'll be working for that lot up at The Manor. Gone over to the other side! I bet that took a bit of swallowin'!"

"Well, let him swallow. I'm going to have to swallow plenty – my Doris getting raped like that and now expecting a mule! How do you think I feel? I'm still going to put the squeeze on that cow, riding around on her sex-mad stallion. She should make it wear a muzzle or whatever you do to keep a horse's thing in its pants."

That last remark made them both laugh as they down the remains of the bottle of special offer Port and began thinking about bed.

The Rector was about to take a cup of cocoa up to Caroline, who had retired early, exhausted by having written eighteen Mother's Union invitations for members to come to the coffee morning the following Thursday, when someone rang the front doorbell.

'Whoever can that be?' The Rector asked himself, making sure that he collected a stout walking stick from the hat-stand in the hall as he first switched on the outside light. Too many priests had been assaulted recently. He could make out a large person, whose shape looked vaguely familiar, the other side of the peephole.

Canon Blythe couldn't make out the man's features so he connected the door security chain and opened the ancient portal by the protected seven inches.

Instantly recognising Bertie, he closed the door, undid the chain and pulled the door back to welcome him in.

"Oh dear, Bertie, you look distressed, what's the matter?"

"Thank you, Canon Blythe. Has Melissande come in yet?"

"I don't think she's out. She didn't say anything. I think she's tucked away up there in her office. Perhaps you could run up and see. My old legs find it difficult these days and I don't want to shout because my wife's very tired and has retired early. Do go up, but please be light of foot!"

"Bertie mounted the stairs two at a time, propelling himself as fast as he could, desperate to explain the misunderstanding. Up the second flight of stairs to the attic in a matter of seconds – only to be disappointed: not a sign of a light in any of the attic rooms and no Melissande. On the way down again he even poked his head into her bedroom, where he and she had crept one evening for a surreptitious embrace on the way up to her hideaway. She was not there and there was no sign that she had been there recently.

Back in the hall, Bertie could see Canon Blythe in the kitchen, carrying a cup of something.

"I expect she popped out for some air," suggested Bertie, not wishing to alarm The Rector.

"In *this* weather? Well I suppose she does have her funny ways. I'll tell her you called."

The Rector wanted Bertie to know that visits so late in the evening might not always be welcome, so he added: "it is rather *late*, though, isn't it?"

"Oh yes indeed! I'm so sorry to have troubled you." Bertie let himself out and stood for a moment, wondering what to do.

There now followed one of the low-points in Bertie's life. Never had he felt so desperate – as he walked the road and paths, looking for Melissande. It was hard to see, because of the driving rain, and the air seemed to have an extra sharp chill as it raced in from the North East. He was wet through but kept searching, certain that Melissande must have either had a fall or worse.

Hours later he had still found nothing, but throughout the night he continued – looking behind gateways, walls and into two bus shelters, finding nothing and no one.

It was nearly dawn when he was plodding along by the river, hoping *not* to find anyone floating there. As he finally neared the bridge at Chippenham he saw the flashing light of an ambulance heading out of town in the direction of the village he'd just left and he knew instinctively that Melissande must have either been found or had called for help.

There was no way he could contact the speeding vehicle but he knew just what to do. In the grey, dismal dawn he turned round and raced back to The Manor, letting himself into the Gate Lodge, casting off his wet coat and soggy jumper.

"Reg?"

"Ello!" Came the answer from the kitchen. Reg was giving the cat her morning saucer of milk. "Where the 'ell 'ave you been? I didn't hear you come in last night."

"I've only just come in now – I've been looking for Melissande. She's missing."

"Missing? However's that?"

"She was very upset last night about something and ran off into the darkness. I've been looking for her ever since. I'm really worried – and now I've seen an ambulance coming from out this way."

"Oh Gawd! What are you going to do?"

"I'll go up to Swindon – that's where they'd go, isn't it?"

"I reckon they would: up to A and E, where I went that day, thanks to you!"

"Have you got the car keys? Lady V won't mind, will she?"

"I'm sure she won't! Here you are." Reg took the keys from the hook on the dresser and handed them over. "She's got plenty of petrol on board. You'd better change those trousers, too – they're soaked! It must have been bloody wet out there. All night, you say?"

"It hasn't stopped – and blowing a gale, too. It's rough!"

"You'd better get going, then. Do they know, over at The Rectory?"

"No, I didn't tell them what had happened."

"Well you can tell me all about it when you find her. I'll get some soup going for lunchtime. Give me a call if you find anything."

Bertie changed at record speed and was on the road to Swindon in no time, not pressing the old vehicle too hard for fear of breakdown.

"I must ask for your name and relationship," said the receptionist at the hospital.

"I'm a colleague and close friend of Miss Blythe," said Bertie, impatient for news. "We both live at Tytherton Kellaway – she's from The Rectory and I'm at The Manor."

The receptionist politely explained the need for patient confidentiality and was quietly insistent that she could only give out information of any admissions to the next of kin. Bertie pleaded that he had seen her 'dash off into the night, in a state of some distress, and had been searching for her all night in the foulest weather. There had been no hint of an altercation – no violence – couldn't she give him *any* news at all?

The receptionist thought he looked respectable and recognised an accent that was definitely not 'Bristol', and could see the genuine concern and anxiety in Bertie's eyes. She repeated her request for his personal details and said she would try to enquire.

He spelled out his name, using his title in the hope that it might have its usual effect. It did: and she spent a few moments on the phone before addressing him.

"Well, Sir Bertrand, Miss Blythe was admitted a few minutes ago. She's being examined in A and E but that's all I can tell you for the moment."

"Is she in danger?"

"I didn't get that impression, but I'm so sorry, I won't have any idea until they have finished their assessment. If you don't mind waiting over there, I'll let you know if I hear anything – and we'll give it thirty minutes or so and I might be able to get through to the ward sister to ask."

An hour later – nearly nine o'clock – and there was still hardly any news. Bertie was beside himself with worry. He realised that by this time, The Rector must surely have discovered that Melissande was not at home. At least Bertie knew where she was and he ought to tell her parents. One blessing was that here in Swindon, his mobile worked. He went outside, avoiding two smokers as they dragged sheepishly on their cigarettes – Bertie couldn't bear the smell and went up-wind of them – and phoned The Rectory.

"Canon Blythe, it's Bertie."

The Canon didn't give Bertie time to explain but poured out his own concerns.

"I'm so glad you phoned. We can't find Melissande. After you left last night, I assumed that she must have come in again, after a breather in the garden – she does that sometimes, although I was surprised she should do so in that terrible weather we were having; but this morning I see that her bed has not been slept in. Her mother is most worried and we're wondering what to do."

As calmly as he could, Bertie put The Rector in the picture, emphasising that, as far as he could gather, Melissande was not in danger but had been admitted to Swindon hospital for observation. The only thing he'd been able to discover was that she had been found, suffering from hypothermia and was being treated. No, he had not been allowed to see her because he was not family or guardian.

"We must come up at once," said The Canon.

"I'll wait for you in reception, Canon Blythe. It will probably take you half an hour."

It took an interminable forty-five minutes, during which Bertie attempted to read the newspaper he'd picked up at the hospital kiosk. He found he couldn't get the words on the page to speak louder than the worries in his head. He forced his eyes to move back and forth across the pages taking nothing in. His mind was full of images of Melissande lying on a white bed, her pulse being monitored, her eyes closed and her breathing laboured as her poor body fought feebly for life.

His nightmare was finally interrupted by The Rector's voice, speaking loudly so as not to be misunderstood by the West Indian receptionist; ('one needs to raise one's voice for foreigners – it *does* help', he often said, not being racially prejudiced but simply practical).

"Yes, I'm her father!"

Bertie got up and went to stand beside The Canon.

"Oh Bertie – I'm so glad you're here. We've been so worried. This lady's just going to enquire from the ward how she is."

They stood in silence, watching the receptionist's expression to see whether there was any hint of concern or relief detectable as she listened to the ward sister.

"Yes, it's her father, and a Sir Bertrand Lamotte here at reception. Can they come up. Yes I'll wait."

The receptionist put her hand over the phone's mouthpiece and turned to Canon Blythe.

"Your daughter is stable, and suffering from hypothermia – but she's not in danger. The sister is asking her if she feels well enough for visitors. Excuse me....." She was now paying attention to the telephone.

"Yes, right..... I'll tell him." She put the phone down, with the look of 'I told you so', congratulating herself for being cautious about non-family enquiries. "Miss Blythe would like to see her father but asks that Sir Bertrand does not go to the ward."

This was another body blow to Bertie, the words taking a moment to sink in. Canon Blythe assumed his daughter must be feeling weak. He knew nothing of the gravity of the message.

"Oh well – I'm glad she can at least see me – I'll come and tell you how she is, Bertie. So kind of you to take such concern, I'm sure. I'll tell her you are waiting down here."

"I'll wait here but please give her my love," said Bertie, hopefully.

"Of course!" The Canon didn't realise that such a message might be received like an Exocet – carrying explosive, inflammatory content. Bertie feared it might do damage rather than help but clung to the faint hope that he might be forgiven – even though he was innocent.

As The Rector followed the receptionist's directions to reach the ward, Bertie resumed his attempts at learning today's news but once again failed to connect his eyes with his brain. Holding the newspaper up in front of him did, perhaps, conceal the look of intense anxiety on his face from the growing number of the public who were joining him on the 'please wait here' line of chairs.

"She's not nearly as bad as I feared," said The Rector, on his descent. "It was rather extraordinary, though – she seems to be suffering from loss of memory, perhaps a result of catching a chill. She couldn't explain *why* she had spent the whole night out in such terrible weather, or how she finished up semi-conscious by the roadside. It was lucky someone discovered her and called the ambulance. She seems to be recovering but when I gave her your message she burst into tears! Had you perhaps criticised her work? Found it at fault? I couldn't think of any other reason – you seem to have been spending so much time in each other's company recently. She hasn't complained before."

"Definitely not, Canon Blythe. Melissande has produced a most excellent feasibility report and, more than that, has come up with a succession of brilliant suggestions: I have absolutely no complaints at all! We are all delighted with her work and creativity."

"Well I can't think what was the matter, she seemed inconsolable and I couldn't get her to tell me any more. The nurse advised that it would be better if I let her rest. I think she must be still suffering from the effects of getting so cold and wet. The nurse said the doctor had been most encouraging – he could find no evidence of any serious ailment, which will be of great relief to Melissande's mother."

The next couple of weeks continued to be Hell for Bertie – and indeed for Melissande, although no one else knew of the reason. She refused to see him, avoided any possibility of their meeting, either at The Rectory or the Manor, despite his disguised requests for an audience. He tried to make his enquiries in a casual way, while not showing his disappointment as he received curt answers. He learned from Mrs Blythe that Melissande had resumed her work in her office up at the top of the house, and seemed to be concentrating on completing her report in good time for the launch, the date for which had now been fixed before everyone in the City departed for the Dordogne, Mustique or Padstow.

"She's not seeing anybody," Caroline told him. "Actually I don't think she's quite got over her strange escapade when she finished up in hospital. She won't answer the phone. Asked me to do it. I just take messages."

Mrs Blythe confided that Melissande's behaviour was quite uncharacteristic. She had heard her weeping late at night but got no sensible replies to her enquiries.

"It seems to be some sort of breakdown. I think it must be all the thinking she's put into that report of hers. She hasn't been used to such intense study for some time – looking after us and Arabella's horse. It must have come as a shock to her system. It's strange though – she won't speak to Arabella, or you. She says it's because 'you're too close to the subject' – your views are strongly biased, as are Bella's – and she wants to achieve an objective conclusion to her study: most peculiar!"

For days, Bertie did not catch even a glimpse of Melissande. He was not able to see how she was losing weight or the dark lines under her eyes, the result of so many hours crying alone in her office and bedroom. She had taken to visiting the stable yard at unpredictable hours, making sure she didn't bump into Bertie or Arabella.

Arabella was sure she knew why Melissande was keeping a low profile. Having interrupted a delicate moment between herself and Bertie she must be feeling foolish and embarrassed – perhaps concerned that she'd spoiled Bella's chances of landing a nice beau.

"I don't know what's got into her," she told her aunt. "Bertie and I were just beginning to get on rather well – I'd put on a mini-party in the tack-room to thank him for rescuing the horse and she turned up at the wrong moment – put us right off! She made it worse by creating a fuss, snivelling as she left. I've no idea why, but it ruined our evening. Bertie's keeping out of my way and Melissande won't speak to either of us. She's gone weird if you ask me."

"Arabella, you know she's a very sensitive girl. *Something* must have upset her. She has been working very hard on my dear John's project. I've been so pleased that Bertie and your friend Tristram have taken it up again: it's essential if we're going to stay here at The Manor. I am a little confused, though. What's *Tristram* going to say about you making eyes at Bertie? I thought you were rather keen on *him*: it might not be wise to flirt with both of them."

Aunt Veronica was equally keen for Arabella to 'settle down' as Caroline Blythe was to see Melissande find a 'suitable young man'. Yet here was Bella being fickle. She might miss both opportunities!

"Oh Auntie – it's not like *that!*" Arabella dismissed her aunt's concern and went off for her Saturday morning ride.

At the next meeting of The Board of TGP, Bertie had to make the opening statement. Melissande was not present.

He welcomed members and enquired after her in as casual way as he could manage.

"Has anyone seen Melissande? I thought we'd told everyone about today's meeting?"

"There you go, Bertie," said Reg, with a smile: "women can have their moments too! It was 'er that told us the date and time, and I put it on the calendar – up 'ere at The Manor, eleven o'clock. She would 'ave been 'ere if she'd wanted, but she dropped in at The Gate Lodge when you were out, earlier on, and gave me this package. I said 'see you later' and she looked a bit funny and said 'probably not, Reg. I've got an appointment in Bath.' She was sure we'd manage without 'er and this was the final draft of the report. She gave me this letter as well."

He handed Bertie an envelope addressed to 'The chairman *Amphib 21 Ltd*. Bertie opened it and read it, his face taking on a quizzical frown.

"Go on then, Bertie, what's it say?" Reg wanted to know.

"Oh yes," said Lady Veronica, "do put us out of our suspense!"

"Well – I can't understand this but she's giving in her resignation. She says: 'I'd like to thank The Board for all their co-operation and hereby present the feasibility study I have been working on. My conclusion is that you have a potentially excellent business opportunity in property development of land that would otherwise not be considered suitable for habitation or permanent agriculture. I wish you all well in your pursuit of this aim. Personally, however, I have decided that my career lies in other directions and am resigning from The Board. I shall not be attending today's meeting, or others in the future.'"

"That's rather a shock," said Mr Penworthy. "Miss Blythe has been such a source of information and reliability for this project."

"I wonder what has made her change her mind so suddenly," said Lady Veronica. "I will try to have a word with her mother. Mr Haines, how did she seem? You did speak with her, didn't you?"

"I did, your ladyship, but I didn't know what was in the letter. I thought we'd see 'er later."

"Did she look all right?"

"Pretty as ever, your Ladyship – but come to think of it, rather tired and not too happy. She didn't stay more than a minute. I told her Bertie would be back in a minute and she hurried off."

"Well, it's a mystery, then," lied Bertie. "We shall have to conduct this meeting without her. I think we all know what she's saying in her report by now, having seen the first two drafts and I presume any queries we had, have now been covered in this last one." He unwrapped the package. "Ah yes, she's even given a summary of the latest changes. I think we should take them one at a time, don't you?"

He was forcing himself to appear as businesslike as usual but it was a huge effort. His soul was filling him with pain. Melissande was taking herself completely out of his life and from now on this project was of no real interest to him. Once it was up and running he would get back on the train and use the rest of his year-and-a-day to put as much distance between Tytherton Kellaway and himself as possible.

The meeting continued and as Bertie pushed through necessary decisions about the City launch of TGP in six weeks' time, and noted the various formalities that had been followed and those that still needed attention, Melissande was packing a suitcase over at The Rectory. She was ignoring the tears that periodically splashed on what she was packing.

"I wish you'd talk to us about this," her mother had been saying. "I don't even know where the island of Iona *is*."

"It's a small island next to a larger one – Mull – off the coast of Scotland."

"I know there's a religious community there – because we had a preacher once from there, years ago – it sounded very windswept and chilly! But how long do you think you will stay there?"

"Mummy, I'm not sure. All I know is that I must get away and sort myself out."

"I've been so worried about you, dear. It's not only that your father and I depend on you so much but we shall miss you badly and you have been so unhappy this past week or two. You will keep in touch, won't you? Your Aunt has agreed to stay on for a while but I don't know what we shall do if she wants to go home."

"Don't worry, Mummy; I won't desert you – it's just that I need some time to put things right in my life."

"My dear I'm so sorry. I feel I ought to be able to help in some way but I can't, if you won't let me.."

"It's nothing, Mummy! It's just ..... I feel I've let myself down; you and Daddy, too. I need to come to terms with it."

"Is it this building thing that's upset you?"

"No, Mummy, that's been very interesting and I've learned a lot. Look – I can't tell you about it yet – perhaps one day. Now I must finish my packing. It's a long journey, so I'll take some sandwiches."

CHAPTER 24

The launch was a week away. Bertie and Tristram were back in London. Arabella had just left to get ready for the evening out she'd been promised by Tristram.

"Just a little reward," he'd said to her. "You've worked so bloody hard this past month."

She had. In the absence of Melissande there had been a great deal to do. Some of it was, for her, straightforward: such as putting the word around to editors and correspondents that a novel kind of property development was just around the corner and was going to make quite a splash ('ha ha' – said Tristram).

An extra lure for the launch was the international design competition.

"Everyone will wish they'd thought of it first," said Tristram. "With a bit of luck it will bring a dash for our shares."

Arabella made a few phone calls to favoured editors whom she knew personally, with exclusive 'mini-leaks', giving faint clues about 'very relevant to climate change' or 'a way out for flood plains' and 'ultimate house chic', and these were bringing in yes-please replies.

Several of them decided to cover the story themselves, (because of the promised day-trip). It would be a 'good opportunity to freshen the mind', one remarked.

One or two senior media types, who had at some time spent some exciting hours with Arabella at her flat, signed up in the hopes of having another little run with her. She would not disappoint their hopes until after their stories had been filed.

During this period, she and Bertie, using Melissande's report as handbook, worked closely, drawing up the publicity and (with the help of professionals), devising rules for the architectural competition.

Bertie had gone to a couple of his former colleagues who specialised in sketching imaginative visualisations. They produced rough ideas of how the finished constructions might look, set amongst trees and verdant grassland, both 'dry', and 'wet', when the River Avon had submersed all the land, leaving the houses as an archipelago.

These images were drawn with a background of Wiltshire scenery including The Roman Temple and a distant view of the Manor.

"I like the idea of giving them a surprise trip," Tristram had said. "As long as you warn them there's going to *be* one. We can't just kidnap them!"

"They'll jump at it, won't they?"

"They're jumping! I've already booked up four managing editors," said Arabella. She didn't mention that two of them 'knew' her of old.

"It might be a good idea to invite the MP, what's-his-name, the minister: you know, the chubby one," suggested Bertie. "As Secretary of State for Communities and Local Government he comes across all the people we need to influence. He enjoys a lunch and if we give him a good tale he'll pass it around plenty of councils. In six months we could ask him back to hand out the prizes: give him an incentive to attend the launch."

"Good idea Bertie!" Said Tristram. "I'll dig out a few fund managers. We could take them down to look at the land – let 'em see how drastic things *can* look: then go somewhere nice and show 'em our video."

"Follow that up with a technical session. We can put a panel together: an engineer, perhaps a Dutchman to answer awkward ones; an architect, an artist and then someone from the Green lobby – keep them on side! Then we can give 'em lunch."

"Don't forget the economist, Bertie," said Tristram. "We need someone there to talk about costs and returns – I mean: that's what all this is for, isn't it? What a pity Melissande's buggered off up North. Will she be back by then? She'd be ideal; she's got the figures at her finger tips."

"Never can tell! I'll try to think of someone else, just in case," said Bertie, feeling awful. He had been thinking exactly the same but was sensitive about revealing any bias towards his lost love and her great ability with figures. At least now, since it was Tristram who had suggested it, he had a new reason to contact her.

He dragged his mind away from what was taking up most of his thinking moments, to the matter in hand. He had arranged similar events before, like giving surprised journalists and radio reporters an unexpected day-trip across the Channel to Orleans to visit the statue of Jean D'Arc. The group he was representing on that occasion was a women's organisation seeking government intervention over trafficking of teenage girls from Eastern Europe. He couldn't quite remember the logic but it was something to do with 'even a nineteen-year-old girl with vision and courage can change regimes'. He himself had been moved, learning more detail of how St Joan's heroism had earned world respect.

His attention lagged – St Joan and Melissande merged in his imagination, the latter suffering anguish and distress for equally mistaken causes. Poor Melissande, tied to the stake of misunderstanding, and doubtless, remorse over 'her sinful relationship with that bastard, me!' It was unbearable: he couldn't just let things rest.

A couple of weeks earlier, returning to his London flat in the course of TGP business, Bertie had been pleased to see that his housekeeper might have been expecting him even though he hadn't contacted her since the day he set off to seek his fortune. She knew him well enough to have faith about her salary being paid. The mail was neatly arranged in piles of 'looking like official', 'junk mail' and 'personal'; the fridge had a bottle of fresh milk and some fruit – all looking new and the place was immaculately clean and tidy; as though she were expecting him. It was good to be back, apart from the nagging pain of rejection by the only woman with whom he'd ever truly fallen in love.

He and Tristram met every morning at a coffee bar or hotel and worked together on their laptops and mobiles. Now and again Arabella joined them for lunch, sternly dressed in her range of dark suits and pearls. She was being careful not to make a show of the sizzling private life she was leading with Tristram because she didn't want to embarrass him with displays of her 'ownership' of him.

After work, however, she was making sure that Tristram's body was well serviced in many imaginative and novel culinary and bed-time ways, in both of which she excelled.

This overkill was in case Bertie had spilled the beans to Tristram about her making a blatant pass at him that night in the tack room. She knew they were old mates but she wasn't entirely confident over what details they shared about their personal lives. She had given up on her bid for Bertie. He had plainly not welcomed her assault – which was strange, because such a technique usually succeeded in getting into a man's trousers. Anyone would have thought she was going to rape him, the way he reacted. Given a little encouragement, she might have: but after Melissande had broken the spell, she had been unable to re-kindle any spark of his interest in any of her assets. He'd been reserved and stand-offish. Perhaps he *was* a closet gay? So many of these public school boys – before girls got amongst them in the sixth form – had had to make do with fags, hadn't they? Having given up Bertie's title as a bad job, Bella didn't want to miss out on the other front runner as husband: better demonstrate her devotion to Tristram to keep him on side. She was no believer in the way to a man's heart being through his stomach. A man's heart and brain were governed by another more predictable organ, the management of which she was an expert. She wanted to make him an 'Arabella addict' and this she was working on, with some success.

Tristram had never experienced such practical devotion being combined with professional expertise and hard work. He confided to Bertie:

"Arabella's really putting her back into this project; and she's bloody marvellous in bed!"

"You sound quite keen!" Bertie was not going to reveal the raw wound of his recent loss and made himself sound jolly.

"I am, actually," said Tris. "Haven't ever felt quite like this about a girl. What do you think? Should I consider going long term?" He respected Bertie's instinct about women.

"Ideal, I'd say! You need someone with a bit of steel about her. You're a complete bastard and she'd have to be tough to put up with all your antics."

"I say, that's a bit strong isn't it, Bertie?" Tristram tried to sound offended but knew it was true. "I reckon she's battle-hardened. I haven't managed to incur her wrath yet and she goes out of her way not to upset me but she's pretty unscrupulous, you know!"

He couldn't discuss details of this with his old mate, but he was remembering Bella's plan for discovering Bertie's intentions.

Tristram wasn't aware that she had been considering trading him in for Bertie although he wouldn't have been surprised, had the truth come to light.

"Unscrupulous? That's the impression I had, too," remarked Bertie. She was a hard-nosed bitch, well-bred, in prime condition, wonderful arse and knew how to turn herself out – and use her body to a man's delight. He would hate to be hitched up to someone like that.

He didn't care what happened to Arabella – or Tris, come to that; his whole being was crying out for Melissande and until he could win her back or rid himself of this enchantment he could never rest or be happy. Tristram and Arabella were ideally suited for each other. They had the same aims – money, possessions and appearances.

"I can see her making an ideal wife for you, as long as you let her loose with your credit card: turn up to do your bit when asked, for cocktail parties and so on."

"I was thinking the same – and I must say she'd make a gorgeous wife to hang on your arm. She'd charm the pants of any CEO – could be most beneficial."

"Quite so, quite so," agreed Bertie. What she did to CEOs might turn out to be more literal than metaphorical. That might not bother a man such as Tristram, whose proclivity for 'playing away' would soon become evident to any intelligent wife.

"I think you'd make an ideal match!" Bertie said with conviction.

Tristram nodded in agreement, then asked:

"What about the Manor estate? If our project goes through, are you thinking of hanging about there? Have you got any long term plans in that direction, once you've got your money back?"

"Only in as much as we might be able to replicate the idea all over the show. If you tied the knot with Bella it would be yours and hers, wouldn't it, once the dear old lady popped her clogs? Sad but inevitable and Bella's the heiress."

"... to a red bottom line," added Tristram, with some resignation.

"I like that," laughed Bertie: "A Red Bottom Line! It has a nice ring to it! Make a good title for a book about the perfect match: a fabulous arse and no bank balance!"

"Don't be so bloody insulting about the woman I love!"

Bertie saw his old chum didn't mean it.

"No – I've got no desire to hang around Chippenham or Tytherton Kellaway – except to visit for the christening when you two start reproducing. Regretfully at some stage I'll have to take over from my mother, bless her, and go to live in Suffolk but I hope that's a long way off. Until then I'd like to make a go of TGP and its clones. We could go all over the place."

"We? You and who else?" Enquired Tristram. "Not me! You'll be able to count me out if I tie the knot with Bella. I'd love to settle down and breed – especially at a great spot like Tytherton. I get the impression that's what she wants, too. Even if TGP didn't work out I could manage to keep it afloat if I pottered on in the City. Have you got some bird in mind? I can't see Penworthy wanting to go to York – even Bradford on Avon!"

"Oh, no one in particular!" Bertie was now blushing.

"Couldn't you fancy Melissande? She could be gorgeous if you took off her specs – lovely figure!"

Bertie nearly choked. Had he been rumbled? Or was it just Tristram's eye for the female form? He couldn't reply so he forced a chortle before saying:

"Oh – no one in mind! Live in hopes and all that!"

As he spoke, Bertie knew it wasn't true. He wanted to forget Tytherton and run away from the pain that was making his life such a misery. Any reference to flooding, amphibious anything, Venice, The Church, girlfriends, love – stabbed at him leaving fresh wounds.

Later, back at the flat, he made another grave decision to help him cope with his distress. He wouldn't go back to stay at The Gate Lodge with Reg. Once this project was under way he would eat humble pie and ask Ogle to take him back. They'd agree and he could resume an existence that would keep his mind off things, eventually seeking female company to channel any lust that might one day return.

At present he was running on automatic pilot – navigating his way through permanent unhappiness. He would phone Reg that very evening to make sure he was managing. He'd write a letter to Lady Veronica, explaining that he could support TGP better by staying at his London flat and working from there. Phrases such as 'then I could rustle up the capital we shall be needing' and 'of course, I'll pop down from time to time for board meetings and so on' sprung to mind.

Those decisions made, Bertie poured himself a stiff drink to dull the edges as he watched a tedious quiz show on BBC.

Bertie was not alone in his desolation. Far to the north, Melissande was trying to contemplate the agonies of sin. She had let herself down: she had failed her parents and her Faith, and never had she been so repentant. All those now-repugnant things she had done with Bertie had become disgusting. Worse, she had *revelled* in private orgies of Old Testament magnitude with him. She fought back any longing to repeat all of it.

At the time she had convinced herself it wasn't wrong. How *could* it have been wrong? She had been sure this was to be her life partner, wanting only to be with him, be his anchor and support and bear his child. She had joyfully given herself permission to welcome him into her life, soul and body – indeed she still ached to be held in his arms and feel him inside her: sharing the heat and strength of his body.

She tried to resist the way her mind kept coming back to the passion and love she still felt for Bertie. She knew she must purge it and get back to her previous life of celibacy, yet once again her ungovernable thoughts undermined these resolutions. Was it purity or wasted sterility? Had Jesus preached the denial of our primate origins? Surely not! All his teaching acknowledged, yet advocated positive ways of rising above, our feet of clay. His message was 'do as you would be done by in a spirit of consideration and care'. It was not Jesus, but bigoted men and women who wanted to impose rigid curbs not only on what *they* defined as greed and lust but on what they assumed would be everyone else's. It was we humans who desired to subjugate children and anyone within our power, demanding of them obedience, chastity and guilt, using fear to enforce it with warnings of Hell, stoning, torture and excommunication.

Melissande's head was swamped with thoughts of shame, remorse and grief; and she was *so* tired. Was this Hell, she wondered? It felt like it.

She found moments of peace during the church services on the chill Scottish island. Times when her tears were stopped by calming music, talk of forgiveness and love; silent prayer when her mind could follow liturgies of familiar words, loaded with beauty and meaning.

The staff at Iona could see that their guest was in a state of great unhappiness and they made sure that there was always a smile ready for her and a friendly arm around the shoulder when red eyes and scrumpled handkerchief showed her distress.

At times like this Melissande wanted to give way to her grief and fall into someone's arms but she couldn't allow herself this luxury: it would be so embarrassing. Little did she know how often those arms had offered comfort and healing to others who, like her, were at rock bottom; arms that had saved having to call an ambulance or tell parents and friends of tragedy.

Most of all, Melissande would have given anything to weep in the arms of her mother but she couldn't bear the thought of confessing the reasons for her grief. She had to sort this out for herself and this was the best place in which to work through her ordeal.

The Management, however, seemed to be taking a personal interest in the unhappy couple and intervened in a drastic way. What was it, that drew his/her/its attention to this particular situation rather than far worse ones in Africa, the Middle East or Asia? Could it be there was someone in Iona who had a better direct line than that of the Pope, the Ayatollah or the Archbishop of Canterbury? Or was it Melissande's prayers and Bertie's consuming distress that showed a red alarm on the Heavenly Control Panel? Things got moving when the Angel of Death was despatched to a flood valley near Chippenham in Southern England.

In Tytherton Kellaway, the lives of Lady Veronica, Reg and the cat had begun to resume a routine. Reg and the cat missed Bertie being around, with his jokes, strokes and kindness – and of course, his strength in heaving logs. Like Lady Veronica, they welcomed his occasional visits for board meetings or when he came to supervise Travis's survey, which was turning out to be accurate and intelligently done.

When he wasn't too busy, Tristram came down too, for the odd weekend with Arabella. She went riding while he accompanied Travis, taking photographs of features that the young man was identifying and recording. They got on surprisingly well, considering their first meeting in the shopping arcade. That episode was not something they ever mentioned.

It was on a Monday that the Management's executive angel took action. It was after Tristram and Arabella, now officially designated as his girlfriend, had returned to London following a lusty weekend, during which they had graciously celebrated Reg's birthday – at Lady Veronica's prompting – with several bottles of wine, and some of Arabella's magnificent nibbles. Lady Veronica made a short speech in which she praised Reg's 'irreplaceable role at Tytherton Manor', making him blush at her praise for his devotion.

Next morning, poor Reg, woken by his alarm as usual, went to get out of bed, felt a sharp pain and tightness across his chest as he stood up; thought 'ouch – that's heart, I'll bet a bob' – and then dropped dead on the floor.

An hour later Lady Veronica, looking at her clock, wondered where Reg had got to: he was usually here by now and her breakfast would have been clattering on to the kitchen table. It was ominously quiet downstairs. She got dressed, carefully as usual, and prepared her own breakfast. She even put down a saucer of milk for the cat – who, unusually, was not there to greet her with a rub against her shin.

After a second cup of tea, feeling generally less feeble but by now rather worried, Lady Veronica put on her Barbour and hat – if it wasn't raining now it probably would be by the time she was ready to come home – and set off for the Gate Lodge. She knew Reg never locked his back door and after knocking, let herself in.

The scene she found was distressing. There was Reg, lying beside his bed, admittedly with a serene and content expression on his face – apart from his mouth being open as if snoring. The cat was sitting like an Egyptian sculpture, on guard by her old master's head. She didn't move to greet her other patron but, sitting tall, continued her vigil.

Lady Veronica touched Reg's hand and found it to be cold. She sought a pulse in his wrist and found none. Death was no stranger to her – having found her dear John in a similar state one sad morning like this, in his room. She went to the telephone in the hall and dialled the doctor's out of hours line, which she found in the directory, telling the operator the situation. She then phoned The Rectory, to let them know, too.

She and Caroline had been seeing much more of each other since Melissande had gone away 'on retreat'. It was partly for company and partly because both of them were worried about Melissande's sudden decline and loss of weight.

The doctor certified that Reg had died and told Lady Veronica that there would have to be a post mortem, because it was a sudden, unexplained death, although he was fairly sure it must have been a heart attack. An ambulance took Reg's remains away.

Lady Veronica tried to persuade the cat to come back to The Manor with her but it refused, settling down on the unmade bed in which Reg had lain until that morning.

"Oh well – someone will have to come down and feed you," she said; then wondered: 'but who? I suppose it must be me!' Here indeed was a quandary. How on earth could she do all the things that Reg did? A moment of panic seized her. She couldn't manage on her own; she couldn't afford to pay anyone and she was already beginning to feel light headed.

Borrowing Reg's walking stick from beside the front door, she made her way slowly back to the big house, wondering what on earth to do. Worse – Bertie and Tristram were due to bring a whole group of journalists and politicians to The Manor next week! She telephoned Arabella, breaking the news and expressing her panic.

"Auntie that's frightful! I'm so sorry – but I simply *can't* come straight down – I've got all this to organise! Tell you what, I'll try to get hold of Melissande and see if she'll come back to help out. It really is an emergency and I'm sure she'll understand. I'll call you back when I've made some progress."

As soon as she put the phone down, Arabella realised that she had a problem on her hands. She had heard of The Iona Community and knew it was where Melissande had fled to, but she had no idea where the place was. Management gave her a nudge towards her laptop and slipped a hint into her mind that 'Google will know'; and left her to get on with it. Up popped their website and Bella clicked on 'contact' to find the phone number.

"Damn! No phone number!" She'd have to send an email, asking to be put in touch with Melissande, giving the reason; otherwise, going by recent experience, Melissande would ignore it. She hoped someone checked for messages first thing in the morning. They did: and within minutes her phone rang. It was Melissande.

"Bella – what happened?" Melissande had been snatched out of her introverted state, leaving on one side her grief, anger and resentment for Bella. Sudden death and the call for help now brought all her upbringing and faith back in control and she was instantly at action stations.

As she listened to Arabella she knew what she had to do and within minutes she was on her way to Edinburgh Airport, promising to keep in touch with her mentors at Iona as she faced yet another test of her fortitude. Dragging her wheelie suitcase to Departures, waiting around, wondering whether low cloud and pouring rain would lift; then trailing down long passages to board the aircraft was all an effort, as she forced herself onward.

After take-off she snatched half an hour's restless sleep before rejoining the scrum of suited businessmen and women as they marched in search of their baggage and trekked to find the bus for Reading Station, the train and Chippenham, where it was a relief to find The Rector waiting for her.

Although Canon Blythe always found it more difficult to deal with family members than with parishioners, his approach on this occasion was absolutely right. He gave her a quick hug, and took over her suitcase, leading her straight to his car in the station yard car park.

"Your mother will tell you the whole story – you'll have to forgive me but once we're home I have to dash off for another funeral."

Melissande was glad the urgency prevented her father from discussing her own state. She knew she had to hang on just long enough to feel her mother's arms around her before she could release her pent-up emotion.

When it came to it, Melissande couldn't bring herself to relate her sad story of failure and heart-break: she was simply too tired. After a tearful embrace, she went straight to bed and cried herself to sleep.

CHAPTER 25

"But my darling Melissande, of course I'm not going to be shocked!"

Caroline rocked her beloved daughter to help her finish the torrent of tears and garbled words that had been going on for some minutes.

After dragging herself down, late for breakfast, Melissande had kept control of her emotions during the agonising wait until her father had picked up his leather suitcase containing his vestments and hat and gone off to an outlying church to conduct yet another of what he called 'seasonal' funerals. This was the time of year, when the leaves were coming out and the days were getting longer, for which many elderly folk had been hanging on all winter, before gasping their last.

As soon as he'd left, Caroline led Melissande to the sitting room. She patted the sofa beside her.

"Come and sit here, darling. I've missed you so much! We don't have to worry about Gwen bursting in – she's gone to Bath for the day. You know how she loves the shopping and now they've got this wonderful new centre she has the same 'good idea' every Wednesday morning. There's always a good reason – mostly the weather. She says: 'I can't do anything in the garden because of the rain, so I'll pop into Bath. Expect me after tea – and I'll bring something nice for supper.' She is marvellous and I couldn't have done without her but I have to admit I have enjoyed my Wednesdays; but it's so good to have you back – if only you didn't look so thin and tired. I didn't know that Mr Haine's death would cause you such distress. Were you *so* fond of him?"

It was then that the flood gates had burst and Melissande, after being wracked with sobs and being unable to speak for what seemed like an age, said:

"I miss dear Reg, of course but I've been such a fool! I'm so ashamed and I sometimes wish I was dead!"

"You poor child! You *can* tell me about it."

"I can't, Mummy – you'll be so disappointed in me."

That was when Caroline, almost holding her breath, had offered the promise of being unshockable.

"I fell in love with *Bertie*: and when we went to Venice, we slept together."

The memory of this prompted renewed sobbing. In the romantic hotel by the Grand Canal it had been so beautiful and liberating, but now, sullied and devalued by Bertie's betrayal, it screamed guilt and failure.

"If you're pregnant, it's not the end of the world, my darling – perhaps it's the beginning of a new one!" Caroline's fingers were crossed that this was *not* the cause of Melissande's condition but she felt the girl needed moral support.

"I'm not!"

"So what's the matter, dear? Has he gone off with someone else?"

It was the tensing of Melissande's body that made her go on:

"Men do, you know! I hadn't thought Bertie was like that though – he seemed such a gentleman. Is it someone you know?"

"It's ARABELLA! My best friend! Or so I thought!"

The storm of tears and embracing finally cooled, as Caroline stroked her distraught daughter's back and continued gentle rocking.

"Did she know you and Bertie were lovers?"

"I hope not! That would make it even worse!"

"Well then, to be fair, she couldn't have known she was treading on your toes. You know what she's like!" Caroline knew that Arabella was a flirt – but imagined it was in an innocent way, although her clothing sometimes did seem a little 'brazen', which Caroline put down to 'unfortunate taste', without wanting to criticise her daughter's friend. If she had known the truth about Arabella's bedtime antics she might have thought differently.

"Did Bertie know you felt like this about him?"

"Mummy of course he did! He said he did too!"

"They do! Some men just can't be trusted but I'm still surprised he's like *that*. Did you catch them in an ... uncompromising situation?"

"They were kissing!"

"Well that's not a sin, is it? Perhaps they had something to celebrate. Maybe they were planning a nice surprise for you!"

"Mummy it wasn't that sort of kiss! She was wrapped around his neck!"

"Well perhaps she was trying to catch his attention and he wasn't responding. Was she 'dressed to kill'?

"She was wearing clothes that made her look naked! It was sickening."

"I often disapprove of her attire, darling. She does tend to dress provocatively. I'm not surprised she gets herself into scrapes; but she seems to enjoy them!"

"It's not so much her I'm upset about. It's Bertie – I gave up all my scruples and good intentions because I trusted him. Now I can't go back – I'm ruined!"

"Of course you're not, Melissande! Anyone would think you're the first girl to have been seduced by a predatory man. You'll get over it! Just keep busy and it will soon fade."

"But I don't *want* it too. I can't live without him!"

"Well if that's the case you'll have to establish the true facts of the case and then either forgive him – or forgive him anyway and give him another chance; although it would mean keeping a careful eye open for the rest of your life."

"I can't bear to see him or speak to him. I'd only make a complete fool of myself'"

"But you're bound to see him at poor Mr Haine's funeral. He's moved back to London, now that Mr Haines is better – was better – but he often visits; and Arabella comes down at weekends with that friend of hers, Tristram. I don't think there's anything between her and *Bertie*. She and Tristram behave as though they are madly in love: that's why I'm surprised to hear you say she was kissing Bertie. Perhaps I'm not *so* surprised, having known Arabella for so long; she's never been very 'constant'."

"Mummy what shall I do?"

"Well, events often dictate what we all do in the immediate future. Today we have to go to Mr Haines' funeral. Lady Veronica tells me she has pleaded with Bertie to come back to the Gate Lodge for a while because she simply can't manage by herself, and he arrived today, so it's most likely you will have to face him: she phoned to tell me how relieved she was that he was back. I might add that Arabella has been saying how much they needed you to present your report at the launch of their company next week in London. It seems to me that you have to bite your tongue – behave in a formal way and take each moment as it comes, doing your duty, supporting this little community in the best way you can. It will take some of the pain out of your disappointment over Bertie – although I wouldn't give up on him yet. I feel so sure he's a good man: and to be truthful, I was hoping that you and he might make a match. I've been very taken with him: he's such an attractive person. I've been surprised to hear what you told me."

"But you're not shocked and disgusted?"

"Of course not, my dearest Melissande! You're just a perfectly normal girl!"

"But don't you see how I've let myself down? I've always grown up knowing that marriage is consummated *after* the ceremony and not before."

"That, my darling, is the ideal situation – there's always the risk that the ceremony doesn't take place: men are so fickle! If one is convinced that this man is to be your life's partner, I'm sure God forgives a 'trial run', as it were."

"Mummy, you've never told me *that* before!"

"Haven't I dear?" Mrs Blythe looked a little embarrassed and smiled as she remembered the days when Canon Blythe had been a curate and she a Sunday school teacher, infatuated with him. She still felt a little guilty about the way she had pretended to sprain her ankle when they were alone in the vestry one Saturday – how helping her up had led to the kiss that broke the ice. "I'm sure I *meant* to, when you were old enough." She looked distinctly shifty.

"You didn't, did you? I mean, with Daddy?" Melissande had forgotten her own sorrows for a moment.

"Darling, we're talking about your predicament, aren't we? Not my indiscretions!"

"Don't tell me you two *had* to get married!"

"Of course not, dear, although you were a little premature." Caroline was now in the dock.

Melissande had always rejected her own suspicions, having studied her birth certificate and her parents' marriage licence when applying for a passport. Her birth seemed to have been after a very short pregnancy if her parents had been playing by the rules. In her innocence she had accepted being a premature baby and was grateful it had not affected her consequent development.

"Melissande, there are times when you have to simply 'brave' your way through – behave as though nothing was wrong, press on through the waves of a storm in the hope of tranquil waters ahead. It's the only way to survive – especially if you have a leaky boat! I think it would be magnanimous of you to approach Arabella – offer to take part in the London event, and pretend that you have simply been away on retreat, to freshen your spirit and regain energy. You've put so much into this enterprise – all those late nights in your office – and everyone so full of praise for your work."

The mention of late nights in the office brought it all back. Melissande dissolved into tears again, at which her mother began to lose patience.

"Melissande! You really must take a hold of yourself and control your emotions!" She gave her daughter quite a shake, followed by a loving hug, causing Melissande to stop crying and determinedly blow her nose. Their mother/daughter confidences now exchanged, it was time to face life as though nothing were untoward. A long ring of The Rectory doorbell gave the necessary prompt for action stations.

It was Arabella. She hadn't bothered to change after her ride, but hearing that Melissande was back, had hastened over in the hope of re-opening communications.

"God – you look rough!" Arabella couldn't help her comment – her oldest friend looked awful – red nose and eyes, gaunt, hair limp and lifeless. "Have you had 'flu?"

"You *could* say that?" Said Melissande, truthfully. "Come in, Bella – I must just go to the loo a minute and then I'll be with you." She left Arabella with her mother and disappeared upstairs to wash her face and make some repairs.

"Whatever's wrong with Melissande?"

"My dear, you'll have to have a good talk with her," said Caroline Blythe, determined not to give anything away. "I'm sure she will be fine!"

"We haven't been able to get hold of her at all! Bertie's been tearing his hair out: she's so important to the launch next week."

"I know, dear; I've told her you've been waiting for her to come back – but she really did need some time on her own – after all that brain work. I understand her report was a major achievement. It was, wasn't it?"

"It was! A real hum-dinger: we're delighted with it and that's why everyone's been going bananas about her disappearing!"

"Well do be gentle with her, Arabella. Let her explain in her own time: perhaps she'll talk to you, her oldest friend."

Mrs Blythe couldn't say any more because Melissande had come back and was putting the kettle on. She smiled sweetly at Arabella:

"Coffee or tea?"

"Coffee please: and I wouldn't mind one of The Canon's chocolate biscuits too if they're on offer. I'm a bit peckish after the ride. The stallion's been quite a handful this morning. I'm sure he's remembering that blasted donkey – he keeps trying to go over toward Bunts' caravan."

"I thought it was Miss Marchmont's," said Caroline. "She's been quite friendly, recently, and I've noticed the caravan seems brighter too. Strange, isn't it how situations change? She used to be so po-faced when we met at the shop. I haven't heard any more complaints from her about your housing project. It *was* she who made all that fuss in the papers, wasn't it?"

"That's before Travis began working for us," said Arabella. "But he's turned out to be quite a brick, one way and another. He's doing a good job."

"I wondered how he would fit in – after those first encounters," said Melissande.

Putting on the brave face was actually reviving her interest in TGP and its issues. Her mother noted the change in mood: it was good to see; and it had been quite a thrill to hear Melissande's confession. At last there might be a chance of becoming a grandmother: perhaps with a grandson destined to become a baronet!

She had almost resigned herself to Melissande drifting into being a spinster, but Bertie, if he could be trusted, seemed ideal. He was so handsome and charming; so considerate too.

She could believe Arabella might have made a pass at him, even if it meant competing with her old school-friend, but she found it hard to believe that such a nice man could have been a conspirator in this. She excused herself from the two young women and left them to their coffee, making herself scarce by going up to clean Melissande's office and the other attic rooms.

Since Gwen had been staying, Caroline had become so much more energetic and less of an invalid. Gwen's capability always irritated her, making her feel she ought to be 'doing something', rather than being waited on. After a week or two she forced herself to be more active and, truth to tell, she felt much better.

"Where the bloody Hell have you been?" Arabella had forgotten Mrs Blythe's advice about being gentle with Melissande. Bella's rough approach was something she had always been able to ignore and on this occasion it indicated genuine ignorance. She wasn't trying to be subtle or clever; Bella really wanted to know. "And why did you go off blubbing that night you burst in on Bertie and me?"

"Oh – did I?" Brazened Melissande, offering her friend another of her father's favourite biscuits. "I could see you were 'busy'. I might have had this cold coming on...."

"You wrecked everything! I thought I might be in with a chance of dragging him up the aisle!"

"Why on earth? What about Tristram – is that all over?"

"Not at all! But he's a bit common isn't he? Bertie's got real class – *and* a title. I wouldn't mind being married to someone like that. I thought I'd give it a go – but you came along and fucked it all up!"

"Bella – for goodness sake – you are in The Rectory and my mother's about. Please don't swear like that: we're not in the stable yard!"

"She can't hear – listen to the Hoover! Well you did! Scuppered my chances of becoming the next Lady Lamotte. I've always wanted to be 'Lady' someone – like Mummy. It makes a Hell of a difference to the way people treat you!

Thanks to *you* it doesn't look as though I'll make it, unless Tristram puts half his fortune into the Tories for a peerage."

"But what were you doing with Bertie in the tack room, anyway? Champagne – and you dressed up like a tart!"

"Don't be so bloody insulting! It was a thank-you surprise for saving my horse and I was trying to look 'alluring' – get his trousers off! It was Last Chance Saloon! And what happens? You turn up and turn him off!"

"Was he 'on'?" Melissande was now tense.

"I never found out, thanks to you! I'd only just managed to get him to drink a second glass and it was like trying to seduce a marble statue. After you flounced off, he went really weird – couldn't get away quick enough. He seemed scared out of his wits – kept fussing about the weather – said you had no coat on. I gave up and left him to it. Do you think he's queer?"

"I couldn't possibly know," lied Melissande, rejoicing. "Now – what's all this fuss about me not presenting my paper next week in London?"

Reg's funeral was a sad affair. Lady Veronica had put a notice in the local paper announcing his death and written an obituary to go with it. The Editor of the paper refrained from referring to Reg's connection with the recent controversy over 'flood plain development' at Tytherton Kellaway. He allowed Lady Veronica's piece to be published in full, along with an old photograph that Bertie had found in the Gate Lodge of Reg in the uniform of corporal during his National Service in 1947.

The Rector was surprised at how many people turned out for the service; the church was packed. Mr Haines had plainly been much loved and respected locally.

At The Manor, afterwards, Bertie, Arabella, Tristram and Melissande had to wash glasses, cups and plates in rapid succession – with Tristram having to dash into Chippenham to buy some more sherry and crisps to accommodate all the mourners, who in turn, spent much time discussing how Reg would be missed, Her Ladyship being so aged and apparently lacking in resources.

The general dilapidation and tiredness of the building and its contents was duly observed. People agreed Reg had been holding the place together. As people downed their sherry and wished Reg's spirit a safe journey to Heaven there was murmured speculation as to what would happen to The Manor and its estate.

It was indeed Reg's day, and conversation returned to memories of darts matches won; the shine on old Mr Kelway's car when Reg was chauffeur, and how Reg played a great Left Back for Chippenham, back in the fifties. Mostly though, people remembered his kindness and loyalty to The Manor.

Lady Veronica got Bertie to call for silence so she could say a few words to commemorate his passing. She found this difficult but braced herself to praise his life, and that of Beth his late wife.

"I miss them both, terribly," she concluded. "They kept me going through thick and thin and I am proud to have known them."

Bertie had prevailed on Arabella (who in turn persuaded Tristram) to stay on for a few days to look after Lady Veronica while he dashed over to Suffolk to see his mother. It had been nearly three months since he saw her and while being dutiful son he could keep out of Melissande's way. He knew he had to wean himself from this strong desire to make it up with the young woman who had so disrupted his life. Such disasters must be avoided in future and talking to his mother might help.

Melissande had not expected Bertie to cut himself off from her so completely. She didn't realise he was badly wounded and couldn't risk resuming the role of lover, confidant and companion of someone who behaved so precipitously. For him, once was enough.

Caroline's revelation that her daughter only just scraped into being legitimate, due to her own reckless behaviour, gave Melissande a feeling of being forgiven – for everything. She had hoped that Bertie might be forgiving too and still love her, despite her mistaken outrage.

It was a blow to find that on meeting Bertie now, he had changed towards her. He was formal, polite and courteous but was hiding behind his eyes, not looking at her the way he used to; not offering to seek her company. Any communication was entirely about work. She didn't even dare discuss the matter of her future with TGP, since her contract was due to expire after the launch.

She didn't think she could continue being associated with the company if Bertie was going to be like this. It was awful: she was longing to be in his embrace again but he wasn't having any of it!

In her new intimacy with her mother, she asked for advice.

"He won't have anything to do with me, Mummy. What shall I do?"

"You're going to have to apologise, my darling. You must have hurt him badly, walking out on him then refusing to discuss it."

"But I thought he'd betrayed me!"

"Well he *hadn't*: you know that now. You *do* believe Bella, don't you? Even I can see when she's telling the truth and to be fair, she didn't know you and Bertie were..... close."

Melissande could see that her mother was right: she had to regain Bertie's confidence; but he was an expert at avoiding people he didn't want to see, and was proving elusive. He always had to rush off after board meetings. His duties as Reg's temporary replacement meant working early and late – carrying out 'morning at The Manor', until Lady Veronica was set up for the day; making sure that her needs were met as he worked from her dining room, and, after office hours, retiring to the Gate Lodge to feed the cat and being in bed early.

He promised himself that from now on he was *not* going to get in a position with any woman who might make his life a misery. This experience had taught him: 'don't give your heart to a woman! She'll destroy it!'

He related this decision to his mother during his stay in Suffolk and she listened sympathetically to the whole sad tale.

"I only met Melissande for a very short time, when you were on your way to Holland that time," she said, "but I was *so* impressed. I thought she was such a lovely girl.

"I did too: but look at the way she treated me – it was so unfair: I didn't know Bella was going to do that! Anyone might think I was completely promiscuous!"

"Well, my dear, you *have* had your moments. Remember that house party we had when you first left college. I had to mop up two girls whose hearts you'd broken in just a few days! You were a bit of a Don Juan, at that time."

"That's different, Mummy; they'd been throwing themselves at me and it was hard to refuse."

"Can't you see that Melissande isn't that sort of girl? I haven't met this Arabella but from what you say she's not 'backward in coming forward', whereas Melissande struck me as being very innocent and reserved."

"She told me she'd never been out with a man before," confessed Bertie. "We talked about it a lot, on the way to Holland that time. Her religious upbringing had left her with all sorts of hang-ups and she had to do a lot of soul-searching before she'd even let herself hold hands."

"There you are then, Bertie! Poor girl: she's heard nothing but warnings about men and just when she's allowed herself to have strong feelings for one, she finds you in the embrace of her best friend. What do you *expect* her to think?"

"I do see that, Mummy, but it wasn't *like* that!"

"*You* know that, and *I* know that but the poor girl doesn't! She must think you are a real traitor, unless she's since found out the truth. Won't she have questioned her friend?"

"How do I know? I've decided to keep completely out of her way until I forget her."

"Don't be so petulant! You sound like a teenager! It's a misunderstanding and it needs you two to give each other a chance to sort it out. Shutting yourself off like this won't help and if you've really got strong feelings towards her then what you're doing is *wrong,* and most unfair on Melissande."

"To tell the truth I've never felt worse, Mummy. I can't face the chance of all this happening again. I've decided to get away from that place and those people as soon as I can, even though I've agreed to go back and look after Lady Veronica and the cat until they can find someone else. Once TGP is off the ground I'll get out of that, too, and go back to Ogle. They've been on the phone lately, begging me to go back. The woman they took on is hopeless – serve them right! The chairman was trying to mix business with pleasure – fatal mistake, as now I know!"

"Bertie, hearing you talk about 'Lady Veronica' reminds me of the Lady Veronica we had at school. She was on the staff for a while before she went off to get married. Her father was the Duke of somewhere. We used to be quite friendly. Give me Lady Kelway's phone number, I'll give her a call and see if she's the same one. It would be lovely talk about old times again, if she is."

Lady Lamotte had been impressed with Melissande Blythe, and the way she and Bertie had looked at each other during their brief stay, earlier in the year. At the time she had warmed to the girl and thought what a nice daughter-in-law she might make, once she'd grown up a little. It was time Bertie settled down; perhaps something could be done ......

CHAPTER 26

The weather forecast on the day of the launch was enough to put anyone off travelling. However, media folk, intrepid and indomitable, having set their minds on a day out, turned up for an early breakfast at The Garden Room on the third floor of The Barbican.

"I never guessed there was any kind of garden in this concrete honeycomb!" Bertie had commented as he and the rest of The Board of TGP inspected everything before the guests began to arrive. They had arrived at six-thirty from the hotel in which they had spent the night, close by."

"Well this *is* mostly potted palms, isn't it?" Said Tristram.

"Never mind – it's leafy," said Arabella, defending her choice of venue. And it's no distance from most of the people we want. They'll be able to get here with their eyes shut: it's an early start."

"I thought a lot of them began work at this time anyway," said Bertie.

"Well I suppose they'll need to – the markets in Shanghai and Mumbai have been open for hours – you can't just wake up and expect everyone to have been waiting for you!" Tristram said.

"Oh Tris – you are a bullshitter," Arabella murmured to him. "You're never up before nine!" The others didn't hear as he said out of the corner of his mouth:

"Only when you're around! It's much more fun in bed; otherwise I'm up with the lark!"

"Is everything ready at The Manor?" Asked Mr Penworthy, feeling slightly out of place in these lush surroundings. He rarely visited London and hadn't slept well. The rumble of the city never stopped and he couldn't sleep with the window shut. Car doors were still being slammed at four o'clock in the morning.

"I phoned earlier," said Arabella. "Mel said Auntie wasn't awake yet but we'd hardly recognise the place. They've got the dining room set up for the presentation and the marquee is decked out for the buffet lunch. The caterers were there all day yesterday."

"Have they made sure the coach can get to the front door?" Asked Bertie.

"Yes, Melissande got one of the churchwardens to bring his bus around after the school run, to make sure."

"So even The Rectory Network *can* go commercial!" Commented Tristram.

"Excellent connections with The Management, too!" Said Bertie.

"We'll need help *there*, too, with weather as it is", said Arabella.

It was daunting. Bertie had listened to the shipping forecast earlier on and was glad he wasn't at sea. Storm force winds and poor visibility. The general forecast before *Farming Today* talked of 'amber warnings' and 'be prepared for delays'.

"Well I suppose it will emphasise the point we're trying to make. I wonder whether our site is under water again: it was just going green again last weekend."

"I'll give Travis a ring and we can decide on the best place to take them for a good view," said Bella. "We've got several plans, in case it was like this."

"She's my girl!" Said Tristram, giving her a surreptitious pat on her behind, which she pretended to ignore but rather enjoyed.

They had all been pleased to hear their launch getting a mention on *News Briefing*'s business slot on the radio that morning. The presenter had linked it to the weather forecast.

"Excellent!" Said Tristram. "Have they got someone coming along?"

"Yes – and I made sure she had a full briefing pack yesterday. The others'll get theirs at breakfast." Arabella was showing off her talent in public relations.

It had been Bertie's idea to keep Melissande at Tytherton Kelway, rather than go to London. His real reason was to avoid her, but he made a convincing argument that 'an effective member of the Board' should be there to ensure everything was ready when the coach arrived; everyone agreed it should be her.

At the last Board meeting in Chippenham, Bertie had proposed the programme:

"On arrival they can see the site, witness the problem and hear our solution; then we'll give them coffee and Mel can hold forth on how it can make money for them." First, though, he needed to marshal the diverse group and get them to Chippenham – through near hurricane conditions.

The invited guests began to turn up at the Barbican, dripping in their raincoats and wrestling with inside-out umbrellas. The gale, its blasts magnified by the complex's towers as it raced to keep up with itself, blew rain under doors and tore at the clothes of the leaning Londoners fighting their way to their rendezvous.

Once safe in the calmer air of the reception area the mood was that of a brave group facing daunting odds: good cheer, courage and determination. This was going to be fun, come what may!

"Rather like a Cornish beach holiday," commented Tristram, wryly, "but they seem to be in good form."

The continental breakfast and strong coffee, combined with the central heating, dried people out and kept spirits high. It prepared them for the coach ride to their unknown destination, 'not too far from London', the secrecy of which had added to their adventure.

As everyone finished their second coffee, and before anyone slipped out for a quick fag, Arabella, with perfect timing, called for order.

"Hello everyone!" She was using her 'stable' voice, which normally contained swearwords directed at the stallion for treading on her foot or pushing her against the door. It was a voice that could stop traffic or break glass, and there was instant quiet.

"Lovely to see you here on such a fine morning!"

Pause for laughter.

"I'd like to introduce you to our chairman, Sir Bertrand Lamotte, who will give you a brief over-view of this morning's programme."

Bertie stepped up to the lectern with its light and microphone.

"I think you all deserve a medal for turning up on a morning like this," he began. "But for us, it helps make our point that the time has come when we can no longer expect this to be 'summer'. It might be changing into 'the June monsoon' – or equally, a long period of drought. We simply don't know. All we *do* know is that, according to the best meteo-brains and research findings, in future we're not going to *have* the traditional four seasons."

He was gratified to see that some of the journalists had their notebooks and pencils out and were using them. He went on:

"Many of us have been living in denial about climate change and it has cost a lot of us, a *lot* of money. Just consider, over the past winter, the price paid by the residents of The Somerset Levels! Some of you will have been writing cheques that come straight off *your* bottom line as a consequence. Government, too, has had to dig deep into the Treasury's pocket to pay for dredging, pumping, rescue teams and measures to calm the population. Just imagine trying to sell a property around there!"

At that moment as if on cue, a squall of wind, loaded with horizontal rain, hit the terrace outside the window of the Garden Room. Two palms keeled over and rolled past in a scene reminiscent of hurricane clips from South Carolina. Bertie gestured towards them as they left a trail of earth and broken fronds.

"Let's face it! We've all got to change if we are to thrive in the new world of uncertain climate, floods, droughts and unknown hazards. *That's* what TGP – The Grand Plan – is all about. We all know that every new challenge carries opportunities for the astute – and we like to think we're on to a winner here!"

Bertie stopped to take a sip of his coffee, which he had ledged on the shelf of the lectern. He wasn't using notes but was gratified to see there was hardly a still pencil or Apple Air in the room.

Melissande was dreading today. Last night, she and Lady Veronica had entertained the four visiting speakers in The Royal Crescent Hotel in Bath. They had agreed to an early supper and she had brought Lady Veronica back in time for her usual bedtime.

Melissande had been surprised at how full of life the indomitable octogenarian still was.

"It's been such a relief, having you young people getting involved with The Manor," Veronica had told her. "You've no idea how much better I feel; and John would have been so happy."

Melissande herself had hardly slept. It wasn't the arrangements and preparation that spoiled her rest but the hope that she had an opportunity to win Bertie back.

If she could look her best, make a faultless presentation and somehow get him cornered: force him to talk, perhaps she could make her apology and start rebuilding the relationship that had become the most important thing in her life.

The prospect of failure in this – not TGP – was what kept her awake. Giving up on sleep at around five, she decided to get herself ready; washed her hair, dried it and brushed it until it shone as it hung down, heavy and loose over her shoulders. Wearing her new contact lenses, the frames of her specs no longer concealed her eyebrows and she borrowed her mother's tweezers to give them that last tweak for perfection. Very gingerly she plucked the odd one that interrupted otherwise long, even curves and natural delicacy.

Having lost so much weight, she had had to buy a new outfit for the occasion; and rather than a restricting suit, she'd chosen a close-fitting black dress with three silver buttons, giving her choice as to how much of her cleavage might be displayed. Wearing this, she could reach up to point at graphs and maps during the presentation, without pulling a jacket out of shape or have it rising up above the skirt to reveal a white blouse. This stretchy garment was all one piece, and it showed her contours in a flattering way. She nearly changed her bra because it allowed her other two little buttons to reveal their position if they got alerted: then thought 'why shouldn't they?' They were in exactly the right place each side and she knew Bertie found them hard to resist.

In the past she would never have dreamed of wearing such a dress but knowing now what she did, and still hungry for Bertie's attention and love, she was prepared to live dangerously. She had to, if she was going to overcome his stubborn retreat and make up for her stupidity.

As the coachload of journalists, insurance actuaries, fund managers and bankers headed West towards the M4 motorway through the pouring rain, watching TGP's promotional video on the screens in front of them, Melissande spent a little more time applying make-up the way she had learned two days ago at a salon in Bath where she had decided to spend some of her research fees on a 'summer makeover'. When she was finally ready to face Bertie and his high-powered guests, she knocked on her mother's bedroom door and went in to display the results of her labour.

"Mummy, what do you think?" She stood inside the door and looked at her mother sitting up in bed reading her morning prayers. It was only recently that Melissande had begun to show an interest in her own looks and apparel. Her mother had welcomed this and was finding the new openness between the two to be a great joy. It had brought them together in a warm conspiracy.

Caroline Blythe now knew why her daughter had been pining and was rejoicing that she wasn't giving up and withering away, but taking action to put things right between herself and her erstwhile lover. She longed to be able to help, but now, looking over her reading glasses she beheld a vision that made her gasp with delight.

"My darling you look *beautiful!*" She put down the prayer book and clasped her hands together with pleasure. "Such a lovely dress – and I never realised you had such a perfect figure! Is that a new bra?"

"No, Mummy, there's just less over it! Thank goodness I haven't lost weight there but elsewhere."

"You have a perfect waistline, darling. Have you measured it? And what a difference it makes, now you've taken off those awful schoolmarm spectacles! Can you see properly?"

"Of course I can, Mummy! I've got to be able to read my notes."

They had never been able to talk so easily and frankly. Caroline had always felt sensitive over Melissande's early birth and almost as a penance, made up her mind that her child should be brought up 'keeping these things in perspective'. She still couldn't bring herself to ask one more question: as to whether her daughter might have forgotten pants. Surely not!

Mrs Blythe was not au fait with 'the thong' and Melissande had only recently dared wear such a thing. This dress demanded no lines in the wrong places – especially since she would be spending part of the time with her back to the audience, pointing at charts.

Events of the past few weeks, including the new freedom and closeness between mother and daughter, were giving Caroline more energy and motivation to 'do things'. Melissande's absence and Gwen's irritant presence had done much to make her less of an invalid.

"I think Bertie will find you irresistible! Silly man – it's time he realised you are perfect for each other."

Melissande didn't want to start tearful conversations on this subject immediately before appearing in public so she changed the subject.

"Are you going to be all right, Mummy, coming over to The Manor?"

"Of course I am. Your father will drop me off and I can walk home afterwards."

Caroline Blythe had promised her friend Lady Veronica that she would come to give her moral support. They had agreed to sneak off after the presentation for a quiet cup of tea and perhaps a nap. "They won't want old ladies around during question time."

"I must go and make sure the speakers' transport picks them up from the hotel," Mel told her mother, giving her a departing kiss.

By the time she arrived at The Manor, the place was like a beehive, with last minute details being checked and food being prepared as the invading chefs took over the kitchen. She hurried to the front door as soon as the bell clanged, to greet the speakers.

It was good to see Professor Veerman again. He had been so helpful and welcoming in Holland and now it was Melissande's turn to return the compliment. When inviting him to be one of the judges, on behalf of TGP she had made sure he was generally happy with its aims and plans, although he warned her he might raise some points that needed attention.

The professor had been pleased to see Jonathan Porritt as the 'green' panel member, whose foundation *Forum for the*

Future was proposing a host of progressive ideas on building construction, energy, communities and lifestyle in the face of climate change.

"I've read your book *The World We Made*," Melissande told Jonathan, when she first approached him, "and I think our project would fit in there nicely!"

"It looks as though we are on the same wavelength," he agreed, "and I'm looking forward to seeing the entries we get for the competition. It will be fun trying to pick a winner, but I suspect it's going to be difficult."

The Building Research Establishment had sent Guy Hammersley, the chief executive of their *BRE Ventures* company, which they said was always interested in new techniques and aspects of building. He was going to speak briefly about what his company did and would say he expected architects and engineers to enter the spirit of the competition. He told Melissande he was looking forward to working with the rest of the panel, adding that he was new to the paintings of Ruth Stage, the landscape artist, also on the panel, but had looked her up on Google to be pleasantly surprised. He could see why TGP had invited her to take part: good buildings needed to look right in their settings.

The last to arrive, the evening before, had been the one with the shortest journey, architect Kevin Murphy, from Bath. He had been chosen for his experience of introducing acceptable change into treasured scenery. A director at Aaron Evans Architects, he'd been delayed at a meeting and had to rush to the hotel straight from work.

Melissande, as sixth member and secretary of the panel, had sent each of them an early draft of her report and had taken on board many of their comments and suggestions, incorporating them in the final copy. She was now able to thank them in person for their participation.

The general atmosphere was enthusiastic, and as one of them commented: "the weather's on your side: just look at those clouds – they're truly ominous."

The clouds were indeed unusual, hanging in a sky that resembled a Victorian etching, with vivid, clear-cut rollers of dark grey getting blacker into the distance and for the moment, hardly moving, the wind, for the moment, had died down.

The panel, now assembled, was ready to meet the party from London, which arrived five minutes early, much to Bertie and Tristram's relief, despite the hold-ups on the M4 near Hungerford. During an informal coffee break, TGP directors mingled to ensure everyone was introduced to each other and Bertie was pleased to note that many of the visitors were already acquainted. The conversation centred on the weather and the preview of TGP they'd watched during their stormy journey. It was decided to delay the site visit until later in the hope that the weather may have improved. They would stay indoors at the Manor for the initial proceedings.

Various issues seemed to present themselves and individual editors and reporters were beginning to see the lines they'd like to take in their stories. They had plenty of questions to ask after the briefing that followed.

As Bertie announced Melissande's presentation, dripping water from the ceiling caused a slight movement of chairs to allow one of the catering staff to place a bucket strategically. Bertie was able to pay a short tribute to Reg Haines, 'our sadly missed colleague and board member who died suddenly, quite recently'. He said this diversion would not have occurred if Reg had still been with us: 'He would have already placed a bucket in the right place upstairs – he knew this place so well!'

As the drips tapped their relentless arrival in the bucket, Melissande began her presentation, showing slides comparing investment costs and projected returns in different scenarios over the next five years. She didn't go on long enough to be boring and after ten minutes, drawing attention to various sections of her report, she concluded:

"In Britain's current situation of housing shortage at all price levels and the scarcity of agreed sites for new building, I think you will agree that TGP offers attractive, novel and profitable ways forward for the building and property sectors."

Bertie thanked her and added a few words about other possible enterprises that could be included on The Manor's low-lying meadows next to the River Avon.

"Local farmers with similar low-lying land have been looking for how best to use it, now that the weather seems to be changing. We shall be able to propose profitable solutions for them too – without changing agricultural practice too much, *or* the ecology of the countryside, except by enriching it. Some neighbours have already begun to plant willow beds, which will be harvested every few years as energy crops. The leaves can be used as animal feed and the woody stems – traditionally used for basket-making – can be made into small wood pellets for use instead of fuel oil in domestic central heating boilers."

He paused to allow people to write, and then continued: "We have gone one step further and begun discussing the possibility of including a system of 'district heating' for TGP's first project here, bringing insulated pipes to each house from a combined heat and power plant on higher land, just up-river. It would use willow chips, which are cheaper than the wood pellets. The heating pipes can follow the same service ducts as the drainage and electricity, so although it adds cost, now is the right time to include them in the project."

During the questions, for which Bertie had allowed plenty of time in his programme, it emerged that home-grown energy from short-rotation coppice not only provided excellent habitat for wildlife, especially birds, but also slowed down flood water, extracting from it nitrates and other plant nutrients that might be leached off neighbouring farmland.

Tristram then took the rostrum, spelling out the various ways investors might get involved, suggesting that TGP would have wide appeal. He called for national companies, conservationists and groups such as the RSPB to contact him to see how they might be able to pursue their special interests.

"At this stage, the project is still very flexible and can incorporate many innovative concepts," he said. While summing up the commercial and social benefits of the new scheme, he drew attention to the bucket.

"Ladies and gentlemen – the drips have stopped! I think that after lunch we might even have a little sunshine that will give you the chance to see what a beautiful area this is, and visualise what will become the first of a whole new era of waterside living – even if it's not all year round."

After further discussion, Bertie asked board members to hand out the presentation packs which, he said, contained full details of the competition for architects, designers, engineers and artists, for which the winning entries could receive some fifty thousand pounds in prizes, as well as wide publicity.

"After lunch, we'll go for a tour of the site; you can take pictures and enjoy the scenery. Then we'll have tea and climb back on the coach for London. Looking out of the window, I think it's looking promising: there's at least enough blue sky to make whatever garment a rabbit might want."

From their armchairs by Lady Veronica's bedroom window, she and Caroline Blythe watched the assembly making its way across the lawn over a path of freshly laid dry straw towards the marquee.

"They seem to be very animated," remarked Caroline. "Just look at them, deep in conversation!"

"Let's hope it's positive! It's so important that this thing works," said Veronica; "it's our last chance of saving The Manor. Shall we go down and join them? There's to be a rather nice aperitif and I've been rather looking forward to it. It will be fun to meet so many new people, too."

Melissande helped usher guests to their various tables, but by the time everyone had enjoyed their glass of Pimm's and taken their seats, she was disappointed to find that she was nowhere near Bertie: he had seen to that, placing each board member on a different table. He would have his back to her so she wouldn't even be able to see his face. Lady Veronica however, could, and observed to Caroline that 'he looked rather drawn and sad'.

"I'm in touch with his mother, you know," she confided. "She telephoned the other evening, wondering whether I had taught at her school, just after the War.

"I didn't know you'd been a teacher," said Caroline.

"Well it wasn't for long. I helped on the sporting side until John came along and swept me away to come here. I lost touch with all my girls. It was so nice to hear from one of them after all these years. Bertie's mother was Cecily Akenfield – such a nice girl and very useful with a hockey stick!"

"I'd like to *brain* him with a hockey stick," said Caroline. "Poor Melissande is distraught, pining after him. I don't know if you were aware, but she and Bertie fell for each other on their recent trip to Europe; but when they got back, she found him and Arabella apparently in a passionate embrace. It upset her so

318

much she nearly had a breakdown and that's why she fled to Scotland. It was only Mr Haines' funeral and this launch that brought her back. I made her realise she had misunderstood what she'd witnessed and she's been making efforts to put things right between herself and Bertie – but he's not having any of it. He's being formal and cold and keeping a heartless distance from her. The poor girl's beside herself, not knowing what to do."

"Well I learned a little of that from Bertie's mother," said Lady Veronica. "I think that was the real reason for her telephoning. He'd mentioned his involvement here and spoken of me, making her remember her school days. If I turned out to be the right Veronica, she was hoping I might know *you*. Then perhaps we could intervene to get Bertie to see sense. She had been very much taken to Melissande when they popped in to see her on their way to Holland. She was hoping they might make a match."

"Melissande certainly returned from that expedition looking very pleased with herself and it's heartbreaking to see her suffering now, all due to a misunderstanding: so unnecessary!" Caroline spoke with exasperation.

"Cecily Lamotte saw how unhappy Bertie was, after some tiff with Melissande. He had set his mind on forgetting her – such a lovely girl – and we began talking about what we might do."

"Isn't that rather risky, interfering?" Caroline Blythe was inexperienced in such matters, knowing more of family break-ups and divorce. It had often involved The Canon calling her in to comfort a weeping woman while he talked to an angry husband or partner.

"Of course it is: but I can see why Bertie doesn't need to be at home on his estate – not while his mother is around. She's a very enterprising woman. She had some ideas that I thought might be very effective in getting this young couple to see sense."

"Really? I'd be so pleased if that happened. Melissande will be ill if she loses any more weight."

"She does look ravishing today, though, doesn't she?" Said Lady Veronica, admiringly.

"That's kind of you – but I have to agree. She's never looked glamorous until now. She was always a sober dresser but since she met Bertie she's changed completely and now she's dressed to kill! But you can see how he's keeping his distance: so well that she can't get near enough to kill him! It's such a pity!"

"Well," said Veronica conspiratorially, "Cecily came up with an idea which sounded most promising."

It was getting quite hard for the two women to hear each other, as tongues were loosened by red wine, and then white (to go with pudding). Conversation in the marquee had increased in volume by several decibels.

"I don't think they'd miss us if we left them to their coffee and went back to my room, do you? I can tell you all about it," said Lady Veronica.

They excused themselves 'to rest after all the excitement': and to plot.

CHAPTER 27

The coach, on its way back to London, must have been sending out 4G signals all across Britain as the media transmitted their stories to newsrooms, blogs, Twitter and Facebook.

Everyone had his or her own take on their memorable visit to Tytherton Kellaway and the Manor's flooded meadows, the muddy River Avon flowing into and out of them. The BBC *Farming Today* reporter was editing her interviews on willow coppicing and district heating; the *Financial Times* columnist was picking quotes from Melissande's feasibility study and suggesting that green-minded investors and ethical fund managers should take a good look; *Country Living* was going through the rich choice of photos his photographer had gathered; and architectural bloggers and magazine staff were going big on this new competition, predicting a new era of wooden and lightweight construction.

Later that evening, Tristram and Arabella opened a bottle of champagne, cock-a-hoop over the launch. They had given up on Bertie, who, after accompanying the guests back to London on the coach, pleaded pressure of work and went back to his flat alone.

"I can't wait for the morning," said Bella. "Fingers crossed we're going to make a hit in the press and media. I've rarely seen them so enthusiastic, and that final cloudburst was so spectacular they won't forget their day at Tytherton!"

"I thought someone had copped it when lightning struck the telegraph pole," said Tristram. "Then when it hit that tree by the Marchmont caravan."

"Travis says the tree only just missed it," said Bella. "Bloody lucky!"

"Travis did a good job, though, didn't he? I'd never have expected he could present himself so well."

"Shows you what a job can do for a man," said Bella, nodding sagely.

"I must try it!"

Next day, the pair were indeed able to celebrate. Both the weather and TGP made headlines and TV bulletins. One report read:

NEW HOPE FOR BRITAIN'S FLOOD VALLEYS
Venice rises from the mud in Wiltshire.
Plagued recently by annual overflow from the River Avon a landowner has given up trying to farm low-lying meadows and is transforming them into a luxury housing development with amphibious homes that will rise above the flood water.

With Britain facing ever more unpredictable and extreme weather, planners, builders and investors are seeking ways in which home-owners can remain secure.

Insurance underwriters visiting the scheme said it also gave hope to home-owners on the Somerset Levels, the Vale of Evesham, Tewkesbury, and York. No longer will they have to see their property and possessions disappear beneath muddy water as rivers force their way into the house through doors, windows and, worst of all, from sewers and drains.

"This is going to bring down property insurance premiums very significantly," one broker told our correspondent.

Similar techniques offer new opportunities in other parts of the UK and Europe, claimed Amphib 21 Ltd, unveiling a design competition for the novel houses.

The buildings will be comparatively light-weight and will rise above the floods without becoming cut off from services such as clean water, electricity and drainage. They won't rock or make occupants seasick but residents will be able to live and commute as usual, because during floods the Amphib 21 ferry, manned by estate staff, will carry them to their cars parked on higher ground. It is part of the 'Community package' service charge for the new properties.

Amphib 21 has studied amphibious structures in Holland, Italy and further afield, adapting techniques to fit in with Britain's strict planning regulations.

"We are also respecting the local people's desire to keep the countryside green and beautiful," a spokeswoman said. "What we need now are imaginative and beautiful designs for modern living."

Last night, insurance companies and investors showed their approval as they signed up for the project, which already has planning permission and government backing.

Chief Executive of the new company, Sir Bertrand Lamotte, formerly of Ogle Associates, speaking at the launch of the competition at Tytherton Kellaway Manor, told the press and investors that the company was receiving more than £2m from the recently announced £6bn funding for local governments, designed to boost local economies.

The new 'Growth Deal' fund, which is to be matched by private investment, will go towards supporting local businesses, creating jobs, building new houses and local infrastructure improvements.

"Wiltshire Council along with The City of Guildford are amongst the first to be taking up this initiative by the Coalition," Sir Bertrand told our reporter.

"Councillors and planning staff have given us full co-operation and support," he said; attributing much of this to Amphib21's principle of complete transparency over its aims and objectives, which had proved so beneficial in winning local support.

Reading it out loud to Arabella as they ate croissants and cherry jam in bed, Tristram laughed.

"Some *support*! That's what they think!" He chortled. "But it was certainly local! The reason that bloody Marchmont woman shut up was nothing to do with transparency! It was your randy stallion, plus Bunt washing her caravan and us employing his son! But if the media believe Bertie, good luck to 'em!"

"Travis has been OK, though: you've got to acknowledge that!" Said Bella.

"He's been the biggest surprise of the whole affair," said Tristram. "Turned out to be great! The way he's paddled about for the last few months – bloody marvellous. All those little flags: damn good idea: the journalists could make out exactly where we were."

"Bertie did well to get hold of the grant, didn't he?"

"He did – but he bloody well should have – he knows everyone up there in Whitehall and TGP is just the kind of thing they're looking for. It's all very well splashing money about but finding something sensible to *spend* it on is another matter."

He read on as the next paragraph caught his imagination:

"Hang on, there's more about those grants. I might have been wrong about Bertie and his friends in high places. Apparently it's *not* decided in Whitehall but at county level. Listen:

"The £6bn is the first instalment of £12bn the coalition is investing in a series of local initiatives. Prime Minister David Cameron describes 'Growth Deals' as 'a crucial part of our long-term plan to secure Britain's future.' He has said that for too long the UK economy has been too London-focused and centralised. 'Growth Deals will help change all that. They are about firing up our great cities, towns and counties so they can become powerhouses. By trusting local people, backing business and investing in infrastructure, skills and housing, we can create thousands of new jobs.'

"The government says it expects the investment to lead to work on more than 150 roads, 150 housing developments and 20 railway stations, as well as kick-starting super-fast broadband networks. The project at Tytherton Kellaway is one of the first schemes to be announced, following decisions by Wiltshire Council."

"Someone's on the ball, anyway," commented Tristram. "They got this out pretty quickly, didn't they?"

"I remember seeing Nick Clegg banging on about it on TV," said Arabella. "Bertie must have chased it up fast!"

"That's more than he did for you, isn't it?" Laughed Tristram. "You couldn't even get his hand on your bum!"

"Don't be so common, Tris," rebuked Arabella. "My action was in the cause of commercial intelligence."

"Your allure was a complete failure. I'm amazed, because Bertie's never been able to resist a nice arse!"

"Well he resisted mine. I thought he must be 'of other inclinations'. He told *you* what he had in mind for The Manor, didn't he? Have you two got something I didn't know about?"

"Certainly not! I'd much rather roll around with you!" He squeezed her knee. "I just asked him – and he told me. I suspect you had ulterior motives: wanted to see whether you could nail him. You fancy a title, don't you? Then you'd have dumped me!"

At this perceptive remark Arabella had the grace to redden a little, to hide which, she slipped out of bed to fetch the coffee pot.

"Don't be so beastly!" Even her departing rear looked outraged as she headed towards the kitchen.

She did, however, make a mental note that Tristram knew her better than she had imagined. He didn't seem to mind and it added to her hunch that he might be the perfect life partner.

Alone in his flat, Bertie was feeling worse. Whisky had not been a solution to his unhappiness the night before. His head was thumping and his underlying depression was still sapping his will to live. He was pining for Melissande but still resolute to erase her from his heart. What was making it all the more difficult was that she wasn't letting him go: yesterday she had still been making attempts to approach him.

She had looked stunning and was the star of the show, outshining the other well-dressed and shapely women from London – even Arabella, who looked fantastic (but perhaps just a little gaudy).

Bertie, however, had resisted as she kept turning up next to him: so close at one stage that he caught a memory-filled whiff of her rosewater scent. He had done his best to be polite and courteous, despite his longing to take her in his arms and express his undying love and forgiveness. He couldn't allow himself that luxury.

Now, he faced another miserable day, hoping things might improve as time passed. He must wean himself away from Tytherton Kellaway, TGP and everyone connected. He would phone Ogle and accept their offer of a directorship: it would keep him occupied. He took two paracetamol and tried to go back to sleep.

"They need their heads knocking together and *Bertie* needs a good shake," said his mother to Lady Veronica on the telephone later that morning. After reading about yesterday's triumph at Tytherton Kellaway, dramatised by one of the worst storms in living memory, she had phoned her old friend with congratulations. She had already spoken with Bertie but found him unexpectedly subdued and unwilling to talk. She mentioned this to Veronica, wondering why, after such a successful event, her son wasn't more chirpy.

"I think he and Melissande might still be harbouring some disagreement," Lady Veronica suggested. "I was talking to Caroline Blythe last night and she told me quite a lot. Did you know they had become very 'close' – your Bertie and Melissande?"

"I did – and had great hopes for it," said Cecily. "Such a lovely girl, and so cultured. I thought she would be ideal for Bertie: he needs someone like that: graceful as well as clever."

"I know what you mean. I often wish my niece were more like her. Arabella does tend to be – how shall I put it – brassy. She's got bags of spunk and *go*, but is rather self-centred and demanding: such a pity, because she is so good-looking and *ought* to be able to marry anyone."

"Bertie remarked that she seemed to be keen on his old friend Tristram."

"Oh yes, I think she is: a pity really because he doesn't have quite the same .... breeding..... as your boy, does he?"

"He *is* very enterprising and has done *so* well in the City," said Cecily in Tristram's defence; "and he's been very loyal to Bertie ever since they were teenagers: very different characters, but they seem to complement each other."

"Well that's like Melissande and Arabella; they've been friends for years – but are like chalk and cheese! I think they've been good for each other, and even yesterday were working well together. Bella's always very bossy but normally Melissande takes no offence – except recently, when I've noticed she seems to be avoiding us. I put it down to her being so busy with her report."

"My morning newspaper is terribly complimentary about that, too," said Cecily. "It's partly why I'm phoning. I wanted to congratulate you. Your fortunes look as though they're about to turn for the better."

"If they do, it's entirely because of your son, Cecily. He's been marvellous – having just turned up out of nowhere, he saved poor Mr Haine's life and looked after us all so magnificently. I'd hate to lose him and I'm glad you phoned, because Caroline Blythe has been telling me the whole sad story of what went wrong between him and Melissande."

Without giving away too many confidences Lady Veronica then related what her friend had told her the night before: how she had had to stay up late with Melissande trying to comfort her, following the girl's failure to make it up with Bertie.

"Caroline is very worried," said Veronica. "Her daughter has lost too much weight, and although it made her look so magnificent yesterday, if it goes on it won't be healthy. She seems to have lost interest in everything and has been moping about the house, going over to the stables at funny times and hardly speaking. The atmosphere at The Rectory has not been at all conducive to heavenly love and thankfulness."

Lady Veronica didn't often gossip but she felt that Cecily needed to hear the whole story: "Caroline's sister has been staying for several weeks and both Caroline and her husband find her very irritating, despite her essential helpfulness. It seems to have stirred Caroline to rise miraculously from her sick-bed and do more for herself, which I think she *should* have been doing before, although I didn't like to say so. She could probably manage The Rectory without either Melissande *or* Gwendoline. She and The Rector would, of course, miss Melissande if she got married, but Caroline's desperate for grandchildren."

"I have to admit I would love some, too!" Lady Lamotte confessed. "Bertie needs to settle down and I had high hopes that it might be with Melissande. Do you think we might intervene in some way?"

"Let's put on our thinking caps," said Veronica. "Then I'll have a word with Caroline."

Danielle and Trevor had been reading the local paper. The near miss, when the tree had come thundering down close to the caravan – in full view of the nation's press – had been widely reported, and the local journalist who later approached Danielle for her views on 'flood-plain development' was hoping he might be able to resurrect her protest. He had promised to quote her at length. Danielle wanted to check he hadn't misconstrued whatever she might have said.

"I was hoping we could fade into the background again," said Danielle. "We don't want them coming round saying we've got to get off of here. I had another letter last week, demanding this and that. I can see we're going to have to go!"

"I told you the caravan didn't stand out so much when it was sort-of greeny coloured but you wouldn't let it stay like that, would you? You had to make me scrub it up. Now it sticks out like a sore thumb!"

"Well, you can't see the van any more: not with that fallen tree in front of it," said Danielle. "Lucky it didn't flatten our little home! Spoiled the view a bit, though, didn't it?"

"Never mind the bloody view!" Trevor was a great believer in 'out of sight, out of mind', especially when it came to planners and other busybodies. "Now we can't be seen they'll forget all about us,"

"Until the leaves drop off!"

"The van will be green again by then, won't it?"

Trevor folded the paper and put it by the miniature wood-burner.

"By the way, that donkey of yours is looking bloody enormous!"

"Poor Doris! She's like a barrage balloon – can't hardly walk. The vet says she's due any day."

"Well if she doesn't produce soon she's going to burst and that will be the end of it," said Trevor.

"And if that happens I shall definitely put in a claim. Your Travis will have to help, now he's working for them. They can certainly afford it: all that government money!"

"Bertie, dear, is that you?"

It had been quite an effort, groping to find the phone beside his bed and recognising his mother's voice he made no great effort to sound bright or polite.

"Yes."

"You took so long I thought I'd got the wrong number. You are usually such an early riser. Are you well?"

"I'm fine, thank you."

"Well you don't sound it! But I'm glad I've caught you. I thought you might have gone out. Your launch must have gone so well: I saw it on the news *and* in the papers. You ought to be on top of the world, collecting all those investors."

"There's not all that much for me to do, now. Tristram and his girl-friend are seeing to all that. I'm just wondering what to do next – probably going back to Ogle."

By now he was sitting up.

"Why so gloomy then? It can't be all bad, can it?"

"I'm fine, really! Mummy, what do you want? I'd really like to make some coffee, now that you've woken me up!"

"Shall I call you back when you've had some? Perhaps you'll be easier to talk to! I've got to go out and see the men before I have my breakfast – we've got to do something about all the blackgrass – our crop consultant's had a few spraying ideas."

"I thought grass was green."

"Oh dear – you've got so much to learn before I retire," said Lady Lamotte. "It's not the grass itself, Bertie – it's the black seed heads that make dark patches in fields of cereals. It's getting worse and no one seems to have the answer."

"Fascinating!"

"But that's not why I'm phoning, Bertie. However, what you've told me is very helpful because I was going to ask a favour but was worried you might be too busy. You could spare your poor old mother just a couple of days, couldn't you?"

"Do you want me to come down? Something wrong?"

"Nothing wrong, dear; but you know we've discovered that Lady Veronica was at my old school – on the staff? Well, we've been catching up on old times and I'd very much like to go and visit her. Knowing that you visit them frequently I thought I might come down with you. I could catch the train up to Liverpool Street, if you would meet me, and we could get a cab over to Paddington and be in Tytherton by lunchtime, couldn't we?"

"Can't you go on your own?"

"I could if I *had* to, Bertie, but I find crossing London from Liverpool Street to Paddington so trying. It would be so much nicer if you were with me – I hardly ever see you these days!"

"When do you want to go?"

"I'm all ready to leave as we speak."

"What – today? You'd have to get your skates on!"

"Well tomorrow then."

"I can't spend long down there. I'm trying to let them run it themselves, now everything's taken off. I was going to deal with the design competition entries from here. The money's coming in and the others are quite capable of overseeing the ground-works contracts."

"Does 'the others' include that nice Melissande?"

"Yes – and Mr Penworthy. They're very competent."

"Do you see her often?"

"Who?" Bertie pretended not to know, although the mention of her name stabbed him.

"Melissande! She's on the board, isn't she?"

"She is, but ... no, why?"

"I just thought you might. Such a nice girl!"

"Yes, charming – but no." Bertie wanted to sound disinterested but his mother could hear that Lady Veronica's analysis had been on the mark.

"I see: oh well; let's agree on which train you can meet tomorrow."

Cecily's railway timetable showed she could avoid peak hour fares by catching the seven fifty-eight from Halesworth. She emailed her itinerary and ETA to Bertie.

'Oh well,' thought Bertie as he noted the details: 'it will be one more day to cross off before going back to work.'

His year and a day still had some time to run, and something *might* turn up to reverse the current bad fortune. This unhappiness was the worst challenge he'd had so far. Perhaps it was one of the dragons he had to face: 'I'd rather have fought a couple of real ones and seen off robber bands than go through all this: at least it would have been decisive', he complained.

On reflection, perhaps he'd been dealing with a coven of wicked witches disguised as beautiful temptresses, but he couldn't simply give up seeking his fortune at this late stage, having made himself the pledge that day in the London park. There was still time for some genie or wizard to rescue him. 'I deserve a bit of a break,' he told himself: 'a chap's got to win sometimes.'

During this last week or two, time had begun to drag and he was considering packing his knapsack again and setting off, perhaps even for Scotland, in search of a bit of peace. People there would be too busy arguing about their forthcoming referendum on independence to bother him.

He would avoid pubs, abbeys and religious communities and stick to hotels and whisky. Perhaps westerly gales and pouring rain might wash away his unhappiness; yet part of him, resist as he may, thrilled at the thought of possibly seeing Melissande tomorrow. With luck she wouldn't know of his visit, so he could avoid her; and with a bit more luck, if she *did* find out, she would leave him alone.

It had rubbed salt into his wounds, the way she tried to 'talk about things'. He knew it would be best to make a clean break and put this episode down to experience. He ought to have known better: mythical sirens often made themselves beautiful and hard to resist: all those blissful days and nights in Venice – and in The Rectory attic – they must have been trials of temptation he had failed. Now, he was suffering the consequences: the shock and grief of her rejection for no good reason.

Tomorrow's test must surely be the last: but he was determined that Melissande was not going to lure him onto the rocks of despair again: the whole thing was too painful to repeat.

The young baronet, with no armour and no fine white horse, was, however, unprepared for the next trial to confront him. He had barely time to shave and drink two cups of black coffee when the phone made him jump again. This time it was Lady Veronica.

"Bertie – it's about the cat!"

"Oh dear! Is she all right? Someone's been feeding her, haven't they?"

"Yes of course: Melissande's been very good about that: she does it when she comes over to do the stable – although I'm never sure when that will be: she's been so irregular lately."

"So what's the matter?" Bertie was trying not to sound impatient. Fond as he was of Lady Veronica this did seem rather a fatuous conversation, especially when he wanted to continue his introspective and miserable wallowing.

"I'm having to consider having her put down."

The stark statement shook him out of his black mood.

"How frightful! Why ever's that?"

Bertie had been missing the unconditional friendship the animal had given him: suiting herself as to when she graced his lap with warmth and purring before returning to the comfort of the Manor drawing-room fireplace. A vet destroying his four-legged friend was unthinkable. His headache was now throbbing again.

"I simply can't manage to look after her," Lady Veronica went on. "Since you went back to London, Melissande has been looking after her parents, me, the horse *and* the cat, and it's too much for her. She's now talking about leaving altogether – returning to Scotland: goodness knows what for, although things aren't easy at The Rectory – that sister of Caroline's was very trying and Melissande is becoming visibly run down. I feel I must reduce her workload by any way possible and getting rid of the cat would certainly help."

"Lady Veronica, I'm very sorry but what is all this to do with me?"

"I was wondering whether, since you are going to bring your mother here tomorrow, you might stay on for two or three days. I simply can't manage on my own and you are so capable. Your mother says she would love to stay so we can talk about the old days: we haven't spoken for nearly half a century! I thought perhaps you might assist me in finding someone to come and help at The Manor and, as part of the rent, live in The Gate Lodge. I can't think of any other way of saving the cat."

Lady Veronica paused to let Bertie take it all in. Then she deployed her next weapon of persuasion: yet another hard-to-refuse reason for him to prolong his visit.

"One more thing; someone has to go through poor Mr Haines' belongings and clothes: some of them can go to *Save the Children* and we could leave furniture and utensils for the staff we find to work here. You never know, it might be exactly what someone's looking for: part-time work in return for low rent. I do feel it's a man's job to sort Haines' personal items: I wouldn't want to embarrass his spirit, if that's what happens to us when we leave this earth."

Bertie found himself in an awkward spot. It was a small service to perform for his now-departed friend. If he came across anything that might prove detrimental to Reg's memory he could dispose of it discreetly and preserve the image of such a wise and kind man. Here, too, was a chance of reprieve for the cat. He had grown fond of the animal, which, like that of Dick Whittington's, had become an icon of his self-imposed ordeal, offering him companionship as he faced the perils of the world. It would be disloyal to stand by and do nothing to prevent a vet, hypodermic in hand, from destroying his part-time ally.

"Well, I suppose it would give me the chance to tie up some odd ends with TGP before I go back to my old job," he told Her Ladyship. "I need to see Mr Penworthy."

"And we need to repay that money we owe you."

"I'm sure that will all be taken care of. Things are looking very promising for the new company and there's no particular hurry. It will take only a couple of years. I wouldn't be surprised if we didn't get an offer from one of the big construction companies to buy us out. With the economy picking up they're all looking for new avenues. Our shares will go whizzing up."

"So you *will* stay on? Just a few days?"

"How can I resist? I must try to save my friend the cat."

As she put the phone down Lady Veronica, clenched her fist and gave it a little shake.

"Yes!"

CHAPTER 28

It was the first sunny day for weeks. The contrast between the dark green of trees along by the river and the emerald grass on the higher ground was vivid. The sparkling waters, still covering parts of the meadows, added a brightness to the scenery and reflected a sky so blue that it gave residents of Tytherton Kellaway hope that summer might at last have begun. The forecast for the next week, and possibly longer, was for an area of high pressure to be stationary above the British Isles. Travel reports warned of roads to the West Country being congested as people headed for last minute holidays.

Caroline Blythe had surprised The Canon by having his breakfast ready by the time he had finished his daily ritual of reading Matins. As he opened the study door the smell of frying bacon beckoned him to the kitchen where he found the table laid and his wife, fully dressed, taking warmed plates from the oven.

"My goodness how nice: a full English breakfast! What brought this about?"

"Had you forgotten? It's your birthday, Edward: many happy returns of the day, my dear!"

"But you are usually.... I mean ....."

"I've decided I'm not nearly as poorly as I thought I was; and it's about time I got back on my feet and took a more active part in running this house and looking after us both."

"So where's Melissande?"

The Rector's morning routine had only recently been resumed. Melissande would have toast and cereal with him in the kitchen, after first having delivered a tray to her mother's bedroom.

"I looked in and she was sleeping so peacefully I switched off the alarm clock and closed her door. She really needs to rest: I'm quite worried about her. Last night she was talking of going back to Iona and I can't help thinking that would be such a waste."

"Hardly a waste, Caroline. I'm sure they do important work there and if she finds happiness joining their community, it can only be for the good."

"Edward, of course you are right but let's celebrate your birthday and my recovery. Just enjoy your breakfast and I'll tell you about something that Veronica and I have devised regarding our dear daughter."

"Oh – very well, my love." The Rector went to sit down.

"Shut the door would you dear, before you say Grace? I don't want to be overheard."

"I can't think who by – there's only us and Melissande in the house – but as you wish; and thank you for my birthday breakfast. It looks delicious – such a pleasant surprise!"

At the District Council offices, a rare early morning meeting was just concluding.

"Everything ready?" Asked the chief planning officer.

"Enforcement officers have just radioed in: yes, the machines are in place and the police are standing by."

"Are you *sure* they need diggers and a crane?"

"I can't see any other way of moving it: the tow-bar and wheels have long since been replaced by piles of bricks; and we can't get at it without removing a large fallen tree."

"It could be messy, though; and I don't just mean mud!"

"Well they should have thought of that, shouldn't they? We've given them enough warning. Sometimes the law has to be enforced."

"Do you think we might have timed it better?"

"The Chairman thinks we've waited long enough, what with the elections coming up; anyway, I can't think it's going to get much better than this. The weather's fine for a change. It's less wet under foot and the newspapers are full of these floating houses – artists' impressions and all that. With a bit of luck we can get in there and finish the job without them becoming martyrs. At the moment it's an illegal blot on the landscape. Councillors are fully behind it, especially the greenies."

"Before we set out, I'd just remind you that we are only there to offer legal and technical advice. We must not get involved – that's the job of the contractors and the police, who may have to restrain the occupants."

"We'll get the blame though!"

"Of course: one of the hazards of the modern civil servant!"

When Melissande woke, she was shocked at how late it was. The alarm had failed – most unusual. Fearing she might bump into Bertie, who had arrived yesterday at The Manor with his mother, she scrambled into her clothes, ready to dash over to the stables to complete her morning tasks before anyone was around.

At the Gate Lodge, Bertie, after a restless night, conscious he was only a few minutes away from the only person he wanted to be with, yet repressing the urge to go and fall at her feet, decided to get up and go for a walk. Perhaps the sunshine and fresh air would clear his head and give him the moral courage to play the part of Dutiful Son and Manor Handyman for just a couple more days before returning to the oblivion of London.

He didn't even stop for a shave before putting on his boots and setting off towards the River Avon. It would be interesting to see how high or low, the floods were. The coming dry period might allow diggers to create the necessary trenches and groundworks connecting all the carefully chosen plots. After that it would be all systems go.

The night before, as his mother and Lady Veronica chattered twenty to the dozen about hockey matches and school scandals of the previous Century, Bertie sensed that the cat must know of his action to save its bacon, because the moment he'd finished putting a log on the drawing-room fire and sat down opposite the two ladies, it came and sat on his lap, rubbing its face against his hand before stretching out and going to sleep 'safe in his arms'.

He was quite touched by its show of affection. If only it could have been Melissande snuggling up against him! *That* dream, which sneaked into his mind when he wasn't looking, had to be dismissed smartly, so he tried to listen as his mother related highlights of 'when we thrashed Benenden'.

The cat then followed him back to the Gate Lodge, eventually onto his bed, where it kept waking him up – hence his early rise. If it had still been raining he might have felt worse, but the sunshine gave him hope that today might not be as miserable as yesterday: a walk would do him good.

The peaceful dawn at Tytherton Kellaway was shattered by something between a fearsome scream and a agonised roar. The hideous sound of a large animal in pain reverberated around the caravan and across the valley, waking Trevor and Danielle with such a start that Danielle thought she was going to have a panic attack. She sat gasping for air as Trevor leapt from the bed and fell into his trousers and shirt. He was getting ready for flight or a fight, but after half a minute in which the terrifying noise was not repeated, his reasoning caught up with him.

"Don't worry, ducks," he said. "That must have been our Doris – I bet she's started labour."

"Oh my god! Poor thing – and her baby's going to be enormous! Someone will have to call the vet. Phone Travis!"

"Why him?"

"I've lost the number but he'll know about vets – that's what he went to college for – countryside and all that."

Trevor, always ready to take the easier course, did as he was bid and called Travis's mobile.

"Can you get round here, son: quick as you can. Danielle's in a tizzy about Doris giving birth; and *she's* outside making 'orrible noises. We've got to get a vet – can you fix that?"

"You want the vet *and* me? What am *I* for? I've got to go to work."

"Well it *is* your work, in'it? The donkey's in trouble because of your boss's 'orse! If anything 'appens we need a witness. You know how Danielle loves that bloody animal: there'll be Hell to pay if it dies in child-birth."

"I hope it's not child-birth, Dad! We're expecting a hinny!"

"I thought it was a mule."

"No, Dad, technically, it's a hinny – offspring of a horse stallion and jenny donkey."

"Where d'you learn that?"

"On my course, Dad, in Animal Husbandry."

"It's *that* all right; and it sounds like the wages of sin goin' on outside. You'd better come, at least 'til the vet gets 'ere. I can't cope with Danielle *and* Doris at the same time."

Trevor decided Danielle's needs were greater than those of the donkey, whose contractions must have paused because she was, for the moment, quiet.

"I'll make you a nice cup of tea," he told his partner as she sat, holding her anxious face, frozen in a look of fear, tears streaming down her cheeks, "have my 'ankie."

He handed over his red spotted handkerchief and was relieved to hear Danielle's trumpeting as he busied himself at the kitchen end of the caravan: at least she wasn't cataleptic. He'd spent some time as a care worker in a psychiatric unit and knew some of the symptoms. Blowing the nose indicated she wasn't seized up inside her head but was taking action to relieve a physical need.

"That *poor* animal!" She sniffed.

Doris' first blood-curling cry had been so loud that even Melissande heard it when she was half way up the lane on her way to the stables. No wonder it had woken Trevor and Danielle. Two days ago Travis had mentioned to Melissande that the donkey was nearing parturition. That's what this cry must be. Melissande now felt duty bound to be of assistance: holiday jobs at stables during her teens had taught her some of the equine facts of life.

She changed direction. The stallion, like many expectant fathers, would have to wait for his breakfast and she would have to risk running into Bertie later, when she had time to do her chores at the stables. Her presence might be important at the caravan, if she could reach it quickly. From where she was, the most direct route would mean crossing where the River Avon overflowed into the Manor meadows, if she wanted to avoid a two-mile detour around the road.

With the past couple of days having been dry, she might be able to wade across: she had her wellies on.

At the caravan, Danielle had finished her mug of tea and was feeling better. The donkey had uttered no more horrifying cries and seemed to be getting on with the job. Danielle was confident that Travis and the vet would soon be there.

Within minutes she heard what must be the vet arriving but couldn't understand why he should need to arrive in something that sounded like a tractor. Then, as the powerful engine stopped, yet another one could be heard, also drawing closer.

She was going to open the caravan door to see whether they had decided to send an animal ambulance, when there was a loud banging on the side of the aluminium wall of her home.

"Hello, hello! Anyone in there?"

"Travis, whatever's the matter with you!" Trevor bellowed angrily as he went to the door. "Of course we're bloody in 'ere! I just phoned you, didn't I?"

But it wasn't Travis facing him when he threw open the door. Instead, a large man in bright orange waterproof and crash helmet confronted him.

"Is Miss Marchmont there?" demanded the man.

"Wot if she is?" replied Trevor, determined to protect his loved one.

"We're from the Council: and we're going to tow this caravan off this site, where it is has been illegally parked despite frequent warnings."

"It can't move," intervened Danielle, pushing past Trevor. "The tyres are shot, the bearings are gone and the whole thing's resting on bricks."

"We're ready for that, madam," said the man politely. "We have a crane and a low-loader, as well as a tractor and winch in case either of them get stuck. I suggest you pack a few things and be ready to be moved out within the next few minutes."

"How can I move out when I've got a donkey in labour – about to give birth? Have you got no heart?"

"I have, madam, but I can't be responsible for the behaviour of wildlife or domestic animals."

By now, a police car with two female officers and a sergeant had arrived, parking next to the vehicles gathered on the bright green meadow grass. As they gathered by the caravan Danielle addressed the growing group of officials from the top of its steps.

"In the interests of animal welfare, I refuse to budge until the vet has arrived!"

Melissande, arriving the other side of the water from the drama, found the level of the Avon not quite low enough to allow her to wade across to the caravan, partly hidden behind the fallen tree. She could just see Danielle's hand gesticulating, above the leaves and hear her impassioned oration. The flashing blue light of the police car, twinkling between the limbs of the stricken tree, then caught her eye. It was all mysterious and alarming.

She was wondering what to do when the donkey issued its second agonised bray. It prompted Melissande to take a risk and step forward into the fast-moving current of the Avon's new tributary: she must at least try to reach the poor animal. With luck the water wouldn't be too deep.

"Don't do it! Melissande – my darling – please stop!"

Bertie's voice halted her forward motion as she turned, hardly believing her own ears.

Minutes earlier, the sun and light breeze had begun to lift Bertie's mood as he strode towards the river. Life, perhaps, might not be as desolate as he had feared, and he had almost reached the stage of calling a meeting with himself. The agenda was forming in his mind. First he must leave this soggy country and go abroad. If the worst came to the worst he could join the French Foreign Legion and distinguish himself in combating mad extremists in the deserts of Northern Africa. That would help erase Melissande from his memory: wretched woman! Talk about intransigent! So she thought she could come *back*, after treating him like *that*, did she? Bloody Hell! Talk about feminine guile: he had fallen for it this time – but never again. Butter wouldn't melt in her mouth – innocent virgin that she'd been, until he'd relieved her of that little barrier.

Seeing that Bertie was tempted to relive the memory of that delicious moment, his other, better self took control of the meeting:

'Perhaps you *did* take advantage of her,' hinted his conscience: 'and maybe she really *did* think you'd been mucking about with Bella that fateful evening' it nagged.

'Let's be reasonable, Bertie,' he told his self-generated accuser. 'It must have *looked* as though I was playing away – that bottle of fizzy and her sexy outfit. How could Melissande know I'd had nothing to do with it – except rescue Bella's bloody horse from a bucket?'

He allowed his reason and his conscience time to reconsider, before adding: 'I didn't know Bella was going to throw herself at me! I don't fancy her a bit! She's such a hard-nosed ...... not at all like Melissande....'.

'Don't start all that again: you've written her off, remember,' he rebuked himself. He was finding it very hard to keep the meeting in order, with his thoughts sliding back to Melissande's gentle loveliness and an ever-increasing feeling of guilt gaining ground. Perhaps he *had* been over-hasty in rejecting her apologies.

'Bertie, you've been a bloody idiot!' His conscience told him, decisively.

'I say, steady on!' Bertie answered himself. 'That's a bit much: she was damned unkind, wasn't she? No explanation – no chance to defend myself!'

'OK, she was mistaken – but we all make mistakes,' his conscience persisted.

The interrogation was halted suddenly by Doris' second, ear-splitting cry.

It happened precisely as he emerged from behind a hedge into the meadow by the river, opposite where the lightning had struck the tree on that dramatic launch day.

Heavenly Management had given TGP a send off to remember by intervening with a spectacular storm at exactly the right moment in front of the world's press: it intervened for a second time now for Bertie's own good.

The blood-chilling noise set him into emergency mode and, his heart racing, he took in the scene in front of him in a millisecond. The fallen tree, men in orange jackets, a police car, its blue light flashing, shouting, chaos; and then – horror of horrors – Melissande wading out into the muddy waters of the Avon.

She was plainly going to do away with herself: feeling as inconsolable as he. Thank God he had arrived when he did!

The Management had indeed needed some ingenuity to make everything happen with such split second timing and various angels would be praised for their part in the action but now, matters could be left in Bertie's capable hands.

"Don't do it! Melissande – my darling – please stop!" he roared, his bass voice in top gear as his words fired out across the meadow, causing her nearly to lose her balance as she turned to see him, racing towards her across the squidgy grass.

She was still only one pace into the flowing water, hoping against hope that it wouldn't get any deeper. The donkey's distress and the chaotic situation on the other side of the water seemed so desperate she ought to press on. Bertie's bellow changed all that!

Before she could retrieve her other foot from in front of her to begin turning back, Bertie had grabbed her hand and hauled her back on to drier land. He didn't say a word but took her forcefully into his embrace, nearly squeezing the breath right out of her.

"How could you?" he demanded, releasing her a little.

"How could I what?" responded a furious Melissande, giving Bertie a sharp smack across the jaw. "Let me go! How dare you?"

"Throw yourself into the river! I thought you were made of stronger stuff!"

"I wasn't and I am! So there!" She exploded. "I was going to see what I could do for that poor donkey. It's plainly in trouble and someone has to help."

"Well by the look of it they've got half the county over there – police and all! Whatever's going on?"

They both looked across the water and saw the crane about to hitch itself to the fallen tree and a policewoman walking purposefully towards the caravan steps. Next, a motor scooter speeded up behind the police car and Travis, familiar in his black leather jacket, dismounted and stood, hands on hips, assessing the situation.

"Look, Travis is there – I'm sure he can cope," said Bertie. "It's nothing to do with us but you and I have some *talking* to do!"

"That's what I tried to tell you, you stupid man!"

"But there's no need to drown yourself! You'll get over it! So will I!"

"I don't *want* to get over it! I want you back, Bertie! I love you and you've no idea how much!"

"Yes I have, dammit! I love *you* madly and I've been going through unspeakable withdrawal ever since you buggered off blubbing into the night,."

"Well I thought you were having it off with Bella! And please don't swear!"

"Well you thought wrong, didn't you?"

"I realise that, now; and yes, I was mistaken. It was all down to her." Melissande had the grace to lower her eyes and look at the Barbour brand on his jacket.

"She didn't know," said Bertie, "that we'd been ..... well .... more than colleagues, did she?"

"No! She was just having a go to see whether she could marry a baronet and get a title like her mother. If she'd known about us she wouldn't have 'approached' you."

"That's what you think! She's as hard as tungsten! Tris is welcome to her!"

"He's just *like* her! She'll soon find *that* out." Melissande had her own opinion of Tristram. He had already made a casual pass at her when Bella's attention was distracted.

"She won't care, as long as she produces an heir for The Manor," said Bertie. "She'll use him as some kind of stud-cum-banker."

He had still not let go of Melissande's hand, and they both noticed. Despite irreparable differences and angry exchanges, here they were, holding hands. Bertie's cheek stung a little but the slap had snapped him out of his hopelessness. Suddenly he was full of exuberance.

"You hit me!" He said, feigning outrage.

"You deserved it!"

"What for?"

"For giving me the wrong impression!" She replied, stiffly. "But I'm prepared to discuss it." The warmth and strength of Bertie's hand undermined her wrath. She abandoned her outrage and giggled.

That did the trick: it was infectious and they both nearly fell over with their mirth. They held on to each other for support and were about to kiss when a puff of diesel smoke and loud engine noises from across the water took their attention.

"Whatever's going on? That poor donkey!" Melissande's concern had returned.

"I've no idea," said Bertie. "My guess is that she's about to give birth and that Trevor and Danielle have some issue with the authorities. I don't think the events are connected but they both seem to be happening at the same time. It's certainly nothing to do with you and me."

"Well I'm grateful to that donkey, for bringing you to your senses?" Melissande's confidence was returning.

"Blast me! I never heard such rubbish. The donkey had nothing to do with my being here. I was simply out for a stroll. Then I came across you – about to do away with yourself."

"I most certainly wasn't!"

"Well I'm glad! It would have been terrible!"

"And I'm glad you're glad; but you nearly made me lose a wellie, hauling me out like that."

"Let's find somewhere else to talk, away from here." Bertie wanted Melissande on her own, away from the developing drama.

"Where shall we go? I can't go to The Rectory – there'll be too much explaining to do."

"And I can't go to The Manor – my mother's there and she's been getting together with Lady Veronica – and I bet they've been talking to *your* mother."

"Let's go to the Roman Temple – no one's going to be there at this time of morning."

Ignoring the shouts, brays and revving engines so near, yet so inaccessible, Bertie and Melissande retreated behind the hedge, making their way hand in hand back to the higher ground.

Reaching the steps up to the temple, they stopped and looked back. The diesel smoke was still rising above the distant trees but any sound effects were drowned out by the rustle of leaves, the loud and melodious song of a blackbird enjoying the sun, which had risen sufficiently to make itself felt. It was now pleasantly warm.

"Look at that! The sun's streaming in right on to the altar," said Melissande.

The said 'altar' had been conveniently placed to act as a low table and sideboard for 'Roman Orgies' organised by Bella's ancestors a century earlier when everyone dressed up in togas and wore laurel wreaths as they imbibed Chianti.

Melissande turned to face Bertie and without speaking, reached out to undo the zip of his jacket. He did the same for her and they slipped out of the heavy garments. He spread his on the warm stone.

"I've only got a tee-shirt on," said Melissande. "I wasn't expecting to meet anyone. I usually dress properly after seeing to the horse and lady Veronica."

Bertie stood back and looked at her. Her hair was tied back, her eyes were bright and smiling and her lips needed no makeup, they were full, rose-pink and irresistible. Looking down at the tee-shirt he saw how its thin blue cloth was skin tight over her breasts, whose little peaks were showing distinct interest in life.

Melissande took his hand and brushed it across her left breast. He needed no further invitation but began tracing and caressing, finishing up with his thumb and finger teasing the point. This sent the most delicious weakness throughout Melissande's body and she relaxed into Bertie, allowing him to take her weight as he pressed his mouth against hers. She met his tongue with her own and, reaching up, took his head in her hands, pulling him down to her as they tasted each other and resumed the intimacy that had been so cruelly interrupted the other side of the Hell they had both been through.

Their passion rose as the kissing became more urgent. Bertie was now pressing her against the side of the altar with his hips and she was responding. He released her, took her coat, rolled it up into a cushion, and laid it at the top of his own. He then lifted Melissande to lie on his coat, her head resting on the pillow, and resumed the kiss, his hand now free to seek direct contact with the breast it had been appreciating. He slipped it up under her tee-shirt, sending electric shocks that centred on that part of her body that was now crying out for attention. After stroking the breast for a little longer, Bertie's hand now moved down, arriving at the triangle of dark curls. Without taking his lips from hers, Bertie began the lightest of searches with his middle finger. First it travelled down one side of her vulva, then back up the other side, tenderly spreading Mother Nature's lubricant as he introduced his finger. Softly, it found the little button that it had been seeking and began circling, with the occasional touch of pressure that made Melissande thrill with lust.

She felt for Bertie's trousers and found what she sought there, straight and hard – larger than she remembered. She pressed and stroked it with her fingers through the coarse cloth of his outdoor kit; then found the zip and, slipped her hand inside to find the way through his pants to grasp him. Once free, projecting from his trousers, she ran her fingers up and down it, gently pulling and caressing, until he too, produced a droplet which she spread around to make things ready.

Bertie had to back away, to prevent instant ejaculation. He wanted to save it until he could be deep inside her. She understood and pulled up her tee-shirt inviting his lips to kiss her breasts, his tongue playing and his mouth tasting them, returning repeatedly to the nipples. This was now becoming too much for Melissande to bear, unless he was filling her. She sat up, her legs over the side of the altar and edged out of her pants, pushing them towards her knees. Bertie took over and removed them completely, dropping them on to the sunlit floor. He undid his belt, letting his trousers fall, and then stood between Melissande's knees, pulling him towards her. Her arms around his shoulders and her legs wrapped around his body, Bertie let her slip down himself until he felt his penis come up against her. He held her tightly and she moved her pelvis until she too, felt it arrive where she needed it so much. After pressing down for a moment, she felt his erection slide into the heat and tightness of her vagina and allowed herself to descend, taking the full length into herself. Her heels were now pressing against his hard buttocks and he was holding each of hers, soft and round, in his hands, taking her weight and using it to rise and fall as he moved up and down inside her.

They were now kissing again, uttering soft sounds of love and oblivious to anyone and anything. When it came, their climax was in perfect synchronisation. Bertie was unable to hold back any more. His body gave a tremendous shudder and he could feel himself dissolving into the depths of his darling love. She, experiencing the same release, gave way to wave after wave of contraction as her body responded. Something of great importance was happening – she knew it. She wished it could last for ever: and in that moment, knew it was going to.

For Bertie, it was like being saved from a desert of unhappiness. As his body completed its ecstatic reunion, he rested his face on Melissande's neck, breathing in her scent, still so intoxicating. He spoke to her, softly, almost in tears:

"I have missed you unbearably. I couldn't bear it much longer."

"Nor me! I've been such an idiot! Will you forgive me?"

"I already have: but I've been so bloody stupid – I'm *so* sorry; but we're together again, connected all over – can we stay like this for always?"

"Well perhaps not *exactly* like this, delicious as it is," whispered Melissande, "this stone slab's a bit hard, but I'd like to re-enact it as often as we can. That was FANTASTIC, Bertie! We must go somewhere softer: back to my office – it's more comfortable indoors. Then we can do it again. I'll explain to Mummy afterwards: she thinks we're still not speaking."

"Will you marry me – straight away – before anything else awful happens?"

"I'll probably have to anyway – I stopped the pill as soon as I went to Scotland and you have just delivered a fresh lot of seed to exactly the right place!"

CHAPTER 29

The bright sun and freshness in the air had woken Arabella and Tristram too, that morning. On the spur of the moment they decided to spend the day at Tytherton Kellaway, away from the grime and noise of London's traffic. After a rapid shower and much hilarity they jumped in the car and left the metropolis before commuters had blocked its streets with their grumpy crawl to work. Even the M4 flowed harmoniously, with most of the traffic coming the other way. They reached their destination in record time, only exceeding the speed limit when absolutely necessary to put an insolent BMW behind them.

On arrival at The Manor, Bella fancied a ride and suggested that Tristram could jog beside her.

"Can't I sit behind you? It could be fun!"

"We shall have to get you a horse – perhaps a nice mare."

"Your randy steed would always be after her! You'd have to get him gelded!"

"Why shouldn't he have his oats? You enjoy yours!"

"Meanwhile I have to jog along on foot, aye?"

"Do you good! Get rid of that paunch!"

They were walking towards the stable exchanging this banter, having deposited their overnight bags in the hall.

Lady Veronica, looking at the clock wondered why she hadn't heard Bertie doing the fire downstairs or clattering the dishes as he laid the table for breakfast. She had expected him to, now that her ruse to have the cat put down had lured him back to take poor Haines' place during his mother's stay. She was about to investigate when she heard Arabella's snorty laugh and the front door creak. It made her put on her slippers and dressing gown, ready for action.

This was not the first time a bright morning had brought her niece to The Manor before breakfast and on this occasion it might complicate things later in the day. She put her head outside her bedroom door and was amused to see Cecily doing the same, along the passage.

"Do you fancy a cup of tea?" Veronica called to her old friend.

"That's what I was hoping for," came the reply. "I thought Bertie might bring it and I heard someone downstairs and was going to let him know I was awake."

"That was Arabella – and I think she must be with Tristram. I expect the fine weather has tempted her out of town. She will have gone straight down to the stable. I hope it won't disrupt things!"

"We shall just have to play it by ear, Veronica; but let's go down and make ourselves the tea. We will have to work out how to get Bertie over to The Rectory; Caroline says she doesn't think she will be able to convince Melissande to come here, once she's fed the horse. She knows I've got Bertie back to help out for a day or two and she will avoid us, I'm afraid. We'll have to chat with Caroline – go over there for coffee – and see what we can arrange."

"We're like the three old witches in Macbeth!"

"It's in a good cause! Anyone can see Bertie and Melissande are made for each other and although I'd never normally interfere in 'young love', I think on this occasion they're not *that* young and they do need a little help from their elders and betters. They're both behaving very foolishly."

"Well at least Arabella seems to have brought Tristram with her, so she won't be flirting with Bertie," said his mother.

"Even that isn't out of the question – she's so... indiscreet... sometimes," said Veronica.

Arabella, arriving at the stable, was not pleased:

"Where the Hell's Mel? My poor horse hasn't been fed and his stable's disgusting. She hasn't even *been* here this morning!"

"Perhaps she's ill?" Offered Tristram.

"Suppose so – she's been weird lately," Arabella conceded. "I'll find him something to eat if you'll muck out – OK?"

"Anything to oblige, madam!"

By the time their delayed ride and jog began, the sun was well up, warm enough for Tristram to leave his track-suit top in the tack room. They set off towards the higher ground, on the path that passes the Roman Temple.

Catching their breath, in the moments after their passionate and exhausting insemination, Bertie and Melissande didn't hear the stallion's hooves, or Tristram's trainers trotting over the firm turf. There being no door to the temple and with the sun streaming in, the tableau presenting itself to Arabella was quite startling.

Bertie's bottom had not benefited from the sun's rays for many a long moon, and its whiteness between Melissande's brown knees made a colourful contrast.

Arabella recognised Bertie's backview – that broadness of shoulder and ample hair. Her reaction was to stop the stallion for a better look – and avoid embarrassing whoever he was 'addressing', by not getting any closer.

She was longing to know who it was, underneath: she might know her. It had already answered her question over Bertie's sexuality. Those knees and that position were definitely 'missionary hetero'.

Tristram caught up and stood by the horse. Arabella shushed him with her finger to her mouth and turned the stallion away from the temple, taking them out of sight of the doorway. Once out of earshot, she and Tristram had a good laugh.

"Caught in the act, aye? Bertie's not going short of *his* oats, either!" Chortled Tristram.

"I wonder who *she* is?" Said Arabella, curious and a little peeved that she had missed out on those magnificent buttocks – *and* a title!

"It was *me!*" Confessed Melissande, confessed to her, a few minutes later.

Regaining her wits after the sunny interlude in the temple, The Rector's daughter had remembered her morning duties and hastily found her pants and dashed back to the stable.

Bertie, looking at his watch, thought he'd better see how 'the older generation' were getting on, at The Manor.

Arabella was already taking off the stallion's saddle, and gave Melissande a sniffy look when she finally arrived, still slightly flushed.

"Are you ill or something? You look red."

No – I'm just .... a bit late..., sorry. Got distracted."

"Well you missed a bit of a laugh. We caught Bertie bonking some woman up in the Roman Chapel – right there in the open!"

With much mirth she was about to relate the sordid details. The time had come for Melissande to stand up and be counted: she braced herself.

"It was *me*!"

"*Never*!" Bella could *not* believe her *ears*!

"It *was*! We've been lovers ever since we went to Venice – well.... until that night when I caught you and him in the tack room."

"But you're not *like* that! You've never been. Was that really you, rutting like a hussy out in the open in a Roman chapel for the whole world to see? Melissande I'm really shocked!"

"It was an emergency: we'd just made it up – after weeks and weeks apart!"

"I had no *idea*!" Arabella dumped the saddle on its stand and sat down heavily on the boot box. She was truly stunned and had gone quite pale.

"I *know* that, *now*," Melissande continued; "but I didn't *then* and I thought it was *him* being unfaithful."

"So have you been knocking off men like that for years without me knowing? You're an even darker horse than I thought!"

"No of course not, Bella! I was never like that – until I met Bertie. Then we, sort of ... fell for each other, down at the stable, when he was changing a light bulb."

"No wonder you threw a wobbly when I was giving him a thank-you party – it must have looked awful! I admit I *was* having a go – but I had no idea you'd got there first. He's such a catch! So are you going to be the next Lady Lamotte?"

"Well yes, actually! I am – he asked me just before we heard you snorting; and I'd said 'yes'."

"Oh God! You didn't hear us, did you? We thought you were too busy and we'd crept off like mice. I hope it didn't put you off. We were killing ourselves!"

"It didn't – anyway I didn't care! We'd just had the most fantastic time I could ever imagine."

"Melissande – all my images of you being a saintly virgin are completely shattered! Here's me, feeling guilty and common, all these years and now you 'come out' as quite shameless: not even worried about shagging in public!"

"Bella don't be so *common*! You may be my oldest friend but there's no need for that. What you don't know is how I've envied you, all this time – being so 'uninhibited'. I knew it was wicked (and all that) but I couldn't help wondering what it might be like: and now I know! I've got to make up for lost time."

"But isn't it still sinful?"

"Not with us! I've decided it's only wrong if it's with the wrong *person*."

"Was it Bertie who made you change your mind?"

"It was, really. We had long talks on the way to Maasbommel."

"Is that when you started bonking him?"

"Ara*bella* – please! But no – we were chaste until Venice."

"But you had separate rooms. Tris and I were at least honest about it!"

"Well, yes, but....".

"You crafty....!"

They both laughed: and as old barriers were removed their unlikely friendship began a new era. From then on they were to know each other better, sharing joys and sorrows even when living counties apart.

"Where's Tristram?"

"He's gone for a bath. I'm going up to join him."

"*Really* Bella!"

Melissande looked round to see what still needed doing, and Arabella made her way back to The Manor trying to come to terms with the new image of her oldest girlfriend, and itching to tell Tristram as she lathered his back before 'getting hold of him' to relieve her gathering lust.

Danielle was in floods of tears. Trevor was wondering what to do. They were standing by the white van, which Travis had summoned, in which their meagre belongings had been packed before the mighty machines of the local authority finally crunched the caravan.

It hadn't been planned like that by the officers, but the dwelling had long since lost its rigidity. It could no longer be towed and at the first lift of the crane, it collapsed on itself to the sound of bending aluminium, breaking glass and cracking timber struts and roof supports.

That's when Danielle's tears had begun. The caravan had looked so sweet, parked amongst the trees down by The Avon – not hurting anyone – especially since Trevor had given it a wash.

The scene was now so different. The surrounding grass, churned into green-flecked mud by huge wheels, was sprinkled with white sawdust from the fallen tree, which was unrecognisable after being sliced, ready to split into logs; its dead leaves stacked for burning. Next to that was a pile of bent panels, broken windows and a shattered door. This sad heap had been her happy home.

"What shall I do?" She bewailed. "And what about poor Doris and her baby?"

"Let's ask Travis," said Trevor.

The donkey had been haltered and tethered at a safe distance from all the destruction. She had given birth without the assistance of the vet, whose advice was not to intervene unless she had problems. He had stood at a respectful distance from the straining donkey, along with the orange-clad drivers and one of the police-women, marvelling at this wonder of nature as they delayed going into action. After the birth the destruction began.

By the time Danielle and Trevor's home had become two unrecognisable piles, Doris' offspring was being much admired by the visitors for its size and long ears. It had begun to suckle and wasn't going to wander off. The donkey herself, feeling better after unloading such a heavy burden was content to rest.

The vet, after cursory examination of the new mother and hinny, went off to write his bill.

Travis, always the pragmatist, was having discussions with the council officers. Part of his new role with TGP was to liaise with them, making sure all the ground plans and services followed Building Regulations and environmental restrictions.

Tristram had been so pleased with the launch, he had promised Travis the use of a Land Rover. He had felt Travis deserved a reward and further incentive, and Travis was looking forward to the status this would give him. He could see himself parking outside the Council offices in the future, striding in to meet the planners or visiting experts. He'd buy himself some suitable outdoor clothes to match the vehicle and perhaps even a Labrador to complete the image.

"Dad: you take Danielle down the town for a cup of tea and some breakfast, and I'll see what I can do," Travis told the distressed couple. "I'll have a chat with these officers."

He was enjoying being treated like a responsible human instead of a troublesome youth. In the back of his mind he had a plan that was worth a try. First, he wanted to make sure that the authorities were going to call it a day with no further action being taken – no bills for 'services rendered'.

Caroline Blythe ushered her two friends into The Rectory dining room and closed the door behind her.

"We won't speak too loudly because they're still up in Melissande's office."

"Who are?" Asked Cecily Lamotte.

"Why – Melissande and Bertie! I was going to tell you: I think they're reunited: the job's done. I don't have any details but Melissande breezed in about an hour ago looking radiant and saying 'it's all right, Mummy – will you send Bertie up when he gets here?' I hardly had time to say anything but I gathered they've got over their squabble. She disappeared upstairs saying something like 'we've so much to catch up on' – I imagine they're still opening letters. Piles have been arriving. Please keep your voices down while I go to make some coffee: I'd hate them to think we'd been plotting!"

As soon as the door closed behind Caroline Blythe's purposeful back, Cecily and Veronica enjoyed a private laugh.

"I expect they'll emerge when they're ready!" Said Veronica. "Oh the joys of youth! It takes me back."

"Seeing Caroline it's no wonder Melissande has grown up the way she has – but such a lovely girl," said Cecily. "I think Bertie has found someone who can manage him at last; we can leave Mother Nature to do the rest. We'd better explain to Caroline what's likely to happen, if it hasn't happened already: we don't want her to be shocked. Emphasise the grandchildren. I know she's as keen as I am."

It was nearly lunchtime when the three ladies ended their coffee morning. Caroline Blythe pretended to be somewhat surprised by the conclusions reached by her two friends. They didn't know Melissande had already told all, and the prospect of becoming a grandmother had already ameliorated her disapproval of the behaviour of 'today's young people'.

Caroline Blythe, however, found what Veronica had revealed about Arabella and Tristram distasteful.

"Do you mean they *regularly* visit each other's rooms at night?", she asked in astonishment. Melissande and Bertie's lapse was forgivable, understanding the circumstances; *theirs* was surely an exceptional case. Her daughter had been seduced by a most charming and attractive man who might evolve into a son-in-law: a distinguished one at that. That the *others* should indulge repeatedly was downright *wrong*.

"I think there is every possibility that they do," said Lady Kelway, trying not to smile. "My niece has always been somewhat precocious and Tristram is very much 'a man about town'. I'm hoping they may make a match and I'm prepared to turn a blind eye to their indiscretions as long as they are not blatant."

"Do you think it possible that Melissande and Bertie might have been indulging in more than office work in our attic?" Caroline found this hard to contemplate.

"It's certainly a possibility! Youth today can be very uninhibited!"

"And amoral by the sound of it. I can't possibly think it's right!" Caroline felt quite giddy: that Melissande might be repeating her transgression was deplorable.

"Let me pour you some more coffee, my dear. I don't think you need worry – the girls all take 'the pill' these days."

Caroline felt worse. That Melissande might have sunk to this!

"Shush, someone's coming," said Cecily. They froze, listening to the footsteps on the stairs. It sounded like more than one person.

"Mummy! Where are you?" Melissande's voice was in a higher key than recently.

"I'm in here, dear – with Veronica and Cecily! In the dining room!" Caroline's voice was strained but the effort of having to call out, restored the blood supply to her head.

Seconds later the door opened and Melissande breezed in, dishevelled but a picture of happiness. Close behind her, Bertie, grinning broadly, placed his hands on her hips, giving her his backing as he stood, smiling over her shoulder.

"How lovely! You're all here!" Said Melissande. "I can tell you our amazing news: we're engaged! And we want to be married by special licence before we have any more silly rows!"

There was a moment's silence as the three ladies digested the news. Caroline was the first to speak, feeling she ought to advocate caution: such rash decisions could so often lead to trouble.

"Do you think that's wise, dear?"

Melissande knelt by her mother's chair.

"Mummy I *know* it is!"

Caroline, not used to such flamboyance, was embarrassed by this unexpected gesture but, conscious of her two friends' motherly smiles, patted Melissande's shoulder, leaned over and kissed her, before stroking the fair hair into a semblance of order.

"Very well, dear: we'll have to talk with your father. Speaking of whom, I really must excuse myself: he'll be back soon from his meeting and I have to get some lunch."

As she released herself from Melissande's public affection, to put cups back on the tray, she decided an early wedding would indeed be desirable since her daughter had jumped the gun in such an uncharacteristic way. Caroline's own love-life with The Rector, though similar in inception, had long since ended, making her bedtime excuses no longer necessary. The whole messy business was best not remembered or discussed. The Rector now had his own room.

"We ought to be making our way, too," said Lady Veronica.

"Why don't I invite you all to lunch in town," suggested Bertie.

"That's a good idea," said his mother. "You could leave a note for The Rector to catch us up, couldn't you?" She asked Caroline.

The change of subject was welcome: it stopped Caroline asking herself where she had failed in her daughter's upbringing. The thought of lunch 'out' cheered her instantly; it was not something they could often afford on The Rector's stipend.

"How nice! I'm sure he'd enjoy that too; as long as we are back for Mother's Union at four."

"I suppose I ought to invite Batty and Bella, hadn't I?" Bertie asked Melissande.

"Tell them it's an engagement lunch!" She agreed, standing to give him her first public kiss – more of a peck, compared to those endless ones they had so recently been exchanging, upstairs.

As Lady Veronica and her two friends adjusted their hair in the powder room before lunch at the restaurant, they expressed their pleasure over the promised union.

"And we didn't have to do a thing!" Said Cecily. "I was prepared to give Bertie a good wigging but it seems that The Management had everything under control."

"The management? What's that Cecily?" Caroline was curious.

"Oh it's just a term we use in our family for 'fate' or 'Mother Nature'. I've no doubt you call it 'God'."

"I hope that doesn't mean you'd want them to have a Registry Office wedding?" questioned Caroline, with an anxious look: what would the parish say? Or the clergy?

"I'm sure Melissande would never agree to *that*! She's far too considerate," said Lady Veronica.

Calm was restored and they made their way to join the celebration.

At the next board meeting of TGP, Mr Penworthy followed Bertie's introduction with a request that 'any other business' could be moved to the top of the agenda; particularly for one matter he wished to air.

"I don't see why not, Mr Penworthy," said Bertie. "Go ahead!"

"I propose that it be recorded in the minutes of this meeting that The Board offers hearty congratulations to both you, Sir Bertrand and Miss Blythe on your engagement; and to you, Mr Heath-Cohen and Miss Kelway, for yours."

"That's most kind of you! Is there anyone against?" Bertie was only half joking and hoped it didn't show, but any fears that Bella might say something facetious were unfounded and the motion was carried.

"And I'd also like to pay tribute to our dear departed friend and board member, Reg Haines, without whose down-to-earth common sense and kindness none of us would be attending this meeting."

At this point Bertie recalled the fact that it was Arabella's backview that had led him to find poor Reg at the opportune moment. So much for 'fate'!

The tribute – to Reg – was endorsed by everyone and Bertie proceeded with the agenda as listed.

"So to the first item: Tristram – how is the market responding to all our publicity?"

"Well Mr Chairman, I'm delighted to report that the four biggest insurance companies have expressed great interest, especially Legal & General and Aviva. The NFU Mutual seems pretty keen too, because TGP's going to put new value on their members' low-lying land. The builders too, have moved fast and we've already got two more sites being planned in Kent and Yorkshire. It's land they bought years ago, which has only recently started flooding and they were wondering what to do with it: they'd never get permission for conventional housing after all the flooding. I've also arranged for us to meet a group of investment bankers early next month. Meanwhile, Bertie and I propose to put enough into the kitty to get things off the ground."

"I won't be comfortable until you get re-paid all we owe you," said Lady Veronica, still concerned about her debt to Bertie. The episode with the bailiffs had been *so* awful.

"Absolutely!" said Arabella, still suspicious of Bertie's intentions regarding The Manor.

Tristram handed round a sheet of figures with a healthy number of commas and noughts, which indicated that companies and investors agreed with The Board about amphibious houses having an important future in a world where extremes of weather were likely to become the norm. Board members received this document with satisfaction.

Bertie moved on to the next item: 'the Design Competition'.

"My fiancée and I have been handling this together," he said, with a broad smile to Melissande, who blushed. She hoped he wasn't going to elucidate on just how closely their collaboration had been. Her father had expressed concern at the long hours she and Bertie spent in the office, warning her that over-work had led to her last 'breakdown'; and, much as he approved of her association with The Iona Community, he would prefer her to 'develop a more sustainable work profile' such as advocated in an article he'd read on human resources.

Bertie continued: "I'll ask her to tell us about progress so far. I think it's true to say we are very pleased with the number and quality of entries. Many of them would look fantastic on our meadows, dry or wet!"

Melissande had printed out some of the sketches and designs they'd already received, saying a few words about each before passing them round.

"I really liked this one," she said, holding up a French-style 'pavillion' with a central tower. "The master bedroom is up in the tower and I can imagine it having a lovely all-round view. You could watch your neighbours and see who's beginning to float."

There was another that received enthusiastic comments. It was in the style of a three-story Swiss chalet with wooden balconies between the sloping sides of the roof.

"You could sit out even if it were raining – those verandas are wide enough to make an 'outside upstairs room'. I like that," said Bertie.

"Are you sending them *all* to the judges," asked Cecily. "Some of them look a bit 'odd'."

"But so did the design for Sydney Opera House," said Tristram.

"Which turned out almost impossible to use until they worked out how to put a stage and seats in it!" Retorted Arabella.

"I think we should leave it for the judges to decide how practical the entries are, don't you?" said Melissande. "I'm just pleased there's such a wide choice and so much diversity of design. They're going to look so much nicer than that row we saw in Holland."

"I agree we leave it to them," said Lady Veronica, who had actually studied Melissande's report. "It's looking most promising and I'm sure they will enjoy seeing *everything* that is submitted. Our meadows will be a most unique place to live. I can't wait to see it!"

CHAPTER 30

The Wiltshire Council's social services provided emergency accommodation for Trevor and Danielle, the first night after their eviction. The RSPCA found somewhere for Doris and her hinny 'on a very temporary basis' and some kind of calm was restored to the foursome.

To prolong this, Travis needed to implement his plan as soon as possible. He decided to start with Tristram, because he had observed that Arabella tended to listen to her fiancé more than to others at Tytherton Kellaway. Also, Travis liked to see himself as 'the same kind of bloke' as Tristram – swashbuckling and courageous, prepared to live dangerously.

"Excuse me, Tris," he said, as they walked out of Chippenham station after seeing off a party of potential plot buyers; "can we 'ave a chat?"

"Let's have a beer!" Tristram, not waiting for a reply, veered away from the car-park towards the pub.

Two half-pints and a packet of crisps later they had worked out an excellent solution to various problems facing their nearest and dearest.

Although not eloquent, Travis had summed up Lady Veronica's predicament:

"She ain't so young any more, and old Reg really looked after 'er. Now Bertie's doing it but I can't see *that* goin' on for long, can you? He told me it was to save the cat – I don't know what that meant – but I fink he wants to get *out* more."

"You've certainly got something there," said Tristram. "*We* need him to. He's going to be doing most of our marketing and we're hoping he and Mel will move over to Suffolk to cover that side of England – the Continent as well; and you're right – Lady V has a problem. I doubt she can manage on her own."

"Well I've been chatting to my dad and his girlfriend. They've got nowhere to go – especially with the donkey an' all; and Danielle says she wouldn't mind bein' a carer for the old girl."

"Lady Veronica, you mean?" Tristram wasn't sure whether he meant the donkey.

"Exact! And Dad could do odd jobs – there's a lot needs doin' and he's 'ad a go at most things."

"What an excellent suggestion: and they could live in the Gate Lodge!"

"Exact! That's just what I fought." Travis was showing yet another of his hidden talents, personnel management: 'let the other person think it was their idea'.

It was not long before life for Travis began improving in other aspects, too. TGP gave him a year's contract; the Land Rover was exactly the one he'd fancied and he found an empty cottage to rent on the Green at Tytherton Kellaway. Having moved in, he discovered that living in a bedsit required all kinds of extras, like furniture and curtains. By a stroke of luck one evening he met a girl he'd known at Lackham. She happened to drop in at the same wine bar as him in Bath. They had always got on OK – even been to a couple of raves together – and were pleased to see each other.

He told her about his new job and she liked his dog, which found her shoes fascinating – she must come from somewhere with loads of animals, every whiff told a story. She was in digs near Melksham and worked as an assistant manager at the new holiday complex at Beckhampton. Her job was to devise and run 'Ecotrips: enjoying nature from the saddle' in which participants were allocated a horse, a 4G Kindle Fire, binoculars and a magnifying glass.

"They stay bed and breakfast; we meet up at the stables every morning and trek for an hour to somewhere interesting, like a clump of trees or a stone circle," she told Travis. "Then we stop and look at plants, birds, prehistoric remains – and I help them look stuff up on their tablets. They take photos and make little videos on their phones and then in the evenings, they go off and whack it up on Facebook."

"I suppose their friends see it and want to come on the next holiday: good idea!" Travis nodded with approval. As the evening progressed, he told her about TGP and his role in its development. He mentioned that a couple of the directors – the future owners of Tytherton Kellaway Manor – were also horsey. To make her laugh he told her about the misdeeds of Arabella's stallion.

"My Dad's girlfriend owned this donkey and Bella, when it was flooding, fell off 'er 'orse, which got together with the donkey and Bobs-yer-Uncle, they got this little chap with long ears and a funny voice."

"What did they do with it?" She asked, curious.

"They've kept it – the stallion's got a mare to go with him now, as well as his bit of donkey on the side."

"What do you mean 'funny voice'?"

"Well a hinny *sounds* funny. It's not like a horse *or* a donkey: it's got a squeaky hee-haw: like this!" he made an imitation, to her amusement; "and a mule has more of what my vet book calls a 'brayin' squeak'.

"Don't do it!" She pleaded, in fits of mirth. "I ask you! A hinny-whinny! Whatever next?"

Before long they'd made a date. One thing led to another and now she was moving in, taking over the decor and making it like home. Travis had rarely lived so happily.

POSTSCRIPT: JUNE 2017

"Bertie! There's another letter from Ogle," Melissande calls from the bottom of the stairs at their new home in Suffolk.

"God! They're not still trying, are they?" Bertie looks up from his *Financial Times*. He is normally up by this time of the morning but their pretty little daughter, Matilda has kept him up half the night with 'a tummy ache'. When he's home, Bertie has to take 'night duty' with Matilda to give Nanny a break.

It was Bertie's suggestion – the name Matilda – and although Melissande hasn't mentioned it she thinks it's a subconscious thing on his part because he's always whistling 'Waltzing Matilda' when he's happy. He always has, according to his mother and Melissande is pleased to hear it as an indicator of his wellbeing. It also gives her a frisson of amusement when she recalls the effect of his whistling on her ex-rival and still-best-friend.

If all with Matilda is not well, Daddy must *do* something: *be* there, bring her some water or be sympathetic. She has her grandmother's drive, Bertie's eyesight, (which is excellent, not like Mummy's) and her mother's looks, which Bertie still believes are perfect, even when she puts on her reading glasses in the evening having popped her lenses into their night-cases.

She has her mother's light blonde hair with added fluffy curls. When she smiles, the world becomes a better place; when she thunders, look out! Her grandmother is confident that her stormy side can be tamed and intends to ensure it.

Granny Cecily loves having family around her and it has been worth holding the fort until Bertie came back to take on his father's social and property legacy, even if it is still she who has to run the farm – and Matilda.

They say a child chooses its own name, and when the child was already showing signs of leadership at four-months old, her parents discovered that 'Matilda' means 'mighty in battle'.

It looks as though she might grow up fulfilling the promise of her name and needs Granny's firm hand to curb her commanding ways. Bertie can't say 'no' to her and Melissande doesn't have that kind of assertiveness but the senior Lady Lamotte, having moved into the dower house near the lake, takes command of Matilda and her nanny when Bertie and Melissande are away on one of their trips.

During the week they often visit flood plains and estuaries around the British Isles and Western Europe, leaving Granny in charge. At weekends Cecily Lamotte enjoys a peaceful break and concentrates on the estate and going to church, while Matilda's parents benefit from the discipline and training she has picked up during the week. It's a happy arrangement.

When they moved to Suffolk, Melissande had been given free hand to redecorate the Elizabethan family pile, which she enjoyed immensely, while being sensible about the expense. She gave extra attention to insulation and energy saving, making sure that the place could be kept warm and dry in the keen East Anglian winds. She did this while restoring some of the Elizabethan features that had been covered over in the fifties.

This interior design activity coincided with her natural instinct to make a nest prior to giving birth to Matilda, which occurred rather earlier than residents at Tytherton Kellaway might have expected so soon after the spectacular double wedding, held there in the autumn, three years ago. That glittering event had taken place precisely a year and two days after Bertie had made his decision to 'disappear and seek his fortune'.

"*And* I got my princess!" He boasted to Melissande.

"My knight rescued me from The Rectory – and then made me pregnant," she concurred.

The Rector had found preparing the two couples for Christian Marriage quite exhausting. His daughter was the only one of the four who didn't press him for further explanations and 'firm data' to back up what he was saying. He concluded that Arabella was what he described to Caroline as 'a heathen hoyden, but very attractive'. Bertie was 'a gentleman with an unorthodox set of beliefs', and Tristram worshipped Mammon but was charming.

Caroline Blythe had been relieved when Bertie whisked her daughter off to Suffolk, out of sight of parish ladies and members of the MU who would undoubtedly have discussed the expansion of Melissande's waistline 'so soon after that expensive wedding'.

Caroline's energy levels have remained sufficiently high for her to resume many of the duties of Rector's Wife, and Matilda's grandmother. Melissande has friends living on 'The Meadows' development and brings Matilda to stay fairly frequently when Bertie flies to places that Melissande doesn't fancy, like the Pest suburbs of Budapest where *Amphib 21* has three large housing projects.

The Danube and its excesses are proving profitable for TGP, whose quaint and popular residences, during the past two winters, have been providing owners with all kinds of water-borne excitement at no extra cost. Internationally, major builders are requesting exploratory visits from Sir Bertrand Lamotte, the English baronet, to discuss his *Amphib 21* turnkey packages. Promising clients are invited to Suffolk, thence to Tytherton Kellaway where they can see the original 'part-time Venice'. This usually leads to contracts being signed before they return to the Czech Republic, Hungary and other exotic places whose names Cecily has had to Google (to find where they were), before joining Bertie and Melissande at dinner with the guests on their final evening, (leaving Nanny to manage the ever vivacious Matilda.)

Lady Veronica has found repose in her frail old age. After the wedding, Arabella, now with access to Tristram's bank balance, gave up work, except part-time on TGP, and devoted herself to bringing Tytherton Kellaway Manor back to its Georgian and Queen Anne splendour. Her first act was to settle Lady Veronica's debt to Bertie, thus removing any claim that he might have to equity in the property: a niggle that had for so long irked Bella.

She converted part of the west wing into a self-contained apartment for her aunt, installing a lift (after a dispute with English Heritage in which concessions had to be made on both sides) that allowed easy access to the drawing room and its welcoming hearth for Her Ladyship's regular glass of port.

Arabella, too, employed a nanny, but not until eleven months after the wedding. This had caused some banter between Bertie and Batty Heath-Cohen.

"Better get on with it, Batty!" Taunted Bertie, when his old chum remarked on Melissande's changing shape.

"At least I didn't jump the gun!"

"Oh no? You were at it far sooner than we were! Bella told Mel and she told me! Mel was quite shocked."

"She was always bloody shocked in those days! She doesn't even *blush* now – what have you done to her, you cad!"

"We just worked things out logically," Bertie said, preening an imaginary moustache. "It worked a treat: we're still very happy!"

"I must say we are, too – apart from the squalling kids! Thank God for nannies!"

"Well if you must produce two at a time, that's your fault. You'll have a rugger team in no time if you go on like this."

"This time it was a slip-up." Tristram complained.

Arabella is expecting their next batch any time soon. The scan shows twin boys again. This pleases both her and her aunt: at least one of her brood might have what it takes to keep The Manor thriving for another generation. It will keep the family name alive, too, because her pre-nuptial agreement, drawn up by Mr Penworthy's assistant with much interference from Arabella, decrees that 'any children from the union shall keep the Kelway surname, as shall their mother.

The same document ensures, too, that if Tristram decides to leave the marriage he will have to leave a good fifty per cent of his wealth with Arabella and her offspring. It's a risk Tris is prepared to take.

Bertie suspects that Arabella's current 'mistake' might be intentional, as back-up insurance. She would have preferred a title to go with the marriage but a team of sons and money to support The Manor, herself and the children would have to suffice.

"A good job you've got plenty more bedrooms," says Bertie.

"And a good job TGB's making a bob or two so we can afford to do them up," adds Tristram.

It's true, Tytherton Meadows has already made more than a bob or two for *Amphib 21 Ltd* and its investors. The design competition produced so many imaginative entries that TV channels across the Western World and even China signed up for a series on the lines of *'Strictly Come Dancing'* where teams showcased their projects with computer-generated images and descriptions of how the houses would respond to rising flood waters. Some had clever innovations like 'a fishing patio' and 'rear dinghy dock'. The original judges took part in each show, making comments and awarding points. The royalties from this were all good for TGP's balance sheet.

Prof Veerman has become quite a celeb, his political and academic confidence charming both audience and panel. The general public votes at the end of each show and the popularity weighting is taken into consideration for the last five designs.

The final shows, at which winners are chosen, bring record viewing numbers. The first English final occurred on a night when near-hurricane winds and torrential rain were driving the population indoors, in front of the TVs.

By the time the competition's winner was announced, every plot on Tytherton Meadows was sold and proud owners had already chosen the design they liked best. As luck would have it, one of them backed the winner, an Austrian artist with a passion for Scandinavian pine. He had negotiated a deal with one of the first new residents who had seen the unique design on the TV show. Apart from one or two changes to the interior layout, the buyer went ahead with the original external appearance, which was like a modernised child's fort, painted to look like stone, with a turret at each corner, a light-weight roof garden and a drawbridge into the garage. The concrete floating cellar supporting this whole edifice is the largest on the development and has room for a sound-proof rock studio, gymnasium and squash court.

As floodwater subsides, Travis deals with any floating log – or even dead animal – that might get wedged between the amphibious cellars and the concrete bases on which they rest, causing a house to tilt or smell awful. In the event of a drifting branch or worse becoming lodged, Travis tows it off with the launch. This is part of his role of 'Estate Manager and Harbour Master', a title that gives him a choice of hats depending on the season.

Newscasts recorded what happened to the winning fort the first time the floods rose in Tytherton Meadows. When the River Avon began to relieve itself onto the low-lying land, the owner of this now famous building drove his car down the drawbridge on to the raised access road and up to the communal car park next to the blocks of luxury apartments to the West of The Manor (though not visible from Lady Veronica's apartment, due to a belt of trees).

On this momentous day, the owner's children raised a flag on one of the corner towers, racing around the ramparts to cheer their father as he jogged back 'aboard' to be there as the castellated house rose for the first time above the muddy water that was submerging the surrounding lawn. There was a ceremonial raising of the drawbridge. Next morning, the fort's resident, along with other commuters, was filmed being picked up by Travis in the launch.

Never was a flood more welcome. The fact that The Avon now had somewhere to 'unload' some of the relentless rain meant that conventional house-owners further downstream would not have to face sleepless nights placing sandbags and carrying valuables upstairs.

The flood-relief payment (FRP) that the land-owner receives from Government for providing an area of floodable land to protect other more vulnerable sites downstream is most welcome. It adds to Lady Veronica's rapidly recovering bank balance. Each plot sold has made such a difference that she now receives a free magazine from the bank each month, packed with investment suggestions.

The Country Landowners Association has featured this FRP source of income in its journal, bringing in a host of new enquiries from owners of low-lying farms: even the Crown Estate, interested in developing some of its foreshore property.

"Bring on the bad weather," says Arabella, rubbing her hands each time rain is forecast. "Let's hope the climate doesn't change its mind and go dry!"

Trevor has discovered a new interest. He never thought much about gardens or gardening until Lady Veronica asked him to drive her over to Stourhead house, near Frome, in her new Renault 'Twingo RS', which, though small, is distinctive and decidedly sporty, appealing to the octogenarian's flamboyant side.

"What do you think, Mr Bunt?" She asks him, on arrival as he helps her towards a bench with a good view over the lake by the Palladian mansion.

"Beautiful, your Ladyship," he says. "It wouldn't take too much to make your place like this."

This was exactly the response she had been hoping for. Part of Tytherton Meadows, where they had excavated soil to raise the level of access roads around the development, had been landscaped to form a permanent lake.

'Tytherton Lake' itself is designed to be floodable and rise well above its usual level without causing any problems, except to the lawns, which go brown for a while after submersion. It's not a problem because within a week or two of The Avon resuming its 'normal' banks, estate staff can again mow the grass and clean up the paths and benches. Mother Nature soon restores the verdant surroundings, ready for summer visitors, which include walkers, fishermen and family picnickers.

The lake lies between the Manor and Tytherton Meadows, providing privacy from 'the public', for the residents. The luxury apartments have a view of it from their elevated position near the Roman Temple.

On the Manor side of the lake, more lawns have replaced the scruffy pastures either side of the drive, which still descends into the green tunnel of the lane, now free of mud and traffic. This shady lane now forms part of the 'green experience' walks, mapped out in Tytherton Manor's brochure.

Under Arabella's direction, Travis, wearing his countryside hat and followed by his dog, supervises the visitor facilities at The Manor. His dad, as well as driving Lady Veronica, acting as her butler and 'man with pliers and screwdriver', nominally comes under Travis's command and at busy periods helps out in the Manor Tearoom, (tastefully designed by Bella and a couple of friends from Town).

Originally the tearoom was the estate workshop beyond the stable yard. The adjoining coach house, now converted into a souvenir shop, sells locally-made jam, biscuits, pottery, maps and books.

To amuse younger visitors while their parents browse in the shop, a glass panelled door connects to the stable yard, where they can stroke the noses of various animals penned there during the tourist season, including a donkey and its equine young, now larger than Doris herself.

The stallion and mare are kept out of reach in case they nip anyone but a few sheep and goats provide something to stroke and pat, while numerous bantam hens and cockerels add movement and colour.

Being under cover in the stables, the diversions for the young work even better during rainy weather, allowing parents the peace to decide which jam or map they will buy. During dry periods a closed circuit TV system with screens in the shop, gives them supervision of their kids playing on the slides and swings the other side of the menagerie, all helping to make the 'Tytherton Manor Experience' highly repeatable.

Bertie and Melissande have kept the house in Bayswater. The housekeeper leaves it ready for instant occupation and the facility is useful if they arrive back from abroad too late to go home to Suffolk. It's also appreciated by friends and relatives for 'the occasional night in town'.

"What's Ogle saying this time?" Asks Melissande. "Do they still want you back?"

Bertie has been reading the hand-written letter with some amusement.

"No! It's just The Chairman keeping me up to date with his love-life. He's split up with his bird. She's made a real hash of Exec Director and he's found a younger model. He says he's looking for someone else to run the show and he'll keep the new girl's role as 'purely domestic'.

"Well his last mistake did you a favour, didn't it? Melissande took away his FT.

"She did!" Said Bertie, reaching for his beloved as she kicked off her shoes. "Life's a succession of consequences, isn't it? If The Chairman hadn't appointed his totty instead of me, I'd never have been whistling 'I'm off to see the Wizard' – and Arabella wouldn't have told me off and I might not have noticed her bum – and then I'd never have met you!"

"And then there was the light bulb......"

"Mm....".

THE END

By the same author:

Fiction:

BAGAMOYO SPRING
A novel

Bagamoyo Spring begins as weather and climate become more extreme, and world leaders discover that their countries are under threat from starving and desperate neighbours, led by extremists. Action is needed before civilisation falls apart. War has proved a failure in solving such crises: it's imperative to find constructive solutions that create jobs, provide food, water and world security. The US, Russian and Chinese presidents turn to the UN Security Council, which takes action, mobilising blue-beret personnel and resources; calling experts and specialists out of retirement to launch an unprecedented bid to avoid meltdown.

Bagamoyo Spring records these events, following the fortunes of Arun Gillies, half-Burmese, half-Scottish, in his late sixties, as he's recalled from retirement and appointed to oversee the project in the Horn of Africa, parched by years of drought. In his years working with villagers in the Third World, he has never before had to face murdering insurgents and migrating populations. Arun never meant to return to work in the tropics. Events at home, with his abusive and alcoholic wife, precipitated this, forcing him into new chapters of life. Then he meets Laura.

Knowing that there's no fool like an old fool, Arun resists the temptation to fall in love with this university student who is determined to become France's first woman president. She has other plans for him.

Bagamoyo Spring, an international novel for today is fast-moving and frank, expressing the anger of oppressed people and the passion of those who have at last found love.

Since publication of Bagamoyo Spring in 2013, world events, especially population migration and extremist invasion, have, uncannily, seemed to parallel many elements of this book.

Available from Amazon as paperback or full-length Kindle e-book. Download a free sample.

OKAVANGO - ANOTHER LIFE
A novel by George Macpherson

A story of adventure and love in Botswana, at a time when the historical prejudices and injustices, still entrenched in all its neighbours, were being challenged as the new African nation emerged in 1967. By overcoming the dangers of wild animals, the power of traditional beliefs; hatred and love between races and tribes, as well as the hazards of international politics, Botswana was to become a unique social, political and commercial melting pot for the Africa of the future.

Alan Black is a third generation white Rhodesian, starting his career in Botswana's Ngamiland, one of the world's last unspoiled habitats that encompasses the vast Okavango Swamps. His job, as a Botswana Government employee, is to work with the newly independent Batswana people to achieve a higher standard of living, in this vast area of the Northern Kalahari.

He becomes close to an Afrikaner family whose safari company faces radical challenges; and to a beautiful African woman whose natural boldness has been given the extra confidence of university education. Together they experience success in their work and their passionate relationship: but how can it all end? There's someone else in Alan's life with whom he seems inevitably and mysteriously linked.

This is African enchantment in the most exotic of settings, in which love challenges racial boundaries breached only by the few despite the conflicts of religion, politics, race and class. *Available as a full-length Kindle e-book or paperback from Amazon. Download a free sample.*

THE FLOATING ISLAND – A TALE OF AFRICA
A novel by George Macpherson

In 1961 newly-independent Tanzania is set for change – Africans are taking power. They intend to raise people out of poverty, combat superstition, and stamp out corruption. A few disgruntled whites are leaving for Rhodesia and South Africa. Other, more dedicated ex-patriates, stay on. In the villages, little has changed in half a century, but newcomers from Europe and Asia are arriving in this tropical setting of contrasting lifestyles, keen to contribute. They have a lot to learn about 'maendeleo' - development.

Two young people from very different backgrounds become entangled in this melange of language, work and cultures. Charles Johnson, product of an English public school is, despite his veneer of confidence and boyish enthusiasm, still unsure of who he is or what he wants from life. Leaving Carol Libby, his first love, in England, has been a wrench, but they both know that his restless nature needs wider vistas than those offered by a Cornish fishing village.

In Northern China, Yi Zhang Li is training as an anthropologist. Her interest in prehistoric wall paintings leads her to help plan the railway from Dar es Salaam to Kapiri Mposhi in Zambia's Central Province. She has much to lose if she fails to uphold Communist Party principles, but her natural charm and classical beauty ensure her acceptance amongst villagers, officials and fellow workers. One person who desperately seeks her attention and approval is Charles. To Zhang Li he appears to be a conceited young 'foreign devil'.

The story begins at a Catholic mission school on the shores of Lake Victoria Nyanza.

The Floating Island *is available as a full-length Kindle e-book or paperback from Amazon. Download a free sample.*

EXPRESSIONS OF LOVE

A love story by George Macpherson

In the years after World War II a Dorset boy finds himself victim to class prejudice at an early age, when the daughter of The Manor decides *he* is what she wants.

Both children are the product of their history. Harriet is one of several sisters in a family of landed gentry. Jeremy's father is the respected local carpenter and his mother, the village schoolteacher. As love for each other develops, it meets opposition – but only from one side.

Despite ambitious, devout parents, sexual hang-ups and the wide gulf between their classes and religions, their love endures. It shapes their lives and careers.

Their mutual passion for playing chamber music brings them friends and social recognition – in some quarters. They also learn how to give each other what Mother Nature demands.

They discover that the dedication and patience needed to perfect their playing of stringed instruments can also be applied to overthrowing barriers of class and religion. The supreme satisfaction of playing in a quartet is matched in their working lives and personal relationships, as the lovers follow their training, logic and instincts.

Available as a full-length Kindle e-book or paperback from Amazon. Download a free sample to your reader, tablet, smartphone or desktop computer.

THE GLEBE FIELD – A NOVEL SET IN CORNWALL
By George Macpherson

What does it take to make humanity take notice of what Nature is telling us? Heatwaves and forest fires, summers with floods and no sun? Or will disappearing islands and foul air convince us? And what can we as individuals do about all this?

The Glebe Field is about natural resources - and the way people exploit the planet, on which we all depend. It's about economic, emotional and romantic aspects of life, and how people's behaviour, in different walks of life, can make a difference.

Successful artist Rose Yi Johnson is elected to the local District Council in Cornwall, despite her mother being from Northern China. Her illegitimate daughter, Emily, is a Fine Arts graduate working for a London gallery. She has inherited her mother's oriental good looks and deep intellect.

Councillor Johnson is incensed when she learns that The Church is applying for planning permission to build a car-park and ice-cream kiosk on an ancient and legally-protected meadow, (SSSI and AONB) known as The Glebe Field. The application is supported by influential landowner and womaniser Hugh Olver-Blythe, who has much bigger plans in mind. He has been buying farms along the Cornish coast, amalgamating the land and refurbishing the buildings as holiday lets and cottages for sale. He wants to diversify further.

Rose Johnson's passionate concern for the environment, aided by an astounding stroke of family fortune, brings a personable young barrister and his famous father into the picture. This has dramatic repercussions.

This book is a sequel to *The Floating Island – a tale of Africa*. It recognises that human behaviour has changed little over the centuries. Set within the context of a modern love story, it suggests that while our acquisitive and greedy instinct drives us to plunder and wreck this planet – and even attack Mother Nature herself, bringing mass self-destruction – money, in itself, need not be evil. Great riches can bring many good things and much happiness.

Available as a full-length Kindle e-book or paperback from Amazon. Download a free sample of **The Glebe Field** *to your reader, tablet, smartphone or desktop computer.*

Non-fiction:

Home-grown energy from Short Rotation Coppice
Hardback, (214 pages) Published in 1995 by Farming Press Books, distributed in North America by Diamond Farm enterprises. ISBN 0 85236 289 7.

With a foreword by Derek Wanless, this is a handbook for those interested in planting, tending and harvesting willow and other woody biomass crops for energy. 'Wood is the purest fuel in the world' and there are all kinds of benefits from cultivation of short rotation coppice – such as flood prevention, water recycling, sewage recycling, buffer-strips to prevent fertilizer run-off polluting water-ways; provision of wildlife habitat – and basket making uses the same type of willow. The book is generously illustrated with photographs and is of a very practical nature.
   Available from Amazon and some bookshops

First Steps in Village Mechanisation
Published by Tanzania Publishing House in 1975

When George Macpherson was a UN International Labour Organisation technical advisor to the Government of Tanzania, he wrote this handbook for those starting rural workshops, using easily available materials and tools. It begins with basic black-smith skills, and goes on to the design and construction of wheelbarrows, cultivators, donkey and ox harness, and other farm tools and machinery. Illustrated with photos, artist drawings and diagrams.
   Available in paperback, second-hand, from Amazon and some bookshops

Namna ya kujitengenezea gari la gurudumu moja

(How to make a wheelbarrow for yourself)

Published by Tanzania Publishing House in 1975

Written in Swahili, this is a photographic description, with commentary, on how to make a wheelbarrow from pieces of wood and a strip of lorry tyre. It can easily be followed by someone not understanding Swahili.
   (Not currently available from Amazon).

Computers in Farm Management
By Barry Wilson and George Macpherson
Published by Northwood Books in 1982, following a series of farming conferences organized by the magazine Big Farm Management

 An early textbook on the use of computers on the farm, it asked farmers of that era 'Do I need a computer? How quickly could I recoup its cost? Would my staff need special training to use it? Should I buy my own on-farm computer or buy in computing services from a bureau?
   Examples of hardware available at the time, and the programs being developed by pioneering software companies make the book of historic interest.

   This book is occasionally available on Amazon and in some bookshops.

Farming with the BBC
(In Bulgarian – BBC World Service)
Out of print

Farming with the BBC
(In Romanian – BBC World Service)
Out of print

Farming with the BBC

(In Albanian: 40-part radio soap opera – BBC World Service)
Out of print

About the author

Award-winning writer and journalist George A Macpherson was educated at St Paul's School, London and Seale Hayne Agricultural College (now the University of Plymouth).

He worked for the United Nations' International Labour Organisation in Africa as a technical advisor on appropriate technology before joining BBC World Service, as a producer in the Science Unit, later becoming Programme Organiser of the Swahili Service.

Leaving BBC staff to become editor of a monthly farming magazine, he continued his broadcasting on a freelance basis, on radio and television, before going fully independent, starting his own daily rural news service on The Internet for the Farming Online website. He continued presenting and producing farming and wildlife, medical and musical programmes for BBC World Service, BBC 5 Live and BBC Radio 4 before moving with his wife Jane, to France to write novels. In his spare time he learned the cello at the local music conservatoire at Ribérac and took part in amateur musical events in the Dordogne.

George and his wife, Jane, have a large, rainbow family and moved back to Somerset in 2014 to be nearer them.

While working in journalism UK George was a Fellow of the Royal Society of Arts; Fellow of the Royal Agricultural Society; Fellow of the British Institute of Management; and an Honorary Associate of the British Veterinary Association.

Published by Grande Vigne Press

Made in the USA
Charleston, SC
24 November 2015